Praise for *Funeral in Blue*

"One of Perry's best . . . [Her] talent for history is in full view."
—*The Globe and Mail* (Toronto)

"What a pleasure it is to pick up the latest from Perry! She delivers some of the best mysteries in the genre: Her writing is solid, her characters are intriguing and multilayered, and her plots are inventive and intelligent. . . . Serious entertainment, the novel offers a thoughtful look at the dark puzzles of the human heart."
—*Tampa Tribune*

"*Funeral in Blue* captures and retains the reader's undivided attention. . . . The plot is intriguing on its own, but it becomes fascinating as Perry, with each new avenue of the investigation, seamlessly explores the nature of truth and the price at which it comes. Perry is a prolific writer. Her fans will be delighted."
—*The Virginian Pilot*

"Highly recommended . . . another gripping Victorian spellbinder . . . Perry's deep, sympathetic characterizations help cement the complex plot, as she explores Victorian class distinctions, hypocrisy, duty, and morality."
—*Library Journal*

"William Monk is an intriguing character in Perry's pantheon: a Victorian private investigator who has no memory of his life before an accident that took place some six years ago. The nature of truth, or lies, or memory is at the heart of Perry's writing, and she never permits the answers to be simple."
—*Booklist*

FUNERAL IN BLUE

A WILLIAM MONK NOVEL

Anne Perry

Ballantine Books Trade Paperbacks
New York

To Meg MacDonald, for her wonderful ideas,
her work, and her belief in me.

2011 Ballantine Books Trade Paperback Edition

Copyright © 2001 by Anne Perry

Published in the United States by Ballantine Books, an imprint of
The Random House Publishing Group, a division of Random House, Inc., New York.

BALLANTINE and colophon are registered trademarks of Random House, Inc.

Originally published in hardcover in the United States by Ballantine Books,
an imprint of The Random House Publishing Group, a division of
Random House, Inc., in 2001.

Library of Congress Cataloging-in-Publication Data
Perry, Anne.
Funeral in blue / Anne Perry.
p.   cm.
ISBN 978-0-345-51414-1
1. Monk, William (Fictitious character)— Fiction. 2. Private
investigators—England—London—Fiction. 3. London (England)—
Fiction. 4. Nurses—Fiction. I. Title.
PR6066.E693 F86 2001
823'.914—dc21
2001037481

Printed in the United States of America

www.ballantinebooks.com

2   4   6   8   9   7   5   3   1

FUNERAL IN
BLUE

CHAPTER ONE

———

The operating room was silent except for the deep, regular breathing of the gaunt young woman who lay on the table, the immense bulge of her stomach laid bare.

Hester stared across at Kristian Beck. It was the first operation of the day, and there was no blood on his white shirt yet. The chloroform sponge had done its miraculous work and was set aside. Kristian picked up the scalpel and touched the point to the young woman's flesh. She did not flinch; her eyelids did not move. He pressed deeper, and a thin, red line appeared.

Hester looked up and met his eyes, dark, luminous with intelligence. They both knew the risk, even with anesthesia, that they could do little to help. A growth this size was probably fatal, but without surgery the woman would die anyway.

Kristian lowered his eyes and continued cutting. The blood spread. Hester swabbed it up. The woman lay motionless except for her breathing, her face waxen pale, cheeks sunken, shadows around the sockets of her eyes. Her wrists were so thin the shape of the bones poked through the skin. It was Hester who had walked beside her from the ward along the corridor, half supporting her weight, trying to ease the anxiety which had seemed to torment her every time she had been to the hospital over the last two months. Her pain seemed as much in her mind as in her body.

Kristian had insisted on surgery, against the wishes of Fermin Thorpe, the chairman of the Hospital Governors. Thorpe was a cautious man who enjoyed authority, but he had no courage to step outside the known order of things he could defend if anyone in power were to question him. He loved rules; they were safe. If you followed the rules you could justify anything.

Kristian was from Bohemia, and in Thorpe's mind he did not belong in the Hampstead Hospital in London with his imaginative ways and his foreign accent, however slight, and his disregard for the way things should be done. He should not risk the hospital's reputation by performing an operation whose chances of success were so slight. But Kristian had an answer, an argument, for every-thing. And, of course, Lady Callandra Daviot had taken his side; she always did.

Kristian smiled at the memory, not looking up at Hester but down at his hands as they explored the wound he had made, look-ing for the thing that had caused the obstruction, the wasting, the nausea and the huge swelling.

Hester mopped away more blood and glanced at the woman's face. It was still perfectly calm. Hester would have given anything she could think of to have had chloroform on the battlefield in the Crimea five years ago, or even at Manassas, in America, three months back.

"Ah!" Kristian let out a grunt of satisfaction and pulled back, gently easing out of the cavity something that looked like a dark, semiporous sponge such as one might use to scrub one's back, or even a saucepan. It was about the size of a large domestic cat.

Hester was too astounded to speak. She stared at it, then at Kristian.

"Trichobezoar," he said softly. Then he met her gaze of in-credulity. "Hair," he explained. "Sometimes when people have cer-tain temperamental disorders, nervous anxiety and depression, they feel compelled to pull out their own hair and eat it. It is beyond their power to stop, without help."

Hester stared at the stiff, repellent mass lying in the dish and felt her own throat contract and her stomach gag at the thought of such a thing inside anyone.

"Swab," Kristian directed. "Needle."

"Oh!" She moved to obey just as the door opened and Callandra came in, closing it softly behind her. She looked at Kristian first, a softness in her eyes she disguised only as he turned to her. He gestured to the dish and smiled.

Callandra looked startled, then she turned to Hester. "What is it?"

"Hair," Hester replied, swabbing the blood away again as Kristian worked.

"Will she be all right?" Callandra asked.

"There's a chance," Kristian answered. Suddenly he smiled, extraordinarily sweetly, but there was a sharp and profound satisfaction in his eyes. "You can go and tell Thorpe it was a trichobezoar, not a tumor, if you like."

"Oh, yes, I'd like," she answered, her face melting into something almost like laughter, and without waiting she turned and went off on the errand.

Hester glanced across at Kristian, then bent to the work again, mopping blood and keeping the wound clean, as the needle pierced the skin and drew the sides together, and finally it was bandaged.

"She'll feel a great deal of pain when she wakens," Kristian warned. "She mustn't move too much."

"I'll stay with her," Hester promised. "Laudanum?"

"Yes, but only for the first day," he warned. "I'll be here if you need me. Are you going to stay? You've watched her all through, haven't you?"

"Yes." Hester was not a nurse at the hospital. She came on a voluntary basis, like Callandra, who was a military surgeon's widow, a generation older than Hester, but they had been the closest of friends now for five years. Hester was probably the only one who knew how deeply Callandra loved Kristian, and that only this week she had finally declined an offer of marriage from a dear friend because she could not settle for honorable companionship and close forever the door on dreams of immeasurably more. But they were only dreams. Kristian was married, and that ended all possibility of anything more than the loyalty and the passion for healing and justice that held them now, and perhaps the shared laughter now and then, the small victories and the understanding.

Hester, recently married herself, and knowing the depth and the sweep of love, ached for Callandra that she sacrificed so much. And yet loving her husband as she did, for all his faults and vulnerabilities, Hester, too, would rather have been alone than accept anyone else.

It was late afternoon when Hester left the hospital and took the public omnibus down Hampstead High Street to Haverstock Hill, and then to Euston Road. A newsboy shouted something about five hundred American soldiers surrendering in New Mexico. The papers carried the latest word on the Civil War, but the anxiety was far deeper over the looming cotton famine in Lancashire because of the blockading of the Confederate States.

She hurried past him and walked the last few yards to Fitzray Street. It was early September and still mild, but growing dark, and the lamplighter was well on his rounds. When she approached her front door she saw a tall, slender man waiting impatiently outside. He was immaculately dressed in high wing collar, black frock coat and striped trousers, as one would expect of a City gentleman, but his whole attitude betrayed agitation and deep unhappiness. It was not until he heard her footsteps and turned so the lamplight caught his face that she recognized her brother, Charles Latterly.

"Hester!" He moved towards her swiftly, then stopped. "How . . . how are you?"

"I'm very well," she answered truthfully. It was several months since she had seen him, and for someone as rigidly controlled and conventional as Charles, it was extraordinary to find him waiting in the street like this. Presumably, Monk was not there yet or he would have gone inside.

She opened the door and Charles followed her in. The gas lamp burned very low in the hall, and she turned it up and led the way to the front room, which was where Monk received prospective clients who came with their terrors and anxieties for him to attempt to solve. Since they had both been out all day, there was a fire laid but not lit. A bowl of tawny chrysanthemums and scarlet nasturtiums gave some light and an illusion of warmth.

She turned and looked at Charles. As always, he was meticulously polite. "I'm sorry to intrude. You must be tired. I suppose you have been nursing someone all day?"

"Yes, but I think she may get better. At least, the operation was a success."

He made an attempt at a smile. "Good."

"Would you like a cup of tea?" she offered. "I would."

"Oh . . . yes, yes, of course. Thank you." He sat gingerly on one of the two armchairs, his back stiff and upright as if to relax were impossible. She had seen so many of Monk's clients sit like that, terrified of putting their fears into words, and yet so burdened by them and so desperate for help that they had finally found the courage to seek a private agent of enquiry. It was as if Charles had come to see Monk, and not her. His face was pale and there was a sheen of sweat on it, and his hands were rigid in his lap. If she had touched him she would have felt locked muscles.

She had not seen him look so wretched since their parents had died five and a half years ago, when she was still in Scutari with Florence Nightingale. Their father had been ruined by a financial swindle, and had taken his own life because of the ensuing disgrace. Their mother had died within the month. Her heart had been weak, and the grief and distress so soon after the loss of her younger son in battle had been too much for her.

Looking at Charles now, Hester's similar fears for him returned with a force that took her by surprise. They had seen each other very little since Hester's marriage, which Charles had found difficult to approve—after all, Monk was a man without a past. A carriage accident six years ago had robbed him of his memory. Monk had deduced much about his past, but the vast majority of it remained unknown. Monk had been in the police force at the time of his meeting with Hester, and no one in the very respectable Latterly family had had any prior connections with the police. Beyond question, no one had married into that type of social background.

Charles looked up, expecting her to fetch the tea. Should she ask him what troubled him so profoundly, or would it be tactless, and perhaps put him off confiding in her?

"Of course," she said briskly, and went to the small kitchen to riddle the stove, loosen the old ashes and put more coal on to boil the kettle. She set out biscuits on a plate. They were bought, not homemade. She was a superb nurse, a passionate but unsuccessful social reformer, and as even Monk would admit, a pretty good detective, but her domestic skills were still in the making.

When the tea was made she returned and set the tray down, poured both cups and waited while he took one and sipped from it. His embarrassment seemed to fill the air and made her feel awkward as well. She watched him fidget with the cup and gaze around the small, pleasant room, looking for something to pretend to be interested in.

If she was blunt and asked him outright, would she make it better or worse? "Charles . . ." she began.

He turned to look at her. "Yes?"

She saw a profound unhappiness in his eyes. He was only a few years older than she, and yet there was a weariness in him, as if he no longer had any vitality and already felt himself past the best. It touched her with fear. She must be gentle. He was too complex, far too private for bluntness.

"It's . . . it's rather a long time since I've seen you," he began apologetically. "I didn't realize. The weeks seem to . . ." He looked away, fishing for words and losing them.

"How is Imogen?" she asked, and instantly knew from the way he avoided her eyes that the question hurt.

"Quite well," he replied. The words were automatic, bright and meaningless, as he would answer a stranger. "And William?"

She could bear it no longer. She put down her cup. "Charles, something is terribly wrong. Please tell me what it is. Even if I cannot help, I would like you to trust me at least to share it."

He was sitting forward, his elbows on his knees. For the first time since he had come into the room he met her gaze directly. His blue eyes were full of fear and absolute, total bewilderment.

She waited.

"I simply don't know what to do." His voice was quiet, but jagged with desperation. "It's Imogen. She's . . . changed . . ." He stopped, a wave of misery engulfing him.

Hester thought of her charming, graceful sister-in-law, who had always seemed so confident, so much more at ease with society and with herself than Hester was. "How has she changed?" she asked gently.

He shook his head. "I'm not really sure. I suppose it must have been over a while. I . . . I didn't notice it." Now he kept his eyes down on his hands, which were knotted together, twisting slowly, knuckles white. "It seemed just weeks to me."

Hester forced herself to be patient. He was in such obvious distress it would be unkind, and on a practical level pointless, to try to concentrate his mind. "In what way has she changed?" she asked him, keeping the emotion out of her voice. It was extraordinary to see her calm, rather pompous brother so obviously losing control of a situation which was so far merely domestic. It made her afraid that there was a dimension to it beyond anything she could yet see.

"She's . . . unreliable," he said, after searching for the word. "Of course, everyone has changes of mood, I know that, days when they feel more cheerful than others, anxieties, just . . . just unpleasant things that make us feel hurt . . . but Imogen's either so happy she's excited, can't keep still . . ." His face was puckered with confusion as he sought to understand something which was beyond him. "She's either elated or in despair. Sometimes she looks as if she's frantic with worry, then a day later, or even hours, she'll be full of energy, her eyes bright, her face flushed, laughing at nothing. And . . . this sounds absurd . . . but I swear she keeps repeating silly little actions . . . like rituals . . ."

Hester was startled. "What sort of things?"

He looked embarrassed, apologetic. "Fastening her jacket with the middle button first, then from the bottom up, and the top down. I've seen her count them to make certain. And . . ." He took a breath. "And wear one pair of gloves and carry an odd one that doesn't match."

It made no apparent sense. She wondered if he could possibly be correct, or if in his own anxiety he was imagining it. "Did she say why?" she asked aloud.

"No. I asked her about the gloves, and she ignored me, just spoke about something else."

Hester looked at Charles, sitting in front of her. He was tall and slender, perhaps a little too thin now. His fair hair was receding, but not much. His features were regular; he would have been handsome if there were more conviction in his face, more passion, even humor. His father's suicide had wounded him in a way from which he had never recovered. He was marked with a pity he did not know how to express, and a shame he bore in silence. He would have felt it a betrayal to offer explanations of such a private grief. Hester had no idea what he had shared with Imogen. Perhaps he had tried to shelter her from it, or imagined it would be helpful to her to see him as invulnerable, always in control. Perhaps he was right!

On the other hand, Imogen might have wanted passionately to have shared his pain, to have known that he trusted her with it, that he needed her kindness and her strength to bear it with him. Perhaps she had felt excluded? Hester would have, she knew that absolutely.

"I suppose you have asked her directly what troubles her?" she said quietly.

"She says there is nothing wrong," he replied. "She changes the subject, talks about anything else, mostly things that neither of us care about, just anything, a wall of words to keep me out."

It was like probing a wound; you were afraid to strike the nerves, and yet knew you must find the bullet. She had done it too many times on the battlefield and in military hospitals. She could smell blood and fear in her imagination as the simile came to her mind. Only months ago she and Monk had been in America and had seen the first pitched battle of the Civil War.

"Do you really have no idea what is causing it, Charles?" she asked.

He looked up wretchedly. "I think she may be having an affair with someone," he answered hoarsely. "But I've no idea who . . . or why."

Hester could have thought of a dozen reasons why. She pictured Imogen's lovely face with its soft features, wide dark eyes, the hunger and emotion in her. How much had she changed in the sixteen years since she had been so excited to marry a gentle and respectable young man with a promising future? She had been so full of optimism, thrilled not to be one of those still desperately seeking a husband, and perhaps paired off by an ambitious mother with someone she would find it difficult even to like, let alone to love.

Now she was in her mid-thirties, childless, and perhaps wondering with even more desperation what life offered beyond mere safety. She had never been cold or hungry or outcast from society. Maybe she did not value her good fortune very much. To be loved, provided for and protected was not always enough. Sometimes to be needed counted more. Could that be what had happened to

Imogen? Had she found someone who offered her the intoxication of telling her she was necessary to him in a way Charles would never say, no matter how much it might actually be true?

Would she do more than flirt? She had so much to lose; surely she could not be so infatuated as to forget that? Society did not frown on adultery if it was conducted with such discretion that no one was forced to know about it, but even a married woman could lose her reputation if she was indiscreet. And, of course, a divorced woman, whatever the reason for the divorce, simply ceased to exist. A woman put away for adultery could very easily find herself penniless and on the streets. Someone like Imogen, who had never fended for herself, might not survive.

Charles would not divorce her unless her behavior became so outrageous that he had no choice, if he was to preserve his own reputation. He would simply live side by side with her, but separated by a gulf of pain.

Hester wanted to touch him, but the distance of time and intimacy between them was too great. It would be artificial, even intrusive. "I'm sorry," she said softly. "I hope that isn't true. Perhaps it's only a momentary thing and it may die long before it becomes any more." How false that sounded. She winced at herself even as she heard her own words.

He looked up at her. "I can't just sit by and hope, Hester! I need to know . . . and do something. Doesn't she realize what will happen to her . . . to all of us . . . if she's found out? Please . . . help me."

Hester was bewildered. What could she do that Charles had not already done? There was no easy cure for unhappiness that she could produce and persuade Imogen to take.

Charles was waiting. Her silence was making him realize more acutely just what he had asked of her, and already embarrassment was overtaking hope.

"Yes, of course," she said quickly.

"If I just knew for certain," he started to rationalize, filling in the silence with too many words. "Then perhaps I would understand." He was watching her intently, in spite of himself, part of him still clinging to the belief that she could help. "I don't know the right questions to ask her. She might be able to explain to you, then . . ." He tailed off, not knowing what else to say.

If only understanding were the answer! She was afraid it would increase the hurt, because he would see that there was no way to escape the fact that Imogen did not love him the way he had assumed, and needed.

But then perhaps he did not love her with the passion or the urgency that she wanted?

He was waiting for Hester to say something. He seemed to think that because she was a woman she would understand Imogen and be able to reach her emotions in a way he could not. Maybe she could, but that did not mean she could change them. Even if the truth would not help, however, it was a certainty that nothing else would.

"I'll go to see her," she said aloud. "Do you know if she will be in tomorrow afternoon?"

Relief ironed out his face. "Yes, I should imagine so," he said eagerly. "If you go early enough. She may go calling herself, at about four o'clock." He stood up. "Thank you, Hester. It's very good of you. Rather better than I deserve." He looked acutely uncomfortable. "I'm afraid I haven't been very . . . considerate lately. I . . . am sorry."

"No, you have almost ignored me," she said with a smile, trying to make light of it without contradicting him. "But then, I am equally guilty. I could easily have called upon you, or at least written, and I didn't."

"I suppose your life is too exciting." There was a shadow of disapproval in his voice. He might not have intended it this moment, but it was too deeply ingrained in his habit of thought to get rid of it in an instant.

"Yes," she agreed with a lift of her chin. It was the truth, but even if it had not been, she would have defended Monk and the life they shared to anyone. "America was extraordinary."

"About the worst time you could choose to go," he observed.

With an effort of will, she smiled at him. "We didn't choose. We went in order to help someone in very desperate trouble. I am sure you can understand that."

His face softened, and he blinked a little. "Yes, of course I can." He colored with embarrassment. "Do you have the fare for a hansom for tomorrow?"

With a considerable effort, she resisted snapping. After all, it was possible she might not have. There had certainly been those times. "Yes, thank you."

"Oh . . . good. Then I'll . . . er . . ."

"I'll come and see you when I have anything to say," she promised.

"Oh . . . of course." And still uncertain exactly how to conduct himself, he gave her a light kiss on the cheek and went to the door.

When Monk returned home in the evening, Hester said nothing of Charles's visit. Monk had solved a small case of theft and collected the payment for it, and consequently was pleased with himself. He was also interested in her story of the trichobezoar.

"Why?" he said with amazement. "Why would anyone do something so . . . so self-destructive?"

"If she knows, she can't or won't tell us," she answered, ladling mutton stew into bowls and smelling the fragrance of it. "More probably, she doesn't know herself. Some pain too terrible for her to look at, even to acknowledge."

"Poor creature!" he said with sudden, uncharacteristic pity, as if he had remembered suffering of his own and could too easily imagine drowning in it. "Can you help her?"

"Kristian will try," she said, picking up the bowls to carry them to the table. "He has the patience, and he doesn't dismiss all hysterics as hopeless, in spite of Fermin Thorpe."

Monk knew the history of Kristian and Fermin Thorpe, and he said nothing, but his expression was eloquent. Silently, he followed her to the table and sat down, hungry, cold and ready to eat.

In the morning, Hester went back to the hospital, and found Mary Ellsworth in a great deal of pain as the laudanum wore off. But the wound was clean, and she was able to take a little beef tea and to rest with some ease of mind.

In the early afternoon, Hester returned home and changed from her plain blue dress into the best afternoon gown she owned. The weather was mild, so she did not need any kind of coat or cape, but a hat was absolutely necessary. The dress was a soft shade of bluish green and very becoming to her, although it was certainly not fashionable. She had never kept up with exactly how full a skirt should be, or how a sleeve or a neckline should lie. She had neither the money nor, to be honest, the interest, but now it was an issue of pride not to visit her sister-in-law looking like some poor relation, even though that was exactly what she was. Perhaps that was why it mattered.

It was also possible that Imogen might very well have other callers, and Hester would not wish to be an embarrassment to her. For one thing, it would get in the way of her purpose in being there.

She went out into the dusty street and walked the short journey to Endsleigh Gardens. She did not look at the facades along the London streets. She was barely aware of the sounds of hooves, of the passing traffic or the rattle of wheels over the cobbles and the clink of harness, the shouts of irate drivers, or peddlers calling their wares. Her whole attention was inward, wondering how she could do anything at all to help Charles and not seriously risk actually making the matter worse. She and Imogen had once been close, before Hester's professional interests had separated them. They had shared many hours together, laughter and gossip, beliefs and dreams.

She had still come to no useful decision when she reached the house and went up the steps to pull the doorbell. She was admitted by the maid, who showed her into the withdrawing room. She had not been there for some time, but this was the house she had grown up in, and every detail was familiar, as if she had walked straight into the past. The opulent dark green curtains seemed not ever to have been moved. They hung in exactly the heavy folds she remembered, although that must be an illusion. In the winter, at least, they would be drawn every evening. The brass fender gleamed, and there was the same Staffordshire pottery vase with late roses on the table, a few petals fallen onto the table's shiny surface. The carpet had a worn patch in front of the armchair her father had used, and now Charles.

The door opened and Imogen came sweeping in, her skirts fashionably full, a beautiful pale plum-pink which only someone of her dark hair and fair skin could have worn well. Her jacket was a deeper shade and perfectly cut to flatter her waist. She looked radiant and full of confidence, almost excitement.

"Hester! How lovely to see you!" she exclaimed, giving her a swift, light hug and kissing her cheek. "You don't call often enough. How are you?" She did not wait for an answer, but whirled around and picked up the fallen petals, crushing them in her hand. "Charles said you went to America. Was it awful? The news is all about war, but I suppose you're used to that. And the train crash in Kentish Town, of course. Sixteen people were killed, and over three hundred injured! But I suppose you know that." A frown flickered across her face, then disappeared.

She did not sit down, nor did she offer Hester a seat. She seemed restless, moving around the room. She rearranged the roses slightly, collapsing one altogether and having to pick up more petals. Then she shifted one of the candlesticks on the mantelpiece to align it with the one at the opposite end. She was quite clearly in the last sort of mood for a confidential discussion of any kind, let alone on a subject so intimate as a love affair.

Hester realized what an impossible task she had undertaken. Before she could learn anything at all she would have to reestablish the friendship they had had before Hester had met Monk. Where on earth could she begin without sounding totally artificial?

"Your dress is lovely," she said honestly. "You always had a gift for choosing exactly the right color." She saw Imogen's quick look of pleasure. "Are you expecting someone special? I should have written before I came. I'm sorry."

Imogen hesitated, then rushed on, speaking rapidly. "Not at all. I'm not expecting anyone. Actually, I'm going out. It's I who should apologize, leaving so soon after you have arrived. But of course I'm delighted you came! I really should call upon you; it's just that I'm never sure when it will be convenient." There was too much enthusiasm in her voice, but she met Hester's eyes only momentarily.

"Please do," Hester responded. "Let me know, and I shall make certain I am at home."

Imogen started to say something, then stopped, as if she had changed her mind. In a way they were like strangers, and yet the bond that tied them together made it more uncomfortable than had they known nothing of each other.

"I'm pleased you called," Imogen said suddenly. Now she looked directly at Hester. "I have a gift for you. I thought of you as soon as I saw it. Wait, and I shall fetch it." And in a swirl of skirts she was gone, leaving the door open, and Hester heard her feet lightly cross the hall.

She returned within minutes, carrying an exquisite trinket box of dark wood inlaid with gold wire and mother-of-pearl. She held it out in both hands. It looked vaguely Oriental, perhaps Indian. Hester could think of no reason why it should have made anyone think of her. She hardly ever wore trinkets, and she had no particular connection with the East. But then, perhaps to Imogen the Crimea was close enough. Regardless, it was a charming thing, and certainly expensive. She could not help wondering where Imogen had come by it. Had it been a gift from another man, and so she dared not keep it? It was hardly a thing she would buy for herself, and it was certainly not Charles's taste, nor his extravagance.

"It's beautiful," she said, trying to put a warmth of enthusiasm into her voice. She took it from Imogen's outstretched hands and turned it slowly so the light shone on the inlaid pattern of leaves and flowers. "I can hardly imagine the time it must have taken someone to make it." She looked up at Imogen. "Where does it come from?"

Imogen's eyes widened. "I've no idea. I just thought it was pretty, and sort of . . . full of character. That's why it seemed right for you; it's individual." She smiled. The expression was charming, lighting her face, bringing back the shared moments and the laughter of only a few years ago.

"Thank you," Hester said sincerely. "I wish I hadn't allowed preoccupation with other things to keep me away so long. None of them were really important, compared with family." As she said it she was thinking of Imogen, but more intensely of Charles. He was the only blood relative she had left, and suddenly she had been forced to see that he was far more fragile than she had realized. She thought of Monk, and how alone he was. He said nothing, but she knew he ached to have ties to a past he understood, roots and a belonging. Family gave you bearings, an anchorage in who you were.

Imogen turned away and started to speak in a rush. "You must tell me about America . . . on another visit. I've never been to sea. Was it exciting, or terrible? Or both?"

Hester drew in breath to begin describing the extraordinary mixture of fear, hardship, boredom and wonder, but before she could say anything, Imogen flashed her another brilliant smile and then began rearranging the loose cushions on the sofa. "I feel dreadful not asking you to stay to tea," she went on. "After you've come so far. But I'm due to call on a friend, and I really can't let her down." She raised her eyes. "I'm sure you understand. But I'll call on you next time, if I may? And we'll exchange news properly. I know you're terribly busy, so I'll send you a note." Almost unconsciously, she was urging Hester towards the door.

There was no possible civil answer except to comply.

"Of course," Hester said with forced warmth. The opportunity to learn anything was slipping away from her, and she could think of nothing to keep it. One moment, as she held the trinket box, she had felt as if the old friendship was there, and the next they were strangers being polite and trying to escape each other. "Thank you for the box," she added. "Perhaps I could come back for it at a more convenient time?"

"Oh!" Imogen was startled. "Yes . . . of course. I hadn't thought of you carrying it. I'll bring it one day."

Hester smiled. "Come soon." She opened the withdrawing room door, and giving Imogen a light kiss on the cheek, she walked across the hall just as the maid opened the front door for her, bobbing a half curtsy.

The following morning Hester went into the City to report on her visit, and at shortly after ten o'clock she was in Charles's offices in Fenchurch Street. Within minutes he sent for her and she was shown to his room. He looked as stiff and immaculate as he had when he visited her, and his face was just as pale and shadowed by lack of sleep. He stood up as she came in, and gave her a quick kiss on the cheek, inviting her to take the chair opposite the desk. He remained standing, his eyes fixed on her face.

"How are you?" he asked. "Would you like tea?"

She wanted to reach across the gulf between them and say something like "For heaven's sake, ask me what you want to! Don't fidget! Don't pretend!" But she knew it would only make it more difficult for him. If she tried to express any of her feelings, or break his own concentration of effort, it would delay the moment rather than bring it closer.

"Thank you," she accepted. "That's most thoughtful."

It was another ten minutes of polite trivia before the tray was brought and the clerk left, closing the door behind him. Charles invited Hester to pour, then at last he sat back and looked at her.

"Did you visit Imogen?" he asked.

"Yes, but not for very long." She was acutely aware that his eyes were studying her face as if he were trying to read something deeper than her words. She wished she could tell him what he so desperately wanted to hear. "She was about to go out, and of course I had not told her I was coming."

"I see." He looked down at his cup as if the liquid in it were of profound interest.

Hester wondered if Imogen found him as difficult to talk to as she did. Had he always been this stilted about anything that touched his emotions, or had Imogen made him this way? What had he been like five or six years ago? She tried to remember. "Charles, I don't know what else to do," she said helplessly. "I can't suddenly start visiting her every day, when I haven't done so for months. She has no reason to confide in me, not only because we are no longer close, but I am your sister. She must know my first loyalty is to you."

He was staring out of the window. Neither of them had touched their tea. "Just as I arrived home yesterday, I saw her leaving. She didn't notice me. I . . . I stayed in the cab and told the driver to follow her."

Hester was too startled to speak. And yet even as she was rejecting the thought, she knew that in his place she might have done the same thing, even if she had hated herself for it afterwards. "Where did she go?" she asked, gulping and struggling to keep her voice level.

"All over the place," he answered, still looking out of the window, away from her. "First she went through a string of back streets to somewhere near Covent Garden. I thought at first she was shopping, although I can't think what she would find there. But she went into a small building and came out without anything." He seemed to be about to add something, then changed his mind, as if he thought better of saying it aloud.

"Was that all?" Hester asked.

"No." He kept his back to her. She saw the rigid line of taut muscles pulling his coat tight. "No, she went to two other places, similar, and came out again within twenty minutes. Lastly she went to a street off the Gray's Inn Road and paid her cabbie off." At last he turned to face her, his eyes challenging. "It was a butcher's shop. She looked . . . excited. Her cheeks were flushed and she ran across the pavement clutching her reticule . . . as if she were going to buy something terribly important. Hester, what could it mean? It doesn't make any sense!"

"I don't know," she admitted. She would like to think Imogen was simply visiting a friend and had perhaps looked for an unusual gift to take to her, but Charles had said she appeared to carry nothing except her reticule. And why go in the evening just as Charles came home, albeit a trifle early, but without telling him?

"I'm . . . I'm afraid for her," he said at last. "Not just for my own sake, but for what scandal she could bring upon herself if she is . . ." He could not say the words.

She did not leave him floundering. "I'll call on her again," she said gently. "We used to be friends. I shall see if I can gain her confidence sufficiently to find out something more."

"Will you . . . will you please keep me . . ." He did not want to say "advised." Sometimes he was aware of being pompous. At his best he could laugh at himself. This time he was afraid of being ridiculous, and of alienating her as well.

"Of course I will," she said firmly. "I would rather be able to tell you simply that she had made a rather unlikely friend of whom she thought you might disapprove, and so she did not tell you."

"Am I so . . ."

She made herself smile. "Well, I haven't seen the friend. Perhaps she's very eccentric, or has fearfully common manners."

He blinked suddenly. "Yes . . . perhaps . . ."

The clerk came to the door and said apologetically that Mr. Latterly's next client was still waiting. Hester excused herself, walking out into the street and the busy traffic, the errand boys, the bankers in their dark suits, the carriages with harnesses gleaming in the sun, a sense of oppression closing in on her.

CHAPTER
TWO

—

Hester was clearing away the dishes after luncheon and had just put the last one into the sink when the front doorbell rang. She allowed Monk to answer it, hoping it might be a new client. Also, she was wet up to the elbows and disliked doing dishes quite enough not to have to make two attempts at it.

She heard Monk's step across the floor and the door open, then several moments of silence. She had dried the first plate and was reaching for the second when she was aware of Monk standing in the kitchen doorway. She looked around at him.

His face was so grave it startled her. The clean, hard lines of it were bleak. The light shone on his cheekbones and brow; his eyes were shadowed.

"What is it?" she said with a gulp of fear. It was more than a new case, however tragic. It was something that touched them in the heart. "William?"

He came a step further in. "Kristian Beck's wife has been murdered," he answered so quietly that whoever was waiting in the sitting room would not have heard him.

She was stunned. It hardly seemed believable. She had a picture in her mind of a thin, middle-aged woman, lonely and angry, perhaps attacked by a thief in the street.

"Does Callandra know?" She asked the thing that was of most importance to her, even before Kristian himself.

"Yes. She's come to tell us."

"Oh." She put down the towel, her thoughts whirling. She was sorry anyone should be dead, but no matter how ashamed she was of it, her imagination leaped ahead to a time when Kristian would feel free to marry Callandra. It was indecent . . . but it was there.

"She'd like to see you," Monk said quietly.

"Yes, of course." She went past him into the sitting room and immediately saw Callandra in the center of the floor, still standing. She appeared bereaved, as if something had happened which she could not begin to understand. She smiled when she saw Hester, but it was a matter of friendship and without any pleasure at all. Her eyes were bright and frightened.

"Hester, my dear," she said shakily. "I'm so sorry to call at such a silly time of the afternoon, but I have just heard dreadful news, as I expect William has told you."

Hester went to her and took both Callandra's hands in her own, holding them gently. "Yes, he did. Kristian's wife has been killed. How did it happen?"

Callandra's fingers tightened over hers and held her surprisingly hard. "No one really knows yet. She was found this morning in the studio of the artist Argo Allardyce. He was painting a portrait of her." Her brow puckered faintly, as if she found it difficult to believe. "The cleaning woman came and found them . . . both . . ."

"Both?" Hester said with a catch in her breath. "You mean the artist as well?" It seemed incredible.

"No . . . no," Callandra said quickly. "Mrs. Beck and the artists' model Sarah Mackeson."

"You mean Allardyce killed them both?" Hester was struggling to make sense of it. "Yesterday afternoon? Why?"

Callandra looked totally confused. "No one knows. There was nobody there from midday until this morning. It could have happened at any time."

"She would not have a sitting in the evening," Hester replied. "He wouldn't paint after the light was gone."

Callandra colored faintly. "Oh no, of course not. I'm sorry. It's

22

ridiculous how deeply it shocks one when it is someone connected, however . . ."

Monk came in from the kitchen. "The kettle is boiling," he told Hester.

"Oh, for goodness' sake!" Callandra said with a tight little laugh. "You can make a cup of tea, William!"

He stopped, perhaps realizing for the first time how close to hysteria she was.

Hester turned to him to see if he understood. She saw the flash of comprehension in his eyes, and left him to attend to tea. She looked at Callandra. "Sit down," she directed, almost guiding her to the other chair. "Have you any idea why this Allardyce did such a thing?" Now that she was met with the necessity of thinking about it more rationally, she realized she knew nothing at all about Mrs. Beck.

Callandra made a profound effort at self-control. "I don't know for certain that it was Allardyce," she answered. "They were both found in his studio. Allardyce himself was gone." Her eyes met Hester's, pleading for some answer that would make it no more than a sadness far removed from them, like an accident in the street, tragic but not personal. But it was not possible. Whatever had happened, this would change their lives irrevocably simply by the violence of it.

Hester tried to think of something to say, but before she could, Monk came back into the room with tea on a tray. He poured, and they all sat in silence for a few moments, sipping the hot liquid and feeling it ease the clenched-up knots inside.

Callandra set her cup down and faced Monk with more composure. "William, she and this other woman were murdered. It is sure to be very ugly and distressing, no matter how it happened. Dr. Beck will be involved because he is . . . was her husband." She picked up her tea once more, but her hand wobbled a trifle and she set the cup down again before she spilled it. "There are bound to be a lot of questions, and not all of them will be kind." Her face looked extraordinarily vulnerable, almost bruised. "Please . . . will you do what you can to protect him?"

Hester turned to look at Monk also. He had left the police force with extreme ill feeling between himself and his superior. One could debate whether he had resigned or been dismissed. Asking him to involve himself in a police matter was requiring of him a great deal. Yet both he and Hester owed Callandra more than was measurable in purely practical terms, regardless of loyalty and affection, which would in themselves have been sufficient. She had given them unquestioning friendship regardless of her own reputation. In lean times she had discreetly supported them financially, never referring to it or asking anything in return but to be included.

Hester saw the hesitation in Monk's face. She drew breath in to say something that would urge him to accept. Then she saw that he was going to, and was ashamed of herself for having doubted him.

"I'll go to the station concerned," he agreed. "Where were they found?"

"Acton Street," Callandra replied, relief quick in her voice. "Number twelve. It's a house with an artist's studio on the top floor."

"Acton Street?" Monk frowned, trying to place it.

"Off the Gray's Inn Road," Callandra told him. "Just beyond the Royal Free Hospital."

Hester felt her mouth go dry. She tried to swallow, and it caught in her throat.

Monk was looking at Callandra. His face was blank, but the muscles in his neck were pulled tight. Hester knew that the studio must be in Runcorn's area, and that Monk would have to approach him if he were to involve himself. It was an old enmity going back to Monk's first days on the force. But whatever he felt about that now, he masked it well. He was already bending his mind to the task.

"How did you hear about it so soon?" he asked Callandra.

"Kristian told me," she replied. "We had a hospital meeting this afternoon, and he had to cancel it. He asked me to make his excuses." She swallowed, her tea ignored.

"She can't have been home all night," he went on. "Wasn't he concerned for her?"

She avoided his eyes very slightly. "I didn't ask him. I . . . I believe they led separate lives."

As a friend, he might not have pressed the matter—it was delicate—but when he was in pursuit of truth neither his mind nor his tongue accepted boundaries. He might hate probing an area he knew would cause pain, but that had never stopped him. He could be as ruthless with the dark mists of the memory within himself, and he knew with bone-deep familiarity just how that hurt. He had had to piece together the shards of his own past before the accident. Some of them were full of color, others were dark, and to look at them cost all the courage he had.

"Where was he yesterday evening?" he continued, looking at Callandra.

Her eyes opened wide, and Hester saw the fear in them. Monk must have seen it also. She looked as if she were about to say one thing, then cleared her throat and said something else. "Please protect his reputation, William," she pleaded. "He is Bohemian, and although his English is perfect, he is still a foreigner. And . . . they did not have the happiest of marriages. Don't allow them to harass him or suggest some kind of guilt by innuendo."

He did not offer her any false assurances. "Tell me something about Mrs. Beck," he said instead. "What kind of woman was she?"

Callandra hesitated; a flicker of surprise was in her eyes, then gone again. "I'm not certain that I know a great deal," she confessed uncomfortably. "I never met her. She didn't involve herself with the hospital at all, and . . ." She blushed. "I don't really know Dr. Beck socially."

Hester looked at Monk. If he found anything odd in Callandra's answer there was no sign of it in his expression. His face was tense, eyes concentrated upon hers. "What about her circle of friends?" he asked. "Did she entertain? What were her interests? What did she do with her time?"

Now Callandra was definitely uncomfortable. The color deepened in her face. "I'm afraid I don't know. He speaks of her hardly at all. I . . . I gathered from something he said that she was away from home a great deal, but he did not say where. He mentioned once that she had considerable political knowledge and spoke German. But then, Kristian himself spent many years in Vienna, so perhaps that is not very surprising."

"Was she Bohemian, too?" Monk asked quickly.

"No . . . at least I don't think so."

Monk stood up. "I'll go to the police station and see what I can learn." His voice softened. "Don't worry yet. It may be that the artists' model was the intended victim, and only a tragic mischance that Mrs. Beck was also there at that moment."

She made an effort to smile. "Thank you. I . . . I know it is not easy for you to ask them."

He shrugged very slightly, dismissing it, then put on his jacket, sliding it easily over his shoulders and pulling it straight. It was beautifully cut. Whatever his income, or lack of it, he had always dressed with elegance and a certain flair. He would pay his tailor even if he ate bread and drank water.

He turned in the doorway and gave Hester a glance from which she understood thoughts and feelings it would have taken minutes to explain, and then he was gone.

Hester bent her attention to Callandra and whatever comfort she could offer.

Monk disliked the thought of asking any favor of Runcorn even more than Callandra was aware. It was largely pride. It stung like a burn on the skin, but he could not possibly ignore either the duty, both moral and emotional, or the inner compulsion to learn the truth. The purity and the danger of knowledge had always fascinated him, even when it forced him to face things that hurt, stripped bare secrets and wounds. It was a challenge to his skill and his courage, and facing Runcorn was a price he never seriously thought too high.

He strode along Grafton Street down to Tottenham Court Road and caught a hansom for the mile or so to the police station.

During the ride he thought about what Callandra had told him. He knew Kristian Beck only slightly, but instinctively he liked him. He admired his courage and the single-mindedness of his crusade to improve medical treatment for the poor. He was gentler than Monk would have been, a man with patience and a broadness of spirit that seemed to be almost without personal ambition or hunger for praise. Monk could not have said as much for himself, and he knew it.

At the police station, he paid the driver and braced his shoulders, then walked up the steps and inside. The duty sergeant regarded him with interest. With a wave of relief for the present, Monk recalled how different walking into a station house had been the first time after the accident. Then it had been fear in the man's face, an instant respect born of the experience of Monk's lacerating tongue and his expectation that everyone should match his own standards, in precisely his way.

"Mornin', Mr. Monk. What can we do for yer terday?" the sergeant said cheerfully. Perhaps with the passage of time he had grown in confidence. A good leader would have seen to that. But it was pointless regretting past inadequacies now.

"Good morning, Sergeant," Monk replied. He had been thinking how to phrase his request so as to achieve what he wanted without having to beg. "I may possibly have some information about a crime which occurred late yesterday in Acton Street. May I speak with whoever is in charge of the investigation?" If he were fortunate it would be John Evan, one man of whose friendship he was certain.

"You mean the murders, o' course." The sergeant nodded sagely.

"That'd be Mr. Runcorn 'isself, sir. Very serious, this is. Yer lucky as 'e's in. I'll tell 'im yer 'ere."

Monk was surprised that Runcorn, the man in command of the station and who had not worked cases personally in several years, should concern himself with what seemed to be an ordinary domestic tragedy. Was he ambitious to solve something simple, and so be seen to succeed and take the credit? Or could the case be important in some way Monk could not foresee, and Runcorn dare not appear to be indifferent?

He sat down on the wooden bench, prepared for a long wait. Runcorn would do that simply to make very sure that Monk never forgot that he no longer had any status there.

However, it was less than five minutes before a constable came and took him up to Runcorn's room, and that was disconcerting because it was not what he expected.

The room was exactly as it had always been, tidy, unimaginative, designed to impress with the importance of its occupant and yet failing, simply because it tried too hard. A man at ease with himself would have cared so much less.

Runcorn himself also was the same, tall with a long, narrow face, a little less florid than before, his hair grizzled and not quite so thick, but still handsome. He regarded Monk cautiously. It was as if they were catapulted back in time. All the old rivalries were just as sharp, the knowledge precisely where and how to hurt, the embarrassments, the doubts, the failures each wished forgotten and always saw reflected in the other's eyes.

Runcorn looked up and regarded Monk steadily, his face very nearly devoid of expression. "Baker says you know something about the murders in Acton Street," he said. "Is that right?"

Now was the time to avoid telling the slightest lie, even by implication. It would come back in enmity later on and do irreparable damage. And yet the whole truth was no use in gaining any cooperation from Runcorn. He was already tense, preparing to defend himself against the slightest insult or erosion of his authority. The years when Monk had mocked him with quicker thought and more agile tongue, an easier manner, lay an uncrossable gulf between.

Monk had racked his mind all the way there for something clever and true to say, and had arrived still without it. Now he was standing in the familiar surroundings of Runcorn's office, and the silence was already too long. In truth, he knew no information about the murders in Acton Street, and anything he knew about Kristian Beck, and the relationship between himself and his wife, was likely to do more harm than good.

"I'm a friend of the family in Mrs. Beck's case," he said, and even as the words were on his tongue he realized how ridiculous and inadequate they were.

Runcorn stared at him, and for a moment his eyes were almost blank. He was weighing up what Monk had said, considering something. Monk expected a withering reply and braced himself for it.

"That . . . could be helpful," Runcorn said slowly. The words seemed forced from him.

"Of course . . . it may be a simple case," Monk went on. "I believe there was another woman killed as well . . ." He was undecided whether to make that a question or a statement and it hung in the air unfinished.

"Yes," Runcorn agreed, then rushed on. "Sarah Mackeson, an artists' model." He said the words with distaste. "Looks as if they were killed pretty well at the same time."

Monk shifted his weight a little from one foot to the other. "You're handling the case yourself . . ."

"Short of men," Runcorn said dryly. "Lot of illness, and unfortunately Evan is away."

"I see. I . . ." Monk changed his mind. It was too abrupt to offer help.

"What?" Runcorn looked up at him. His face was almost expressionless, his eyes only faintly belligerent.

Monk was annoyed for having got himself into such a position. Now he did not know what to say, but he was not prepared to retreat.

Runcorn stared down at the desk with its clean surface, uncluttered by papers, reports, or books of reference. "Actually, Mrs. Beck's father is a prominent lawyer," he said quietly. "Likely to run for Parliament soon, so I hear."

Monk was startled. He masked it quickly, before Runcorn looked up again. So the case had a different kind of importance. If Kristian's wife had social connections, her murder would be reported in all the newspapers. An arrest would be expected soon. Whoever was in charge of the investigation would not escape the public eye, and the praise or blame that fear whipped up. No wonder Runcorn was unhappy.

Monk put his hands in his pockets and relaxed. However, he did not yet take the liberty of sitting down uninvited, which irked him. He would once have sat as a matter of course. "That's unfortunate," he observed mildly.

Runcorn looked at him with suspicion. "What do you mean?"

"Be easier to conduct an investigation without newspaper writers trampling all over the place or the commissioner expecting results before you begin," Monk replied.

Runcorn paled. "I know that, Monk! I don't need you to tell me! Either say something helpful or go back to finding lost dogs, or whatever it is you do these days." Then instantly his eyes were hot with regret, but he could not take back the words, and Monk was the last man to whom he would admit error, let alone ask for help.

At another time Monk might have relished Runcorn's discomfort, but now he needed his cooperation. However much they both disliked it, neither could see how to achieve what he wished without the other.

Runcorn was the first to yield. He picked up a pen, although he had no paper in front of him. His fingers gripped it hard. "Well, do you know anything useful, or not?" he demanded.

Monk was caught out by the directness of the question. He saw the recognition of it in Runcorn's eyes. He had to allow him to taste the small victory. It was the only way he could take the next step. "Not yet," he admitted. "Tell me what you have so far, and if I can help, then I will." Now he sat down, crossing his legs comfortably and waiting.

Runcorn swallowed his temper and began. "Number twelve, Acton Street. Cleaning woman found two bodies this morning when she went in around half past eight. Both roughly in their late thirties, the sergeant guessed, and both killed by having their necks broken. Looks like there was a struggle. Carpet rumpled up, chair on its side."

"Do you know which woman was killed first?" Monk cut in.

"No way to tell." There was resentment in Runcorn's voice but none in his face. He wanted Monk's help, whatever the emotions between them; he knew he needed it, and at the moment that overrode all past history. "The other woman was apparently Allardyce's model, and she sort of half lived there." He let the sentence hang with all its ugly judgments.

Monk did not skirt around it. "So it's going to look like jealousy of some sort."

Runcorn pulled the corners of his mouth down. "The model was half undressed," he conceded. "And Allardyce was nowhere to be found this morning. He turned up about ten and said he'd been out all night. Haven't had time yet to check if that's true." He put the pen down again.

"Doesn't make sense," Monk observed. "If he wasn't there, why did Mrs. Beck go for a sitting? If she arrived and found him gone, is she the sort of woman to have sat around talking to the model?"

"Not if that's all she went for." Runcorn bit his lip, his face full of misery. He did not need to explain the pitfalls for a policeman faced with proving that the daughter of an eminent figure was having an affair, one so sordid in its nature that it had ended in a double murder, with an artist.

There would also be no way whatever of avoiding dragging Kristian into it. No man would take lightly his wife's betraying him in such a way. In spite of himself, Monk felt a twinge of pity for Runcorn, the more so knowing his pretensions to social acceptability and the long, hard journey he had made towards being respected, rather than merely tolerated, by those he admired. He would never achieve what he wished, and it would continue to hurt him. Monk had the polish in his manner, the elegance of dress to pass for a gentleman, partly because he did not care if he succeeded or not. Runcorn cared intensely, and it betrayed him every time.

"Would it help if I were to see what I can learn in a roundabout way?" Monk offered casually. "Through friends, rather than by direct questioning?" He watched Runcorn struggle with his pride, his dislike of Monk, and his appreciation of just how awkward the situation could become and his own inadequacy to deal with it. He was trying to gauge what help Monk would be and how willing he was to try. What did he want out of it, and how far could he be trusted?

Monk waited.

"I suppose if you know the family it might avoid embarrassment," Runcorn said at last. His voice was matter-of-fact, but his hands were clenched on the desk. "Be careful," he added warningly, looking up at Monk directly at last. "It may not be anything like it seems, and we don't want to make fools of ourselves. And you're not official!"

"Of course not," Monk agreed, keeping the amusement out of his expression, bitter as it was. He knew why Runcorn did not trust him. Given the circumstances, he would have despised him if he had. It was a large enough admission of his vulnerability that he had confided in Monk at all. "I suppose you're looking for witnesses? Anyone seen near the place? Where does Allardyce claim to have been?"

Runcorn's face reflected his contempt for the unorthodox and bohemian life. "He says he was out drinking with friends in Southwark all night, looking for some kind of . . . of new light, he said. Whatever that may mean. Bit odd, in the middle of the night, if you ask me."

"And do these friends agree?" Monk enquired.

"Too busy looking for new light themselves to know," Runcorn replied with a twist of his mouth. "But I've got men following it up, and we'll find something sooner or later. Acton Street's busy enough—evenings, anyway." He cleared his throat. "I suppose you'd like to see the bodies? Not that the surgeon has much yet."

"Yes," Monk agreed, trying not to sound eager. His affection for Callandra and his regard for Kristian made it imperative he do what he could to help, but it also made it a personal tragedy too close to his own emotions.

Runcorn stood up, hesitated a moment as if still undecided exactly how to proceed, then went to the door. Monk followed him down the stairs and out past the desk. It was less than half a mile to the morgue, and in the density of traffic, easier to walk than try to find a hansom.

The pavements were crowded and the noises of hooves and wheels, the shouts of drivers and street hawkers, the creak and rattle of harnesses filled the air. Sweat and horse manure were sharp in the nostrils, and they could go only a few yards before having to alter course to avoid bumping into people.

They walked in silence, excused from trying to converse by the conditions, and both glad of it. They passed a seller of peppermint water on the first corner, and had to wait several moments for a lull in traffic before they could cross, dodging between carts, carriages and drays, and a costermonger's barrow being pushed, oblivious of pedestrians. Runcorn swore under his breath and leaped for the curb.

A newsboy was shouting the headlines about Garibaldi's campaign in Naples and the fact that there had been no further major battles in America since the bloody encounter at Bull Run two and a half months ago. No one was paying him the slightest attention.

The few bystanders who had no urgent business were listening to the running patterer whose entertainment value was far higher.

"Double murder in Acton Street!" he called in his singsong voice. "Two 'alf-naked women found broken-necked in artist's rooms! Stop a few minutes an' I'll tell yer all abaht it!"

Half a dozen people accepted his invitation, and coins chinked in his cup.

Runcorn swore again and plunged on, pushing his way between a large City gentleman in pinstriped trousers who blushed at being caught listening to the gossip, and a thin clerk clutching a briefcase who only wanted to attract the attention of the ham sandwich seller.

"See what I mean?" Runcorn said furiously as they reached the morgue and went up the steps. "Story's got arms and legs even before we've said a word to anyone. I don't know who tells them these things! Seem to breathe it in the air." He pushed the door open and Monk followed behind him, tasting the sweet-and-sour odor of death, which was always made worse by carbolic and wet stone. He saw from the tightness in Runcorn's face that it affected him the same way.

The police surgeon was a dark, stocky man with a voice like velvet. He shook his head as soon as he saw Runcorn. "Too soon," he said, waving a hand. "Can't tell you any more than I did this morning. Think I'm a magician?"

"Just want to look," Runcorn replied, walking past him towards the door at the other end of the room.

The surgeon regarded Monk curiously, raising one eyebrow so high it made his face lopsided.

Runcorn ignored him. He chose not to explain himself. "Come on," he said to Monk abruptly.

Monk caught up with him and went into the room where bodies were kept until they could be released to the undertaker. He must have been in places like this all his professional life, although he could remember only the last five years of it. It always knotted his stomach. He would not like to think he could ever have come to such a place with indifference.

Runcorn moved over to one of the tables and pulled the sheet off the face of the body, holding it carefully to show only as far as the neck and shoulders. She was a tall woman, her flesh smooth and blemishless. Her features were handsome rather than beautiful, and the bones of her cheek and brow suggested her eyes had been remarkable, and now her lashes stood out against the pallor of her skin. Her thick hair was tawny red-brown and lay about her like a russet pillow.

"Sarah Mackeson," Runcorn said quietly, keeping his face averted, his voice catching a little as he tried to keep emotion out of it.

Monk looked up at him.

Runcorn cleared his throat. He was embarrassed. Monk wondered what thoughts were going through his mind, what imagination as to this woman's life, the passions that had moved her and made her whatever she was. Artists' models were by definition disreputable to him, and yet whatever he meant to feel, he was moved by her death. There was no spirit, no consciousness in what was left of her, but Runcorn seemed discomforted by her closeness, the reality of her body.

A few years ago Monk might have mocked him for that. Now he was annoyed because it made Runcorn also more human, and he wanted to retain his dislike for him. It was what he was used to.

"Well?" Runcorn demanded. "Seen enough? Her neck was broken. Want to look at the bruises on her arms?"

"Of course," Monk replied curtly.

Runcorn moved the sheet so her arms were shown, but very carefully held it not to reveal her breasts. Without wishing to, Monk liked him the better for that, too. It didn't occur to him that it could be prudery rather than respect. There was something in the way Runcorn held the cloth, the touch of his fingers on it, that belied the idea.

Monk bent and looked at the very slight indentations on the smooth flesh, barely discolored.

"Dead too quickly for it to mark much," Runcorn explained unnecessarily.

"I know that," Monk said. "Looks as if she fought a bit." He picked up one of the limp hands and looked to see if she might have scratched her killer, but none of the nails were broken, nor was there any skin or blood underneath them. He put it down and looked at the other, finding nothing there either.

Runcorn watched him silently, and when he had finished, pulled up the sheet again and walked over to the next table. He lifted the sheet from the face and shoulders of the woman there.

Monk's first reaction was to be angry that Runcorn had made such a disturbing mistake. Why couldn't he have been careful enough to have got the right body? This could not be Kristian Beck's wife. She was very slender, and must have been almost as tall as Kristian. Her cloud of dark hair was untouched by gray, and her face, even without the spark of life in it, was beautiful. Her features were delicate, almost ethereal, and yet haunted by an element of passion that remained even now in this soulless place with its damp air and smells of carbolic and death.

He did not care in the slightest what Runcorn thought of her, yet he had to look up at him to see.

Runcorn was watching him. Through the trouble and the uncertainty in his eyes there was a sudden spark of triumph. "You didn't know her, did you? You were expecting someone else. Don't lie to me, Monk!"

"I didn't say I knew her," Monk replied. "I know her husband."

The momentary satisfaction died from Runcorn's face. "He's still too shocked to make any sense, but we'll have to question him again. You know that?"

"Of course!"

"That's why you're really here, isn't it? You're afraid he did it. Found her with Allardyce and killed her. . . ." His voice was harsh, as if he were angry with his own vulnerability, and deliberately hurting himself by saying something before anyone else could.

But she had the kind of face that affected people in such a way. It was that of a dreamer, an idealist, someone intensely alive, and it twisted some secret place inside to see her broken. He looked up and met Runcorn's angry gaze with an equal anger of his own. "Yes, of course I'm afraid he did it! Are you saying you've only just realized that?"

Now Runcorn had to say yes, and look stupid, or no, and leave himself no reason to change his mind about seeking Monk's help. He chose the latter, and without a struggle, betraying just how worried he was, how far beyond his depth. "She died of a broken neck also," he said flatly. "And two of her fingernails are torn. She put up more of a fight. I'll bet someone has a few bruises and maybe a scratch or two . . . and . . ." He indicated her right ear and pulled back the hair to show the torn flesh where an earring must have been ripped from her. "And this."

"Did you find it?" Monk asked.

"No. Searched the place, even the cracks between the floor-boards, but no sign of it."

"And you've searched Allardyce?" Monk said quickly. He found himself shaking with anger that this woman had been destroyed, and confused by how different she was from anything he had imagined.

"Of course we have. Nothing. At least nothing that counts. He's got the odd cut and scratch on his hands, but he says he has them all the time, from palette knives, blades to cut canvas, nails and things to stretch them, that kind of thing. He said to ask any artist and they'd say the same. He swears he never even saw her that night, much less killed her. He looks shattered by it, and if he's acting, then he should be on the stage."

The chill of the morgue began to eat into Monk and the smell of it churned his stomach. He reminded himself he had known men before who had killed—in rage, jealousy or wounded pride—and then been as horrified as anyone else afterwards. And a woman as hauntingly beautiful as Kristian's wife might have woken all kinds of passions in Allardyce, or anyone else, especially Kristian himself.

"Seen enough now?" Runcorn's voice cut across his thoughts.

"Clothes," Monk said almost absently. "How were they dressed?"

"The model had on a loose kind of gown, a sort of . . . shift, I suppose you'd call it," Runcorn said awkwardly. His embarrassment and contempt for her style of life and all he imagined of it were sharp in his voice. His lips tightened and a faint color washed up his cheeks. "And Mrs. Beck wore an ordinary sort of dress, high neck, dark, buttoned down the front. It fitted her very well, but it's not new."

"Boots?" Monk asked curiously.

"Of course. She didn't go there barefoot." Then understanding flashed in his face. "Oh—you mean had she them on? Yes."

"Actually, I meant were they old or new?" Monk replied. "I assumed that if she had taken them off you'd have mentioned it."

The color deepened in Runcorn's face, but this time it was irritation. "Oldish—why? Doesn't Beck make a decent living? Her father's Fuller Pendreigh. Very important man, and bound to have money."

"Doesn't mean he gave any of it to his daughter," Monk pointed out. "Now that she's a married woman, and has been for . . . do you know how long?"

Runcorn raised his eyebrows. "Don't you know?"

"No idea," Monk admitted testily. Except that it had to be longer than he had known Callandra, but he would not say that to Runcorn.

"I suppose you want to see them. They won't tell you much. I've already looked." But Runcorn did not argue. He covered the white face again, tucking in the corner of the sheet as if it mattered, then he led the way across the floor, his footsteps echoing, to the small room where property of the dead was kept. It was locked away. He had to get a clerk to open up the drawers for him.

Monk picked up Sarah Mackeson's shift. There was still a faint aroma of her clinging to it, almost like a warmth. The sense of her reality came over him like a wave, more powerful than actually seeing her body. His hands were shaking as he put it down. There was no underwear. Had she been so confident in her beauty she was happy to dispense with the privacy more conventional dress would have given her? Or had she been sitting for Allardyce and simply slipped these things on while he took a break, expecting him to resume? Why hadn't he?

Or had she gone to bed for the night, either alone or with someone, when Mrs. Beck had arrived? For that matter, did she often spend the night at Allardyce's studio? There were a lot of questions to be answered about her. The most important in Monk's mind, and becoming more and more insistent with every moment, was, had she been the intended victim, and Kristian's wife only an unwilling witness who had been silenced in the most terrible way?

"Is there really nothing to tell which one died first?" he said, putting the shift back and beginning to go through the next box, which was Mrs. Beck's. He found it difficult to think of her by that name, she was so different from anything he had envisioned, and yet he knew no other.

"Nothing so far." Runcorn was watching him as if every move he made, every shadow across his face, might have meaning. He was desperate. "Surgeon can't tell me anything, but we know from the tenant on the floor below that he heard women's voices at about half past nine in the evening."

"Presumably Mrs. Beck arriving?" Monk observed. "Or whoever killed her? At least one or both of them were alive then."

"Presumably," Runcorn agreed. "Maybe you'll make something more of it if you speak to the man."

Monk hid a very slight smile. Runcorn still had that inner belief that there was always something hidden that Monk would find and he would not. It had happened so many times in the past it was the pattern of their lives.

Mrs. Beck's clothes were good quality, he could feel it in the fabric under his fingers, fine cambric in the undergarments, even though they had been laundered so many times they were worn almost threadbare in places. The dress was wool, but the slight strain on the seams of the bodice betrayed that it had been worn several years, and altered at least once. The boots were excellent leather and beautifully cut, but a cobbler had resoled and reheeled them again and again. Even the uppers were scuffed now and had taken a lot of polishing to make them look good. Was that poverty or thrift? Or had Kristian been meaner than Monk had imagined?

He picked up the thin, gold wedding ring, and one delicate earring which might have been gold or pinchbeck. It was a pretty thing, but not expensive. He looked up at Runcorn, trying to judge what he made of it, and seeing confusion in his eyes.

"Well?" Runcorn asked.

Monk folded the clothes and closed the box without answering.

"I suppose you want to see the studio?" Runcorn pursed his lips.

"What do you make of Allardyce?" Monk asked, following him out, thanking the surgeon and going into the street. This time Runcorn stopped a hansom and gave the Acton Street address.

"Hard to say," Runcorn replied at last, as they jolted along and joined the traffic. "Bit of a mess, actually."

Monk let it go until they arrived in Acton Street, as the light was beginning to fade. It was a reasonable-sized house. The ground floor was let to a jeweler who was presently away on business, the second floor to a milliner, who repeated to Monk exactly what he had told Runcorn. There had been a loud cry, a woman's voice, at about half past nine.

"Was it a scream?" Monk asked. "A cry? Fear? Or pain?"

The man's face puckered. "To be honest, it sounded like laughter," he replied. "That's why I thought nothing of it."

"Can't shake him from that," Runcorn said in disgust. "Got men out in the street. Might turn up something."

40

There was a constable on duty on the landing outside the door. Runcorn greeted him perfunctorily and then went in, Monk on his heels.

"This is it," Runcorn told him, stopping in the middle of the room and gazing around. There were three large woven rugs of different colors on the floor, their edges touching. Windows faced out over the rooftops, but even this late, most of the illumination came from skylights to both north and south. It was immediately obvious why an artist appreciated the studio's almost shadowless clarity. An easel was set up in one corner, a couch on the far side, and a selection of chairs and other props were huddled in the third corner. A second doorway led to the rest of the rooms beyond.

"Mrs. Beck was found lying there." Runcorn pointed to the floor just in front of where Monk was standing. "And Sarah Mackeson was there, at the join of those two carpets. They were scuffed up a bit where she must have fallen." He indicated another place a couple of yards away, closer to the main door.

"Looks as if someone had just killed Sarah Mackeson as Mrs. Beck came in from the street and saw him, and he killed her before she could escape," Monk observed. "Or else someone killed Mrs. Beck, not realizing the model was here, and she disturbed him and got killed for her pains."

"Something like that," Runcorn agreed. "But nothing so far to say which. Or a three-cornered quarrel between Allardyce and the two women which got out of hand, and then he had to kill the second woman because of the first."

"And you found nothing?" Monk assumed.

"Searched the place, of course," Runcorn said unhappily. "But nothing of any meaning. No one was obliging enough to leave bloodstains, except a few drops on the carpet where Mrs. Beck was, from her torn ear. Hunted everywhere for the earring, but never found it. No footprints or bits of cloth, or anything so convenient." He pursed his lips. "No weapon needed. Whoever it was came in through the door, like anyone else. Allardyce said it wasn't often locked."

"And we presume Mrs. Beck was here and alive at half past nine, because the milliner heard women's voices, possibly laughing. Did anyone see her outside in the street?"

"Not so far, but we're still looking."

"Did she come by cab? For that matter, where does she live?"

"Thought you knew Dr. Beck." Runcorn was sharp.

"I do. I've never been to his home."

"Haverstock Hill."

"Three miles at least, so she must have come by cab, or in a carriage, and Beck doesn't have a carriage."

"We're looking. It might help for time, if nothing else."

The far door opened and a disheveled man in his late thirties stood leaning against the frame. He was tall and lanky with very dark hair which flopped forward over his brow. His eyes were startlingly blue, and at the moment he was badly in need of a shave, giving his face a look both humorous and faintly sinister. He ignored Monk and regarded Runcorn with dislike. "What do you want now?" he demanded. "I've already told you everything I know. For God's sake, can't you leave me alone? I feel terrible."

"Perhaps you should wash and shave and sober up, sir?" Runcorn suggested with ill-concealed distaste.

"I'm not drunk!" Allardyce replied, his blue eyes hard. "I've just had two friends murdered in my home." He took a deep breath and shivered convulsively. He turned to Monk, regarding his jacket with its perfectly tailored shoulders and his polished boots. "Who the devil are you?" He had obviously dismissed the possibility of his being police.

"He's assisting me," Runcorn said before Monk could reply. "Now that you've had time to gather yourself a bit, I'd like to ask you a few more questions."

Allardyce slumped into the only chair and sat with his head in his hands. "What?" he asked without looking up at either of them.

"How long did you know Mrs. Beck?" Monk said before Runcorn did.

Allardyce took no notice of the fact that it was Monk who spoke. He seemed still deeply shocked and in a kind of despair. "A few months," he answered. "I'm not sure. What does it matter? What is time anyway, except what we put into it? It's like space. Who can measure nothingness?"

Was the man being deliberately contentious, or were his words a reflection of how deeply he had cared for Kristian's wife? From the wretchedness of his body, the sagging shoulders, the feet sticking out, the bowed head, Monk could easily believe it was the latter. "So you knew her well?" he said aloud.

"Infinitely," Allardyce answered, looking up at Monk now as if he perceived some glimmer of understanding where he had not expected it.

"Was her husband aware of that?" Runcorn interrupted.

"Her husband was a philistine!" Allardyce said bitterly. "As you are!"

Runcorn colored faintly. He knew he was being insulted but he was not quite sure how. If it were his morality, then from such a man it was a compliment, even if not intended as such.

"Did you know him well?" Monk enquired conversationally.

"What?" Allardyce was startled.

Monk repeated the question.

Allardyce's face tensed, and he retreated a little into himself. "No. Actually, I never met him."

"So why is it you think he is a philistine? Did she say so?"

Allardyce hesitated. Admitting this would paint him in an ugly light, and he was obviously aware of it. "He didn't appreciate her anymore, didn't see the depth of her, the mystery," he tried to explain. "She was a remarkable woman—unique."

"She was certainly beautiful," Monk agreed. "But perhaps beauty wasn't his chief criterion?"

Allardyce climbed to his feet, glanced at Monk for a moment, then walked over to a pile of canvases in the corner behind his easel. He picked out two or three and turned them face out so Monk could see them. They were all of Beck's wife. The first was quickly done, a simple sketch of a woman sitting in the sun, painted in afterwards to catch the spirit of light and shade, the spontaneous smile of someone caught in a moment of enjoyment. It was excellently done, and Monk immediately saw Allardyce in a different light. He was a man with acute perception and the gift to capture it with his hand and eye. He was an artist, not merely a craftsman.

The second, a far more formal portrait of a woman very obviously posing, was unfinished. She wore a gown of rich plum color which faded into the warm, dark tones of the background, throwing her face and shoulders into prominence as the light gleamed on her skin. She looked delicate, almost fragile, and yet there was extraordinary strength of passion in her features. Now Monk knew what she had been like when she was alive. He almost imagined he could hear her voice.

But the last picture was the one which affected him the most. It was painted with a limited palette, mostly blues and grays with barely a touch of green in the foreground. It was a city street in the evening in the rain. The shop signs were suggested rather than depicted in detail, but there was enough of the writing to show it was German. In the foreground was Beck's wife, younger than now, and the haunting quality of her beauty and the strength of her passion and sorrow were enhanced by the misty half-light from the street lamps. Horses with black plumes—again, suggested more than painted in full—made it plain that she was watching a funeral; and the shadows of other mourners—almost the ghosts, as if they, too, were dead—ringed the cortege. But all the emphasis was upon her and her feelings, everything else was merely to enhance the power and mystery of her face.

Monk stared at it. It was unforgettable. From what he had seen of her in the morgue, it was an excellent likeness, but far more than that, it had caught the spirit of an extraordinary personality. To have painted such a portrait the artist must have felt for her deeply and understood far more of her nature than mere observation could have taught him. Unless, of course, he was investing in her some passionate experience of his own?

But Monk had seen Beck's wife; the former was easy to believe. "Why this?" he asked Allardyce, indicating the painting.

"What?" Allardyce forced his attention back. "*Funeral in Blue?*"

"Yes. Why did you paint it? Did her father ask for this, too?" He would not have believed Allardyce if he had said he had. No man could create a picture like this on the request of someone else.

Allardyce blinked. "No, I did it for myself. I won't sell it."

"Why Germany?"

"What?" He looked at the painting, his face filled with grief. "It's Vienna," he corrected flatly. "The Austrians speak German."

"Why Vienna?"

"Things she told me, in her past." He looked up at Monk. "What has that got to do with whoever killed her?"

"I don't know. Why were you so long painting the portrait her father commissioned?"

"He was in no hurry."

"Apparently neither were you. No need to get paid?" Monk allowed his voice a slight edge of sarcasm.

Allardyce's eyes blazed for a moment. "I'm an artist, not a journey-man," he retorted. "As long as I can buy paints and canvas, money is unimportant."

"Really," Monk said without expression. "But I assume you would take Pendreigh's money when the picture was completed?"

"Of course! I need to eat . . . and pay the rent."

"And *Funeral in Blue*, would you sell that?"

"No! I told you I wouldn't." His face pinched and the aggression in him melted away. "I won't sell that." He did not feel any need to justify himself. His grief was his own, and he did not care whether Monk understood it or not.

"How many pictures of her did you paint?" Monk asked, watching the anger and misery in his face.

"Elissa? Five or six. Some of them were just sketches." He looked back at Monk, narrowing his eyes. "Why? What does it matter now? If you think I killed her, you're a fool. No artist destroys his inspiration." He did not bother to explain, either because he thought Monk incapable of understanding or because he simply did not care.

Monk looked across at Runcorn and saw the struggle for comprehension in his face. He was foundering in an unfamiliar world, afraid even to try to find his way. Everything about it was different from what he was accustomed to. It offended his rigid upbringing and the rules he had been taught to believe. The immorality of it confused him, and yet he was beginning to realize that it also had standards of a sort, passions, vulnerabilities and dreams.

The moment he was aware of Monk's scrutiny he froze, wiping his expression blank. "Learned anything?" he said curtly.

"Possibly," Monk answered. He pulled out his pocket watch. It was nearly seven o'clock.

"In a hurry?" Runcorn asked.

"I was thinking about Dr. Beck." Monk replaced the watch.

"Tomorrow," Runcorn said. He turned to Allardyce. "It'd be a good idea, sir, if you could be a bit more precise in telling us where you were last night. You said you went out of here about half past four, to Southwark, and didn't get home until ten o'clock this morning. Make a list of everywhere you were and who saw you there."

Allardyce said nothing.

"Mr. Allardyce," Monk commanded his attention. "If you went out at half past four, you can't have been expecting Mrs. Beck for a sitting."

Allardyce frowned. "No . . ."

"Do you know why she came?"

He blinked. "No . . ."

"Did she often come without appointment?"

Allardyce pushed his hands through his black hair and looked at some distance only he could see. "Sometimes. She knew I liked to paint her. If you mean did anyone else know she was coming, I've no idea."

"Did you plan to go out or was it on the spur of the moment?"

"I don't plan, except for sittings." Allardyce stood up. "I've no idea who killed her, or Sarah. If I did, I'd tell you. I don't know anything at all. I've lost two of the most beautiful women I've ever painted, and two friends. Get out and leave me alone to grieve, you damn barbarians!"

There was little enough to be accomplished by remaining, and Monk followed Runcorn out into the street again. Monk was startled how dark it was, more than just an autumn evening closed in. There was a gathering fog wreathing the gas lamps in yellow and blotting out everything beyond ten or fifteen yards' distance. The fog smelled acrid, and within a few moments he found himself coughing.

"Well?" Runcorn asked, looking sideways at him, studying his face.

Monk knew what Runcorn was thinking. He wanted a solution, quickly if possible—in fact, he needed it—but he could not hide the edge of satisfaction that Monk could not produce it any more than he could himself.

"Thought so," Runcorn said dryly. "You'd like to say it was Allardyce, but you can't, can you?" He put his hands into his pockets, then, aware he was pushing his trousers out of shape, pulled them out again quickly.

A hansom cab was almost on them, looming up out of the darkness, hooves muffled in the dead air.

Monk raised his arm, and the cab pulled over to the curb.

Runcorn snorted and climbed in after him.

* * *

Hester's eyes met Monk's with enquiry as soon as he was through the door into the sitting room. She looked tired and anxious. Her hair was straggling out of its pins and she had put it back too tightly on one side. She had taken no handwork out, as if she could not settle to anything.

He closed the door. "Runcorn's on it," he said simply. "He's frightened and he's letting me help. Did you ever meet Kristian's wife?"

"No. Why?" Her voice was edged with fear. She was searching his face to know why he asked. She stood up.

"Did Callandra?" he went on.

"I don't know. Why?"

He walked further into the room, closer to her. It was difficult to explain to anyone the quality in Elissa Beck's face that disturbed one and remained in the mind long after seeing her. Hester was waiting, and he could not find the words.

"She's beautiful," he began, touching her, absently pulling the tight strand of her hair looser, then moving his hand to the warmth of her shoulders. "I don't mean just features or color of hair or skin, I mean some inner quality which made her unique." He saw her surprise. "I know! You thought she was boring, perhaps cold, even that she had lost her looks and no longer took care of herself. . . ."

She started to deny it, then changed her mind.

He smiled very slightly. "So did I," he admitted. "And I don't think the artist killed her. He was at least half in love with her."

"For heaven's sake," she said sharply. "That doesn't mean he didn't kill her! In fact, if she rebuffed him it could be precisely the reason."

"He painted several pictures of her," he went on. "I don't think he would destroy his inspiration, whether she rebuffed him or not. And I had the feeling . . ." He stopped.

"What?" she said urgently.

"That . . . that he held her in some kind of awe," he finished. "It wasn't simply lust. I really don't think Allardyce killed her."

"And the other woman?" she said softly. "People have killed even those they loved to protect themselves—especially if the love was not equally returned."

"I don't know," he answered. "You are right. Very probably someone killed her, and Elissa Beck was just unfortunate enough to witness it."

"Or it could be the other way . . . couldn't it?" She held his gaze steadily.

"Yes," he agreed. "It could be almost anything. But Allardyce says he wasn't there. He says she sometimes came without telling him, and they talked, or he painted her for his own pleasure, not to sell. There was a picture of her, set in Vienna. It was called *Funeral in Blue* and it was one of the most powerful things I've ever seen." He did not continue. He could see in her face that she had already understood the darkness, the possibilities on the edge of his mind.

She stood in front of him. "You're still going to help, though . . . aren't you." It was a statement, not a question.

"I'm going to try," he said, putting both arms around her and feeling the tension in her body under the fabric of her dress. He knew she was more afraid now than she had been when he left to see Runcorn. So was he.

CHAPTER
THREE

Monk left home early the next morning, and by half past seven he was already walking smartly down Tottenham Court Road. There was a cold wind and the fog had lifted considerably. He heard the newsboys shouting about the American War, and there had been another outbreak of typhoid in the Stepney area, near Limehouse. He remembered the fever hospital there, and how terrified he had been that Hester would catch the disease. He had wasted so much effort trying to convince himself he did not really love her, at least not enough that he would be unable to carry on perfectly well with his life even if she were no longer there. How desperately he had struggled not to give any hostages to fortune . . . and lost!

He wondered about Kristian Beck. He had seen Beck work night and day to save the lives of strangers. His courage never seemed to fail him, nor his compassion. At first thought it was not difficult to see why Callandra admired him so much, but how well did she know him? Was it anything more than his professional character? What of his thoughts that had nothing to do with medicine? What of his fears or his griefs? What of his appetites?

He saw an empty hansom and stepped off the curb to hail it, but it hurried on blindly, the driver muffled in scarves, and he rounded a lamppost up onto the pavement again.

He increased his pace, suddenly angry, energy surging up inside him. He found his hands clenched and he all but bumped into the sandwich seller standing idly on the corner watching for custom.

The streets were already busy with brewers' drays and delivery carts with vegetables for the market. A milkman was selling by the jug or can on the corner of Francis Street, and two women were waiting, shivering in the wind and the damp.

Another hansom came by, and this one stopped. He climbed in, giving the driver the address of the police station and telling him to wait while he picked up Runcorn, then to take them both on to Haverstock Hill.

Runcorn was there within moments. He came down the steps with his jacket flapping and his cheeks still ruddy from the scraping of the razor. He climbed in beside Monk and ordered the driver on sharply.

They rode in silence. Half a dozen times Monk almost asked Runcorn for his opinion on some aspect of the case, a possibility, and each occasion he changed his mind. At least twice he heard Runcorn also draw in his breath as if to speak, and then say nothing. The longer the silence remained, the harder it became to break it.

As they went uphill out of the city, the fog lifted further and the cleaner air was sharp with the smell of damp earth, wood smoke, fallen leaves and horse manure.

When they reached the corner of Haverstock Hill and Prince of Wales Street, the hansom stopped and they alighted. Runcorn paid the driver. The house in front of them was substantial but not ostentatious. Monk glanced at Runcorn and saw the respect in his face. This was the sort of home a man of moral quality should have. The curtains were lowered. There were black crepe ribbons on the door. Monk smiled, and forced back his own thoughts.

Runcorn went ahead and yanked the bellpull, then stepped away.

After several moments the door was opened by a middle-aged maid in plain stuff dress and a white apron that was wet around the bottom. Her hands were red, and a faint line of soap showed white on her wrists. It was plain from her face that she had been weeping and was controlling herself now only with the greatest effort.

"Yes sir?" she enquired.

It was not far off nine o'clock. "May we see Dr. Beck, please?" Runcorn asked. "I'm sorry, but it's necessary." He produced his card and offered it to her. "I'm from the police," he added as she ignored it, and he realized she probably could not read.

" 'E can't see yer," she said with a sniff.

"I'm aware of his bereavement," Runcorn said quietly. "It's about that that I must speak."

"Yer can't," she repeated expressionlessly. " 'E in't 'ere."

Monk felt his heart beat faster. Runcorn stiffened.

" 'E's gorn ter the 'orspital," the maid explained. "Up 'Ampstead. Poor soul, 'e don't know wot ter do wif 'isself, but 'e don't never forget the sick." She blinked rapidly but the tears still ran down her rough cheeks. "You gotta find 'oo done this to 'im. If yer worth sixpence of a decent person's money, yer can do that!"

Runcorn drew in his breath to be reasonable, then changed his mind. Perhaps he was conscious of Monk a step behind him, watching, listening. He would be patient. "Of course we will, but we need his help . . ."

"Up the 'orspital." She waved her arm, indicating the direction. "I can't do nothin' for yer 'ere. An' yer'd best 'urry, afore 'e starts operatin', 'cos 'e won't stop fer nothin' then, not you ner me, ner Gawd 'isself."

Runcorn thanked her and went back to the street to look for a hansom, Monk a couple of steps behind him, finding it difficult to follow graciously, but if he wanted to be included he had no choice but to comply. He was certain Runcorn was conscious of it, and enjoying it.

"Better get a cab, Monk," Runcorn said after a moment or two.

Monk knew why he did that. Hansom drivers could spot the self-assurance of a gentleman fifty yards away. A man with breeding would have more money, more appearance of position to keep up and therefore more generosity. Whatever Runcorn wore, whatever rank he attained, he would never have that air, the unconscious arrogance that Monk was born with. That was the core of his loathing all the years they had known each other: the fact that they were both aware of the differences between them, and Monk had never yielded a word of honest praise, or stayed his tongue. He was not proud of that now, but the pattern of years was too deep to erase.

Again they rode in silence, this time as a matter of necessity. They alighted at the hospital some half an hour later, and Monk led the way, being familiar with the place from the times he had been there to see Hester.

As soon as he was inside he smelled the familiar odors of carbolic and lye and another odor, sweeter and different, which might have been blood. His imagination raced to the morning he had woken up after his own accident, and to the battlefield in America where he had seen for the first time what it was that Hester had really done in the Crimea, not the English imagination of the horror and the helplessness but the reality of flesh and pain.

Runcorn was a step behind him. The difference in experience was a gulf between them that could never be crossed. All the telling in the world, even supposing Runcorn were to listen, could not convey things for which there were no words.

They passed a middle-aged woman carrying two heavy slop buckets, her shoulders dragged down by the weight. Her eyes did not meet theirs. She was a nurse, a hospital skivvy to fetch and clean, stoke fires, launder, roll bandages and generally do as she was told.

Three medical students stood in earnest conversation, shirts spattered in blood. One had a neat incision in the side of his black frock coat, as if it had somehow got caught up in the speed of a surgical procedure. There was blood around that also, but dried dark, so not today's events.

"We're looking for Dr. Beck," Monk said, stopping beside them.

They regarded him with slight disdain. "The waiting room's

over there." One of them pointed, and then returned his attention to his colleagues.

"Police!" Monk snapped, stung by the attitude, as much for the patients treated with such cavalier manner as for himself. "And we have no intention of waiting."

The student's expression barely changed. He was a professional man, and he considered police to be on a level both of skill and in society equal to that of a bailiff, dealing with the detritus of the world. "You'll have to wait," he said dryly.

Runcorn looked at the student, then at Monk, his hope that Monk's razor tongue had not lost its edge plain in his face.

"If the operating room is still where it was, I shall find it for myself," Monk replied. He surveyed the young man's coat. "I see you have something yet to learn regarding accuracy with the knife. Unless, of course, you were intending to remove your own appendix? If so, I believe it is on the other side."

The student flushed with anger, and his colleagues hid a smile. Monk strode on with Runcorn at his heels.

"How did you know that?" Runcorn asked as soon as they were out of earshot.

"I've been here before," Monk answered, trying to remember exactly where the operating rooms were.

"About the . . . appendix!" Runcorn corrected.

"Man called Gray published a book on anatomy about three years ago," Monk answered. "Hester has a copy. Here." He reached the door he thought was the correct one, and went in.

It was empty but for Kristian Beck standing beside a table. He was in shirtsleeves, and there was blood on his rolled-up cuffs, but his hands were clean. It had been a long time since Monk had seen him, and he had forgotten the impact of the doctor's appearance. He was in his early forties, of average height, with hair receding a little, but it was his eyes which commanded the attention. They were dark and of such remarkable intelligence as to be truly beautiful. His mouth suggested passion, but there was a sense of inner control, as if the intense emotions there were seldom unguarded.

He drew in his breath to protest the intrusion; then he recognized Monk and his face relaxed, but nothing could take from it the marks of shock.

"I'm sorry," Monk said, and the sincerity with which he felt it was clear in his voice.

Kristian did not answer, and a glance at his face showed that for a moment loss overwhelmed him and he was incapable of speech.

It was Runcorn who salvaged the situation. "Dr. Beck, I'm Superintendent Runcorn. Unfortunately, we need to ask you several questions that can't wait for a better day. Have you time now? I expect it'll take an hour or so."

Kristian composed himself. Perhaps it was a relief to be practical. "Yes, of course. Although I don't know what I can tell you that will help." He spoke with difficulty. "You did not tell me how she was killed. I saw her, of course . . . in the morgue. She looked . . . unhurt . . ."

Runcorn swallowed as if there were something blocking his throat. "Her neck was broken. It would have been very quick. I daresay she would have felt very little."

"And the other woman?" Kristian said softly.

"The same." Runcorn glanced around as if to find a more suitable place to speak.

"We won't be interrupted here," Kristian said wryly. "There's no one else operating today."

"Is that why you came?" Runcorn asked. "Surely, in the circumstances . . ."

"No," Kristian said quickly. "They'd have found someone. I . . . I had no wish to sit around and . . . think. Work can be a blessing . . ."

"Yes." Runcorn was embarrassed by grief, especially when he could understand but not share it. His discomfort was clear in his face, his eyes studiously avoiding the array of instruments laid out on the table near the wall, and in the way he stood, not knowing what to do with his hands. "Did you know Mrs. Beck was having her portrait painted by Argo Allardyce, Doctor?"

"Yes, of course. Her father commissioned it," Kristian replied.

"Have you ever been to the studio or met Allardyce?"

"No."

"Not interested in a portrait of your wife?"

"I have very little time, Superintendent. Medicine, like police work, is very demanding. I would have been interested to see it when it was completed."

"Never met Allardyce?" Runcorn insisted.

"Not so far as I know."

"He painted several pictures of her, did you know that?"

Kristian's face was unreadable. "No, I didn't. But it doesn't surprise me. She was beautiful."

"Would it surprise you if he was in love with her?"

"No." A faint smile flickered around Kristian's mouth.

"And that doesn't anger you?"

"Unless he harassed her, Superintendent, why should it?"

"Are you sure he didn't?"

The conversation was leading nowhere, and Runcorn was as aware of it as Monk. There was a note of desperation in his voice and his body was tense and awkward, as if the room oppressed him, the pain and the fear in it remaining after the events were over. He still kept his eyes fixed on Kristian, to avoid the other things he might unintentionally see, the blades and clamps and forceps.

"Did you know she was going to Acton Street that evening?" Monk asked.

Kristian hesitated. The question seemed to cause him some embarrassment. Monk saw Runcorn perceive it also.

"No," Kristian said, glancing from one to the other of them. He seemed about to add something, then changed his mind.

"Where did you think she was going?" Monk hated pressing the issue, but the fact that it caused discomfort was an additional reason why he had to.

"We did not discuss it," Kristian said, avoiding Monk's eye. "I was visiting a patient."

"The patient's name?"

Kristian's eyes flicked up; only momentarily was he startled. "Of course. It was Maude Oldenby, of Clarendon Square, just north of the Euston Road. I suppose you have to consider that I might have done this." His body was tense, the muscles standing out in his neck and jaw. His face was ashen pale, but he did not protest. "Do I need to say that I did not?"

For the first time, Monk was embarrassed also. He spoke uncharacteristically. "There are regions in all of us unknown not only to others, but even to ourselves. Tell us something about her."

There was absolute silence. The distant noises from beyond the door intruded, footsteps, the clink of a pail handle falling, indistinguishable voices.

"How do you describe anyone?" Kristian said helplessly. "She was . . ." He stopped again.

Thoughts raced through Monk's mind about love and obsession, boredom, betrayal, confusion. "Where did you meet her?" he asked, hoping to give Kristian a place to begin.

Kristian looked up. "Vienna," he said, his voice taking on a sudden vibrancy. "She was a widow. She had married very young, an Austrian diplomat in London. When he returned home, naturally she went with him. He died in 1846, and she remained in Vienna. She loved the city. It is like no other in the world." He smiled very slightly, and there was a warmth in his face, his eyes soft. "The opera, the concerts, the fashion, the cafés, and of course the waltz! But I think most of all, the people. They have a wit, a gaiety, a unique sophistication, a mixture of east and west. She cared about them. She had dozens of friends. There was always something happening, something to fight for."

"To fight for?" Monk said curiously. It was an odd word to use.

Kristian met his eyes. "I met her in 1848," he said softly. "We were all caught up in the revolution."

"Is that where you lived then?"

"Yes. I was born in Bohemia, but my father was Viennese, and we had returned there. I was working in one of the hospitals and I knew students of all sorts, not just medical. All over Europe—Paris, Berlin, Rome, Milan, Venice, even in Hungary—there was a great hope of new freedoms, a spirit of courage in the air. But of course, to us Vienna seemed to be the heart of it."

"And Mrs. . . ."

"Elissa von Leibnitz," Kristian supplied. "Yes, she was passionate for the cause of liberty. I knew no one with more courage, more daring to risk everything for victory." He stopped. Monk could see in his face that he was reliving those days, sharp and fresh as if they were only just past. There was softness in his eyes, and pain. "She had a brighter spirit than anyone else. She could make us laugh . . . and hope . . ." He stopped again, and this time he turned away from them, hiding his face.

Monk glanced at Runcorn and saw an instant of pity so naked it stunned him. It did not belong to the man he thought he knew. It felt intrusive for him to have seen it. Then it was gone and nothing but embarrassment remained, and an anger for being forced to feel something he did not wish to, a confusion because things were not as he had supposed, and not easy. He rushed into speech to cover the silence and his own awkwardness. "Were you both involved in the revolutions in Europe then, Dr. Beck?"

"Yes." Kristian straightened up, lifting his head a little, then turned around slowly to face Runcorn. "We fought against those who led the tyranny. We tried to overthrow it and win some freedom for ordinary people, a right to read and write as they believed. As you know, we failed."

Runcorn cleared his throat. The politics of foreigners were not his concern. His business was crime there in London, and he wanted to remain on ground he understood. "So you came home . . . at least you came here, and Mrs. Beck . . . Mrs. . . . what did you say?"

"Frau von Leibnitz, but she was my wife by then," Kristian replied.

"Yes . . . yes, of course. You came to London?" Runcorn said hastily.

"In 1849, yes." A shadow passed over Kristian's face.

"And practiced medicine here?"

"Yes."

"And Mrs. Beck, what did she do? Did she make friends here again?" Runcorn asked, although Monk knew from the tone of his voice that he had no purpose in mind, he was foundering. What he wanted to know was were they happy, had Elissa taken lovers, but he did not know how to say it so the answer was of value.

"Yes, of course," Kristian answered. "She was always interested in the arts, music and painting."

"Was she interested in your work?" Monk interrupted.

Kristian was startled. "Medicine? No . . . no she wasn't. It . . ." He changed his mind and remained silent.

"When did she first meet Allardyce?" Runcorn went on.

"I don't know. About four or five months ago, I think."

"She didn't say?"

"Not that I remember."

Runcorn questioned him for several more minutes but knew he was achieving nothing. When there was a sharp knock on the door and a medical student asked if Kristian was ready to see patients again, both Monk and Runcorn were happy to leave.

"Was Maude Oldenby the only patient you visited?" Runcorn asked as Kristian stood at the door.

The ghost of a smile touched Kristian's lips. "No. I also saw Mrs. Mary Ann Jackson, of 21 Argyle Street." He went out and closed the door quietly. They heard his footsteps down the corridor.

Neither of them remarked that Argyle Street was rather a long way from Haverstock Hill, but only a few hundred yards from Acton Street.

"He's lying," Runcorn said when they were outside on the pavement again.

"What about?" Monk said curiously.

"I don't know," Runcorn said, beginning to walk rapidly and avoiding Monk's gaze. "But he is. Don't you know what your wife is doing and who her friends are?"

"Yes . . . but . . ."

"But what? But nothing. He knows. He's lying. Let's take the omnibus back."

They did, and Monk was glad of it; it made conversation impossible, and he was able to concentrate on his own thoughts. He would have defended Kristian to Runcorn, out of loyalty to Callandra, but he also was convinced that Kristian was lying. Without saying as much, he had affected to know almost nothing of Elissa's daily life. Certainly he was dedicated to medicine, but he was also a warm and emotional man. He was deeply moved by his wife's death, and when he had spoken of their days in Vienna the passion of it was still there in him, taking him back to it whether he wished or not.

What had happened since then? It was thirteen years. How much did people change in that time? What did they learn of each other that became unbearable? Infatuation died, but did love? What was the difference? Did one learn that too late? Was it Elissa that Kristian still so obviously cared for, or the memory of the time when they had fought for liberty and high idealism on the barricades of Vienna?

Did Callandra know anything of this? Had she ever even met Elissa? Or, like Monk, had she imagined some tedious woman with whom Kristian was imprisoned in an honorable but intolerably lonely marriage of convenience? He had a cold, gripping fear that it was the latter.

What if she had then discovered this woman Argo Allardyce

had seen, the woman whose beauty haunted him and stared out of the canvas to capture the imagination of the onlooker?

What did one love in a woman? Love was surely for honor and gentleness, courage, laughter and wisdom, and a hundred thoughts shared. But infatuation was for what the heart thought it saw, for what the vision believed. A woman with a face like Elissa Beck's could have provoked anything!

Hester went to the hospital early, in part to see how Mary Ellsworth was progressing. She found her weak and a little nauseous, but with no fever, and no swelling or suppuration around the wound. However, even if the operation were entirely successful, she knew even better than Kristian did that that was only the beginning of healing. Mary's real illness lay in her mind, the fears and anxieties, the introspection and the numbing boredom that crippled her days.

Hester spoke with her for a little while, trying to encourage her, then went to find Callandra. She looked in the patients' waiting rooms and was told by a young nurse that she had seen Callandra in the front hall, but when Hester got there she met only Fermin Thorpe, looking angry and important. He seemed about to speak to Hester, then with a curt gesture of irritation he turned on his heel and went the other way. Callandra came from one of the wards, her hair flying up in a gray-brown streamer, the main coil of it askew.

"That man is an interfering nincompoop!" she said furiously, her face flushed, her eyes bright. "He wants to reduce the allowance of porter every day for nurses. I don't approve of drunkenness any more than he does, but he'd get far better work out of them if he increased their food ration! It's drink on an empty stomach that does it." She blinked. "Talking about stomachs, how is Mary Ellsworth?"

Hester smiled a little bleakly. "Miserable, but there's no infection in the wound."

"And no heart in her," Callandra said for her. All the time she was speaking her eyes were seeking Hester's, looking desperately for some reassurance, some inner comfort that this nightmare would be brief and any moment they would all waken and find it was explained, proved sad, but some kind of release.

Hester longed to be able to tell her so, but she could not bring herself to, even for a day or two's ease. "No, no heart," she agreed. "But perhaps when it doesn't hurt quite so much she'll be better."

"No more laudanum?" Callandra asked, pity softening her face.

"No. It's too easy to depend on it. And it can be caustic, which is the last thing she needs with that wound in her stomach. Believe me, she'd sooner have the pain of the moment!"

Callandra hesitated, as if she were reading double and triple meanings into the words, then she smiled at her own foolishness and poked her flying hair back into the knot on the back of her head and went purposefully towards the apothecary's room, leaving Hester to take a quick cup of tea with one of the nurses and then catch the omnibus back to Grafton Street.

In the afternoon Hester busied herself with housework, a large part of which was quite unnecessary. Her housekeeper came in three days a week and did most of the laundry, ironing and scrubbing. Everything that mattered had already been done, but she was too restless to sit still, so she began to clean out the kitchen cupboards, setting everything from them onto the table. Surely it must have been the artists' model who was killed, and Kristian's wife the unfortunate witness? It was the only answer that made sense.

Except that of course it wasn't obvious at all.

She had every cupboard empty and a bowl full of soapy water on the bench, ready to begin scrubbing, when the doorbell rang and she was obliged to go and answer it.

Charles was on the step, looking even more haggard than three days ago, with hollows around his eyes like bruises, and a cut on his jaw, but this time he was at no loss for words.

"Oh, Hester, I'm so glad you're home." He came inside, moving stiffly, without waiting for her to ask. "I was afraid you might be at a hospital . . . or something. Are you still . . . no, I suppose you're not. I mean . . . it's . . ." He stood in the center of the room, and took a couple of deep breaths.

Hester interrupted him. "When you followed Imogen the other evening, you said it was somewhere in the direction of the Royal Free Hospital, didn't you?"

"Yes, Swinton Street. Why?"

"Do you now know of someone she might have been visiting?" Hester asked.

"No." The word came so quickly it almost cut off the question, but if anything, the fear in his eyes increased. He started to say something else. It seemed to be a denial, then he stopped. "I suppose you heard that there was a double murder in Acton Street, just beyond the hospital?" He was watching her intently.

"Yes, a doctor's wife and an artists' model."

"Oh my God!" His legs folded, and he sank down into the armchair.

For a moment she was afraid he had collapsed. "Charles!" She knelt in front of him, clasping his hands, intensely relieved to feel strength in them. She was about to say that the locality didn't mean anything and could have no connection with Imogen when, like a drench of cold water, she realized that he was afraid that it did. He was lying by misdirection and evasion. He was refusing to look at whatever it was that hovered just beyond his words.

"Charles!" she started again, more urgently. "What do you know about where she is going? You followed her to Swinton Street, which is a block from Acton Street . . ."

He jerked his head up. "That's not where she went the night of the murders!" he said abruptly. "I know that, because I followed her myself."

"Where did she go?" she asked.

"South of High Holborn," he said immediately. "Down Drury Lane, just beyond the theater, nowhere near the top of the Gray's Inn Road." He stared at her almost defiantly.

Why was he so quick to deny that Imogen had been there?

She stood up and moved away, turning her back to him so he would not see the anxiety in her face. "I understand they were killed in an artist's studio," she said almost lightly. "The model worked for him and spent quite a lot of time there, and the doctor's wife went for a sitting because he was painting a portrait of her."

"Then the artist did it," he said quickly. "The newspapers didn't say that."

"Apparently, he wasn't there. A misunderstanding, I suppose."

He sat silently.

"So you don't need to worry," she continued, as if she had dismissed the matter. "Anyone walking about in the evening is in no more danger in Swinton Street than anywhere else."

She heard his intake of breath. He was frightened, confused, and now feeling even more alone. Would it persuade him at last to be more open?

But the silence remained.

Her patience broke and she swung around to face him. "What is it you are afraid of, Charles? Do you think Imogen knows someone who might be involved with this? Argo Allardyce, for example?"

"No! Why on earth should she know him?" But the color washed up his face, and he must have felt its heat. "I don't know!" he burst out. "I don't know what she's doing, Hester! One day she's elated, the next she's in despair. She dresses in her best clothes and goes out without telling me where. She lies about things, about where she's been, who she's visited. She gets unsigned messages about meeting someone, and she knows from the handwriting who it is and where to go!"

He fished in his pocket and pulled out a piece of paper, offering it to her. She took it. It was simply an agreement to meet, no place given, and unsigned. Charles pressed his hands over his face, leaving white marks on his cheeks, and he winced sharply when he touched his jaw. "She's changed so much I can hardly recognize her sometimes, and I don't know why!" he said wretchedly. "She won't tell me anything . . . she doesn't trust me anymore. What can I think?" His eyes were hot and desperate, begging for help.

Hester heard all the details of what he said, but overriding it all she heard the panic in him, the knowledge that he had lost control and for the first time in his life his emotions were in a chaos he could not hide.

"I don't know," she said gently, going over to him again. "But I'll do everything I can to find out, I promise you." She looked at him more closely, seeing the darkening bruises. "What did you do to your face?"

"I . . . I fell. It doesn't matter. Hester . . ."

"I know," she said gently. "You think perhaps you would rather not find out the truth, but that isn't so. As long as you don't know, you will imagine, and all the worst things will be there in your mind."

"I suppose . . . but . . ." He stood up awkwardly, as if his joints hurt. "I'm really not sure, Hester. Perhaps I'm worrying . . . I mean . . . women can be . . ."

She gave him a withering look.

"Well . . . not you, of course . . ." He foundered again, his face pale, blotches of dull color on his cheeks.

"Don't be ridiculous!" she contradicted. "I can be as irrational as anybody else, or at least I can appear so to a man who doesn't understand me. If you recall, Papa thought so. But that was because he didn't wish to understand that I wanted something to do just as much as you or James."

"Oh, far more!" The faint ghost of a smile crossed his mouth. "I never wanted anything with the fierceness you did. I think you terrified him."

"I shall go and see Imogen this afternoon," she promised.

"Thank you," he said softly. "At least warn her. Tell her how dangerous it is. She doesn't listen to me."

When she arrived in Endsleigh Gardens she was let in by Nell, the parlormaid she had known for years.

"Oh, Miss Hester!" Nell looked taken aback. "I'm afraid Mrs. Latterly's out at the minute. But come in. She'll be back in half an hour or so, and I'm sure she'd want to see you. Can I get you anything? A cup of tea?"

"No, thank you, Nell, but I will wait, thank you," Hester accepted, and followed her to the drawing room to possess herself with patience until Imogen should arrive. She sat down as Nell left, then, the moment after the door was closed, stood up again. She was too restless to remain on the sofa with her hands folded. She began to wander around the room, looking at the familiar furniture and pictures.

How could she gain Imogen's confidence sufficiently to learn what it was that had changed her? Surely her husband's sister was the last person Imogen would trust with the confidence that she was betraying him. And if Hester asked her a question to which the answer was a lie, it would only deepen the gulf between them.

She stopped in front of a small watercolor next to the mantelpiece. It was attractive, but she did not recognize it. Somehow in her mind she had seen a portrait there, a woman wearing a Renaissance pearl headdress.

She lifted it slightly and saw underneath a darker oval on the wallpaper. She was right, the portrait had been there. She looked around the room and did not find it. She went through to the dining room and it was not there, either, nor was it in the hall. It hardly mattered, but its absence occupied her mind while she waited.

She noticed other small differences: a vase she did not recognize; a silver snuffbox, which had been on the mantelpiece for years, was not there now; a lovely alabaster horse was gone from the side table near the hall door.

She was still wondering about the changes when she heard the front door close, a murmur of voices, and a moment later Imogen's footsteps across the hall.

She threw the door open and swept in, her skirts wide, a lace fichu around her neck. Her dark eyes were shining and there was a flush on her cheeks. "Hello, Hester," she said cheerfully. "Twice in the space of four days! Have you suddenly taken to visiting everyone you know? Anyway, it's very pleasant to see you." She gave her a quick kiss on the cheek, then stepped back to look at the table. "No tea? I suppose it's far too early, but surely you'd like something? Nell says you have been here for three quarters of an hour. I'm so sorry. I'll speak to her . . ."

"Please don't," Hester said quickly. "She offered me tea and I declined. And don't go to any trouble now. I expect you have only just come from luncheon?"

"What?" Imogen looked for a moment as if nothing had been farther from her mind, then she laughed. It was an excited, happy sound. "Yes . . . of course." She seemed too restless to sit down, moving around the room with extraordinary energy. "Then if you don't want to eat or drink, what can I offer you? I'm quite sure you don't want gossip. You don't know any of the people I do. Anyway, they are the most crashing bores most of the time. They say and do the same things every day, and nearly all of them are completely pointless." She whirled around, sending her skirts flying. "What is it, Hester? Are you collecting support for some charity or other?" She was speaking rapidly, the words falling over each other. "Let me guess! A hospital? Do you want me to see if I know any friends whose daughters want to become respectable, hardworking young ladies in a noble cause? Miss Nightingale is such a heroine they just might! Although it's not quite as fashionable as it was at the end of the war. After all, we aren't fighting with anyone just now, or are we? Of course, there's always America, but that's really none of our business." Her eyes were bright and she was staring at Hester expectantly.

"No, it never occurred to me to solicit help from any of your friends," Hester replied with a slight edge. "People have to go into nursing because they care about it, not because anyone asked them, or they couldn't marry the people they wished to."

"Oh, please!" Imogen said with a sharp wave of her hand. "You sound so pompous. I know you don't mean to, but really . . ."

Hester kept her temper with difficulty. "Do you know Argo Allardyce?" she asked.

Imogen's eyebrows rose. "What a marvelous name! I don't think so. Who is he?"

"An artist whose model has just been murdered," Hester replied, watching her closely.

"I don't read newspapers." Imogen shrugged very slightly. "I'm sorry, of course, but things like that happen."

"And a doctor's wife was murdered at the same time," Hester continued, watching her face. "In Acton Street, just around the corner from Swinton Street."

Imogen froze, her body stiff, her eyes wide. "A doctor's wife?"

"Yes." Hester felt a flutter of fear inside her like nausea. "Elissa Beck."

Imogen was sheet white. Hester was afraid she was going to faint. "I'm sorry," she said swiftly, going to Imogen to support her in case she staggered or fell.

Imogen waved her away sharply and stepped back to the sofa, sinking down on it, her skirts puffing around her. She put her hands up to cover her face for a moment. "I was there," she said hoarsely, her voice scratching as if her throat ached. "I mean, just around the corner! I . . . I called on a friend. How awful!"

Hester hated pursuing matters now, but the thought of Charles drove her. "What kind of friend?"

Imogen looked up, startled. "What?"

"What kind of friend do you have in that area?"

68

A flash of temper lit Imogen's eyes. "That is not your concern, Hester! I have no intention of explaining myself to you, and it is intrusive of you to ask!"

"I'm trying to save you from getting involved in a very ugly investigation," Hester said sharply. "You were in Swinton Street, one block from where the murders took place. What were you doing there, and can you explain it satisfactorily?"

"To you? Certainly not. But I was not murdering people! Anyway, how do you know where I was?" This was a demand, challenging and offended.

There was no reasonable answer but the truth, and that was going to make things worse, perhaps stop all practical help in the future.

"Because you were seen," Hester replied. That was a good compromise.

"By somebody who told you?" Imogen said disbelievingly. "Who would you know in Swinton Street?"

Hester smiled. "If it's respectable enough for you, why not for me?"

Imogen retreated very slightly. "And are you visiting your friends in Swinton Street as well, in case they are investigated?"

"Since they live there, there's not much point," Hester retorted, going along with the invention. "And you are my sister-in-law, which is rather more than just a friend."

Imogen's expression softened a little. "You don't need to worry about me. I had nothing whatsoever to do with murdering anyone. I was just shocked, that's all."

"For heaven's sake! I never imagined you did," Hester said, and the moment she said it, she realized it was not true. The darkest fear inside her was that somehow Imogen had been involved, and worse, that she had drawn Charles in as well, although she could not think how.

"Good." Imogen's eyes were still wide and bright. "Is that what you really came for? Not luncheon? Or afternoon tea? Or a little gossip about the theater, or fashion, but to find out if I was involved in some sordid murder?"

"I came to try to help you stay out of the investigation," Hester said, with anger, the deeper because it was unjustified.

"Thank you for your concern; I can care for my own reputation," Imogen replied stiffly. "But had I witnessed anything to do with the murders, no one could protect me from the necessity of doing my duty regarding it."

"No . . ." Hester felt foolish. She was caught in a trap of her own words, and it was perfectly apparent that Imogen knew it. "Then I'm sure you have other calls to make, or visitors to receive," she went on awkwardly, trying to retreat with some grace and knowing she was failing.

"I suppose you saw it as your duty to come," Imogen replied, swirling towards the door to show her out. Her words could have meant anything at all, or nothing, merely the formula for saying good-bye.

Hester found herself out in the street feeling inept and still afraid for both Charles and Imogen, and with no idea what to do next to be any help at all. She was not even sure whether she wanted to tell Monk anything about it.

She started to walk in the mild, damp breeze, knowing that the fog could easily close in again by nightfall.

Monk and Runcorn went from Haverstock Hill to Ebury Street to see Fuller Pendreigh, Elissa Beck's father. It was a courtesy as much as anything. They did not expect him to have information regarding the crime, but it was possible she might have confided in him some fear or anxiety. Regardless of that, he deserved to be assured that they were giving the tragedy the greatest possible attention.

The house in Ebury Street was magnificent, as fitted a senior Queen's Counsel with high expectations of becoming a Member of

Parliament. Of course, at the moment the curtains were half low-ered and there was sawdust in the street to muffle the sound of horses' hooves. The house was further marked out from its neigh-bors by the black crepe over the door to signify the death of a mem-ber of the family, even though she had not been resident there.

A footman with a black armband received them unsmilingly and conducted them through the magnificent hallway to the somber, green-velveted morning room. The curtains hung richly draped, caught up with thick, silk cords. The walls were wood pan-eled, the color of old sherry, and one wall was entirely covered with bookshelves. There was a fine painting of a naval battle above the mantelpiece; a small brass plate proclaimed it to be Copenhagen, one of Nelson's triumphs.

They waited nearly half an hour before Fuller Pendreigh came in and closed the door softly behind him. He was a very striking man, lean and graceful, far taller than average, although standing to his full height seemed to cost him an effort now. But it was his head which commanded most attention. His features were fine and regular, his eyes clear blue under level brows and his fair hair, un-touched by gray and of remarkable thickness, sweeping up and back from a broad brow. Only his mouth was individual and less than handsome, but its tight-lipped look now might have been the shock of sudden and terrible bereavement. He was dressed totally in black except for his shirt.

"Good morning, gentlemen," he said stiffly. "Have you news?"

"Good morning, sir," Runcorn said, then introduced them both. He had no intention of allowing Monk to take the lead on this occasion. It was very much police business, and Monk was there only as a courtesy and would be reminded of such should he forget it. "I am afraid there is little so far," he went on. "But we hoped you might be able to tell us rather more about Allardyce and save time, as it were."

Pendreigh's fair eyebrows rose. "Allardyce? You think he might be involved? It seems likely, on the face of it. The model was surely the intended victim, and my poor daughter simply chanced to arrive at the worst possible moment . . ."

"We must look at all possibilities, sir," Runcorn replied. "Mrs. Beck was a very beautiful woman. I daresay she awakened admiration in a number of gentlemen. Allardyce certainly appears to have had intense feelings for her."

"She was far more than merely beautiful, Mr. Runcorn," Pendreigh said, controlling the emotion in his voice with obvious difficulty. "She had courage and laughter and imagination. She was the most wonderfully alive person I ever knew." His voice dropped a little to an intense gravity. "And she had a sense of justice and morality which drove her to sublime acts—an honesty of vision."

There was no possible answer, and it seemed trivial and intrusive to express a regret which could be no more than superficial compared with Pendreigh's grief.

"I believe she met Dr. Beck when she was living in Vienna," Monk remarked.

Pendreigh looked at him with slight surprise. "Yes. Her first husband was Austrian. He died young, and Elissa remained in Vienna. That was when she really found herself." He took a very deep breath and let it out slowly. He did not look at them but somewhere into the distance. "I had always believed her to be remarkable, but only then did I realize how totally unselfish she was to sacrifice her time and youth, even risk her life, to fight beside the oppressed people of her adopted country in their struggle for freedom."

Monk glanced at Runcorn, but neither of them interrupted.

"She joined a group of revolutionaries in April of '48," Pendreigh went on. "She wrote to me about them, so full of courage and enthusiasm." He turned a little away from them, and his voice grew huskier, but he did not stop. "Isn't it absurd that she should face death every day, carry messages into the heart of the enemy offices and salons . . . walk through the streets and alleys, even over the barricades in October, and live through it all with little more than a few scratches and bruises—and then die in a London artist's studio?" He came to an abrupt halt, his voice choking.

Runcorn waited a moment as he felt decency required, glancing severely at Monk to forbid him from interrupting.

"Is that where she met Dr. Beck?" he said at last. "In a hospital there?"

"What?" Pendreigh shook his head. "No, not in a hospital. He was a revolutionary as well."

Monk drew his breath in sharply.

Pendreigh looked at him, frowning a little. "You only see him now, Mr. Monk. He seems very quiet, very single-minded in serving the poor and the sick of our city. But thirteen years ago he was as passionate for revolution as anyone." He smiled very slightly as memory stirred, and for a few moments the present was swallowed in the past. "Elissa used to tell me how brave he was. She admired courage intensely. . . ." A strange expression of pain filled his eyes and pulled his lips tight, as if a bitter memory momentarily drowned out everything else.

Then he moved his hands very slightly. "But she certainly wasn't foolish or unaware of the dangers of speaking out against tyranny, or of making friends with others who did. She marched with the students and the ordinary people in the streets, against the emperor's soldiers. She saw people killed, young men and women who only wanted the freedom to read and write as they chose. She knew it could be she at any time. Bullets make no moral choices."

"She sounds like a very fine lady," Runcorn said unhappily.

Pendreigh turned to him. "You must suppose me prejudiced in my opinion. Of course I am; she was my daughter. But ask anyone who was there, especially Kristian. He would tell you the same. And I am aware of her failings as well. She was impatient, she did not tolerate foolishness or indecision. Too often she did not listen to the views of others, and she was hasty in her judgment, but when she was wrong she apologized." His voice softened and he blinked rapidly. "She was a creature of high idealism, Superintendent, the imagination to put herself in the place of those less fortunate and to see how their lot could be made better."

"No wonder Dr. Beck fell in love with her," Runcorn said.

Monk was afraid he was beginning to suspect Kristian of jealousy, because he could not keep the thought from his own mind.

"He was far from the only one." Pendreigh sighed. "It was not always easy to be so admired. It gives one . . . too much to live up to."

"But she chose Dr. Beck, not any of the others." Monk made it a statement. He saw Runcorn's warning look and ignored it. "Do you know why?"

Pendreigh thought for several moments before he replied. "I'm trying to remember what she wrote at the time." He drew his fair brows into a frown of concentration. "I think he had the same kind of resolve that she did, the nerve to go through with what he planned even when circumstances changed and the cost became higher." He looked at Monk intently. "He was a very complex man, a disciple of medicine and its challenges, and yet at the same time of great personal physical courage. Yes, I think that was it, the sheer nerve in the face of danger. That appealed to her. She had a certain pity for people who wavered, she entirely understood fear. . . ."

Monk looked quickly at Runcorn and saw the puzzlement in his face. This all seemed so far away from an artist's studio in Acton Street and the beautiful woman they had seen in the morgue. And yet it was easily imaginable of the woman in the painting of the funeral in blue.

Pendreigh shivered, but he was standing a little straighter, his head high. "I remember one incident she wrote about to me. It was in May, but still there was danger in the air. For months there had been hardly anything to buy in the shops. The emperor had left Vienna. The police had banished all unemployed servants from the city, but most of them had come back, one way or another." Anger sharpened his voice. "There was chaos because the secret police had been done away with and their duties taken over by the National Guard and the Academic Legion. There was an immediate crime wave, and anyone remotely well-dressed was likely to be attacked in the street. That was when she first noticed Kristian. Armed only with a pistol, and quite alone, he faced a mob and made them back down. She said he was magnificent. He could easily have walked the other way, effected not to notice, and no one would necessarily have thought the worse of him."

"You said he was complex," Monk prompted. "That sounds like a fairly simple heroism to me."

Pendreigh stared into the distance. "I knew only what she told me. But even the most idealistic battles are seldom as easy as imagined by those not involved. There are good people on the enemy side also, and at times weak and evil people on one's own."

Runcorn shifted position a little uncomfortably, but he did not interrupt, nor did he look away from Pendreigh.

"And battle requires sacrifice," Pendreigh continued, "not always of oneself, sometimes of others. She told me what a fine leader Kristian was, decisive, farsighted. Where some men would see what would happen one or two moves ahead, he could see a dozen. There was strength in him that set him apart from those less able to keep a cause in mind and understand the cost of victory as well as that of defeat." His voice was edged with admiration, and now even his shoulders were straight, as if an inner courage had been imparted to him by the thought.

Monk admired it, too, but he was confused. Pendreigh was painting a picture of a man utterly unlike the compassionate and scrupulous person Monk had seen in the fever hospital in Limehouse, or all that he had heard from Callandra. The leader of such inner certainty and strength was of a nature unlike the doctor who labored without judgment of any kind, risking his own life as much for the fever- and lice-ridden beggar as for the nurse like Enid Ravensbrook. How had Hester seen him? A man of compassion, idealism, dedication, moral courage perhaps, but not a man capable of the ruthless leadership Pendreigh described. The Kristian Beck that Hester saw would not have raised his hand against anyone, much less with a sword or a gun in it.

He looked at Runcorn. His face was only slightly puckered. But then he did not know Kristian, he had not even met him until today. This picture that Pendreigh had received from Elissa, and re-created for them, did not contradict any image in his mind.

Could Kristian have changed so much in thirteen years? Or was he a man of two natures, and showed the one that suited his purpose or the need of the time?

Runcorn was staring at him impatiently, waiting for him to say something.

Monk looked directly at Pendreigh. "I'm deeply sorry for your loss, sir. Mrs. Beck was obviously a person of extraordinary courage and honor."

"Thank you," Pendreigh said, turning at last to face them fully. "I feel as if the world is darkening, and there will not now be another summer. She had such laughter, such hunger for life. I have no other family left. My wife has been gone many years, and my sister also." He said the words with very little expression, which made their impact the greater. It was not self-pity but a bleak statement of fact. He spoke with neither courage nor despair but a kind of numbness.

Monk was overtaken by anger on Pendreigh's behalf, for the profound foolishness of an action which in a moment's violence had robbed him of so much. He turned to Runcorn, expecting to see him preparing to make their excuses and leave. He was startled to see a confusion of emotions in his face, embarrassment and alarm, an acute knowledge that he was out of his depth. Monk turned back to Pendreigh. "I assume that had you any idea who might be responsible you would have spoken of it?" he asked.

"What? Oh, yes, of course I would. I can only imagine that there was some quarrel with the other poor woman, a lover or whatever, and Elissa was unfortunate enough to witness it."

"You commissioned the portrait?" Monk continued.

"Yes. Allardyce is a very fine artist."

"What do you know about him personally?"

"Nothing. But I've seen his work in several places. I wasn't interested in his morality, only his skill. My daughter did not sit alone for him, Mr. Monk, if that is what you are wondering. She took a woman friend with her."

"Do you know who?"

"No, of course I don't! I imagine it was not always the same person. If I knew who it was this time, I would have told you. I assume she went to some assignation of her own, and is too shocked and ashamed of having left Elissa to come forward yet."

Runcorn turned abruptly to Monk, annoyance in his eyes. He should have thought of that himself. "Naturally!" he said, looking back to Pendreigh. "We'll see if we can learn who it was. We will ask Dr. Beck for a list of possibilities. Thank you, sir. We'll not disturb you any further."

"Please . . . let me know what else you learn?" Pendreigh asked, his face stiff with the effort of control.

"Yes sir. As soon as there is anything," Runcorn promised. "Good day."

Outside on the pavement, Runcorn started to speak again, then changed his mind and marched down the street in the hope of finding a hansom. Monk followed after, deep in thought.

CHAPTER
FOUR

———

The funeral of Elissa Beck was held the following day, and Monk and Hester attended, although they were unrelated to the deceased. Hester went largely to support Callandra, who would go as someone who had long been a friend of the widower and had worked beside him at the hospital. No one else would know the crushing loneliness she could feel, watching him in this agonizing ritual and excluded by propriety from offering more than a few formal phrases. She must not linger or show more than the usual emotion anyone might feel.

Monk went to observe, in the vague hope that he might see an expression or overhear a word which would lead him closer to the truth. He hoped profoundly it was as Fuller Pendreigh had said: Sarah Mackeson was the intended victim, Elissa only a tragic intrusion at the worst possible moment.

It was a very moving affair, held in the High Anglican Church with all the weight of spectacle accorded the death of someone who had been brave and beautiful, and deeply loved.

The fog had closed in again, thick yellow-gray in the weak daylight. One of the feathermen waving the black ostrich plumes began to cough as the chill of it caught in his throat. Another stood red-nosed and shivering.

Like everyone else, Hester was dressed in black, not the dead, light-consuming fabric of true mourning, where one was not permitted even a faint gleam in case it should be considered not to be taking bereavement seriously enough. After a year a widow might wear silk, but still black, of course. Petticoats should also be black, and boots and hose, and as plain as possible. If a lady in mourning should lift a skirt to avoid a puddle, there would be considerable talk should she thereby exhibit a petticoat of some lighter shade.

The cortege had not yet arrived, but Kristian and Pendreigh were standing outside the main entrance of the church receiving the mourners and accepting condolences. The magnificent stone archway was carved with angels and flowers. The facade soared above until it faded and all but disappeared in the clinging, motionless fog, only here and there a gargoyle face leering downward.

Pendreigh looked haggard. His fair hair was still smooth and thick, but his face had sunk as if the flesh had withered, and in spite of standing as to attention on parade, there was still something within him that sagged, giving an illusion of emptiness. He was dressed in perfect black, so dark it absorbed even the little light there was, making his hair look the brighter. He spoke with the same gesture to everyone, courteous and mechanical.

Beside him, Kristian also looked stunned and pale. He seemed to be making an effort to say something individual to people, but after a little while he, too, began to repeat himself.

Hester saw Callandra move forward in the line to express her sympathies, and for a moment their eyes met. Callandra was dressed in unrelieved black, but her hat was uncharacteristically stylish, very simple in line, and it became her very much, accentuating the strength in her face, and for once her hair was immaculate. She gave a tiny smile of recognition, but Hester saw the pain of exclusion in her eyes, the misery of not being able to share this whole area of Kristian's life which cut to the heart. All she could do was offer the same polite words as everyone else. She was merely one of the hospital's chief benefactors and was possibly representing them all.

She took her turn, speaking first to Kristian, then to Pendreigh. It was brief. In a matter of moments she was followed by Fermin Thorpe, his fleshy face smooth, his manner meticulous. He expressed his horror and his sympathy, shaking his head and looking rather more to Pendreigh than to Kristian. Then he moved on and his place was taken by the next mourner.

The church was filling. The cortege must be due soon. Hester was shivering in spite of her heavy black coat. She moved forward a step, ready to pay her own respects, and found herself immediately behind a very dark man she guessed to be in his forties. His face was striking, with strong, generous features, but she would have paid him no further attention had she not seen Kristian's reaction to him. To that point his face had been pale and almost expressionless, like that of a man exhausted but unable to sleep, driven to stand upright only by the utmost self-discipline. Now suddenly there was a flash of light in his eyes and something close to a smile.

"Max!" he said with obvious amazement and just as clear pleasure. "How good of you to come! How did you know?"

"I was only in Paris," Max replied. "I read it in the newspapers." He clasped Kristian's hand in both of his. "I'm so desperately sorry. There are too many things to say, a whole world for which there are no words. Something immeasurable has gone out of our lives."

Kristian nodded without speaking, still clinging to Max's hand. For the first time he looked close to losing his composure. It cost him a visible effort to turn to Pendreigh, clear his throat, and introduce the two men.

"This is Max Niemann, who stood with us in Vienna in the uprising. He and Elissa and I had a bond . . ." He cleared his throat and coughed, unable to continue.

Pendreigh stepped into the momentary silence, his own voice thick with emotion. "How do you do, Herr Niemann. I am deeply grateful for all that you have been to my daughter in the past. She spoke of you with the profoundest admiration and affection. It is a great comfort to me, and I am sure it is to my son-in-law as well, that you should be here. Little in the world matters as much as friends at a time like this."

Niemann bowed slightly, bringing his heels together, but without sound. He looked up at Pendreigh, met his eyes with the ghost of a smile, then turned away to allow Hester and Monk to offer their condolences also.

Kristian had regained control of himself sufficiently to speak to Monk, who was now side by side with Hester.

"Thank you," he said quietly. He managed to sound as if he meant it. "It was good of you to come. I know you are doing all you can to help, and we appreciate it." He did not look towards Pendreigh, but his inclusion of him was obvious. He looked at Hester, and suddenly speech was difficult for him again. Perhaps it was memory of the experiences they had shared, the long nights in the fever hospital, the battles for reform, the victories and the failures they had felt so deeply. She spoke quickly, to save him the necessity. The words did not matter.

"I'm so sorry. You know we are thinking of you all the time."

"Thank you," he murmured, his voice cracking.

To spare him, she turned to Fuller Pendreigh, and Kristian introduced them. She would have liked to say something original that would still have sounded sincere, but nothing came to mind except the usual platitudes.

"I'm so sorry, Mr. Pendreigh." She meant it, but there was nothing to add that made it more comforting. She could remember the stunned feeling she had had when she came home to her parents' empty house, the place where they should have been and were not anymore.

"Thank you," he murmured. It was five days since Elissa's death, but she imagined it would be months before it no longer surprised him. It was still new, a wound, not an ache. He would be going through the ritual because it was expected of him. He was a man who did his duty.

Even as she turned to move on, the hearse arrived, drawn by

four black horses, hooves muffled by the fog, black plumes waving. It loomed suddenly, as if it had materialized out of the smothering vapor. The undertaker climbed soundlessly to the pavement. Not a breath of air stirred the long, black weepers trailing from his tall hat. Six pallbearers carried the coffin into the church.

Hester and Monk were now obliged to go in by the side door as the music of the organ shivered through the aisles between the columns of stone and echoed high in the Gothic arches above, and the service began.

Charles had taken care of the funeral of their parents. She wondered now if she had ever thanked him properly for that. She looked around her at the ceremony. It was magnificent, almost frightening in its power, and yet as the music swelled, the familiar words pronounced and all the appropriate responses made, it was comforting also. Here at home, death was always a version of something like this, rich or poor, town or country. There was more splendor or less, but the same ritual. It made it decent, allowed people to do the right thing and have some feeling that it was complete.

Except for those whose grief remained.

It had been different in the Crimea. She had seen so much of it, young men in the flower of their lives, broken on the battlefield or rotted by disease. There were too many to hold funerals for, no churches, no music except a few ragged voices singing for courage rather than the glory of sound.

But the dead went into eternity just the same. This pomp and solemnity, the black feathers and ribbons, the elaborate performance of sorrow, was for the living. Did it really make people feel better, or just that they had done their best and were acquitted?

As the service proceeded, Hester looked sideways to watch Callandra, to their left and a row in front, next to the aisle. Hester wondered what thoughts teemed inside her. A widow could not marry again for years, but a widower could remarry almost immediately, and no one thought the worse of him. It was expected his new wife would wear black in mourning for her predecessor, and Hester wondered with a note of hysteria inside her if her wedding night-gown should be black as well.

She must discipline her thoughts. Callandra had said nothing so unseemly. But Hester knew it was in her mind. The very way she spoke Kristian's name betrayed her.

Had she any idea what kind of a woman lay in the coffin? Could she imagine the beauty, the vitality and the courage she had had when she was alive, according to Fuller Pendreigh—and Kristian himself?

The service was over at last, and the mourners must leave in the proper order. There was a ritual to be observed. Only the men would go to the graveside, a custom she was sometimes grateful for, but today she found it both patronizing and irritating. Women were considered good enough to nurse the sick and dying, to wash them and lay them out, but not strong enough in temperament or spirit to watch the coffin lowered into the earth.

However, she could attend the funeral meal afterwards. It was to be held at Fuller Pendreigh's home, not Kristian's. Had he usurped that right? Or had Kristian yielded it willingly? They had been invited because of the help Monk had offered in attempting to solve the crime.

It seemed like an interminable wait between leaving the church and arriving at Pendreigh's house in Ebury Street for the funeral meal. The guests were assembled in the splendid hall and in the even more beautiful withdrawing room. Hester noticed immediately that Callandra was not among them. Perhaps that was better, even if faintly hurtful. She had not known Elissa, and since she was representing the hospital, her only connection was with Kristian. Courtesy had been amply met, and for her to have been there might suggest a personal relationship. As Hester knew very well, funerals, even more than weddings, were places for rumor to abound and all kinds of speculation to be given birth.

The whole house was hung with crepe. All the servants were in unrelieved black, and their sorrow seemed genuine. Maids had red eyes and looked shocked and tired. Even the footmen, carrying trays of wine and small tidbits for the guests to eat, spoke softly and stood for the most part in silence.

Hester knew no one else present, other than Monk and Kristian, and it was impossible to speak to Kristian except briefly. This was Pendreigh's house, but Kristian was equally involved since he was legally Elissa's closest relative. He had to be seen to speak to everyone, to make them welcome and thank them for their tributes of time and words, and in many cases flowers as well. But standing in the corner, of choice by herself, she watched.

The people appeared to be largely Pendreigh's friends. They were grave and polite to Kristian, but it was Pendreigh they knew. When they spoke to him there was emotion in the attitudes of their bodies, their bent heads and solemn expressions. They were his generation, and the cut and fabric of their clothes spoke of great wealth and a certain authority. She even recognized a few of them from photographs in the newspapers. At least two were Members of Parliament.

Did Kristian feel as much a foreigner as she felt for him? Was his reserve a matter of a grief he could barely control, or did he know few of these mourners at his wife's funeral?

The marked exception to that was the striking figure of Max Niemann. While Monk was speaking to Pendreigh and finding himself introduced to varying other people, Hester managed to move closer to Kristian and still unnoticed by him; she listened to their conversation.

". . . good of you to come," Kristian said warmly.

"For heaven's sake, man, did you imagine I would stay away?" Niemann said in amazement. "The past means too much not to have come this short distance. It's absurd, isn't it, that after all we've seen and done together, that one of us should die in an artist's studio in London?"

Kristian smiled very slightly, but there was gentleness in it, and no bitterness that Hester could see. "I think she would have preferred something a little . . . more dramatic," he said wryly. Then his voice dropped. "And to some purpose, not the idiotic accident of calling at an artist's studio at the wrong moment."

Niemann put his hand on Kristian's arm with only the barest hesitation, just a flicker across his face that vanished again. "I'm sorry," he said fervently. "Elissa, of all people, should have gone out in a blaze of glory. There's so much futility in the world, so many idiotic tragedies that strike from nowhere. All I can think of is the emptiness now that she's gone." His voice was thick with emotion, and he did not move his hand from Kristian's arm, as if in touching him he could share some bond which was precious to him.

"Another day . . . later . . . we must talk about the past," Kristian responded. "It's been far too long. Present crises press and I've allowed them to crowd out too much."

Niemann smiled and shook his head. "Still the same!" He gave Kristian's arm another swift clasp, then moved on to allow the next person to speak.

A little later Hester was standing a yard or two from Pendreigh. He was a remarkably striking man. Even in repose his face had power in it, a balance of nose and brow. If he were aware of other people looking at him he gave no sign of it, yet even in his present grief he did not neglect his duty as host.

"May I offer you something more, Mrs. Monk?" He had remembered who she was.

"No thank you, Mr. Pendreigh," she declined. She wanted to say something to draw him into conversation, and yet the tragedy which had brought her there was one which inner decency treated in silence. "You must be very tired of trying to think of courteous things to say to people." She smiled impulsively. "I imagine you would far rather be alone, and yet custom requires you do all this." She half gestured to the room full of people all talking, nodding discreetly, murmuring meaningless words no one was really listening to, and drinking Pendreigh's excellent wine. They all wore black; the only difference was in the cut and the fabric, some denser than others, some softer and more exquisitely cut.

He looked at her for a moment as if he actually saw her. The spell of retreat was broken, and a bottomless pain filled his face. "Actually, I'm not sure," he said quietly. "I think this has a . . . a sort of comfort about it. It's . . . ghastly . . . and yet perhaps it's better than being alone."

"I'm sorry," she said. "I shouldn't have spoken so intrusively. I beg your pardon."

The formal smile was back again. "You don't need to, Mrs. Monk. Forgive me, I need to bid Mr. and Mrs. Harbinger good-bye. They seem to be about to leave." He gave a slight shrug as if he did not know what he wished to say, and with the faintest bow, he left.

Hester turned to look for Kristian, and saw him standing alone by the door into the withdrawing room. His face was set in a blank, inner concentration that isolated him. He looked utterly confused, as if he had lost sight of the duty Pendreigh strove so hard to fulfill.

Then an elderly woman approached him, and he recalled his obligation, forcing himself to smile at her and say something trivial and polite.

Half an hour later, Hester and Monk excused themselves, but all the way home Hester wondered why the reception had been at Elissa's father's house and not at her husband's, which was, after all, where she had lived for the last thirteen years.

"Perhaps Pendreigh was afraid Kristian would not be well enough to carry the occasion himself," Monk suggested.

She looked sideways at him in the hansom as they moved through the streets muffled by fog, passing from the thick, yellow-gray density which caught in the throat and out into a paler, thinner patch where the light broke through and she could see the black lattice of branches above. There was a pallor of tiredness in his face, and he was staring ahead as if half his attention were in his own thoughts.

"Have you any idea who killed her?" she asked.

"No," he answered without turning.

"But you don't think Runcorn will imagine it was Kristian, do you?" she pressed.

The hansom jolted to a stop at the intersection, then started forward again. The vehicles passing in the opposite direction were visible only as shadows in the gloom.

"He has to consider it," he replied. "We don't know yet if Elissa Beck was the intended victim or simply an unfortunate witness."

"What do you know about the other woman?"

"Very little. She was an artists' model, entirely for Allardyce over the last few years. She was in her middle thirties, already past her prime for such a job. Runcorn's got men trying to find out as much as possible about her, lovers, anyone to whom she owed money. Nothing that means anything yet."

"But surely she was more likely to be the intended victim, and Elissa Beck only a witness?"

"Perhaps."

She wanted to pursue it, but she saw the tight line of his lips and knew it would serve no purpose. She almost had to bite her tongue to keep it still. She had found none of the comfort or assurance she expected. Why had he not said at least that if Runcorn were stupid enough to suspect Kristian, then Monk would prove him wrong? She wanted to ask him, but she knew she did not want the answer.

In the late afternoon Monk went out again, without saying where to. He had not changed out of his best black, almost as if for him the funeral were not over.

Hester waited an hour, trying to make up her mind, then, also still in her black, she took a hansom and gave the driver Kristian's address in Haverstock Hill. She did not know if he had returned home, but she felt compelled to seek him. Why had he not held the reception in Elissa's own house? Why had he allowed Fuller Pendreigh to take control of so much? The whole of the funeral arrangements was out of character for the man she knew, or thought she did. She had worked with him as Monk had not. The black feathermen, the ostrich plumes, the hearse and four, were far from the simple dignity of life and death as he had known it in the hospital or the fever wards they had set up in Limehouse. He was a man too used to the reality of physical death to wrap it in ceremony, and too genuine in his emotion. His pity and his grief needed no display to others.

Was Elissa's death really so different, so shattering, that he had changed utterly? Or had Hester misread him all the time? Had there always been a ritualistic high churchman beneath the uncluttered man she had known?

It seemed an endless journey through the fog-shrouded streets, but eventually she reached the house and requested the driver to wait while she ascertained that Kristian was there. She had no intention of having to search for another cab were he not. She rang the doorbell three times and was about to leave when Kristian himself opened it. His face looked eerie and his eyes enormous in the light from the street lamp. The hall behind him was in darkness, except for a single gas bracket burning low at the foot of the stairs.

"Hester? Is something wrong?" There was an edge of alarm in his voice.

"No," she said quickly. "No one is ill. I came because I was concerned for you. I barely had the opportunity to speak with you earlier."

"That is most thoughtful of you, but I assure you I am merely tired." The ghost of a smile touched his lips, but there was no echo in his eyes. "It is an effort to accept people's sympathies graciously and think of something to say in return which is not so bland as to be a kind of rebuff. I think we are all reminded of our own losses. A hundred other griefs come far too close to us at such times."

"May I dismiss my hansom?" It was an oblique way of inviting herself in.

He hesitated.

She blushed to do it, but with her back to the light he could not have seen. "Thank you," she accepted before he spoke, and turned around to go back and pay the driver.

He was left with no alternative but to invite her in. He led the way to a small morning room where he reached up and turned the gas a little higher. She saw that the room was pleasantly furnished. There were three armchairs, all odd, but of similar rusty shades, lending an illusion of warmth which in fact was not there. The old Turkish rug was full of reds and blues. The fire did not appear to have been used recently. There was a worn embroidered screen in front of it and no poker, coal tongs or shovel in the hearth.

Kristian looked ill at ease, but he invited her to sit down.

She accepted, beginning to realize just how crass she had been in forcing her way in. It was inexcusably intrusive. She had allowed her concern to rob her of all sensitivity. She did not know him nearly well enough to be placing herself there.

What could she possibly say to redeem the situation?

Honesty—it would either make her actions excusable or condemn her beyond recall. She plunged in. "William is working with Superintendent Runcorn to try to find out who is responsible for this. They loathe each other, but they both want to know the truth enough to bury their feelings for the time being."

Kristian's face was almost expressionless as he sat opposite her. Was it from exhaustion at the end of one of the worst days of his life, and was he too in debt to old friendships to throw her out, as most men would have done in the circumstances? Or was he really concealing a very different self he did not wish her to see, more particularly did not wish her to report back to the clever, perceptive, ruthless Monk, who never let go of a case, no matter who was destroyed by the truth?

An icy fear gripped her for Callandra, and she was ashamed of it. She knew Kristian better than that.

"Kristian, was Elissa very religious?"

"What?" He looked totally startled, then the dull color spread up his cheeks, but he offered no explanation.

"The funeral was very High Church." She knew she was hurting him, although not how.

"That was my father-in-law's wish," he said. He was not looking directly at her but somewhere a trifle to her left.

She was aware of feeling cold. The room was too chilly for comfort. Surely he had been sitting somewhere else when she had rung the doorbell. Was he keeping her there in the hope that the cold would persuade her to leave? If so, he had forgotten most of what he had learned about her. Did he really not remember the long, exhausting nights of labor and despair they and Callandra had spent together in Limehouse?

"And you conceded to it?" she asked with a lift of surprise.

"He is deeply grieved!" he replied a trifle sharply. "If it comforts him it does no harm, Hester." It was a reproof, and she felt its sting.

"I'm sorry," she apologized. "It is very generous of you. It did not seem your way, and it is an enormous expense."

Now it was his turn to blush painfully. It startled her to see it. She had no idea what she had said to provoke it. He was obviously acutely embarrassed. He looked down at his hands as he answered. "None of it is my way, but if it helps him to go through the ritual, how could I deny him that? They were unusually close. She admired him intensely." He raised his eyes to meet hers at last. "He had great physical courage also, you know? When he was still little more than a boy he was a mountaineer. There was an accident, and at great risk to his own life, he rescued the three other members of his party. Climbing was very fashionable then, and the incident became well-known. One of the men he rescued wrote a book about it." He half smiled. "I think in a way Elissa was trying to live up to him."

In spite of herself, Hester found her eyes suddenly filled with tears. "I'm sorry," she whispered.

He shrugged and shook his head a little.

"Was that why you allowed him to host the funeral meal also?" she asked.

He looked away again. "In part. They are a Liverpool family, not London. He has only been here a year or so, but he has many friends here, people I don't know, and he wished them to be invited. As you saw, a great number came."

Without thinking, she gazed around the room. Even in the meager light of the one lamp, she could see it was shabby. The fabric on the arms of the chairs was worn where hands and elbows rested. There was a track of faded color across the carpet from the door to each of the chairs. This was a room as one might furnish for the servants to sit in during the brief times free from their duties.

She looked again at Kristian, and saw with a rush of horror that his eyes were hot with shame. Why had he brought her to this room? Surely any other room would be better? Was it nothing to do with desiring her to leave? Was it conceivable . . . She stared at him, and a flood of understanding opened up between them. "The rest of the house?" she said in almost a whisper.

He looked down at the floor. "This is the best," he answered. "Apart from the hall and Elissa's bedroom. The rest is empty."

She was stunned, ashamed for herself and for him because she had exposed something immeasurably private. At the same time it was incomprehensible. Kristian worked harder than any other man she knew. Even Monk did not work consistently as long. A great deal of it was done without payment, she knew that from Callandra, who was very familiar with the hospital's finances, but his ordinary hours were rewarded like any other doctor's.

It flickered through her mind that he could even have given certain things away, but that would have been a noble thing to do. He would have looked her in the face and said it with pride, not down at the floor in silent misery.

"What happened?" She said the words hoarsely, conscious of a terrible intrusion. Had Elissa not been murdered, she would never have deepened such a pain by seeking explanation, but like probing for a bullet in torn flesh, it might be the only way towards healing.

"Elissa gambled," he said simply. "It was only a little to begin with, but lately it became so she couldn't help it."

"G–gambled?" She felt as if she had been struck. Her mind staggered, trying to retain balance. "Gambled?" she repeated pointlessly.

"It became a compulsion." His voice was flat, without expression. "At first it was just a little excitement, then, when she won, it took hold of her. Then it went on, even when she began to lose. You think the next time you will make it up again. Reason doesn't have any part in it. In the end, all you think about is the next chance to test your luck, to feel the excitement in the mind, the blood beating as you wait for the card, or the dice, or whatever it is."

She looked around the room, her throat tightening in misery for the emptiness of it. "But it can cost you everything," she said, her voice choking in spite of herself. Anger boiled inside her at the futility of it. She turned to face him. "And you can't ever win unless somebody else loses."

This time his eyes did not waver. He was not evading the truth anymore, and there was a mark of defiance in him. "I know. If there were no real danger, no loss, it wouldn't make the heart go faster and the stomach knot inside. If you are a real gambler, you must risk more than you can afford to lose. I don't think it was even the winning that mattered anymore; it was the defying of fate and walking away."

But she had not. She had lost. It had taken from her the warmth and beauty of her home, then even the necessities of it, and it had cost her husband grief, exhaustion and the comfort of a home he had labored to provide, and a shame that was almost insupportable. All social life had been swept away. He could not accept an invitation from anyone, because he could not return it. He was cut off, isolated, and surely terrified of ever-increasing debt he would not be able to meet. This would become public disgrace, perhaps eventually even the utter despair of debtor's prison, as other bills of life could not be met and creditors closed in, angry and vengeful.

It was like a disease of the mind—a madness! Elissa was a woman he had once loved, perhaps still did, but there was a part of her he could not reach, and it was destroying both of them.

She did not want to think of it, still less to face it. But it was blazingly, luminously clear even to her, with all her friendship for Kristian and her love for Callandra, that he had a supreme motive for killing Elissa. It was so powerful, so totally understandable, that she did not deny to herself the possibility that in a moment of engulfing panic, as ruin faced him, he could have done it. She felt grieved and guilty and frightened, but above all she felt wrenchingly sorry.

"Did Pendreigh know?" she asked.

"No. She always managed to keep it from him. She only called on him when she was winning, and she managed to find excuses never to invite him here. I think that was easy enough. She used my work as excuse." He shivered and pushed his hand over his brow, hard back, as if the pressure of it eased some pain inside. "She wouldn't have to explain," he went on, his voice husky. "She didn't know much about it; I never really shared it with her. I brought her here from the passion and excitement of Vienna, and expected her to be happy in a domestic life amid people she did not know, and with no cause to fight, no admiration, no danger, no loyalties . . ."

"There are plenty of battles to fight here," she said softly. "Not at the barricades, not with plain enemies, and not always with any glory, but they are real."

He pressed his hands over his eyes. "Not for her. I did nothing to help her find them. I was too drawn into my own work. I expected her to change. You should never expect that . . . people don't."

She struggled for something to say, a way of denying it to offer some comfort. But there was an element of truth in it, and that was all he could see. All the ways in which Elissa could have found causes worth all her efforts, he would see only as excuses for his own failure to make her happy.

"Perhaps we all have something of that hunger in us," she said at last. "But when we love someone we do learn to change its direction. I went to the Crimea to nurse, but I also went for the adventure. It's wonderful to be so very alive, even if some of it is horror and rage, and grief. Not to have lived is the worst death of all." She smiled briefly. "I was going to say that we have the right to make those dreams only for ourselves, not for others, but there's hardly anything we do that doesn't take others along with us, in some way. If I'd stayed at home my family's lives would have been different, and their deaths." It hurt to say that. She had never allowed herself even to think it before. Perhaps life would be different for Charles if she had been there to share the burden instead of leaving him alone with the loss of a brother, then a father. Only now, sitting quietly in this room with Kristian Beck, did she try to imagine how Charles had coped with all that grief, trying to think of anything to say or do to ease his mother's sorrow.

Did he blame himself that he had failed and she had died, too? Did Imogen ever even think of that? Hester was furious with her, and then with herself. She had not been there either. Love, loyalty, the bonds of family should mean more than simply writing good letters now and again.

She lifted her hand and touched Kristian's arm. "I'm so sorry. I can't say that I know how you feel. Of course I don't, no one does who has not been where you are. But I know what pain is, and the knowledge afterwards that you might have added to it, and I am truly sorry."

"Thank you," he said quietly. He bit his full lower lip, bringing blood to it. "I'm not sure I can say I am glad you came, but I am certainly glad you care." His eyes were soft, a profound honesty in them, and a depth of emotion she preferred not to name.

It was pointless offering to do anything for him. All anyone could do was find the truth and pray it did not hurt him any more profoundly. No one could lift the darkness yet, or share it.

She stood up and excused herself, and he collected his hat and coat and walked through the fog with her along Haverstock Hill towards the City until he found a hansom for her, but they did not speak again.

All the way home through the fog-choked streets her mind whirled around the new knowledge she had stumbled on so insensitively. She blamed herself for the pain she had caused, and yet it was woven into every part of the life of the dead woman. Elissa Beck was nothing like the person any of them had imagined. Monk had said she was beautiful, not just attractive but hauntingly, unforgettably beautiful. Kristian himself had said she was brave. Now it seemed she was also driven by a compulsion which devoured not only her own happiness but Kristian's as well. He was taken to the brink of ruin, and had she lived, surely it would soon have been beyond it into an abyss.

How would Callandra feel when she knew—and there would be no way of protecting her from it—that Kristian had had an urgent, compelling motive to kill his wife?

When she arrived home Monk was in the sitting room, pacing the floor.

"Where have you been?" he demanded. "It's after ten o'clock! Hester . . ." He stopped abruptly, staring at her face. "What's happened? What is it? You look awful!"

"Thank you!" she said, deciding in that instant that she could not tell him what she had learned. It was too difficult, too vulnerable. "It has not been a pleasant day."

"Of course it hasn't been pleasant," he responded. "But you looked a lot better at the funeral. What's happened since then? You're as white as paper!"

"I'm tired." She started to walk past him.

He put out his hand and grasped her arm, not hard, but firmly enough to stop her and swing her slightly around. "Hester! Where have you been?" His voice was not rough, but there was no yielding in it, no acceptance of denial.

"I went to see Kristian," she replied, intending to tell him only that much.

His eyes narrowed. "Why? You've already seen him."

She hesitated. How little could she tell him and be believed? "I was concerned for him."

"So you went to his house, after the funeral of his wife?" he said with open disbelief. "Didn't it occur to you that he might wish to be alone?"

She was stung by his belief in her insensitivity, partly because she had been intrusive exactly as he accused. "Yes, of course it did! I didn't go imagining I could comfort him. I went because I needed to know . . ." Then she stopped. She did not want to tell him yet what she had seen. He would know that Kristian could be guilty, then sooner or later he would have to tell Runcorn.

"What?" he said sharply. "What did you need to know?"

She was angry at being caught, having either to tell him the truth or to think of a convincing lie that would not stand between them forever. Or she could simply refuse to answer. "I would prefer to speak about it at another time," she said a little primly.

"You would what?" he said incredulously, his grasp tightening on her arm.

"Let go of me, William. You are bruising me," she said coldly.

He loosened his grip without removing his hand. "Hester, you are deliberately being evasive. What have you discovered that is so ugly that you are prepared to compromise yourself for it?"

"I'm . . ." she began, then the truth of what he was saying bit more deeply. She *was* compromising herself, and also the trust between them. He would find out soon anyway. She was not really protecting Kristian by hiding what she knew from Monk. If Kristian had killed his wife, nothing would protect him, or Callandra; and if he had not, then only the whole truth would do any good.

She looked at Monk's face and met his eyes squarely. "I went to find out why the funeral meal was held in Pendreigh's house, not Elissa's own home," she answered.

"And why was it?" he said softly, a shadow in his face.

"Because Elissa gambled," she replied. "Compulsively. Kristian has hardly anything left, no furniture, no carpets, no resident servants, nothing but her bedroom and one shabby sitting room, without a fire."

He stared at her, absorbing what she had said. "Gambled?" he repeated.

"Yes. It became so she couldn't help it, no matter how much she lost. In fact, if she weren't risking more than she could afford, it didn't have any excitement for her."

He looked very pale, his face tight. He did not say anything of how he understood all that that meant, but he did not need to. It stood like a third entity, a darkness in the room with them.

CHAPTER
FIVE

———

Monk was profoundly disturbed by what Hester had told him. He set out early, walking head down, through the still-shrouded streets. If it were true, then Kristian had a far deeper and more urgent motive for killing Elissa than any of them had realized before.

If she were driving him beyond poverty into ruin, the loss of his home, his reputation, his honor, even a time when debts could not be met, with the prospect of debtors' prison, then Monk could very easily imagine panic and desperation prompting anyone in Kristian's position to think of murder.

The Queen's Prison was still kept exclusively for debtors, but all too often they were thrown in with everyone else: thieves, forgers, embezzlers, arsonists, cutthroats. They might remain there until their debts were discharged, dependent upon outside help even for food, and upon the grace of God for any kind of protection from cold, lice, disease, and the violence of their fellows, never mind the inner torments of despair.

Kristian was a man who in the past had faced injustice and fought it with violence, but then he had not stood alone. Half of Europe had risen in revolution against oppression, but perhaps the memory of it lay so deep in him that he would believe it was the answer again. Violence could have been instinctive rather than reasoned, and then, when it was too late, understanding and remorse returned.

It was too easily believable to discard. If he were honest, Monk could even understand it. Were anyone to threaten all he had spent his life building—his career, his reputation, the core of his own integrity and independence, his power to follow the profession he chose, to exercise his skills and feel of value to the things he believed in—he would fight to survive. He was not prepared to swear what weapons he would use, or decline, however bitter the price, or the shame afterwards.

There was an icy wind that morning, and he bent his head against it, feeling it sting his face. A newsboy was calling out something about a dispatch bearer for President Davis of the Confederacy in America who had been arrested in New Orleans, about to embark for England. It barely touched the periphery of Monk's mind. He still had to know the truth, all of it, and he had to be aware of what Runcorn knew. If Kristian were not guilty, he would defend him to the last stand.

But if he were guilty, then such defense as there might be was different. Except there was no moral defense. Had it been only Elissa, some plea of mitigation might have been possible. He was certainly not the only man to have a wife who had driven him to the edge of madness, and violence lurks in many, if they are frightened or hurt enough. But whoever it was had then killed Sarah Mackeson also, simply because she was there. Nothing could justify that.

He would not yet tell Runcorn anything about what he had learned. It was still reasonable to assume that Sarah Mackeson was the intended victim, and even that Argo Allardyce was lying when he said he had not been back to Acton Street all night. They should begin by finding the woman companion that Elissa Beck had undoubtedly taken with her to her portrait sittings. She could have valuable testimony as to what had happened that night, at least up to the point when she and Elissa had parted. Where had she left Elissa, and for what reason? No doubt Runcorn had thought of that, too.

He stopped abruptly, causing the man behind him on the footpath to collide with him and nearly lose his balance. The other man swore under his breath and moved on, leaving Monk staring into the distance where one of the new horse-drawn trams loomed out of the thinning mist.

Runcorn would naturally begin with the assumption that Elissa had taken her maid, and he would go to Haverstock Hill to find her. And of course there was no lady's maid there. A man who had sold all his furniture except the sort of thing a bailiff would leave could not afford such a thing. The scrubwoman who had answered the door the first time was probably the only servant they had, and she might come only two or three times a week.

Would Elissa have taken someone from her father's house? Or a woman friend? Or might she actually have gone alone?

But the question beating in his mind was how to keep Runcorn from finding out about her gambling, or at least the ruinous extent of it. Perhaps he was only delaying the inevitable, but asking Allardyce himself about Elissa's companion would be as logical as beginning at Elissa's home. He quickened his pace. He must find Runcorn and suggest that to him, persuade him to agree.

He glanced both ways at the crossroads, then sprinted across between a dray and a vegetable cart. He reached the police station at twenty minutes past eight and went straight up to Runcorn's office.

Runcorn looked up, his face carefully devoid of expression. He was waiting for Monk to make the first move.

"Good morning." Monk hid his smile and looked back straight into Runcorn's bland eyes. "I thought you'd probably be going to Allardyce again to see who the woman was who went with Mrs. Beck. I'd like to come with you." He thought of adding a request, but that would be rather too polite for Runcorn to believe of him. He would suspect sarcasm.

Runcorn's shoulders relaxed a little. "Yes, if you want," he said casually. There was only the slightest flicker to betray that he had not thought of it. "In fact, it would be a good idea," he added, standing up. "I suppose Mrs. Beck would take someone, wouldn't she? Wouldn't be proper alone with an artist in his studio, especially not when there's living quarters there as well. Who'd it be, a maid?"

"Or a friend," Monk replied. "Which could be anyone. Easier to start by asking Allardyce himself."

Runcorn frowned, taking his coat and hat from the stand near the door. "I suppose the fog's still like pea soup, and it'll be just as fast to walk." It was not really a question because he did not wait for an answer.

Monk followed him down the stairs and fell into step beside him in the street. Actually, the weather was improving all the time and he could now see almost thirty yards in any direction. All the same, they decided to walk rather than try to flag down a hansom from the steady stream of traffic.

"How many sittings do you have to have for a portrait, anyhow?" Runcorn asked after several minutes.

"I don't know," Monk admitted. "Maybe it depends on the style and the artist. Perhaps the model sits in for you some of the time?"

"They didn't look much alike." Runcorn darted a sideways look at Monk. "Still, I suppose for a dress or something it wouldn't matter." He frowned. "What did she do the rest of the time? I mean, every day. A doctor's wife . . . not quite a lady, but certainly gentry . . . at least." He had exposed an ignorance without intending to. Puzzlement was written plainly in his face. "There isn't anything she would actually have to do, is there?"

"I doubt it," Monk lied. Surely without any resident servants she would have to do most of the housework, cooking and laundry herself. Or perhaps with so little of the house occupied, there was far less to attend to. Only sufficient food for Kristian when he was home, and herself if she was not out with friends or at the gambling tables. Maybe Kristian had his shirts laundered at the hospital.

"Then what?" Runcorn asked. They crossed the Gray's Inn Road and walked north. "I was ill once with bronchitis. Took me ages to get back to regular duty. Enjoyed the rest for the first two or three days. Thought I'd get a lot out of a fortnight. Nearly drove me mad! Never been so bored in my life. Came back before the doctor said I should because I couldn't stand it."

Monk could picture it in his mind. Runcorn relaxing with a good book was almost a contradiction in ideas. Again he suppressed a smile with difficulty.

Runcorn saw it and glared at him.

"Sympathy!" Monk said quickly. "Broke my ribs, remember?"

Runcorn grunted, and they went on in silence as far as Acton Street and turned the corner. "Wouldn't like to be a lady," he said thoughtfully. "Imagine I'd rather have work to do ... unless, of course, I didn't know any different." He was still frowning, trying to imagine a world so terrifyingly empty, when they reached the top of the stairs and knocked on Allardyce's studio door.

It was several moments before it was opened by Allardyce himself, looking angry and half asleep. "What in hell's name do you want at this hour?" he demanded. "It's barely daylight! Haven't you got a home?"

"It's nearly nine o'clock, sir," Runcorn answered flatly, his face set in disapproval and studiously avoiding looking at Allardyce's hastily pulled on trousers and his nightshirt tails hanging over them. His feet were bare, and he moved from one to the other on the chilly step.

"I suppose policemen have to be up at this ungodly hour," Allardyce said irritably. "What do you want now? You'd better come in, because I'm not standing out here any longer." And he turned and went back inside, leaving the door open for them.

Runcorn followed him in, and Monk came a step behind. The studio was otherwise unoccupied, but there were canvases stacked against the walls. Half a dozen were in one stage or another of development—four portraits, one street scene, an interior with two girls sitting on a sofa reading. The one painting on the easel was of a man of middle age and a great look of self-satisfaction. Presumably it was a commission.

Allardyce muttered something under his breath and disappeared through the farther door.

Runcorn wrinkled his nose very slightly. He said nothing, but his face was eloquent of his disgust.

Monk walked over to a sheaf of drawings in a folder and opened them up. The first was brilliant. The artist had used only a charcoal pencil, but with an extraordinary economy of stroke he had caught the suppressed energy in face and body as three women leaned over a table. The dice were so insignificant it took a moment before Monk even saw them. All the passion was in the faces, the eyes, the open mouths, the jagged force that held them transfixed. Gamblers.

He turned it over quickly and looked at the next. Gamblers again, but this time with the vacant stare of the loser. It was powerful, desolate. A home or a fortune lost on the turn of a piece of colored cardboard, but all despair was in the eyes.

The third was a beautiful woman, her face alight as if at sight of a lover, her eyes shining, her lips parted, but it was a fan of cards that she stared at, a winning hand, colors and suits blurred, already without meaning as she looked towards the next deal. Victory was so sweet, and the taste of it an instant, and then gone again.

Elissa Beck.

Monk turned the rest, aware of Runcorn at his shoulder, watching, saying nothing.

There were pictures of this woman, some sketched so hastily they were little more than a suggestion, half an outline, but with such power the emotion leapt raw off the paper, the greed, the excitement, the pounding heart, the sweat on the skin, the clenched muscles. Monk found himself holding his own breath as he looked at them one after another.

Had Runcorn recognized Elissa? Monk felt himself hot, and then cold. Could Runcorn possibly imagine Allardyce was so obsessed with her he had placed her there just to draw her again and again? Not unless he was totally naive. Those drawings were from life; anyone with the slightest knowledge of nature could see the honesty in them. He did not want to turn to meet Runcorn's eyes.

There were two more pictures. They were probably just the same, but their blank white edges, poking out beneath the one he saw now, challenged him. What were they? More of Elissa? He could feel Runcorn's presence so vividly he imagined the warmth of his body, Runcorn's breath on his neck.

He turned the page. The second to last was a man, thick-chested, broken-nosed, leaning against a wall and watching the women, who were again playing. His face was brutish, bored. Sooner or later they would lose, and it would be his job to make sure the debts were collected. He would get rid of troublemakers.

Slowly, Monk lifted the page over to look at the last one. It was an expensively dressed man with dead eyes, and a small pistol in his hand.

Runcorn let out a sigh, and his voice was very quiet. "Poor devil," he said. "I suppose he reckons it's the better way. Ever seen a debtors' prison, Monk? Some of them aren't too bad, but when they throw 'em in with everyone else, for a man like that, he's probably right, better off a quick end."

Monk said nothing. His thoughts were too hard, the truth too close.

"I suppose you think he's a coward," Runcorn said, and there was anger and hurt bristling in him.

"No!" Monk returned instantly. "Don't suppose. You've no idea what I think!"

Runcorn was startled.

Now Monk was facing him, their eyes meeting. Had Runcorn recognized Elissa? How long would it be before he realized the cost of her gambling? He knew enough not to imagine it was a game, a few hours of a harmless pastime. If he had not before, it was there in the drawings, the consuming hunger that swept away all other thought or feeling. They destroyed any illusion that it was a harmless, controllable vice.

"She didn't break her own neck," Runcorn said very softly, his voice rough as if his throat hurt. "Debt collectors? And the poor model just got in the way?"

Monk thought about it. Somewhere in his closed memory he must know more about gamblers, violence, ways of extorting money without endangering their own gambling houses, and thus losing more profit than they gained. "We don't know that she owed enough to be worth making an example of," he said to Runcorn. "Does it look that way to you?"

Runcorn's lips tightened. "No," he said flatly. He would like that to have been the answer, even if they never found the individual man responsible; it was clear in his face. "Doesn't really make sense. If she wasn't paying they'd simply ban her from the place . . . long before she got to owe enough to be worth the risk of killing. They'd murder rivals who could drive them out of business, but not losers. Hell, the gutters'd be choked with corpses if they did that." His eyes widened suddenly. "Might kill a winner, though! Win a bit's good to encourage the others, win a lot is expensive."

Monk laughed harshly. "And you don't suppose they have control over how much anybody wins?"

Runcorn grunted, anger flickering across his face, then unhappiness. "Would have been a good answer. Wonder how long she'd been doing it and how much she lost?"

Monk felt the heat under his skin and the sweat drip down his body. Damn Runcorn for making him unable to lie to him anymore. Damn him for being real, and for finding an honesty in himself that made him impossible to ignore. Perhaps he could get by with a half-truth? No, he couldn't! If Runcorn found out, and he would, he would despise Monk for it. He had patronized Runcorn in the past, bypassed him as not worthy of being told the truth, but he had never told him a face-to-face lie. That was the coward's way.

There was no more time.

"A lot," he said, hating the betrayal of Kristian, knowing that Hester had not meant him to tell Runcorn.

Runcorn's eyes widened slightly. "How do you know?"

"Hester went to see Kristian last night. She told me." He tried to make his voice final, closing the subject. Surely, Allardyce would come back any moment now? He had had time to wash and shave and dress fully.

Runcorn hesitated, drew in a long breath. He decided not to press it farther. Something in him sensed a victory, a balance. He turned away. "Mr. Allardyce!" he called.

Allardyce appeared in the doorway holding a mug of tea in one hand. He was shaved and dressed, and he looked composed. "What now?" he said glumly. "I already told you that I know nothing. Hell! Don't you think if I knew who did it I'd tell you?" He waved his free arm angrily, slopping the tea in the other hand. "Look what it's done to my life!"

Runcorn forbore from answering the last question. "This public house you say you were at . . ."

"The Bull and Half Moon," Allardyce supplied. "What about it?"

"Where is it, exactly?"

"Rotherhithe Street, Southwark."

"Rather a long way to go for a drink?" Runcorn raised his eyebrows.

"That's why I spent the night," Allardyce said reasonably. "Too far to come home, and it was a filthy night. Could hear the fog-horns on the river every few minutes. The Pool was thick as pea soup. Never understand how they don't hit each other more often."

"So why go that far?" Monk asked.

Allardyce shrugged. "Got good friends that way. Knew they'd put me up, if necessary. If I stayed home every time there was fog I'd never go anywhere. Ask Gilbert Strother. Lives in Great Hermitage Street, in Wapping. Don't know the number. You'll have to ask. Somewhere around the middle. Has a door with an angel on it. He did a sketch of us all. He'll tell you."

"I'll do that," Runcorn agreed, thin-lipped.

"Look, I can't tell you anything useful," Allardyce went on.

"I've got a friend hurt in that pileup in Drury Lane. I want to go and see him. Broke his leg, poor devil."

"What pileup?" Runcorn said suspiciously.

"Horse bolted. Two carriages got locked together and a dray got turned sideways and lost its load. Must have been twenty kegs burst open at least—raw sugar syrup. Said he'd never seen such a mess in his life. Stopped up Drury Lane all evening."

"When was that?"

Allardyce's face tightened. "The night of the murders." He stared at Runcorn and suddenly his eyes filled with tears. He blinked angrily and turned away.

"Mr. Allardyce," Monk said quietly, "when Mrs. Beck came for the sittings, who did she bring with her?"

Allardyce frowned.

"As chaperone," Monk added.

Allardyce gave a burst of laughter. "A friend, once or twice, but she only came as far as the door. Never knew her name." His face darkened, his mouth turned down a little at the ends. "She met the man here three or four times. I suppose you know about that?"

"What man?" Runcorn snapped.

"Dark. Strong face. Interesting. Wouldn't mind drawing him sometime, but I never met him. Don't know his name."

"Draw him now!" Runcorn commanded.

Allardyce walked over to the table and picked up a block of paper and a stick of charcoal. With a dozen or so lines he created a very recognizable sketch of Max Niemann. He turned it towards Runcorn.

"Max Niemann, Beck's ally in Vienna," Monk told him.

"Why didn't you say anything about this before?" Runcorn was furious, his face mottling with dark color.

Allardyce was pale. "Because they were good friends . . . or more," he replied, his voice rising. "And I have no idea if he was anywhere near here that night. Anyway, I wasn't expecting Elissa, or I'd have been here myself. If she met this man Niemann, it wouldn't be in my studio. I assume the murderer was some old lover of Sarah's, or something of that sort, and Elissa just picked the wrong time to call in. Perhaps she wanted to see if the portrait was finished . . . or something."

Runcorn gave him a withering look, but since it was more or less what he was inclined to believe himself, there was little argument to make. "We'd better find out a great deal more about Sarah Mackeson," he said instead.

"I've told you all I know," Allardyce said uneasily, all the anger draining from his face and leaving only sadness. "I gave all that to your man: where she was born, where she grew up, as far as she told me. She didn't talk about herself."

"I know . . . I know," Runcorn was irritated. It woke a mixture of feelings in him—pity because the woman was dead, duty because it was his task to find out who had killed her and see that the guilty person faced the law to answer for it. At the same time he despised her morality. It offended every desire for decency in him, the love of rules to live by and order he could understand. He turned to Monk. "We'd better get on with it, then." His eyes widened. "If you're interested, that is?"

"I'm interested," Monk accepted.

They bade Allardyce good-bye and went back down the stairs into the street, where Runcorn pulled a piece of paper out of his pocket. "I'm going to start with Mrs. Ethel Roberts, who used to employ her as a milliner's assistant. You can go to see Mrs. Clark, who took her in now and then. I'll leave you to find out for what." His expression conveyed his opinion of the possibilities. "We'll meet up at that pub on the corner of North Street and the Caledonian Road, can't remember what it's called. Be there at one!" And with that he thrust the piece of paper into Monk's hand and turned abruptly to cross the street, leaving Monk standing on the curb in the sun and noise, the increasing rattle of traffic, street vendors' cries for their shellfish, cheeses, razors, shirt buttons, rat poison.

108

He found Mrs. Clark in a boardinghouse in Risinghill Street, north of the Pentonville Road, just beyond a tobacconist's shop with a Highlander on the sign to denote to the illiterate what it was he sold. Inside the boardinghouse, the air in the hall smelled of stale polish and yesterday's cooking, but the house was cleaner than some he had seen, and there was a cheerful clatter of dishes, and a voice singing, coming from somewhere towards the back.

He followed the sound of it and knocked on the open kitchen door. It was a large room with a scrubbed stone floor, a wooden table in the middle and on the stove a pan was boiling briskly, the steam jiggling the lid. In the stone scullery beyond he could see three huge wooden sinks filled with linen soaking, and on a shelf above them big jars of lye, fat, potash and blue. A washboard was balanced in one sink, and in the other was a laundry dolly, used to push the clothes up and down within the copper when they needed to be boiled. He appeared to have interrupted Mrs. Clark on her wash day.

She was a rotund woman, ample-bosomed and broad-hipped, with short, plump arms. Her blue sleeves were pushed up untidily. An apron which had seen very much better days was tied around her waist and slipping to one side. She pushed her hair back off her face and turned from the bowl where she was peeling potatoes, the knife still in her hand.

"Can't do nuthin' for yer, luv," she said amiably. "Ain't got room ter 'ouse a cat! Could try Mrs. Last down the street. Number fifty-six. In't as comfy as me, but what can yer do?" She smiled at him, showing several gaps in her teeth. "My, aren't yer the swell, then? Got all yer money on yer back, 'ave yer?"

Monk smiled in spite of himself. There was a time when that would have been true. Even now there was a stronger element in it than perhaps for most men.

"You read people pretty well, Mrs. Clark," he replied.

"Gotter," she acknowledged. "It's me business." She looked him up and down appreciatively. "Sorry as I can't 'elp yer. I like a man wot knows 'ow ter look 'is best. Like I said, try Mrs. Last."

"Actually, I wasn't looking for lodgings." He had already decided to be candid with her. "I'm told you used to give Sarah Mackeson a room now and then, when times were rough."

Her face hardened. "So what's that ter you, then? Yer got ideas about her, yer can forget 'em. She's an artists' model now, and good at it she is, too." She stopped abruptly, defiance in her stare.

"Very good," Monk agreed, seeing in his mind the pictures Allardyce had painted of Sarah. "But she was killed, and I want to know who did it."

It was brutal, and Mrs. Clark swayed a little before leaning against the table heavily, the color draining from her face.

"I'm sorry," Monk apologized. It had not occurred to him that she might not know and that she had cared about Sarah, and suddenly he realized how much he had concentrated on the reality of Elissa Beck and forgotten the other woman and those who might have known her and would be wounded by her death. On the other hand, if Mrs. Clark knew her well enough to feel her loss deeply, then perhaps she could give him some better information about her.

She fumbled behind her for the chair, and he stepped forward quickly and placed it so she could sit down.

"I'm sorry," he repeated. "I didn't know you were close to her."

She sniffed fiercely and glared at him, ignoring her brimming eyes and daring him to comment. "I liked 'er, poor little cow," she said tartly. " 'Oo wouldn't? Did 'er best. So wot yer want 'ere, then? I don't know 'oo killed 'er!"

He fetched the other chair and sat down opposite her. "You might be able to tell me something about her which would help."

"Why? Wot der you care?" She narrowed her eyes at him. " 'Oo are yer, any'ow? Yer never said. Yer just came bargin' in 'ere like the rent collector, only I don't owe no rent. This place is me own. So explain yerself. I don't care 'ow swell yer look, I in't tellin' yer nothin' as I don't want ter."

He tried to put it in terms she would grasp. "I'm a kind of private policeman. I work for people who want to know the truth of something and pay me to find out."

"An' 'oo cares 'oo killed a poor little cow like Sarah Mackeson, then?" she said derisively. "She in't got nobody. 'Er pa were a navvy wot got killed diggin' the railways an' 'er ma died years ago. She's got a couple o' brothers someplace, but she never knew where."

"The wife of a friend of mine was murdered with her," he replied. There was a kind of dignity in this woman, with her crooked apron and straggling hair, that demanded the truth from him, or at least no lies.

"There were two of 'em done?" she said with horror. "Geez! 'Oo'd do a thing like that? Poor Sarah!"

He smiled at her very slightly, an acknowledgment.

She sniffed and stood up, turning her back to him. Without explaining, she filled the kettle and put it on the hob, then fetched a china teapot and two mugs.

"I'll tell yer wot I know," she remarked while she waited for the water to boil. "Wot in't much. She used ter do quite well sometimes, and bad others. If she were in an 'ard patch she'd come 'ere an' I'd find 'er a bed for a spell. She'd always turn 'er 'and ter cookin' an' cleanin' as return. Din't expec' summink fer nuffink. Honest, she were, in 'er own fashion. An' generous." She kept her back to him as the steam started to whistle in the spout.

He did not press her in what way; he understood it from her turned back. She was not willing to put words to it.

"Anyone in particular?" he asked, quite casually.

"Arthur Cutter," she said, bringing the teapot over to the table and putting it down. " 'E's a right waster, but 'e wouldn't 'ave 'urt 'er. It would 'a bin some o' them daft artist people. I always told 'er they was no good." She sniffed again and reached for a piece of cloth in her apron pocket. She blew her nose savagely and then poured the tea for both of them, not bothering to ask if he wanted milk or sugar, but assuming both. Monk disliked sugar intensely, but he made no comment, simply thanking her.

"How did she get in with the artists?" he asked.

Now she seemed willing to talk. She rambled on, telling and retelling, but a vivid picture of Sarah Mackeson emerged from a mixture of memory, opinion and anger. Fourteen years ago, aged eighteen, she had arrived in Risinghill Street without a penny but willing to work. Within weeks her handsome figure and truly beautiful hair and eyes had attracted attention, some of it welcome, much of it beyond her skill to deal with.

Mrs. Clark had taken her in and taught her a good deal about caring for herself and learning to play one admirer off against another in order to survive. Within a few months she had found a protector prepared to take her as his mistress and give her a very pleasant standard of living.

It lasted four years, until he grew bored and found another eighteen-year-old and began again. Sarah had come back to Risinghill Street, wiser and a good deal more careful. She found work in a public house, the Hare and Billet, about half a mile away, and it was there that a young artist had seen her and hired her to sit for him.

Over a space of a couple of years she had improved her skill as a model, and finally Argo Allardyce had persuaded her to leave Risinghill Street and go to Acton Street to be at his disposal any time he should wish. She kept a room nearby, when she could afford it, but more often than not she had to let it go.

"Was she in love with Allardyce?" Monk asked.

Mrs. Clark poured more tea. " 'Course she was, poor creature," she said tartly. "Wot do you think? Told 'er she were beautiful, an' 'e meant it. So she was, too. But she were no lady, an' she never imagined she were. Knew 'er limits. That were part of 'er trouble. Never thought she were more'n pretty. Never thought no one'd care for 'er once 'er skin and 'er figure went."

In spite of himself, Monk was struck with a stab of sorrow for a woman who thought her only worth was her beauty. Had she really no sense of her value for her laughter or her courage, her ideas, just her gift to love? Was that what life had taught her? That no man could simply like her, rather than want to look at her, touch her, use her?

A vision of fear opened up in front of him. He saw her constant anxiety each time she looked in the mirror, saw a line or a blemish on her skin, an extra pound or two on the rich lines of her body, a slackness real or imagined, that signaled the decline at the end of which lay hunger, loneliness and eventually despair.

Mrs. Clark went on talking, describing a life in which beauty was caught on canvas and made immortal for the pleasure of artists and viewers, yet was strangely disconnected from the woman, as if her face, her hair, her body, were not really her. She could walk away unnoticed, leaving the image of herself, the part they valued, still in their possession.

The loneliness of it appalled him. He pressed her for more stories, more details, names, places, times.

He felt subdued and deeply thoughtful when he arrived to meet Runcorn nearly an hour late. Runcorn was sitting in the corner of a tavern nursing a mug of ale and getting steadily angrier as the minutes passed.

"Mislaid your watch, have you?" he said from between his clenched teeth.

Monk sat down. He had drunk so much tea he had no desire for ale or cider, and the good-natured babble of the crowd around him made it impossible to speak quietly. "Do you want to know about her or not?" he replied, ignoring the remark. He refused to explain himself. He already knew Runcorn's views on the virtues of women, which consisted mostly of being hardworking, obedient and chaste, the last being the necessity which framed all else. He had been too long away from the streets and the reality of most women's lives, perhaps too afraid of his own frailties to look at other people's.

Runcorn glared at him. "So what did you find, then?" he demanded.

Monk relayed the facts of Sarah's parentage and career up to the point of Allardyce's seeing her and then shortly afterwards employing her exclusively. He also gave him the name of her onetime lover, Arthur Cutter.

Runcorn listened in silence, his face heavy with conflicting emotions. "Better see him, I suppose," he said at the end. "Could be him, if he thought she'd betrayed him somehow, but doesn't seem likely. Women like that move from one man to another and nobody cares all that much. No doubt he expected it, and has had half a dozen different women since then."

"Somebody cared enough to kill her," Monk responded angrily. What Runcorn had said was probably true; it was not the fact that cut Monk raw, it was the contempt with which Runcorn said it, or perhaps even the fact that he said it at all. There were some truths that compassion covered over, like hiding the faces of the dead, a small decency when nothing greater was possible. He looked at Runcorn with intense dislike, and all his old memories returned with their ugliness, the narrowness of mind, the judgment, the willingness to hurt. "She's just as dead as Elissa Beck," he added.

Runcorn stood up. "Go and see Bella Holden," he ordered. "You'll probably find her at her lodgings, 23 Pentonville Road. She's another artists' model, and I daresay it's a bawdy house. Unless you want to give up? But looks like you're as keen to find out who killed Sarah Mackeson as you are about Beck's wife." He walked between the other drinkers without looking back or bothering to tell Monk where to meet him again. Monk watched Runcorn's high, tight shoulders as he pushed his way out and lost sight of him just before the door.

The house at 23 Pentonville Road was indeed a brothel of sorts, and he found Bella Holden only after considerable argument and the payment of two shillings and sixpence, which he could ill afford. Callandra would willingly have replaced it, but both pride and the awareness of her vulnerability would prevent him from asking. This was friendship, not business.

Bella Holden was handsome, with a cloud of dark hair and remarkable pale blue eyes. She must have been a little over thirty, and he could see underneath the loose nightgown she wore that her body was losing its firmness and the shape an artist would admire. She was too lush, too overtly womanly. It would not be long before this house, and its like, were her main support, unless she learned a trade. No domestic employer would have her, even if she were capable of the tasks required. Without a character, a reference from a former employer, she would not be allowed over the step, let alone into the household.

Looking at her now as she stared back at him, holding the money in her hand, he saw anger and the need to please struggling against each other in her face, and a certain heaviness about her eyelids, a lethargy as if he had woken her from a dream far more pleasant than any reality. It was three o'clock. He might be her first customer. The indifference in her face was a lifetime's tragedy.

He thought of Hester, and of how she would loathe having a stranger's hand on her clothes, let alone on her naked skin. This woman had to endure intimacy from whoever chose to walk through the door with two shillings and sixpence to spend. Where did the ignorance and the desperation come from that she would not prefer to work, even in a sweatshop, rather than this?

And the answer was there before the thought was whole. Sweatshops required a skill in sewing she might not possess, and paid less for a fourteen-hour day than she could make in her room in an hour. Both would probably break her health by the time she was forty.

"I don't want to lie with you, I want to ask you about Sarah Mackeson," he said, sitting down on the one wooden chair. He was trying to place the faint smell in the room. It was not any of the usual body odors he would have expected, and not pleasing enough to have been a deliberate perfume, even if such a thing had been likely.

"You a rozzer?" she asked. "Don't look like one." There was

little expression in her voice. "Well, yer can't get 'er fer nothin' now, poor bitch. She's dead. Some bastard did 'er in a few days ago, up Acton Street. Don't yer swine never tell each other nothin'? Even the patterers is talkin' about it. Yer should listen!"

Monk ignored her resentment. He even saw the reason for it. She probably saw herself in Sarah Mackeson. It could as easily have been she, and she would expect as little protection before, or care afterwards.

"I know," he replied. "That's why I want to learn what I can about her. I want to catch who did it."

It took a moment or two for her to grasp what he had said and consider whether she believed it. Then she began to talk.

He asked questions and she rambled on, a mixture of memories and observations, thoughts, all charged with so much emotion he was not certain when she was referring to Sarah and when to herself, but perhaps at times they were interchangeable. A painfully clear picture emerged of a woman who was careless, openhearted, loyal to her friends, feckless with money, and yet deeply frightened of a future in which she saw no safety. She was untidy, generous, quick to laugh—and to cry. If any man had loved her enough to feel jealousy, let alone to kill, she certainly had not known it. In her own eyes, her sole value was as an object of beauty for as long as it lasted. Both time and fashion were already eroding it, and she felt the cold breath of rejection.

Bella Holden was walking the same path, and she could offer no clue as to who might have killed Sarah. Reluctantly, she named a few other people who had known her moderately well, but he doubted they could help. Bella would not compromise her own future for the sake of finding justice for Sarah. Sarah was dead, and past help. Bella had too little on her side to risk any of it.

Monk thanked her and left. This time he returned to the police station, and found Runcorn in his office looking tired and unhappy, his brows drawn down.

"Opium," he said, almost as if he were challenging Monk.

Suddenly, Monk placed the smell in Bella Holden's room. He was annoyed with himself for not having known at the time. That was another gap in his memory. He hated Runcorn's seeing it, especially now. "Sarah Mackeson was taking opium?" he asked with something close to a snarl.

Runcorn misread his expression for contempt. His face flushed with anger almost beyond his control. His voice shook when he spoke. "So might you, if you had nothing to offer but your looks, and they were fading!" He gulped air. His knuckles shone white where his hands were pressed on the desk in front of him. "With nothing ahead of you but doss-houses and selling your body to strangers for less and less every year, you might not stand there in your handmade boots looking down your damn nose at someone who escaped into a dream every now and then, because reality was too hard to bear! It's your job to find out who killed her, not decide whether she was right or wrong." He stopped abruptly and sniffed hard, looking away from Monk now, as if his anger embarrassed him. "Did you go and see Bella What's-her-name as I told you? Have you done anything useful at all?"

Monk stood totally still, an incredible reality dawning on him. Runcorn was abashed because he felt defensive of Sarah and had developed a pity for her he had not expected, and it totally confused him. He was not idly defending her, but was instead defending himself and his own nakedness in front of Monk, who he imagined could not share his understanding or his pain.

The fact that he did share it made Monk angry, too. He admired Runcorn for it. It must have required an inner courage to admit an openness to hurt and to change Monk had not thought Runcorn capable of. Now it meant Monk, too, had to alter his judgments—and of Runcorn, of all people.

He was aware that Runcorn was watching him now. "Opium?" he said, forcing his voice to convey interest. "Any idea where she got it from?"

Runcorn grunted. "Could be Allardyce," he said noncommittally. "That could be what all this is about—opium sale gone wrong. Perhaps Mrs. Beck came in on it and they were afraid she would cause a scandal."

"Worth killing her for?" Monk said dubiously. Selling opium was not a crime.

"Might have been a lot of money," Runcorn reasoned. "Or other people involved. Don't know who else Allardyce painted, perhaps society ladies. Maybe they were taking the stuff and wouldn't want their husbands to know?"

It was possible; in fact, the more he thought of it the better it looked. It would mean the murders had nothing to do with Kristian, or with Elissa Beck. "A quarrel perhaps, or a little blackmail?" he added to the idea. "Allardyce was the supplier?"

Runcorn looked at him with something almost like approval. "Well, he probably gave it to Sarah Mackeson, to keep her docile, if nothing else—poor creature. He wouldn't care what it did to her over time. He's only interested in the way she looks now, not what happens to her once he's tired of her and picked someone else." His mouth closed in a bitter line, as if he were angry not only with Allardyce but with everyone else who failed to see what he did or was indifferent to it.

Monk said nothing. There were too many changes whirling through his mind. His fury against Runcorn dissolved, and then was confused with a new one, because he did not want to have to change his opinion of this man, especially so quickly and so violently. It was his own fault for leaping to a cruel conclusion before he knew the truth, but he still blamed Runcorn for not being what he had supposed. Even as he was doing it he knew it was unfair, and that made it worse.

Runcorn flicked through the papers on his desk and found what he was looking for. He held it out to Monk. "That's the drawing Allardyce spoke about. Feller who drew it said it was the night of the murders, and the pub landlord said he was there right enough, and drawing people."

Monk took it from him. He needed only a glance to see an unmistakable portrait of Allardyce. It had not Allardyce's skill at catching the passion of a moment. There was no tension in it, no drama. It was simply a group of friends around a table at a tavern, but the atmosphere was pervasive; even in such a hasty sketch one could imagine the laughter, the hum of conversation, the clink of glasses, and music in the background, a theater poster on the wall behind them.

"They were there all evening," Runcorn said flatly. "We can forget Allardyce."

Monk said nothing; the ugly, choking misery inside him closed his throat.

CHAPTER
SIX

———

Hester went to the hospital again to see Mary Ellsworth. She found her sitting up in bed, her wound healing nicely and the pain definitely less than even a day ago.

"I'm going to be all right!" she said the moment Hester was in the door. "Aren't I?" Her eyes were anxious, and she held the bedclothes so tightly her hands were balled into fists. Her hair was straggling out of the braids she had put it in for the night, as if already she had started to pull at it again.

Hester felt her heart sink. What could she say to this woman that would even begin to heal her real illness? The bezoar had been the symptom, not the cause.

"You are recovering very well," she replied. She reached out her hand and put it over Mary's. It was as rigid as it looked.

"And I'll ... I'll go home?" Mary said, watching Hester intently. "And will Dr. Beck tell me what to do? I mean ... he's a doctor; he'd know better than anyone, wouldn't he?" That was a challenge, almost a plea.

Kristian could tell her not to eat her hair, but that was not what she meant. She was looking for some other kind of instruction, reassurance.

"Of course he will, but I expect most of it you know for yourself," Hester answered.

An extraordinary look came into Mary's eyes: hope, terror, and a kind of desperate anger as if she were newly aware of something which was monstrously unjust. "No, I don't. And Mama won't know! She won't know this!"

"Would it help if we tell her?" Hester suggested.

Now, Mary was quite clearly frightened. She seemed to be faced with a dilemma beyond her courage to solve.

"Is your mother not very good at looking after things?" Hester said gently. She knew Mary's father had been a country parson, a younger son of a well-to-do family.

"She's good at everything!" Mary asserted angrily, pulling the bedclothes more tightly up to her chest. "She always knows what to do." That came out like a charge. Resentment and fear smoldered in her eyes. Then she looked away, down at her hands.

"I see." Hester thought that perhaps she did, just a glimpse. "Well, it doesn't need to be decided now," she said firmly. "But I'm sure Dr. Beck would be happy to tell you what you need to do, and I will also. Will that make you feel better?"

Mary's hands relaxed a fraction. "Will you write it for me, in case . . ."

"Of course. You will have something to refer to," Hester agreed. "And you can practice before you go home."

"Practice?"

"Practice being certain what is the right thing to do."

"Oh! Yes. Thank you."

Hester stayed a few minutes longer, then went to look for Kristian.

Later, she passed Fermin Thorpe in the corridor. He looked impatient as always, and was affecting not to see her, because she made him feel uncomfortable. He had once lost his temper with her, and he hated being out of control of anything, most of all his own behavior. His color was high, and he had a glitter in his eyes as if his last encounter had displeased him.

She found Callandra in the apothecary's room, and the

moment she saw Hester she concluded her discussion and came out. "Have you heard anything?" she said as soon as the door was closed. "What has William found?"

Hester had not seen Callandra since the funeral and the terrible evening afterwards. She had lain awake arguing with herself over whether she would tell Callandra about Elissa and the gambling, and then, when she realized she had to, she tortured herself as to how she would do it and still leave Kristian some privacy, particularly from Callandra's knowledge of his pain.

But there was a chill of fear inside her that they could not afford the luxury of protecting embarrassment, even pride. At the very best, Callandra would have to know one day. It would be easier to tell her in Kristian's own time—his words, and his decision. But at the worst, it might be a matter of survival, and all knowledge was necessary to protect against betrayal by error.

"What is it?" Callandra said quietly.

"Elissa Beck gambled," Hester replied, then, seeing the look of incomprehension in Callandra's face, she went on. "Compulsively. She lost everything she had, so that Kristian had to sell their belongings, even the furniture." Callandra seemed able to take in the meaning of what was said only slowly, as if it were a complicated story. "It's an addiction," Hester went on. "Like drinking, or taking opium. Some people can't stop, no matter what it does to them, even if they lose their money, their jewelry, pictures, ornaments, the furniture out of their houses ... everything. Elissa was like that."

The real horror of it was dawning on Callandra. Perhaps she realized now why she had never been asked to Kristian's house. She must also realize how vast a part of his life she knew nothing of, the pain, the embarrassment, the fears of discovery and ruin. These were at the heart of his existence, every day, and she had had no knowledge of them, shared nothing because he had never allowed her to know.

"I'm sorry," Hester said gently. "If we are to help Kristian we can't afford ignorance."

"Could it have been someone to whom she owed money?" Callandra began.

"Of course," Hester agreed too quickly.

Callandra's face tightened into blank misery. "Kristian would have paid. You said everything was gone, at least you implied it. Ruined gamblers commit suicide. I've known soldiers to do that. Do creditors really murder them? And what about the other poor woman?" She shivered convulsively. "Surely she didn't gamble, too?"

"She was possibly the one they intended to kill." Hester was trying to convince herself as much as Callandra. "They are trying to find out as much as they can about her."

"Perhaps it was a lover's quarrel that went much too far?" Callandra's voice hovered on the edge of conviction. "What about the artist?"

"Perhaps."

"Well, this won't do any good standing here." Callandra forced herself to smile. "How is the woman who had the hairball? I thought only cats got them. For them it's understandable, but I can't think of anything more revolting than eating hair."

"The wound is healing well. I'm wondering what we can do to give her the belief in herself to heal the inside of her."

"Work," Callandra replied without hesitation. "If she stayed here we could find her enough to do so she would be too busy to sit and worry about herself."

"I doubt her mother would allow her to," Hester replied. "Hospitals don't have a very good reputation for young ladies of genteel background." She gave a twisted smile as she said it, but there was too much truth in it to ignore.

"I'll speak to her," Callandra promised.

"I think she would like it, but she'd never have the courage to defy . . ."

"The mother," Callandra supplied. "I'm good with dragons, believe me. I know exactly where the soft spots are."

This time Hester's smile was wholehearted. "I'll hold your shield for you," she promised.

The following day was the funeral of Sarah Mackeson. Monk wondered if anyone but the priest and the gravediggers would attend. There would be no family to hold an elaborate reception afterwards, no one to pay for a hearse and four horses with black plumes or for professional mourners to carry feathers and stand in silence with faces like masks of tragedy.

Someone should be there. He would go. Whatever the need for truth, this was a need also. He would follow Kristian's path on the evening of the murders and check every detail, speak to every peddler, shopkeeper and barrow boy he could, but he would check his watch regularly and make the time for Sarah's funeral.

He left the house at seven. It was a heavy, still morning with a distinct coldness in the air, but the fog had cleared, at least for the meantime. It was easy to believe that winter was ahead, even if there were still leaves on the trees. Dusk was growing earlier and dawn later by a few minutes every day.

It was hardly worth looking for a cab for the short distance to Acton Street, and walking gave him the opportunity to think about what he was going to do. If he traced Kristian's path precisely, there was a possibility that he could prove he could not have been in Allardyce's studio. Then the question of his guilt would not arise. Runcorn's men had already tried to establish this, and failed to do it conclusively.

He passed a newspaper seller shouting that the government in Washington was starting a crusade against anti–Civil War journals, some of which had been seized at a post office in Philadelphia.

By the time he reached Acton Street and found the constable it was a quarter to eight. He rehearsed Kristian's movements as he had recounted them, and found the first witness, a peddler who sold sandwiches and knew Kristian quite well, having often provided him with what served for luncheon or dinner when he was hard-pressed, hurrying from one patient to another.

"Oh, yeah," he said with conviction. "Dr. Beck passed 'ere 'bout quarter past nine the other night. 'Ungry, 'e were, an' rushed orff 'is feet, like most times. Sold 'im an 'am san'wich an' 'e ate 'alf of it and went on wi' the other 'alf in 'is 'and."

Monk breathed a sigh of relief. If Kristian had been on his way to his patient in Clarendon Square at quarter past nine, then he could not have been in Acton Street at just after half past. "Are you sure it was quarter past nine?" he pressed.

" 'Course I'm sure," the peddler replied, pulling his wide mouth into a grimace.

"How do you know?" He had to be certain.

" 'Cos Mr. 'Arreford come by an' bought 'is usual. Quarter past nine on the dot, 'e is, reg'lar as Big Ben."

"You can't hear Big Ben from here," Monk pointed out.

The peddler looked at him crookedly. " 'Course yer can't," he said. "Figure o' speech, like. If Big Ben ain't reg'lar, the world's comin' ter a rare fix!"

"And this Mr. Harreford is never late—or early?"

"Never. If yer knew 'im, yer wouldn't ask."

"Where do I find him?"

"Don't yer believe me, then?"

"Yes, I believe you, but the judge may not, if it comes to that."

The peddler shivered. "Don' wanna tell no judge!"

"You won't need to, if I find Mr. Harreford."

"Works in the lawyer's offices, number fourteen Amwell Street. That way," he said instantly.

Monk smiled. "Thank you."

An hour later Mr. Harreford, a dry, obsessively neat, little man, confirmed what the peddler had said, and Monk left with a feeling of growing relief. Perhaps his fears were unnecessary after all.

Kristian had an excellent witness, one whom Runcorn would take sufficiently seriously that he would dismiss Kristian as a suspect. He walked back towards Tottenham Court Road with a light, swift step. After he had been to Sarah Mackeson's funeral, he would be able to check again on the patient, Maude Oldenby, and that would account for Kristian's time completely.

"Thank you," Monk acknowledged to the peddler.

"Pleasure, Guv'nor," the peddler said with a grin. "Yer owe me, mind!"

"I do," Monk agreed.

"Still followin' the doc's path that night, are yer?"

"I will, when I come back."

"Good, 'cos yer won't find the chestnut seller on 'is patch till 'arter midday."

"Chestnut seller?" Monk asked doubtfully.

"Yeah! Corner o' Liverpool Street and the Euston Road. 'E must 'a seen 'im too, at twenty arter nine, or the like."

"You mean ten past," Monk corrected. Liverpool Street was in the opposite direction.

"No, I don't!" The peddler stared at him, drawing his brows down.

"If he was going from Risinghill Street, beyond Pentonville Road, towards Clarendon Square, he would pass Liverpool Street before here," Monk pointed out with weary patience.

" 'Course 'e would," the peddler agreed. "But as 'e were goin' t'other way, 'e'd pass me first, wouldn't 'e?"

"The other way?" Monk repeated slowly, the relief freezing inside him to a small, hard stone.

"Yeah. 'E weren't goin' ter Clarendon Square, 'e'd bin, an' were comin' back."

"You're sure?" He knew it was stupid to ask even as he said the words. He was fighting against a truth part of him already accepted.

"Yeah, I'm sure." The peddler looked unhappy. "Is that bad?"

"Not necessarily," Monk lied. "It's good to get it right. No room for mistakes. He was going that way?" He pointed towards Gray's Inn Road.

"Yeah!"

"Did he say where to?"

"No. Just took the sandwich and went. Didn't stop an' talk like 'e sometimes does. Reckon 'e 'ad someone real poorly."

"Yes, I daresay he did. Thank you." He walked away. Of course he would have to check with the chestnut seller, but he was already certain of what he would find.

The funeral of Sarah Mackeson was held in a small church in Pentonville. It was very quiet, and conducted so hastily as to be no more than a formality. It was an observance of the decencies for the sake of being able to say duty was done. There was a plain wooden coffin, but it was of pine, and Monk wondered if Argo Allardyce had paid for it, even though he was not present.

He glanced around the almost empty pews, and saw only one middle-aged woman in a plain black coat and drab hat, and he recognized Mrs. Clark, looking tearful. There was no one else present except Runcorn, standing at the back, angry and embarrassed when his eyes met Monk's. He looked away quickly, as if they had not seen each other.

What was he doing there? Did he really imagine that whoever had killed her would be at the funeral? Whatever for? Some kind of remorse? Only if it were Allardyce, and his presence would prove nothing. He had employed her as his model for the last three or four years, painted her countless times. Until Elissa Beck, she was woven into his art as no one else.

In fact, why was he not there? Was he too overwrought with emotion, or did he not care? Was that why Runcorn was standing so quietly at the back, head bowed, face somber? Monk looked at him again, and as Runcorn became aware of him, he turned away and concentrated on the minister and the brief words of the service. He sounded as if he were simply rehearsing something learned by rote, fulfilling his duty in order to be released to something else. His eulogy was anonymous. He had not known her, and what he said could have applied to any young woman who had died unexpectedly.

Monk resented it with a bitterness he could not explain. Then the thought occurred to him that if he had died in the coach crash which had robbed him of his memory, he might have been buried as coldly as this, with no one to mourn, the decencies carried out as a public duty by someone who did not take the time or trouble to learn anything more than his name, someone who had never known him and certainly never cared.

He decided in that moment that he would go to the graveside as well. It was time in which he could have been looking for further evidence of Kristian's movements. He might find something to prove that Kristian had been far enough away from Acton Street for it to be impossible for him to be guilty. But even as the thought passed through Monk's mind, he followed the small procession out of the church and along the street towards the already crowded graveyard.

In the narrow space between the gravestones it was impossible not to find himself next to Runcorn. Whatever had taken him to the church, it could only be some personal emotion which had brought him there. He stood staring at the open hollow in the ground, avoiding Monk's eyes. He still looked angry to be caught there, yet too stubborn to be put off.

Monk resisted the idea that Runcorn could possibly feel the same mixture of pity and resentment for Sarah that he did. He and Runcorn were nothing alike. Yet they were there side by side, avoiding each other's eyes, aware of the chill of the wet ground under their feet and the dark hole gaping in front of them, the ritual words which should have held passion and comfort, if spoken with feeling, and the solitary figure of Mrs. Clark sniffing and dabbing a sodden handkerchief to her eyes.

When it was over, Monk looked once at Runcorn, who nodded curtly as if they were acquaintances met by chance, then hurried away.

Monk left a few minutes after him, headed towards the Gray's Inn Road. He turned his mind back to the question of Kristian's movements on the evening of the murders. He went to the patients Kristian had visited and asked them again for times as exactly as they could recall. The answers were unsatisfactory. Memories were hazy with pain and with the confusion of days which blurred one into another in a round of medicines, meals, naps, the occasional visit. Time meant very little. There was really no meaning in whether the doctor came at eight or at nine, or on Monday or Tuesday this week, or was it last?

He left uncertain as to whether or not Kristian could prove himself elsewhere at the time of the murder. He began to fear more and more that he could not.

What Hester had told him of Elissa's gambling crowded his mind with ugly thoughts. Too easily, he could imagine the fear of ruin spiraling out of control, until one day the self-discipline snapped and violence broke through. The deed would be done before he had had time to realize what he meant. Then he would be faced with Sarah Mackeson, drunk, frightened, perhaps hysterical and beginning to scream. He would silence her in self-preservation, possibly his old fighting skills returning from the revolution in Vienna, where the cause had been great, and war and death in the air mixed with the hope, and then the despair.

Did such events change a man's core, the way he responded to a threat, the value he placed on life?

He was walking more slowly now, turning south down Gray's Inn Road. He passed a gingerbread man, very smartly dressed, smiling broadly. "Here's your nice gingerbread, your spiced gingerbread!"

he called out. "Melt in your mouth like a red-hot brickbat and rumble in your inside like Punch in a wheelbarrow!" He grinned at Monk. "You never heard o' 'Tiddy Diddy Doll'?"

Monk smiled back at him. "Yes I did. Bit before your time, though, wasn't he?"

"Hundred year," the man agreed. "Best gingerbread man in England, 'e were. An' why shouldn't I copy him? Do you good—warm the cockles o' yer 'eart. 'Ere—threepence worth. Keep the cold out o' yer."

Monk handed him threepence and took the generous slice. "Thank you. You here most evenings?"

" 'Course I am. Come by any time. You'll not find better in London," the man assured him.

"Do you know Dr. Beck, Bohemian gentleman, who tends patients all around this area? He's a couple of inches shorter than I am, dark hair, remarkable dark eyes. Probably always in a hurry."

"Yeah, I know the gent you mean. Foreign. Out all hours. Friend o' yours?"

"Yes. Can you remember the last time you saw him?"

"Lorst 'im, 'ave yer?" He grinned again.

Monk maintained his self-control with an effort. "It was his wife who was murdered in Acton Street. When did you see him?"

The gingerbread man whistled between his teeth, and all the humor died out of his face. "I saw 'im that night, but it were about ten-ish. Bought a piece o' gingerbread an' took a cab up north. Goin' 'ome, I reckoned, but maybe not. I went 'ome meself just arter that. 'E were me last customer."

"How was he?"

"Fit ter drop, if yer ask me. That tired 'e could 'ardly stand up. Terrible thing to lose yer wife like that." He shook his head and sighed.

Monk thanked him and moved on. He was not sure if the man's news was good or bad. It tallied roughly with what Kristian had said, but it also placed him within a few hundred yards of Acton Street.

Perhaps rather than trying to follow Kristian he should learn more about Elissa? Obviously, she had been in Allardyce's studio at the time of the murder, but what about before that? Both he and Runcorn had assumed she had gone from her home straight to Allardyce's studio. Maybe she had gone to Swinton Street to gamble? Regardless of that, he should know more of her gambling. He had accepted Kristian's word, given to Hester. If he believed Kristian capable of killing his wife, why did he assume that his account was true in every other particular, simply because it was humiliating and gave him a motive in her death? There might be things he was ignorant of, or mistaken in. He could be lying to conceal something else.

It was not difficult to find the gambling house. The most simple questions, asked with an assured eagerness and a certain glint in the eye, determined that it was the fifth house along from the Gray's Inn Road, in the north side of the street, well concealed behind a butcher's shop.

He walked briskly and went up the shallow step and through the interior, stacked only with a few miserable-looking sausages, and knocked on the door beyond. It was opened by a large-shouldered man with a badly broken nose and a soft, slightly lisping voice. "Yes?" he said guardedly.

"I'm told a man with a little money to spend can find rather better amusement here than in music halls or the local tavern," Monk replied. "Something with a chance to win . . . or lose . . . a bit of involvement."

"Well now? And who told you that, then?" The man still looked dubious, but there was a flicker of interest in his face.

"A lady I know who enjoys some excitement in her life now and then. Gentlemen don't mention names."

The man smiled, showing a chipped front tooth, and asked to see the color of his money.

"Gold—same color as everyone else's! What's the matter? Only cater for silver here, do you? Or copper, maybe?"

"No call to be rude," the man said patiently. "Just a few ladies and gentlemen spending a pleasant afternoon. Causing nobody no fuss. But I think as I'd like ter know your friend's name, gentleman or no gentleman."

"Unfortunately, my friend met with a . . . misfortune," Monk replied.

"A financial one, like?" the man asked with a sigh.

"She met with a few of those, but that's life," Monk replied laconically. "This one was worse. She was murdered."

The man's face tightened around the lips and jaw. "Very sad. But isn't nothing to do with us 'ere."

The fact that he denied it gave Monk a sudden sense of chill, but he knew that a murder which would draw such intense police attention was the last thing a house like this would wish. They would have to close down and set up somewhere else. That would take time and cost money. They would lose business, and while they were closed their custom would go to their rivals, possibly not to return.

It would be such an easy answer if he could think they were guilty of Elissa's murder, but it made no sense.

The man was waiting for him to reply.

He shrugged deliberately. It cost him an effort of will, and the faces of the two dead women stayed in front of his eyes. "Not my business," he said carelessly. "If you can't pay your debts, you shouldn't play. Pity about her, but life doesn't stop . . . at least not for us."

The man laughed heartily, but his eyes remained cold. "You got the idea right," he said with a nod.

"So how long do I stand here debating the philosophy of debt?" Monk asked, matching him stare for stare.

"Until I decide you can go in!"

"And what would make you decide against it?" Monk enquired. He wondered if Kristian had ever been there. Perhaps Runcorn should ask, with the weight of police authority behind him. Except that there was nothing to make this man tell the truth. It would be instinctive to lie, to keep himself out of a murder.

"Maybe you're another bad debtor," the man said sanctimoniously.

"And on the other hand, maybe I'm a big winner," Monk pointed out. "You afraid of that? Watch others, but no stomach to take a chance yourself?"

"You got a vicious tongue in you, sir," the man said with something that sounded like reluctant admiration. He eyed Monk up and down, judging his balance, his physical strength and agility. A spark of interest lit in his eyes. "But I don't see why you shouldn't come in and spend a little time here in pleasant company for the afternoon. Seeing as how you understand the ways o' life rather the same as we do."

The idea that had been lurking at the back of Monk's mind suddenly took form. He was being weighed up as a potential tool for discipline in the future. He would play into that. He smiled at the man, looking straight at him. "Thank you," he said softly. "Very civil of you."

Inside was a large room, probably originally two and now knocked into one. There were half a dozen tables set up, some surrounded by chairs, some with room only for standing. There were already at least twenty people there. No one noticed his arrival. Every eye was undeviating from the roll of the dice or the turn of a card. No one spoke. In fact, there was no sound but the soft flick of cards on the baize cloth, or the very faint thump of the dice falling. There was barely even the rustle of silk or taffeta skirts or the creaking of the bones of a bodice as someone leaned a little farther forward.

Then there was a win, and cheers. Losers turned away, faces filled with chagrin. It was impossible to guess how much they had lost, whether they could afford it, or were ruined.

The game resumed, and again the tension mounted.

Monk looked around at the faces, eyes on the play, some with jaws clenched. He saw one man with a slight tic in his temple and noticed his hands white-knuckled as the cards turned. Another fidgeted silently, stopping his fingers from drumming on the table edge but holding them just short of the surface. His shoulders seemed to be locked in position, a little higher than natural and totally unmoving.

Monk directed his attention to a woman, perhaps thirty-five, with a sharp, pretty face, blond hair pulled a little too tightly back from her brow. She scarcely breathed as the dice rolled and stopped. She won, and glee lit her eyes, a brilliance that was more like a fever. Immediately she played again, moving the dice from one hand to the other four times before blowing on them and rolling them.

Monk became aware of the man from the door watching him. He must play. Please heaven he could win enough to stay an hour or two. He moved over to the dice. He could not remember if he had ever played cards. He could not afford to make a fool of himself by displaying ignorance. This was not a place where any leeway was given. One glance at faces told anyone that each person in the room was obsessed with the game, win or lose. The money represented victory; they hardly saw it for itself or what it could buy, beyond another chance to play.

He watched the turn of the cards for another twenty minutes, and then he was invited to play, and without thinking he accepted. He had won the first hand before he realized with a cold ripple through his body how easily he had done it. An old, familiar needle of excitement pricked inside him. There was a thrill to winning; the danger of loss sharpened it. It was like galloping a little too fast along the white surf where the sea joins the land, feeling the wind and the spray in your face, and knowing that if you fell you could break bones, perhaps even be killed.

He played another hand, and another, and won. He was now ten guineas better off, police pay for over a month. He stood up and made an excuse to leave. He had more than established himself. He was there to find out about Elissa Beck, not to increase his own wealth. Kristian might have murdered her, and be hanged for it. Someone had killed her! And poor Sarah Mackeson as well. This was life and death. Money was a distraction, winning or losing at the turn of a piece of colored cardboard was idiotic!

But it was remarkably difficult to get any sensible conversation from any of the players. The game was everything. They barely glanced at each other. One could have stood next to a brother or sister and been unaware of it while the next play was awaited.

That was how he was so slow in noticing the woman at the table to his left. Her soft dark hair and slender body, bent forward in eagerness, jolted him back to his reason for being here. She was consumed in the game, her eyes fixed on the dice, her hands clenched at her sides, nails biting into her palms. For an instant it could have been Elissa Beck. There was something familiar about her that clutched at his emotions and turned his heart. He could not help staring at her, sharing the moment's exhilaration when she won. Her face was flushed with excitement. She seemed to vibrate life as if her energy could fill the room. She was beautiful with an inner fire.

He watched as she played again, and won again.

"Go play against her!" a voice said at his elbow. He turned to see the man who had let him in. "Go on!" he was urged with a broken-toothed smile. "Do the house good. You can't both win."

"Does she come often?" Monk said quickly.

The man grimaced. "Too damn often. I'd make it worth your while to beat her. I've watched you. You're good. You could do it. Send her somewhere else for a month or two."

Monk decided to play the part. "How much worth my while? I can pick an easier opponent, if she's really so lucky."

The man regarded him with contempt. "Is that what you came for? An easy opponent?"

Monk smiled back at him, showing his teeth wolfishly. "It

doesn't hurt, now and again." But his expression conceded that what mattered was the game. This conversation might be his only opportunity to find out anything useful. "She reminds me of Elissa," he said to the man.

The man gave a sharp bark of amusement. "Except this one wins. Elissa lost. Oh, she won occasionally; you have to see to it that they do, or they don't come back. But this one wins too often. I could do without her. She was good for a while. People liked watching her, pretty thing, and she encouraged others. Time to get rid of her, though. Some bloke hanging around after her. Could be her husband. Don't want any more trouble. Not good for business."

"Husband?" Then suddenly, like a rush of ice, Monk realized why she looked so familiar. Certainly there was a resemblance to Elissa Beck, the same slender body, the same soft dark hair, but this woman's face was gentler, prettier, just without the passionate, haunting beauty he had seen in *Funeral in Blue*. She was less marked by the triumphs and tragedies of life. She was his sister-in-law, Imogen Latterly.

He found his mouth too dry to answer. Did Hester know? Was this what she was afraid of?

There was another game, and this time Imogen lost, and instantly played again.

He turned away quickly, suddenly realizing that if she looked up she would recognize him, too. He found his voice at last. "Her husband plays?" he said in amazement. He could not imagine Charles Latterly playing anything that involved the slightest risk. Surely his father's death and the circumstances around it had driven every gamble of even the mildest sort from his mind?

"No, he was following her," the man said tartly. His respect for Monk's perspicacity had taken a sharp turn downward.

Monk cursed his emotions for getting in the way of his professionalism. He must make up the lost ground. "Not in here?" he assumed, forcing himself to smile again. "Jealous sort, is he? Or worried for his pocket?"

The man shrugged. "Could be either. More like jealous, I'd say."

"Seen him often?" Monk asked as casually as he could. In spite of himself he was aware that his voice had an edge.

"Two or three times." The man looked at him with more intent. "Why? What's it to you?"

Monk returned his look with contempt.

The man lifted his shoulders even higher. "Your affair! Go after her if you want. But she's trouble. Don't know that she's clever, but she's lucky most of the time. And he looked pretty close to the edge, the husband."

Monk stared ahead of him, masking the dread inside him. "Did he? When was that?" He watched the dice without seeing them. He did not want the answer, but he had to know.

"Couple of times," the man replied. "Still, it's your affair. But if you cause any trouble here, I'll have you thrown out. You can believe that."

"Get a lot of angry husbands, do you?" Monk asked, turning back to face him but still hiding his face from Imogen. "Like Elissa's husband, for example?"

The man's eyes narrowed. "What's with all the questions? Why do you care? Woman's dead. I don't know who did it. Allardyce, probably. Lovers' quarrel, I expect. He was obsessed with her. Comes in 'ere to draw all sorts, but 'specially her. Couldn't take his eyes off her when she was playing."

Monk said nothing. It was more than he wanted to know, and yet there seemed a kind of inevitability about it, once he had realized who Imogen was.

He fingered the money in his pocket. Now it was soiled, and he wanted to escape the greedy, excited faces, the closeness of bodies pressed forward across the tables, eyes watching the cards, the dice, hardly seeing people. It was winners and losers, nothing else. He turned on his heel and pushed past the man, leaving him startled, not understanding. He reached the door and went out through the butcher's shop into the early-evening street, gulping in the air, heavy and laden with the smells of refuse and manure, but also the decent sounds of people going about their work, making things, carrying them, buying and selling.

He walked as quickly as he could along to the Gray's Inn Road and, as soon as the traffic allowed him, across it. He saw the gingerbread man in the distance, but ignored him this time.

He was going towards the police station. Even if he slowed his pace he would be there in half an hour. Runcorn might not be alone now, but eventually he would be. Putting off the time would alter nothing. He still had to decide whether to tell him what Hester had discovered about Kristian, or what he had now confirmed for himself. There was no doubt Kristian had both the time and the means to have murdered Elissa, and he had an extremely pressing motive.

Why did Monk hesitate? Did he believe Kristian guilty? The fact that he even asked the question told him the answer. If he could have dismissed it, then he would have. He would not even be thinking about it. He would go straight to Runcorn and tell him that these were the facts, but they meant nothing. They would have to look further.

Where? To Charles Latterly?

Perhaps someone to whom Elissa owed money, a conveniently unnamed person who might or might not exist.

Would Runcorn believe that? Not unless he were a fool. But even if it were likely, they would still have to pursue Kristian as well.

He crossed a side street, making a carriage driver rein in sharply, red in the face with the effort not to use the language that rose to his lips in front of his lady passengers.

Monk was barely aware of the inconvenience he was causing. He walked on, decreasing his pace even more, staying to the left so people could pass him.

Why was he having such difficulty being honest? Because he liked Kristian; he admired him as a doctor and as a man. He could understand how he could have been driven into a corner by a beautiful wife' whose brilliant courage and passion he remembered, but who had now taken him to the brink of ruin, robbing him of everything he had built, not only for himself but for the cause of healing.

And because Monk had a vivid imagination of how deeply it would wound Callandra, whom he cared for perhaps more than anyone else, apart from Hester, and to whom he owed a debt he could never repay because he had nothing she would want—except the power to help Kristian Beck.

And it would hurt Hester for them all. What would she want him to do? What had she believed he would do when she told him about the empty house?

But the bitter and inexcusable thing was the murder of Sarah Mackeson. No understanding mitigated that.

And what about Charles and Imogen?

Would Runcorn find out anyway? Possibly, but also possibly not. Hester had no obligation to tell him. Kristian would not. So far Runcorn had no cause to go to the gambling house on Swinton Street.

All of which was irrelevant. The question was, did Monk tell the truth or did he lie? To achieve what? A concealment of the truth that Kristian had killed the two women? And if he hid it, then what?

The murder went unsolved? Someone else was blamed, perhaps the Austrian, Max Niemann, who had been meeting Elissa secretly? Or some debt collector?

He was almost at the police station. He hesitated, then went on, one more time right around the block. That was what decided him. If he lied now, even by omission, he would spend the rest of his life walking around the long way to evade the truth. It was false to his nature, to the few certain standards he held unviolated. He was not a coward, whatever faced him. Lies built more lies. He would fight to save Kristian, or have the nerve to watch him face trial, even be found guilty. He would not make the decision who was guilty or innocent before he knew the facts. He would find the evidence, all of it, whatever it proved, and then live with the results, regardless of the cost to any of them.

He went up the steps of the police station and in at the door.

"Is Mr. Runcorn in?" he asked.

"Yes, Mr. Monk. Up the stairs, sir."

Damn! Pity he could not have been out, just this once. He gritted his teeth, thanked the sergeant, and went up. He knocked on the door and, as soon as there was an answer, opened it and went in.

Runcorn was sitting behind his tidy table. He looked almost pleased to see Monk. "Where've you been all day?" he demanded. "I thought you were eager to get this case solved!" He made no reference to having seen him at the funeral of Sarah Mackeson. He was watching to see if Monk was going to mention it. He was pretending they had not seen each other, and yet their eyes had met. Monk realized with a sharp savor of satisfaction that Runcorn was embarrassed at having been caught in an act of uncharacteristic compassion. After all, Sarah Mackeson was a loose woman, the kind he despised. He could hardly say he had gone in order to see who else was there, and expect Monk to believe him. He had stayed far longer than was necessary for that. He had been a mourner. He was looking at Monk now to see if he would deny it.

Monk would like him to have. He wanted to speak of it, to force Runcorn to admit his change of heart. But he could see in his eyes that he was not going to.

It was the perfect time to tell the truth. He hated it. It was like having a tooth extracted. All the long history of resentment and misunderstanding between them rose like a wall. He knew his face reflected his anger. Runcorn was staring at him and already hunching his shoulders as if getting ready to ward off a blow. His jaw was clenched. His fingers tightened on the pen he was holding.

"I know it's already been done, but I went to check Dr. Beck's movements on the day of the murder," Monk said quickly.

Runcorn was surprised. Whatever he had expected, it was not that. He looked up at Monk standing in front of him. He was forced to lift his head.

Monk remained steady. He swallowed. "He was on the way back from seeing his patient when he passed the peddler, not on the way out," he said before Runcorn could prompt him.

Recognition of what that meant flashed in Runcorn's eyes, and surprise that Monk should have told him. "Why did you do that?" he said quietly. "Did it take you all afternoon? Or were you debating whether to tell me?"

Monk ground his teeth. Every word of this was as hard as he had expected. Silence was no longer a choice. He must either tell Runcorn the truth or deliberately lie. Perhaps he was deceiving himself if he thought the choice had ever been otherwise. Plunge in!

"Hester went to see Dr. Beck after the funeral meal, which was at Pendreigh's house." He saw the quick flash of incomprehension in Runcorn's eyes. Pendreigh was of a social class Runcorn aspired to and would never understand. The fact infuriated him, and that Monk knew it angered him even more. He waited, and they stared intently at each other.

"Beck's house is a facade," Monk said painfully. "Only the front room and one bedroom are furnished; the rest is empty. Through her gambling Elissa Beck lost him almost everything he had." He saw incredulity in Runcorn's eyes, then pity, instantly masked, but not soon enough. It had been there, real and sharp. Monk was not sure if he felt better or worse for seeing it. How does a man like Runcorn pity someone like Kristian, who gave his life to compassion, who worked all the hours he was awake to relieve the suffering of strangers?

And yet the feeling made them for a moment equal, and how dare he deny that to Runcorn, even if he could have? A tumult of emotions awoke inside him. "I went to a gambling house on Swinton Street," he continued. "Behind the butcher's. That was where Elissa Beck went when she was early or late to Allardyce's studio.

When she lost badly she took refuge with him. That's probably what a lot of her 'sittings' were."

Runcorn said nothing. He seemed to be undecided, searching for the right words and not finding them. The respect he felt embarrassed him. Why? Because he had to realize that Kristian had every reason and opportunity to have killed his wife? Monk felt exactly the same, but it was pain, not respect. Kristian's virtues were not newly discovered.

Runcorn climbed to his feet, almost as if he were stiff. "Thank you," he said, looking away from Monk. He put his hands in his pockets, then took them out again quickly. "Thank you." And he walked past Monk and out of the door, leaving Monk standing alone in the office, realizing with anger and confusion that the respect was not for Kristian but for him, because he had told Runcorn the truth, and Runcorn hated the feeling as much as Monk hated his being capable of it.

CHAPTER
SEVEN

———

Monk went home, knowing he had to face breaking news which would be even more painful. He had not told Runcorn about Imogen, or that Charles had followed her. Part of Runcorn's admiration for him was misplaced, and it stung like a blister on the heel, catching with every step. But he had no intention of rectifying it.

However, he must tell Hester. If it could have remained secret and she would never have had to know, he would have protected her from it. In spite of her courage, almost willingness to battle, she was capable of deep and terrible pain. In fact, perhaps the two things went together; she fought for others precisely because she understood the cost of losing, the physical and emotional wounds.

But if either Charles or Imogen were drawn into this further, if they actually had a part in it, or if Imogen were on the same path of destruction as Elissa Beck . . . He pushed the thought away from him. It was in Imogen's hectic face and brilliant eyes that he had truly seen Elissa. He must tell Hester. There was no alternative. He must also tell her that Kristian had not spoken the truth about his time on the day of the murder, whether by accident or intent.

He went up the steps and unlocked the front door. Inside, the gas lamps hissed faintly and their light spread warmth over the outlines he knew so well he could have drawn them perfectly for anyone, the folds of the curtains, the exact shape and position of the two chairs they had saved so carefully to buy. The round table had been a gift from Callandra. There was a bowl of bright leaves and berries on it now, echoing every shade of red in the Turkish rug. It was a little chilly, and the fire was laid but not lit yet. Hester was economizing, until he came home. She would simply have put a shawl around her shoulders, and perhaps another around her knees.

The kitchen door was open. She was standing in front of the small cooking range, stirring a pot, a wooden spoon in her hand, her sleeves rolled up. In the warmth of the room, and the steam, the loose hair that had escaped from the pins was twisting into a soft curl.

She turned as she heard his step and his shadow fell across the doorway. She smiled at him. Then, before he was quick enough to conceal it, she saw the shadow in his eyes.

"What?" she asked, her other hand lifting the saucepan off the heat so it should not burn while she removed her attention from it.

He had not intended to tell her immediately, but the longer he waited, the more certain she would be that there was something wrong. It was unnerving to be so easily read. It was a position he had never intended to be in. It was part of the cost of intimacy, perhaps even of friendship.

"What is it?" she repeated. "Kristian?"

"Yes . . ."

She stiffened, the color draining from her face. She put the pan down, in case she dropped it.

"I followed his actions on the evening of the murders," he said quietly. "He wasn't where he said. He had the times wrong."

The muscles in her neck tightened, as if she were expecting a blow.

"Not necessarily a lie," he continued. "He may just be mistaken."

There was an edge to her voice. "That's not all, is it?"

"No." Should he tell her about Charles and Imogen now, deal with it all in one terrible stroke? Perhaps honesty was the only healing thing left.

"What else?" she asked.

He knew she was still thinking of Kristian. He answered that first, and because it led so naturally into having seen Imogen. "I went to Swinton Street, to a gambling house the constable told me about." He saw her wince very slightly. He had no idea she found gambling so repellent. Did she not understand it at all? There was a puritan streak in her that he loved only because it was part of her. He both admired it and was infuriated by it. In the beginning of their acquaintance he had thought it hypocrisy, and despised it. Later he had taught himself to tolerate it. Now again he found it oddly narrow and without compassion. But he did not want to quarrel. Perhaps it was memory of her father's speculation, and ruin, which hurt. Although that was hardly gambling, only what any man in business might do, and much of his actual loss was nobly motivated. He had been duped by a man of the utmost dishonor.

She was waiting for him to continue, as if she was afraid to press him.

"Elissa used to go there fairly often," he went on. "She lost a great deal. Even when she won, she put her money back on the table again and played it."

Hester was looking puzzled, a slight frown on her face. "I suppose that's the way gamblers are. If they could stop when they won it wouldn't be a problem. Poor soul. What an idiotic way to destroy yourself—and those who love you."

"I thought you were going to say 'and those you love,'" he observed.

"I was," she replied. "And then I thought it's really the other way. I think Kristian may have loved her more than she loved him. It looks as if she may have lost that ability. If she did love him enough, surely she would never have gone on until she stripped him of almost everything."

"It's a compulsion," he tried to explain. She had not seen the faces of the gamblers, the avid eyes shining with appetite, the rigid bodies, the hands clenched, breath held as they waited for the card or the dice to fall. It was a lust beyond control. "They can't help it," he added aloud. He was thinking of Imogen, trying to soften the thought in her for when she had to face it within her own family.

"Perhaps not." She did not argue as he had expected her to. "But it still kills love."

"Hester, love is . . ." He did not know how to finish.

"What?" she asked.

"Different things." He was still seeking to explain. "Different things for one person from another. It's not always obvious. You can love and . . ."

"If your love remains, you don't place your own needs before theirs," she said simply. "You might, with moral duties, but not with appetite. Maybe they can't help it. I don't know. But if something takes away your ability to sacrifice your own wants for the sake of someone else, then it has robbed you of honor and love. They aren't just nice warm feelings, they are a willingness to act for someone else's good before your own."

He did not answer. He was surprised by what she had said, and even more that he had no argument with any part of it. He could still see Imogen's pale face and bright eyes and the hectic excitement in her.

"I'm not saying she could help it," Hester went on. "I don't know if she could or not. I think after Vienna something inside her was changed. The reason doesn't alter what she did to Kristian."

"What?"

"Aren't you listening to yourself?" Her voice became sharper. "William! What else is it?"

He hated telling her, but he could no longer avoid it. "I saw someone else there that I knew."

"Gambling?" There was fear in her voice as she watched him. She knew that this was what he had been putting off saying. "Who? Kristian?"

"No . . ." He saw the easing of tension in her, and loathed what he was going to do. For an instant he even thought of not telling her after all, but that was only his own cowardice speaking. "Imogen."

"Imogen?" she repeated very quietly. "Imogen . . . gambling?"

"Yes. I'm sorry."

She did not seem startled or disbelieving. He had expected her to reject the possibility, had been afraid he would have to persuade her, argue, even face her anger. But she was standing quite still, absorbing the information without fighting it at all. Certainly she was not angry with him.

"Hester?"

For a few more moments she ignored him, still thinking about what he had told her, taking it into her mind, working out what it meant.

"Hester?" He reached forward and touched her gently. There was no resistance in her, none of the struggle he had expected. She turned her face and looked at him. Then suddenly he realized that she had known! There was no amazement in her eyes, just a kind of relief. He had gone through this agony of decision unnecessarily. She had known about it and said nothing to him. "How long has it been going on?" he demanded roughly, drawing his hand away.

"I don't know." She was looking not at him but into the distance, and someplace within herself. "Only weeks . . ."

"Weeks? And after you discovered about Elissa Beck, you didn't think to mention Imogen to me? Why not? Is your family loyalty to her so great you couldn't have trusted me?" He realized as he said it how much it hurt to be excluded. He spoke from his own wound, like a child hitting back. He felt no ties of blood, that instinctive bond that was deeper than thought. Perhaps it was irrational, bone-deep, but if he had ever felt it, it was gone with all his memory. It left him alone, rootless, without an identity that was anything more than a few years of action and thought.

He envied her. Whether she felt close to Charles or not, whether she liked or admired him, he was a chain to the past which was unbroken, an anchor.

"I didn't know it was gambling," she said with a frown. "I knew there was something exciting and dangerous. I thought it was a lover. I suppose I'm glad it wasn't."

"But you didn't . . ."

"Tell you?" Her eyes were very wide. "That I was afraid my brother's wife was having an affair with someone? Of course I didn't. Would you have expected me to, if you couldn't help?"

He did not want to, but he understood. He would have thought less of her if she had such a vulnerability for anyone else to see, even him. She was protecting her brother, instinctively, without thinking it needed explanation. She had temporarily forgotten that he had no one else but her. He had left his one sister behind in Northumberland when he came to London, however long ago that had been. He hardly ever wrote to her. A world of experience and ambition divided them, and there was no wealth of common memory to bridge it.

"I shall have to tell Charles," she said softly.

"Hester . . ." He was still confused by her, wanting to help and certain that he had no idea how to. "Are you . . ." he began, then did not know how to finish. Charles already knew. He had followed Imogen. Runcorn had not discovered that yet, but when he investigated further into Elissa's playing at the gambling house, it was more than likely that he would. Then he would know that he had praised Monk in his mind for an honesty that was partial, as if he would protect Charles Latterly but not Kristian. He would wonder why. Perhaps he understood family loyalty, or would he only see guilt?

Monk realized with surprise that he knew nothing about Runcorn's parents, or if he had brothers or sisters. Surely he had known before the accident? Or had he never cared?

"Charles is already aware there is something," Hester said, interrupting his thoughts. "I think he would rather it were gambling; most people would. It's . . . it's less of a betrayal. They may still love you as much as they love anyone." She looked away a moment. "Is it only bored people who gamble like that, William? I can't imagine wanting to, but perhaps if I did nothing but manage a house, with no children, no purpose, nothing to gain or lose, no excitement of life, no crises, I might create my own."

He wanted to laugh. "I'm sure you would." Then his smile withered. His agonizing over her pain had been pointless. He was not sure if he was relieved or angry, or both. She was right about an affair, too. He would rather she were obsessed with gambling, ruinous as it could be, than with another man. He was shocked by the knowledge that he was not certain if he could endure that. He had meant never, ever to be so dependent on someone else. Love was acceptable, but not the power to be so hurt, to be crippled beyond ever being whole again.

Was that what Charles Latterly faced? Or Kristian? Did Allardyce have a part in it, other than as a bystander who drew pictures and provided an occasional refuge? One thing was true for certain: somebody had killed both women.

"Why did Charles think it was an affair?" he asked. "Did he tell you?"

"He found some letters, agreeing to meet someone who didn't bother to sign them," she answered. "The way they were phrased made it obvious they met often. Perhaps it was someone she gambled with. . . ." She sounded uncertain.

A smattering of memory came back to Monk. "Some people like to have company, especially someone they think brings them luck . . . and Imogen is lucky, at least so far. But the gambling house will put an end to that. Hester . . . if Charles can't stop her, you must. They won't let her go on winning. The Swinton Street house has already had enough."

"She goes somewhere else as well," she said miserably. "Charles followed her the night of the murders, down in Drury Lane."

"Drury Lane?" he said with a chill of fear. "Are you sure?"

"Yes. Why? Don't they have gambling houses there, too?"

"He didn't go down Drury Lane the night Elissa was killed."

"Yes, he did. He told me . . ." Now she was staring at him with growing alarm. "Why?"

"Drury Lane was closed," he said softly. "A dray slid over and dumped a load of raw sugar kegs, most of which cracked open over the road."

"He just said that direction," she lied. "I assumed he meant Drury Lane." Her mind was whirling, trying to absorb his words and conceal her emotions from him.

The sauce in the pan thickened and went cold, and she ignored it. Why had Charles lied? Only because the truth was dangerous. He was trying to protect Imogen or himself. Either he thought she had been in Acton Street that night, or he knew it because he had been there himself. Vividly she saw again in her mind his ashen face and shaking hands, the fear in him and the rising sense of panic. The stable, safe world he had so painstakingly constructed around himself was falling apart. Things he had believed to be certainties were spinning away out of his grasp. She realized with a sick churning in her stomach that she did not think it impossible that he had killed Elissa Beck, and then also Sarah Mackeson—who had unintentionally witnessed the first crime.

She was almost unaware of Monk watching her as the reason took hideous form in her mind. She remembered the letter Charles had shown her. It was still upstairs in the bottom drawer of her jewel box. It was a strong, firm hand, but not necessarily a man's. What if the person who had introduced Imogen to gambling and set her on her own ruinous course were Elissa Beck? What if Charles had seen them together that night, had followed Elissa when she left, and caught up with her in Allardyce's studio? He might have assumed it was where she lived. He would have challenged her, begged her to leave Imogen alone. She would have laughed at him. It was already too late to rescue Imogen, but perhaps he would not know that, or would refuse to believe it. They could have struggled, and he could have tightened his grip on her neck without even realizing his strength.

Then Sarah would have awakened from her stupor and staggered through just in time to witness what had happened and would have begun screaming, or even flown at him. He would have gone after her to silence her ... and the same swift movement, more deliberate this time.

No! It was nonsense! She must go to Kristian's house and find a letter of Elissa's, compare the writing. That would end it. It could not be Charles! He had not the physical skill, the decisiveness, even the strength ...

That was damning! So condescending. She did not know that side of him at all. She had no idea how deep his passions might run under his self-controlled exterior. That calm banker's face might hide anything.

After all, who looking at her with the saucepan in front of her could imagine the places she had been to, the violence and death she had seen, or the decisions she had made and carried through, the courage or the pain, or anything else?

Monk spoke to her gently, and she nodded without having heard. If Imogen had driven Charles to that, would she now at least stand by him if Runcorn started questioning, probing, and the net tightened around him? What if he were arrested, even tried? Would she leave the gambling and stand strong and loyal beside him? Or would she crumble—weak, frightened, essentially selfish? If she did that, Hester might not find it within her ever to forgive Imogen. And that was a bitter and terrible thought. Not to forgive is a kind of death.

And yet if Imogen could not now be loyal, place Charles before her own fears, it would hurt him beyond his ability to survive, perhaps beyond his desire to. And if that was weak, too, so much the more must Imogen be strong.

That was illogical, perhaps unfair, but it was what she felt as she looked at the congealed mess in the saucepan and started to consider what to do with it.

Callandra stood in the middle of her garden looking at the last of the roses, the petals carrying that peculiar warmth of tone that only late flowers possess, as if they knew their beauty would be short. There were a dozen tasks that needed doing, and the gardener overlooked half of them if she did not tell him specifically. There were dead flower heads to take off, Michaelmas daisies to tie up before the weight of the flowers bent them too far and they broke. The buddleia needed pruning, it was far too big; and there were windfall apples to pick up before they rotted.

She could not be bothered with any of them. She had come out with gloves and a knife, and a trug to carry the dead heads, thinking she wanted to throw herself into the effort of a physical job. Now that she was there she could not concentrate. Her mind was leaping from one thing to another, and always around and around the same black center. About the only thing she was fit for was weeding. She bent down and started to pull, first one, then another, ignoring the trug and leaving the weeds in little piles to be picked up later.

She had acknowledged to herself some time ago that she loved Kristian Beck, even if it would never lead to anything but the profoundest friendship. She would not marry again. Francis Bellingham had asked her. She liked him deeply, and he could have offered her a life of companionship, loyalty and a very considerable freedom to pursue the causes she believed in. He was intelligent, honorable and not in the least unattractive. If she had met him a few years ago she would have accepted his offer.

What she felt for him was affection, kindness, respect, but no more. If she had married him, as many of her friends had expected her to, then she would have had to cut Kristian from her dreams, and that she was not prepared to do. Perhaps she was not even able to do it. She could not commit the dishonor of marrying one man while loving another, not at her age, when there was no need. She had more than sufficient money to care for herself, the social position of a titled widow, work for charity to fill her time, friends she valued. She was perfectly aware of her own foolishness.

Her fingers stopped moving in the cold earth as she remembered what Hester had told her yesterday afternoon. She had known immediately that it was bad news of some kind. She had seen too many doctors with just that expression, the mixture of resolution and pity, the stiff shoulders and pale face, the softness in the eyes.

At the moment it could only concern Kristian. She had not needed to ask what it was about. She was already prepared to hear that he could not prove his innocence. She had always known, from very early in their acquaintance, that there was a loneliness in his life. She sensed it as she felt the deep, hidden pain in her own. She had never asked about his wife and he had not spoken of her. She had not consciously even tried to visualize her, but gradually, unwittingly, she had drawn in her mind a rather ordinary woman with a bitter face, critical of small things, always expecting something she was not given. How could anyone else have failed to offer a man like Kristian all the love she could?

Then Hester had said she was younger, and not just beautiful, but with that haunting quality that stays in the mind, bringing back the eyes, the lips, the turn of the head at unexpected moments, as if the person never entirely left you.

That had been so hard to accept. What manner of woman was she? Why had she not brought happiness? The answer that forced itself upon her was that Kristian loved her but she did not return his feeling. It was comfort for which he turned to Callandra, for the solace of being loved.

And yet going back over every moment they had shared, even in the impersonal times of sitting in management meetings in the hospital, or arguing with Fermin Thorpe, who was enough to try the patience of a saint, she had been certain there was a warmth between them that had dignity to it, and honesty. Kristian was not a man to descend to using someone else merely to make up for a lack in his own life.

Without realizing it, she had stopped weeding.

Then Hester had told her that Elissa Beck was a compulsive gambler, so addicted to the excitement of the game that she had thrown away all she owned, and almost all Kristian owned as well. She had poured out money, pawned or sold her possessions, until finally even the furniture had gone, debts were piled up, the house was cold and dark, and ruin was on the doorstep.

She could not even imagine the fear and the shame that Kristian must have felt, although she did nothing but try to. Elissa's death must have been a bitter loss to him, a part of his life torn away. And yet it had to have been a relief as well. The bleeding out of money was ended; like a patient whose hemorrhage has at last been staunched, he could begin to rebuild his strength.

She closed her hand on a weed and yanked it out, throwing it at the trug and seeing it fly far beyond.

She had worked beside Kristian, caring for the sick, fighting for reform and improvement. She had seen his compassion, knew he had driven himself beyond exhaustion. She could not believe he would have killed Elissa, still less have added to the crime by killing another woman whose only offense was to have seen him.

But everyone has limits to his endurance, his patience or his threshold of pain. You cannot always say what grief or loss, what outrage, will carry anyone over the precipice. It may catch you completely by surprise, desperation erupting and overwhelming you before you know how close it was. She had felt that dark edge of panic brushing her. She did not imagine Kristian was immune. That would be naive and rob him of reality.

But she could not help him if she did not know the truth, whatever it was. Half blind to it, believing what she wanted rather than what was, she could do more harm than good.

Had Fuller Pendreigh known of Elissa's gambling and paid her debts when Kristian could not? Or was it possible she owed more than she could meet and had found some desperate way of her own of raising the money? Could that somehow have led to her murder? She had been beautiful, imaginative and never lacked physical courage. She would not be the first woman to sell herself when it seemed the only resort.

Had Pendreigh's wealth cushioned her or not?

She rose to her feet, leaving the weeds where they were, and went up the lawn to the French door and inside. She dropped the trug and the secateurs on the step and peeled off her gloves. Inside, she took off her shoes and went straight up the stairs to her bedroom.

She was already washed and in fresh underlinen when she finally called her maid to help her lace up her stays and fasten the small buttons of the bodice. Her hair was another matter. No one had ever been able to make that look elegant for more than fifteen minutes, but the maid, an even-tempered woman of endless patience, did her best.

An hour after making the decision, Callandra sat in her carriage on the way to visit Fuller Pendreigh. She would wait for him as long as necessary, or travel into the City if that was where he was, but she would see him.

He was not at Ebury Street, but he was expected very shortly, and she was shown to a most pleasant conservatory. Had she had less on her mind, she would have enjoyed recognizing the various exotic plants and trying to decide where their native habitat might be.

She was looking at a large yellow flower, without really seeing it, when she heard footsteps across the hall, the low murmuring of voices, and the moment after, Pendreigh was in the doorway, regarding her with slight puzzlement. She saw the signs of strain in his face. There was little color to his skin and a shadow about his cheeks almost as if he had not shaved, although actually he was immaculate. It was exhaustion which tightened his lips and hollowed the flesh.

"Lady Callandra?" It was a question not as to her identity, rather a confusion as to what she was doing waiting there, in the middle of the afternoon, and without having sent any letter or card to say that she was calling. They knew each other only by repute. She had worked tirelessly for reform of the way injured and ill soldiers were treated. Her husband had been an army surgeon, and she learned from him of the problems which could be overcome with foresight and intelligence. She had certainly made sufficient complaints, pleas and arguments, and had written to all manner of people for her name to be known. She was intimidated by no one, nor did flattery have any effect upon her.

Pendreigh, she had heard, had campaigned for the reform of the laws pertaining to property. That was largely why he had come from Liverpool to London, and of course to Parliament. It sounded a thing in which she would be little interested. To her mind, human pain had always far outweighed the disposition of wealth.

"Good afternoon, Mr. Pendreigh," she replied, recollecting herself and unconsciously using the enormous charm she possessed, and was quite unaware of because it lay in her warmth and simplicity of manner. "I apologize for calling upon you without writing first, but sometimes events move too rapidly to allow for such courtesy, and I confess I am deeply concerned."

Only for an instant did he wonder why, then knowledge of it was plain in his eyes. He came further into the room. His expression softened a little, but it obviously cost him an effort of will. "Of course. It would be absurd to wait upon convention at such a time. Would you prefer to speak here or in the withdrawing room? Have you taken tea?"

"Not yet," she replied. She did not care whether she had tea or not, but he might be tired and thirsty, and feel more comfortable if he offered hospitality. It gave one something to do with one's hands, time to think of a reply to an unforeseen or difficult question, and an excuse to look away without rudeness. "That would be most agreeable, thank you."

A flicker of relief crossed his face, and he led her back across the hall to the withdrawing room, instructing the maid to bring tea for them both.

On the day of the funeral she had barely noticed the room. Now, empty of people and with the black crepe of the occasion removed except around the pictures, she saw the magnificence of it. It faced south, and there were long windows to the front, which meant that the unusually large amount of blue in curtains and furniture did not make it cold, rather it gave it a depth and a sense of calm that warmer tones would not.

He caught her admiration and smiled, but he made no comment.

She did not wish to open the subject of Elissa until the maid had brought the tea and gone. Until then she would prefer to speak of something of mutual interest but no emotional heat. She remained standing and looked at the very fine portraits on the wall. One in particular caught her eye. It was of a woman with a handsome face and magnificent hair the shade of warm, dry sand, paler even than corn. The style of her gown was of some twenty years ago, and she looked to be in her middle or late thirties. The resemblance was so marked that she assumed it was Pendreigh's sister, or at the most distant, a cousin.

"My sister, Amelia," he said quietly from a few feet behind her. There was a sorrow in his voice she could not miss. She did not know whether he had meant to conceal it or allowed it to be heard because the wound was still raw and it comforted him to share something of it.

"She has a remarkable face," she said sincerely. "Rather more than beautiful."

"She was," he replied. "She had extraordinary courage, and . . ." He stopped for a moment, as if to compose himself. "Generosity of spirit," he finished.

The use of the past tense and the emotion in his voice required she pursue the subject, but with the greatest delicacy. "She looks no more than thirty-five," she said, leaving it open for him to say whatever he pleased, or to pass on to something else, perhaps the next picture.

"Thirty-eight, actually," he answered her. "It was the year before she died."

"I'm so sorry." It would be tactless to ask what had happened. It could be any of a score of illnesses, without even considering accident.

"Poverty!" His voice was so harsh it actually distorted the word so that for a moment she was not sure if she had heard him correctly. She turned to face him, and the pain and the anger she saw in him startled her. It was as fresh as if it had only just happened, and yet from the picture, it must have been a quarter of a century ago.

"You think I can't mean it, don't you?" he asked with a sharp gesture at the room around him, which was obviously that of a wealthy man. "My family had money. My father died quite young, and he was generous to Amelia as well as to me. She was an heiress when she married." He left the conclusion for her to draw, a challenge in his eyes, hard and bright.

Of course, when she married everything she owned would automatically have become her husband's. It was the law; everyone knew that. Only unmarried women owned anything.

"I see," she said very quietly.

"Do you?" he demanded. "He took her to Europe, first to Paris, then to Italy. We did not know that he spent everything and left her with barely a roof over her head, or that she was living on the few meals offered her by compassionate friends, most of whom had little more than she did. And she was too proud to tell us that the husband she adored was a wastrel and had deserted her in every practical sense. She died in Naples, alone and destitute."

She felt the loss as if he had been able to transfer it to her physically. Her imagination painted a terrible picture of the woman in the portrait being thin to gauntness, racked with fever, lips bloodless, skin flushed and sweating, alone in an ill-furnished room in a foreign land.

"I'm so sorry," she said in little more than a whisper. "I'm not surprised you cannot forget it . . . or forgive. I don't imagine I could, either."

"That's why I fight for women to retain some rights in their property," he said harshly. "The law is blind. It gives them no protection. We speak publicly as if we honor and cherish our women, give them safety from the ills and strife of the world, the dark and the sordid battles of trade and politics, the uses and abuses of power—and yet we leave them open to being mere vehicles for gaining money that was intended for their protection from hunger and want, and the law offers nothing!"

"A law for married women to keep rights in their own property?" she said, filled with a sudden blaze of understanding.

"Yes! Both inherited and earned. That swine sent Amelia out to work to provide for his extravagances, but the law gave him the right to her wages even so." The outrage in him was palpable, like a thing in the air.

She shared it—not the passion, because she had not been touched by it personally as he had, but in her mind the injustice was as great, and the need to amend it. "I see," she said, and she meant it.

He drew in breath to argue, then looked at her more closely. "Yes, perhaps you do. I apologize. I was about to deny that possibility. I know you have also fought for reform, and often against extraordinary blindness. We are both seeking to protect those who are vulnerable and need the strong to defend them." There was fury in his voice, and also a ring of pride.

Callandra was glad to hear it. The willingness to fight and courage were exactly what she needed, and her pity for his loss was now touched with admiration as well. "Do you have hope of achieving such a thing?" she asked with some eagerness.

He smiled very slightly. "I've worked towards it for the greater part of my career, and with the recent change in government I believe that it is within sight. There is a by-election coming up. If I can do this, I will have benefited both men and women, though they may not at first accept that. But surely justice is a boon for all."

"Of course it is," she agreed wholeheartedly.

There was a momentary interruption as the maid brought in the tray with the tea and set it out on the low table for them. She poured and then left.

Callandra was surprised how welcome the hot, fragrant drink was after all, and the tiny sandwiches of cucumber, and egg and cress. It gave her time to compose her thoughts.

She must address the purpose of her visit. He could not for a moment have thought she came simply to talk of good causes, however urgent.

She put down her cup. "As you know, I have engaged Mr. Monk to learn all the truth he can as to the events in Acton Street." It was a rather overdelicate way of phrasing it, and the moment it had passed her lips, she wished she had been more frank. "I am afraid that much of what he has discovered is not what either you or I would have wished."

His attention upon her was absolute, his eyes unwavering. "What has he discovered, Lady Callandra? Please be candid with me. Elissa was my daughter; I cannot afford to know less than the truth."

"Of course not. I apologize if I seemed to be prevaricating," she said sincerely. "We believed Dr. Beck could account for his time, that he was elsewhere with a patient, sufficiently far away to have made his involvement impossible. Unfortunately, he was mistaken in the times. I do not believe for an instant that he has any guilt at all, but he cannot prove it. Since he was her husband, naturally the police have to consider him suspect."

"That is a regrettable comment upon human nature," he said with a very slight tremor in his voice. "And more so upon the state of marriage. But I suppose it is true." He ignored his tea, leaning a little forward across the table. He was a very tall man, and his knees were level with its surface. It was a feat of elegance that he could move without looking ungainly. "Please do not try to spare my feelings, Lady Callandra. You say you do not believe for an instant that my son-in-law could be guilty—why not?" He tried to smile, and failed. It was a twisted grimace of pain. "I do not, either, but then I have known him for many years. Why do you not?"

She drew in her breath to answer truthfully, then realized the danger not only to herself but, by implication, to Kristian also.

"Because I have watched his work in the hospital," she said instead. "But it is only my opinion, and will carry no weight with the police, or anyone else. I had hoped Mr. Monk would find some other person with a strong motive, and perhaps some evidence to implicate him, but so far he has not done so. However, another possibility has come to my attention." She hated telling him of the gambling. Already she was all but certain he did not know, at least not the extent of it.

Pendreigh put his cup down and pushed it a little further into the middle of the table. His hand was trembling very slightly. "It seems to me quite obvious that the artists' model was the intended victim, and Elissa was simply unfortunate enough to have witnessed the crime. Surely that is what the police are really pursuing? Any consideration of Kristian must be merely a formality."

"I imagine so. Nevertheless, I would prefer to have forestalled them before this," she answered.

"Exactly what has Monk found?" he asked.

This was the moment she could not avoid. "That Mrs. Beck gambled," she answered, watching his face. "And lost very heavily." She saw his eyes widen and something within him flinch, so deep it was visible more as a shadow than a movement. But she was convinced in that instant that he had not known. No man could have lied with the skill to blanch the color from his skin, to convey such pain within, and yet not move at all. "I . . . I wish I had not had to tell you," she stumbled on. "But the police are aware of it, and I am afraid it provides a very powerful motive. Many men have killed for less reason than to avoid ruin. It occurred to me that perhaps in desperation to pay debts she may have incurred an enmity . . ." She drew in her breath. "Somehow . . ." Did he understand enough not to need the ugly picture detailed?

He said nothing. He seemed too stunned to be able to respond. He stared into the distance, through her, as if seeing ghosts, broken dreams, things he loved taken from him.

"But I saw her regularly over the last half year since I moved to London!" he protested, still trying to push the reality from him. "She was just as well dressed as always. She never seemed in any . . . difficulty!"

Callandra wished she could have avoided reason and gone with hope, but there was none that stood the light. "She will have chosen the times when she was winning to call upon you," she pointed out. "With skill and imagination one can appear well dressed. One has friends. There are pawnshops . . ."

Something died in his face. "I see." The words were a whisper.

"I think she could not help it," Callandra went on gently. She heard herself almost with disbelief. She was defending the woman who had driven Kristian to despair and the shadow of debtors' prison. He was on the verge of being blamed for her murder. "Mr. Pendreigh . . ."

He recalled his attention and turned his eyes to her, but he did not speak.

"Mr. Pendreigh, we must do what we can to help. You have said you do not believe Dr. Beck is guilty. Then someone else must be."

"Yes . . ." he said, then more abruptly, "Yes . . . of course." He focused his attention with difficulty. "What about the artist, Allardyce? I should be loath to think it was he, but it has to be a possibility. Elissa was extremely beautiful . . ." For a moment his voice faltered, and he made an immense effort to bring it back into control. "Men were fascinated by her. It wasn't just her face, it was a . . .

a vitality, a love of life, an energy which I never saw in anyone else. Allardyce loved to paint her. Perhaps he wanted more than that, and she refused him. He might have . . ." He did not finish the thought, but the rest of it was obvious. It did not surprise her that he could not bear to put it into words.

But Monk had told her that Allardyce could account for his time. He had spent the evening at the Bull and Half Moon in Southwark, miles from Acton Street, on the other side of the Thames.

"It was not he," she told Pendreigh. "The police can prove that."

A sharp frown creased his forehead, making two deep lines·like cuts between his brows. "Then we are back to the only answer which makes sense . . . Sarah Mackeson was the intended victim. If the police do not pursue that to the very end, then we must employ Monk to do so. There is something in her life, in her past, which has driven a past lover, a rival, a creditor, to quarrel with her in a way which ended in murder. The reason is there! We must find it!"

"I will speak to William, of course," she agreed with a fervor which was meant to convince herself as much as Pendreigh. "He said that apparently she was a very handsome woman, and her life was a little . . . haphazard." That was a euphemism she hoped he would understand. She did not wish to speak ill of her, and yet she hoped profoundly that the answer was as simple as that.

Pendreigh sighed. There was an unhappiness in him so profound it filled the room with grief more effectively than hanging every picture with crepe had done, or turning all the mirrors face to the wall and stopping the clocks.

"Rejection can make people behave irrationally," she went on quietly. "Even far against anything they really wish for or believe. But remorse afterwards does not undo the act, nor bring back that which has been destroyed."

He dropped his head into his hands, hiding his emotion. "No, of course not," he said, his voice muffled. "We must save what we can from the tragedy."

She was uncertain whether to rise to her feet now and excuse herself, or if it would be kinder to wait a few moments rather than force him to stand, as courtesy demanded, before he had had time to compose himself. She was actually hungry, and would like to have eaten more of the cucumber sandwiches, but it seemed an oddly heartless thing to do, and she left them. Instead she sat straight-backed, upright on the edge of the chair, waiting until he should be ready to bid her good-bye with the kind of dignity he could afterwards remember without embarrassment.

Monk and Runcorn were together in Runcorn's office the following day. They were both tired and irritable after spending a morning and early afternoon plowing through steady rain from one gambling establishment to another in the path of Elissa Beck, and people like her, both men and women. The addiction to the excitement of chance and the small element of skill involved made no discrimination for age or wealth, man or woman. There was something in certain characters that, once they had tasted the thrill of winning, could not let it go, even when part of them was perfectly aware of the destruction it was causing. They saw their winnings as larger than they were, their losses as smaller, and always there was the hope that the next turn of the card would redeem it all.

"I don't understand it," Runcorn said desperately, staring at his sodden boots. He had been obliged to step in the gutter to pass a group of women talking to each other and oblivious of passersby. "It's like a kind of madness. Why do people do it?"

Monk could understand it, at least in part, enough to feel a brush of fear at how easily he might have become one of them if his path in life had been a little different.

"A need to feel alive," he said, and then, seeing the disgust and incomprehension in Runcorn's face, wished he had held his tongue.

"Vermin!" Runcorn said savagely, yanking his boot off and massaging his cold, wet foot.

Monk looked up sharply, then realized Runcorn was referring to the debt collectors, not the gamblers.

"Wish we could catch a few of them and make a charge stick," Runcorn went on. "I'd like to see 'em in the Coldbath Fields, on the treadmill, or passing the shot." He was referring to the worst prison in London and the habitual punishments of walking inside a turning machine, where in order to remain upright a man had constantly to keep putting one foot in front of the other on a step which gave beneath his weight, spinning the wheel and pitching him forward again. Passing the shot was a useless exercise of bending to pick up a cannonball, straightening the back, and passing the ball to the next man, who put it down again. One could be forced to do it for hours until every muscle ached and movement was pain. It was all utterly purposeless, except to break the spirit.

"Yes," Monk agreed with feeling. "So would I. But we haven't found a jot of evidence to suggest any debt collector went after her. In fact, we can't even find anyone who'll admit she owed him. She got the money from somewhere . . . or someone."

Runcorn looked up from the drawer where he was searching for dry socks. "You believe them?" he asked.

Monk did not need to think about it; he already had. "Yes. Not their words, their lack of fear or anger. The emotion isn't there. If anything, they're disappointed to lose a good customer. They thought she was worth more."

Runcorn pursed his lips and pulled out one thick woollen sock, then another. "That's what I thought, too. What about Sarah Mackeson?"

Monk tried to read Runcorn's face, the doubt, the hope, the anger in it, until Runcorn turned away, pulling on his socks one by one. "We've found nothing to suggest anyone cared enough to kill her," he said miserably. He would rather have said there was passion, envy, fear, anything better than indifference. The most feeling she awoke seemed to have been in Allardyce, because she was beautiful to paint. The only other person who cared was Mrs. Clark.

"I wish we knew which of them was killed first," Runcorn said, slamming the drawer shut. "But the surgeon can't tell us a damn thing."

Monk sat on the edge of the desk with his hands in his pockets. He turned over in his mind what possible evidence there could be which would tell them which woman had died first. It would be no use at all going back to the doctor. All he could say was that they had died in the same manner, and common sense said they had been killed by the same person. Only physical facts would make a difference.

Runcorn was watching him. "We never found the earring," he said, as if following Monk's thoughts. It was disconcerting to have him so perceptive.

"Well, if it got caught in his clothing, whoever it was, he'd have thrown it away," Monk replied. "It wasn't on the floor."

Runcorn said nothing, and silence filled the room again.

"The ear bled," Monk said after a while. "It must have. You can't tear flesh like that without leaving marks on something."

Runcorn climbed to his feet, looking beyond Monk to the rain streaming down the window. "Do you want to go to Acton Street again?" he asked. "We didn't see anything on the carpet before, but we can try again. If we could prove Sarah Mackeson died first it would change everything."

Monk stood up also. "It's worth trying. And we could ask Allardyce how often he saw Max Niemann, and when."

"Think he could be involved?" Runcorn said hopefully. "Lovers' quarrel? Nothing to do with the doctor?" His voice sank at the end. If Elissa and Max Niemann had been lovers, that was more motive for Kristian than ever. And Kristian had lied about where he was, even if unintentionally.

But then Niemann had lied to Kristian also, by omission, allowing Kristian to believe that the funeral was the first time he had been to London in years.

"Can you send men to find out where Niemann stayed?" Monk asked, collecting his coat from the stand. "If he stayed at the same place each time, we can see how often he was here."

"You think he paid her debts?" Runcorn said quickly. His face was pinched with unhappiness. "At a price, maybe?"

"Wouldn't be the first woman who felt she had to sell herself to pay her debts," Monk replied, walking to the door and opening it. The thought sickened him, but it was pointless denying its possibility. As they passed the desk, Runcorn gave the sergeant instructions to send men searching the hotels for where Niemann had stayed.

They set out in the direction of Acton Street, intending to pick up a hansom on the way, but they were no more than two hundred yards from Allardyce's studio when they finally saw one that was free. It was not worth the effort or the fare. Runcorn shrugged in disgust and waved it away.

Allardyce was busy, and irritated to see them, but he knew better than to refuse them admittance.

"What is it now?" he said with ill grace.

Runcorn walked into the studio and looked around, his coat dripping water on the floor. Allardyce was working at a picture on the easel; his shirt was smeared with paint where he had wiped his hands.

"You told us you saw Niemann with Mrs. Beck a number of times," Monk began. "Before the night she was killed."

"Yes. They were friends. I never saw them quarrel." Allardyce looked at him challengingly, his blue eyes clear and hard.

"How often altogether, then or earlier?"

"Earlier?"

"You heard me. Did he come over from Vienna just once, or several times?"

"Two or three that I know of."

"When?"

"I don't remember." Allardyce shrugged. "Once in the spring, once in the summer."

"You've moved things!" Runcorn accused, pulling at the sofa. "It used to be over there!"

Allardyce glared at him. "I have to live here," he said bitterly. "Do you think I want it exactly as it was? I need the light. And wherever I live I can't get rid of the memories and I can't bring them back, but I don't have to keep it just as it was. I'll have the sofa and the carpets any damn way I like."

"Put them back," Runcorn ordered.

"Go to hell!" Allardyce responded.

"Just a minute!" Monk stepped forward and almost collided with Runcorn. "We can work out where the bodies lay. Look at the line of the windows; they haven't moved." He faced Allardyce. "Put the carpets where they were—now!"

Allardyce remained motionless. "What for? What have you found?"

"Nothing yet. It's only an idea. Do you know which woman died first?"

"No, of course . . ." Allardyce stopped, suddenly realizing what he meant. "You think someone might have killed Sarah, and Elissa was an accidental witness? Who?" His face was full of disbelief. "She never did anyone any harm. A few silly quarrels, like everybody."

"Maybe she learned something she wasn't meant to know?" Monk suggested.

"Put the carpets back!" Runcorn repeated.

Silently, Allardyce obeyed, moving them with Monk's help. They were neither large nor heavy, and he was almost finished when Monk noticed that just under the fringed edge of one of them there was a knothole in the pine boards. "I didn't see that before!"

"That's why I put the edges there," Allardyce pointed out.

Monk put his foot on the fringe and scuffed it up, showing the hole again. He glanced at Runcorn and saw the flash of understanding in his eyes. "Get me a chisel or one of those heavy knives," he ordered Allardyce.

"What for? What is it?"

"Do as you're told!" Monk said.

Allardyce obeyed, passing him a small claw-headed hammer, and a moment later there was a splintering of wood and the screech of nails prying loose as the board with the knothole came up. Lying in the dust below, glinting in the light, was a delicate gold earring, the loop stained with blood.

"That was Elissa's," Allardyce said after a moment's utter silence. "I painted it; I know." His voice cracked. "But this is where Sarah was lying! It doesn't make sense."

"Yes, it does," Monk said quietly. "It means Elissa was killed first. The earring was torn off when he put his arm around her neck . . . and broke it. It probably caught in his sleeve and in her struggle was ripped from her. He didn't notice it fall. Then when Sarah came out of one of the other rooms and saw Elissa dead, he killed her, too, and she fell onto the floor, over where the earring had disappeared."

Allardyce rubbed his hand across his face, leaving a smear of green paint on his cheek. "Poor Sarah," he said softly. "All she ever did was look beautiful. And be in the wrong place."

Runcorn pushed his hands deep into his pockets and stared at Monk. He didn't say anything, but there was no need. The time had come when they could avoid it no longer. It was not Sarah who was the intended victim; it had been no more to do with her than mischance. It was not gamblers or debt collectors. Max Niemann's visits to London, his meetings with Elissa that Kristian knew nothing of, were more motive, not less. Even the paid debts made it worse. Either it was the very last of Kristian's money, or uglier even than that, it was money Elissa had sold herself for.

"I'm going to the hospital," Runcorn said wearily. "You don't have to come if you don't want to."

"I'll come," Monk replied. He bent and picked up the delicate earring and dropped it into Runcorn's hand. "You can put your carpets any damn way you like, Mr. Allardyce, but if you alter that floorboard I'll jail you as an accomplice. Do you understand?"

Allardyce did not answer but stood, head bowed, in the middle of the floor as Monk and Runcorn went out and down the steps back into the rain.

CHAPTER
EIGHT

———

When Monk left the house early in the morning, almost before his footsteps died away and Hester heard the front door close, her mind was filled again with the fear that Charles was involved in Elissa's death. It loomed so sharp and painful she would almost rather the unsigned letter Charles had left with her were a love letter from some man than proof that it was Elissa who had introduced Imogen to the gambling which had grown into a thing that now raged through her like a destroying fire.

She had to know. As long as it was still unresolved every nightmare was a possibility. And yet it was also possible that the note was not from Elissa, and the two women had never met, and whatever had made Charles lie to her about having driven down Drury Lane was perfectly innocent, at least as far as Elissa was concerned. It could be simply embarrassing, a little foolish.

As soon as Mrs. Patrick, her housekeeper, arrived, Hester explained that she had an urgent errand to run. With the letter in her reticule, she put on her hat and coat and went out into the rain. It was a considerable journey from Grafton Street to the Hampstead Hospital to ask Kristian for any piece of Elissa's handwriting to compare.

All the long journey she sat and twisted her hands together, trying to keep her racing imagination from picturing Imogen and Elissa, Charles's fury when he found out, his incomprehension, and all the violence and tragedy that could have flowed from it. She argued one way, and then the other, hope to terror, and back again. It was so easy to let the mind race away, creating pictures, building pain.

By the time she reached the hospital and alighted she was so tense she stumbled over the curb and regained her balance only just in time to prevent herself from falling. This was ridiculous! She had faced battlefields. Why did it strike into the heart of her that her brother might have killed Elissa Beck?

Because whoever it was had killed Sarah Mackeson as well. There was an element in a crime of desperation to save someone you love from a force of destruction. But killing Sarah was to save himself, an instinctive resort to violence at the cost of someone else's life.

She ran up the steps, all but bumping into a student doctor coming down. He scowled at her and muttered something under his breath. She stopped and asked the porter if Dr. Beck was in, and was told with a nod of sympathy that he was. She thanked him and hurried down the corridor to the patients' waiting room, where there were already three people sitting huddled in their pain and anxiety, now and then talking to each other to ease the imagination and the passing of time.

Hester considered whether to use the prerogative of interrupting, which she could exercise as someone who worked in the hospital. Then she looked at their faces, strained already with hardship far beyond her own, and decided to wait.

She also talked, to fill the time, learning something of their lives and telling them a little of her own, until at last it was her turn, and there were seven more people waiting after her.

Kristian was startled. "Hester? You're not ill? You look very pale," he said with concern. Considering his own ashen face and hollow eyes, at any other time the remark would have held its element of irony.

"No, thank you," she said quickly. "I'm just worried, like all of us." There was no point in being evasive. "I have a letter and I need to compare the handwriting in order to know who sent it, because there is no signature. I am hoping I am mistaken, but I must be certain. Have you anything that Elissa wrote? It doesn't matter what it is; a laundry list would do."

A shadow of humor crossed his eyes, then vanished. "Elissa didn't write laundry lists. I expect I can think of something, but it will be at home, not here. . . ."

"Doesn't matter, if you will give me permission to look for it."

"What is the other letter you wish to compare it with?"

She avoided his eyes. "I would rather not say . . . please . . . unless I have to."

There was a minute's silence. Not even any hospital noises intruded through the thick walls into the room.

"There is a letter she wrote me, some time ago, in the top drawer of the chest in my bedroom. I . . . I would like it back . . ." His voice broke and he gulped in, trying to control it.

"I don't need to take it away," she said quickly. "I don't need to read it . . . just compare the handwriting. They may be quite different, and it will mean nothing at all."

"And if they are the same?" he said huskily. "Will that mean that Elissa did something . . . wrong?"

"No," she denied it, then knew it was a lie. To have an addiction is a grief, but intentionally to introduce someone else to it she regarded as a profound wrong. "I may be mistaken. It is only an idea."

He drew in breath as if to ask again, then changed his mind.

"If it has anything to do with her death, I will tell you," she promised, still looking down. She could not bear to intrude on the pain in his eyes. "Before I tell anyone else, except William."

"Thank you." Again he seemed about to continue, and changed his mind.

"The room is full of people," she said, gesturing towards the door. "What is your cleaning woman's name, so that she knows I have spoken to you?"

"Mrs. Talbot."

"Thank you." And before either of them could struggle for anything more to say, she turned and went out through the waiting room and down the corridor to the entrance, and the street, to look for an omnibus or a hansom back towards Haverstock Hill.

She alighted within a few yards of Kristian's house, and as soon as she knocked Mrs. Talbot opened the door. She had been working on the hall floor, and the mop and bucket stood a few feet inside.

Hester bade her good morning by name and explained her errand. Rather doubtfully, Mrs. Talbot conducted her upstairs, after carefully closing the front door. She remained in the bedroom while Hester went to the chest. Feeling guilty for the intrusion into what was deeply private, Hester opened the top drawer and looked through the dozen or so papers that were there. Actually, there were two letters from Elissa, undated, but from the first line or two she could see that they were old, from when they were immeasurably close.

With fumbling hands she opened her reticule and took out the letter Charles had given her, although she already knew the answer. It was more scrawled, a little larger, but the characteristic curls and generous capitals were the same.

She placed them side by side on top of the dresser, and for a sick, dizzy moment fought off reality, searching for differences, anything that would tell her they were only similar, not the same. On the second one the tails were longer. A b had a loop; the z was different. And even as she was doing it, she knew it was not true. It was time and haste which gave an illusion of difference. It was Elissa who had drawn Imogen into gambling. Of course, she had not forced her, only invited her, but Charles might blame her as if it were a seduction. It is so easy, so instinctive, to bring the fault away from those we love.

Would he have known it was Elissa? He had no other writing to compare. But he did not need it. On his own admission, he had followed Imogen. He needed only to have kept one of the appointments in the letters, and seen whom she met. Why the Drury Lane lie? For the same reason as any lie—to conceal the truth.

"Thank you," she said to Mrs. Talbot. Conspicuously, she folded up Kristian's letter and replaced it, closed the drawer, then put Charles's letter back in her reticule. "I won't disturb you anymore."

"You look poorly, Miss . . . an' cold, if you don't mind me sayin'. If yer'd like a cup o' tea, the kettle's on the 'ob," Mrs. Talbot offered.

Hester hesitated. Part of her was irritated and anxious to face Charles and know the best or the worst. But it would be the same whenever she went, and a hot cup of tea would warm her, perhaps undo some of the knots in her clenched stomach. She looked at the woman's weary face and felt a rush of gratitude. "Yes, please. Let's do that."

Mrs. Talbot relaxed, and a surprisingly sweet smile lit her face. "D'yer mind the kitchen, Miss?"

"I'd like the kitchen," Hester said honestly. For a start it would be a good deal warmer than the ice-cold room she was standing in now, and no doubt the one furnished morning room would be equally chilly.

It was an hour and a half later before she was shown into Charles's office in the City, and that was only after some rather heavy-handed insistence.

Charles rose from his desk and came around to greet her. "What is it?" he demanded, his voice sharp. "My clerk said it was an emergency. Has something happened to Imogen?"

"Not so far as I know." She took a deep breath. "But she is still gambling, even though she now goes alone." She watched his face intently, and saw the dull flush of color and the heat in his eyes. Denial was impossible.

"If it's not Imogen, what is it?"

She hated having to press him. It would have been so much easier if they could have spoken as allies instead of adversaries, but she could not afford to let him evade the truth any longer. "You told me that the night of Elissa's death you followed Imogen south, down Drury Lane towards the river."

He could not retract it. "Yes," he said, his voice cracking a little. "You seemed to be thinking she was involved in . . . in the murders. Or she might have seen something."

"She might have." Hester was hating this. Why did he not trust her enough to tell her the truth? Was it so hideous? "You didn't go down Drury Lane that evening. A dray slid over and dropped all its load of raw sugar barrels, blocking everything. They took hours to clear it up."

He stood motionless, not answering her. She had never seen him look more wretched. The fear bit so hard and deep inside her that for the first time she truly acknowledged the possibility that he was involved in Elissa's death.

"Where was she?" she asked him. "Did you follow her that night?"

"Yes." It was little more than a whisper.

She found herself gulping also. "Where? Where did she go, Charles?"

"Gambling."

"Gambling where?" Now she was all but shouting. "Where?"

He shook his head firmly. "She wouldn't have killed Elissa. She wouldn't have hurt her at all!"

"Possibly not. But would you?"

He looked startled, as if he had not even thought of such a thing. For the first time she hoped. Her heart lurched and steadied.

"No! I . . ." He let out his breath slowly. "How could you think that . . ." He stopped.

"Where were you?" she persisted. "Where did you follow her, Charles? Someone killed Elissa Beck. It wasn't the artist, and it wasn't one of the gamblers. I want above everything else to be able to prove it wasn't you."

"I don't know who it was!" There was desperation in his voice now, rising close to panic.

"Where did Imogen go?" she said again.

"Swinton Street . . ." he whispered.

"Then where?"

"I . . ." He gulped. "I . . . got very angry." He closed his eyes as if he could not bear to say it while looking at her. "I made a complete fool of myself. I created a scene, and one of the doormen hit me over the head with something . . . I think I remember falling. Later I woke up in the dark, my head feeling as if it were splitting, and I lay for quite a little while so dizzy I daren't move." He bit his lip. "When I did, I crawled around and realized I was in a small room, not much more than a cupboard. I shouted, but no one came, and the door was heavy, and of course it was locked. It was daylight when they let me out." Now he was looking at her, no more evasion in his face, only the most agonizing embarrassment.

She believed him. She was so overwhelmed with relief that the stiff, formal office swam around her in a blur, and she had to make an effort not to buckle at the knees. Very deliberately, she walked forward and sat down in the chair opposite his desk. "Good," she said almost normally. "That's . . . good." What an idiotic under-statement. He was not guilty! It was impossible. He had spent the entire night locked up in a cupboard. She remembered the bruises on his face, how ill he had looked when she had seen him after-wards. They would remember him and could swear to it. She would tell Monk, of course, and get their testimony before they realized how important it was. Charles was safe. What was a little humilia-tion compared with what she had feared?

She looked up at him and smiled.

For an instant he thought she was laughing at him, then he read her face more closely and his eyes filled with sudden tears. He turned away and blew his nose.

She gave him a moment, but only one, then she stood up and went to him, putting her arms around him and holding him as tightly as she could. She said nothing. She could not promise that it would be all right, that Imogen was not involved, or even that Imogen would stop gambling now. She did not know any of those things. But she did know that he could not have killed Elissa himself, and she could prove it.

The trip to the hospital was one of the worst journeys Monk could ever recall having made. He and Runcorn took a hansom, intending it to wait outside so they would have no difficulty in obtaining one for the return to the police station with Kristian Beck. Neither of them even mentioned the possibility of taking the police van in which criminals were customarily transported. They sat side by side without speaking, avoiding looking at each other. To do so would have made the silence even more obvious.

Monk thought about how he would tell Callandra that he had failed, and as he tried to work out in his mind what words he would use, each time he discarded them as false and unintentionally condescending, something she deserved least of all from him.

By the time they reached the hospital, and Runcorn had instructed the cabbie to wait, his sense of failure was for having led her to hope so fiercely, rather than warning her more honestly in the beginning, so she might have been better prepared for this.

They went up the steps side by side, and in through the doors to the familiar smells of carbolic, disease, drifting coal smuts, and floors too often wet. The corridors were empty except for three women with mops and buckets, but they did not need to ask their way. They both knew by now where Kristian's rooms were, and the operating room.

"Are we . . ." Monk began.

"Are we what?" Runcorn said tartly, glaring at him.

"Going to wait until he's seen his patients?" Monk finished.

"What the hell do you think I'm going to do?" Runcorn snapped. "Take him away with a knife in his hand, and some poor devil's arm half off?" He drove his fists savagely into his pockets and strode along the corridor ahead of Monk, not looking back at him. He turned the corner and left Monk to follow.

As it happened, Kristian was not operating, but he still had five people in his waiting room, and Runcorn sat down on the bench as if he were the sixth. He gave Monk one glowering look and then ignored him.

The door opened and Kristian came out. He saw Runcorn first, then Monk.

Monk would not lie, even by implication. He wished he could have, because he knew Kristian would see the rest of those waiting for him, and it would have been easier if he had not known why the police were there. But the instant he met Monk's eyes the question existed, and then the understanding. Something inside him faded, as if he had come to the end of a long test of endurance and reached the point at which he could no longer struggle.

"Mr. Newbury?" he said, turning away and looking at a large man with a pale, flabby face and receding hair. "Will you come in, please?"

Newbury stood up and limped across the floor, watched by everyone else in the room.

Monk sat stiffly in his seat, willing himself not to fidget, not to stand up and pace back and forth. The other people were sick, and probably frightened of whatever pain or debility lay ahead of them. Kristian faced God knew what. All Monk had to deal with was the misery of arresting Kristian, and then of telling Hester and Callandra what had happened. Comparatively, it was nothing.

Still the minutes dragged by, and as one patient went in after another, he alternated between anger with Runcorn simply for being there, for knowing what was in Monk's mind because he had worked with him and could remember a thousand things Monk could not, and a desire to say something to him to ease the waiting, because he knew Runcorn also loathed this necessity. He, too, admired Kristian, whether he wanted to or not, and would have given a great deal for it to have been anyone else, preferably someone of a class and type he despised. Best of all if it could have been a gambler, but Allardyce would have done. Far better an artist, living a bohemian and essentially alien and dissolute life, than a doctor who spent his time healing the sick, the ordinary poor who came to this particular hospital. But Runcorn did not have the courage or the imagination not to do his duty.

No, that was unfair, and Monk knew it even as the thought filled his mind. Monk, too, would have arrested Kristian, even if it had not been forced upon him by Runcorn's presence. His own knowledge was enough. He could have forgiven Kristian for killing Elissa. She had provoked him beyond the limits of forbearance. But Sarah had done nothing except be in the wrong place at the wrong moment. There was no sense to it that he could explain, but the fact that no one else had mourned her except Mrs. Clark—and Runcorn, of all people—made it more of an offense in his eyes.

The last patient came out, and after barely a minute Kristian followed. He stood in the middle of the room, stiff and very straight, his head high. There were marks of sleeplessness like bruises around his eyes, and his skin was bleached of color. "I assume you believe that I murdered Elissa," he said very quietly, not looking at either of them. "I did not, but I cannot prove it."

"I'm sorry, Dr. Beck," Runcorn replied. He was acutely miserable, but he would not shirk doing his duty to the letter. "I don't know whether you killed her or not, but the evidence all points that way, and there's nothing to say anybody else did. You'll have to come with me, sir. You are under arrest for the murders of Elissa Beck and Sarah Mackeson."

Kristian said nothing.

Monk cleared his throat. He was surprised how difficult it was to speak steadily. "Would you like me to collect some clothes for you from your home?"

Kristian blinked and turned to him. "I'd be grateful if you would tell the hospital what has happened, and . . . and Mrs. Talbot, who cleans my house for me." The ghost of a smile touched his mouth and echoed in his dark eyes. "Fermin Thorpe will be pleased. It will justify his opinion of me at last." He could not have said anything which would have made Monk feel worse, or more totally inadequate. He saw with a flash of irony that Kristian recognized it, and although possibly he had not intended it, he could not apologize.

"I'll do both," Monk replied, looking at Runcorn.

Runcorn nodded.

Kristian held out his hand with the front door key in it.

"Thank you." Monk took it and turned away, engulfed in misery.

Monk went straight to Haverstock Hill and let himself into the house with the key. Mrs. Talbot had already left, and there was no sound or movement at all. He found it acutely distressing to see the bare, chilly rooms, and to go upstairs to the stark bedroom Kristian occupied. The dressing room held only the necessities of grooming: a plain hairbrush, a wooden-handled open razor and leather strop, cuff links and shirt studs such as a clerk or shopkeeper might have owned. In the dresser he found four clean shirts and the minimum of underwear. There were two other suits in the wardrobe, and one other pair of boots, carefully resoled. This was all that was owned by a man with years of skill and experience, who worked from dawn to dusk and into the night every day of the week.

He took them back to the police station and gave them to the desk sergeant for Kristian. Now he could no longer put off going home and telling Hester that he had failed, and why.

When he went out into the street again it was raining steadily, and he walked for barely a mile, getting thoroughly soaked, before he finally caught a hansom for the last part of his journey. He reached home shivering with cold, wishing there were any way of avoiding what he must do.

Inside the door he took off his wet overcoat and removed his boots to save putting footprints over the carpet. He heard her come through from the kitchen and half expected her to know already. She was so quick to sense things, to understand, he imagined she would be aware of his failure and prepared for it.

He looked up and saw her face, full of relief, as if some burden had been lifted from her, and realized how mistaken he was.

"William . . ." She stopped. "What is it?" The muscles of her face and neck pulled tight. He straightened up, ignoring the wet boots. "Kristian wasn't where he said he was. God knows he had cause enough to kill her. She's bled him of everything, and if she'd lived she would have gone on until he ended up in prison. Queen's if he was lucky. Coldbath if he wasn't."

"For heaven's sake!" she exploded. "Some gambler killed her! Someone she owed . . ."

He took her shoulder, forcing her to face him. "No, they didn't. Do you think we haven't pressed that as far as it will go? No one wants it to be Kristian."

"Runcorn . . ." she began.

"No," he said sharply. "He's stubborn and prejudiced, full of ambition, taking offense where there isn't any, thin-skinned and short of imagination . . . at times. But he didn't want it to be Kristian."

"Didn't!" she challenged, her eyes blazing. "You said 'didn't'!"

"Didn't," he repeated. He shook his head very slightly. "There's nothing we could do to prevent it. The evidence was too much."

"What evidence?" she demanded. "There's nothing except motive. You can't convict anyone because they had a reason. All you know is that he can't prove he was somewhere else!"

"And that he lied about it, intentionally or not," he answered quietly. "No one else has reason to, Hester. Allardyce was in the Bull and Half Moon, on the other side of the river. It doesn't make sense for any of the gamblers to have killed her. Apart from that, her debts were paid anyway."

"Then the other poor woman was the intended victim," she

said instantly. "I don't know why you even think Elissa Beck was the one killed first, and not Sarah Mackeson! Perhaps she was having a love affair with someone and they quarreled? Isn't that far more likely than Kristian following his wife to an artist's studio and killing her there? For heaven's sake, William! He's a doctor . . . if he wanted to kill her there are dozens of better and safer ways of doing it than that!"

He did not bother to argue with her about passion and sense. It was true, but irrelevant to this. "Sarah wasn't killed first," he said, still holding her and feeling her pull against him, her muscles tight. "Elissa was."

"You don't know that! No doctor could tell you which of two people died first when it was within minutes of each other," she retaliated.

"We found Elissa's earring, torn from her ear in the struggle, fallen through a knothole in the floorboard . . . under where Sarah was lying."

She drew in her breath, then let it out in a sigh. "Oh," she said very quietly. The anger drained out of her, leaving only misery, and he pulled her unresisting body closer to him, then held her in his arms, feeling her shiver and struggle to keep from weeping.

It was several minutes, clinging close to him, before she finally drew back. "Then we've got to fight it," she said, gasping over the words. "You . . . you mean Runcorn will arrest him, don't you?"

"He already has. I took his clothes and razor to him."

"He's in . . . prison?" Her eyes were wide.

"Yes, Hester."

"What?" She shuddered. "Don't you dare tell me you think he could have done it!" Her eyes filled with tears. "Don't dare!"

"Why would you think I might?" he asked. He wished passionately that he could say anything other. She looked so frightened and vulnerable, so willing to take on the battle whatever the odds, and be hurt . . . horribly. And yet he could not have loved her so deeply had she been ready to give in, been wiser, more realistic, even more able to cast aside her emotions and arm herself against the loss.

She was furious because the tears slid down her cheeks. "Because you think he could be guilty," she whispered.

"He could be," he said. "Everyone has a breaking point, you know that as well as I do. We all reach a degree where we can't bear it any longer, and either we crumple up and surrender, or we run away, or else we fight back. Sometimes we lose our balance and we do something we thought was outside even our imagination. I've been there. Haven't you?"

She leaned against him again, her voice muffled because her face was buried in his shoulder. "Yes . . ."

It was several moments later before she spoke clearly. She sniffed hard and pulled away from him. "What are we going to do?" Her voice, her face, the angle of her body, all asserted passionately that they were going to do something.

"I don't know." He hated admitting it, but he had already exhausted every possibility he knew, or he would have argued with Runcorn and delayed the arrest even a day.

"Well, if it isn't Kristian, it has to be someone else!" she protested with desperation. "We've got to find out who it is. I've done nothing so far. I don't know how I can have been so stupid! So complacent! I took it for granted since I . . ." She looked away. "Since I refused to believe it could be Kristian. Where can I begin?"

"I don't know," he said again. "Runcorn's sent men to check if Max Niemann came to London more often than the times we know of, but we know of no reason why he would kill her."

"Perhaps they were lovers?" She said the words with difficulty. "And they quarreled? You said Allardyce told you she met Niemann there. That makes sense . . . doesn't it?" There was no conviction in her voice. Maybe she was remembering Niemann clasping Kristian's hands at the funeral. The feeling between them that had looked intensely real. Yet it seemed as if one of them had killed the woman they had both loved, and with whom they had shared a noble and turbulent past. Which of them was lying so superbly, and what agony of emotions was pouring through him?

"Hester . . ." He drew in a deep breath. "Of course it could be someone else, but Kristian's been arrested. He'll stand trial. He'll need a better defense than your belief that it could be Niemann, or someone else we don't know."

"Have you told Callandra?" She shivered.

"No."

"Then I'd better go and do it." She pulled away from him.

"Tonight?" He was startled.

"Yes. It won't hurt any less in the morning."

"I'll come with you." He bent down and picked up his boots again.

Callandra refused to accept it. She had received them in her sitting room with the gas jets blazing, throwing the dark walls into a radiance of warmth, the flames from the fire dancing red and yellow. Suddenly the familiar comfort of it vanished and even the beauty of the paintings seemed no more than a trick of light.

"No," she said, looking at neither of them, her face white, her body rigid. "He might have been tempted to kill his wife, but he could not have killed the artists' model as well. There is another answer. We must find it."

"I'll go on looking," Monk promised. He said it because he could not deny her, but he had no idea where to begin, and no belief that he could succeed. "But we must think how to defend Kristian as well."

"Oliver?" she said immediately. "I'll pay." She did not bother to add how highly Sir Oliver Rathbone had regarded Kristian. Rathbone was more than a colleague or a friend, he was an ally in battles they had fought before, and his passion for justice was equal to their own.

"He is away in Italy," Monk said grimly. "He might be gone

another two or three weeks. We can't afford to wait that long before beginning. Even when he returns, he might be committed."

She looked at him with misery and rising panic. "Who else is as good?"

"I don't know," he admitted. They had always turned to Rathbone, whatever the case, or the difficulty. "We'll have to make enquiries—I'll start in the morning, as soon as there's anyone to ask. We'll need every moment we have." They would need far more than that, but he did not say so.

"I must come with you," she insisted.

He thought of the rejections, those who would point out what a futile struggle it would be, how slight the chance of winning.

"Callandra . . ." he began.

She stared at him. "You will need my influence, William," she said with infinite dignity. "And my money. I am perfectly aware of the arguments we shall receive, and you cannot protect me from them without also robbing me of the chance to be of any effect. If you imagine you can do it without me, then you are being naive."

He surrendered without a pointless struggle. "Pendreigh doesn't believe Kristian is guilty," he said reasonably. "At least he didn't this morning. We could begin by seeking his advice. He will care very much how the case is conducted, for the sake of Elissa's reputation, if nothing else."

"Then we shall begin with him," Callandra said decisively. "I shall send my card at first light, and ask permission to call upon him as soon as possible." She turned to Hester. "Do you wish to come?"

"Of course," Hester responded. "We shall be ready as soon as you send for us." She touched Callandra lightly on the arm, but it was a gesture of extraordinary tenderness. Callandra moved away, as if emotion now was more than she could bear.

"Come." Monk turned towards the door, guiding Hester with him. "It is time we went home and considered what to say when we see Pendreigh." He turned to Callandra. "We shall be ready for eight o'clock. Send word and we will be wherever you wish."

"Thank you." Callandra reached out and rang the bell for the maid, keeping her face turned towards the fire.

Monk followed Hester out as the maid led them to the door and helped them into their coats again. Outside was raw, with wind driving the rain. As soon as they were beyond the shelter of the steps he felt the chill of it through him, but it was only on the periphery of his awareness. Far deeper, as he watched Hester move into the arc of the lamplight ahead of him, and the gusting rain in the glare it shed, was the realization of how deeply Callandra cared. It was immeasurably more than admiration, loyalty or friendship, for all that that was worth. This was a wound which might not heal, a pain within her heart neither he nor Hester could reach to give any ease.

He caught up and put his arm in Hester's, felt her respond, matching her step to his. He knew that she had known this all along, and he understood why she had not told him.

In the morning they ate breakfast early, and Monk went out as far as the corner to buy the morning edition of the newspapers. He scanned the front page, and then the second and third. The North had gained a considerable success in the Civil War. General Butler had taken the Confederate forces on the Hatteras Inlet. Forty-five officers and six hundred men were prisoners of war.

There was no word of Kristian's arrest—in fact, no mention of the case at all. He returned home uncertain whether he was really relieved or if it only pushed ahead the inevitable. Did the silence bring them any time, any chance to find refuting evidence before the press destroyed all innocence or doubt?

It seemed a wasted age of time until there was a polite tap on the door, and Monk strode over to open it and found Callandra's coachman on the step to say they had an appointment with Fuller Pendreigh in his office in Lincoln's Inn, and would they please come.

The journey took some time in the early-morning traffic, the wet streets glistening in fitful sun breaking through the clouds, gutters awash from the night's rain. The air was damp and milder, full of the odors of smoke, manure, leather and wet horseflesh. No doubt, unless the wind rose considerably, there would be fog again by dusk.

They were there only a few minutes early, but Pendreigh received them immediately. He had obviously expected both women, from whatever Callandra had written to him, but it was Monk to whom he addressed his attention. It was apparent that he was unaware of Kristian's arrest, and he was visibly shaken when he was told. His face was already colorless, and he seemed to sway a little on his feet as if the shock was so profound it had robbed him of balance.

"I'm sorry," Monk said sincerely. "I wish I could have prevented it, but there really is no other reasonable person to suspect."

"There must be," Pendreigh said in a quiet, intensely controlled voice. "We just haven't thought of him yet. Whatever the provocation, or the despair, I do not believe Kristian would have killed Elissa. He loved her . . ." He stopped, his voice wavering a little. He turned half away from them, shielding his face. It was the nearest to privacy he could come. "If you had ever known her, you would understand that."

Monk was compelled by reason. All the passion and idealism in the world, the most devoted love possible, could not alter the truth, and only the truth would serve now. There was a cleanness in it, no matter how terrible, a relief in the mind from the struggle of denial. But it took a fearful courage. He did not know, in Pendreigh's place, if he could have done it. He could not afford to think of Callandra, or how she would feel, nor of Hester beside him.

"Fear can drive us all to thoughts and acts we could not imagine when we are safe," Monk said clearly. "We don't know each other when that last boundary has been crossed. We don't even know ourselves. I used to imagine that no one would act against their own interests or do things that are going to result in something they passionately don't want. But that isn't true. Sometimes we just react to the moment, and don't look even to the very next thing after it. We lash out in terror or outrage. Something seems so monstrously unjust we seek reparation, or revenge, without looking further to think what that does to us, or to anyone else."

"Oh, no . . ." Callandra protested, turning to him with an ashen face. "Some people, perhaps, but . . ."

"Elemental emotions can override reason in even the most rational of us," he insisted, holding her eyes and forcing her to meet his. He wanted to find the right words, but there were none. All he could do was be gentle in his tone. "Reasonable men can be passionate as well," he said softly. "You know that as profoundly as I do. I have seen the mildest and most intelligent of men change utterly if, for example, his wife is violated." He saw Hester wince, but ignored it. "Does he stay at home and comfort her, assure her of his love?" he went on. "Or does he go storming off to kill the man he believes responsible—leaving her alone, terrified and ashamed and hurt when she needs him the most?" Pendreigh was staring at him. Callandra tried to interrupt him, but he overrode her. "In his own rage and guilt that he was not there to protect her, he can attack someone who may or may not be responsible, and risk injustice and his own catastrophic blame, almost certainly arrest, and possibly prison or the rope for himself. All of which makes his poor wife's situation unimaginably worse. Is that reasonable or intelligent? Is it going to produce good for anyone at all?" His voice softened suddenly. "Judges know that, even juries. It won't help to pretend it couldn't be, because we believe that Kristian's innocent."

"But no one has been violated!" Callandra protested at last. "And it is Elissa who is dead." Her voice was full of argument, but he could see in her face that she understood what he meant. The parallel was not irrelevant.

"We shall go on searching for some other answer," Monk agreed, still facing Callandra and ignoring Pendreigh and Hester. "But we must accept the fact that Kristian will stand trial."

Callandra closed her eyes. He saw courage and defeat struggling in her face. The daylight in the room was hard and cold; the clear, pale, autumn sun did nothing to disguise the marks of age in her. There was no kindness in it.

"I'm sorry," he said gently. For a moment even Pendreigh's loss did not mean anything to him. He had known Callandra since shortly after his accident, and that was six years now, all the life he could remember. She had always been loyal, brave, funny and kind. He would have done anything within his power to have saved her from this, but the only way he could offer his love was not to make the ordeal harder by drawing it out with lies. "We have to think who we can ask to defend him when the case opens. At the moment that is the most urgent thing." As he spoke he turned to Pendreigh. "That is the principal reason we have come to you, sir."

"I'll do it," Pendreigh answered without hesitation. Obviously he had been thinking of it while they were speaking. It was not a question he was asking, but a statement of intent. "I'll defend him myself. I don't believe he's guilty, and that fact will be apparent to the jury. As Elissa's father, I'll make the best character witness he could have."

Callandra's face filled with relief, and for the first time the tears spilled over her cheeks. She turned to him and was about to speak, perhaps to thank him, when she must have realized how inappropriate that would be, and stopped.

Hester hastened into the silence, perhaps to distract Pendreigh's eye from Callandra's emotion. "That would be excellent! We will do everything we can to find more evidence, seek everything you want, talk to anyone."

Pendreigh looked thoughtful. Now that he had made a decision, his manner changed. Some kind of strength returned. "Thank you." He looked from one to another of them. "I shall do all I can to raise doubt as to the evidence and any conclusions that can be drawn from it, but we need more than that. Someone is responsible for the deaths of these two women. We need to raise at least one other believable alternative in the minds of the jurors." He looked questioningly to Monk. "Is it true that witnesses preclude Allardyce from the possibility of having been there?"

"Yes. They are willing to swear he was in a tavern on the other side of the river all evening."

"And I assume you have thoroughly investigated the people who own the gambling houses?" His distaste was hard in his voice, but he did not flinch from asking.

"Yes. Apart from their wish to draw the attention of the police as little as possible, and to not frighten away their custom, Mrs. Beck did not owe them any significant amount of money. They say all her debts were paid to date. People like her are the main source of their profit. It would make no sense to harm her."

Pendreigh's face tightened. "Then we must look further. We may not be able to prove anyone else's guilt." His voice was strained, and he did not quite meet Monk's eyes. "But we must raise a very believable possibility. We must create so much doubt that they cannot convict Kristian."

Monk wondered how much that was spoken from the desire to protect not only Kristian, but Elissa's reputation as well, which was going to be almost impossible. He felt an intense pity for the man, and a grave respect for his strength that he could even contemplate going into court and keeping his composure sufficiently to fight the case when his only child was the victim. But Fuller Pendreigh had not risen to the position he held without great resources of inner power and remarkable self-discipline. Perhaps his very appearance in court would be the best chance that Kristian had.

They discussed details and ideas for another thirty minutes or so, then left Pendreigh to think over the plans that were already forming in his mind, people he should contact, witnesses who might be called, eventualities to follow or to guard against.

Callandra took her own carriage home, and Monk and Hester called a hansom.

"What do you really believe, William?" Hester asked when they were alone.

He hesitated. Should he try to protect her? Was it what she wanted? He knew there were emotions inside her he could not reach, or understand, because they were to do with old loyalties to Charles, memories of family grief and loss, the passion to shield the weaker. He had only an empty space in his own life where those feelings should have been. His childhood held a few sharp moments, mostly physical memories, of the sea, bright and choppy, of sitting in a boat and the consuming need to be one of the men, to equal their courage and their ability to know what to do in any eventuality—how to tie ropes so they did not undo, how to balance when it was rough, how not to be sick or show fear. He realized with shame that there was no concern for anyone else. Every fear or need was for his own pride, his passion to be respected, to succeed. He was profoundly glad Hester could not see that as he did.

"William?"

"I don't know what I think," he answered. "It would be more comfortable for us to think it had something to do with Max Niemann, but there's very little to suggest it. He said at the funeral that he had come from Paris because he read of her death there, and he's in Vienna anyway, so far as we know."

"I could believe that Kristian could have panicked and lashed out in despair," she said quietly, staring ahead into the darkness. "But not that he killed Sarah Mackeson. I'll never believe that!" They were brave words, said with a tremor in her voice and the edge of tears too close to hide.

He did not argue. He reached across and took her hand, and felt her fingers curl around his, cold in the chill of the hansom and the weariness of her heart, but gripping him with strength.

CHAPTER
NINE

———

Keeping her appointment with Fuller Pendreigh had been difficult for Callandra because of the element of self-control necessary to hide the depth of her emotions. As far as he was concerned, she was no more than a good friend and colleague who wished to help and was quite naturally grieved by the whole matter. For everyone's sake, his perception must remain exactly that.

Now, as she left Lincoln's Inn, she was startled to find herself shaking with release from the tension. Her head was pounding and her hands felt clammy, in spite of the cold.

She had not seen Kristian alone since the death of Elissa, except for moments in the hospital, standing in the corridor with the certain knowledge that someone else might pass at any moment. They had spoken of trivia. She had been thinking a hundred other things that she longed to be able to say, and the frustration of silence was almost unbearable. She was sorry for his pain and his loss. She wanted him to fight back with more passion, to defend himself, at least to speak openly, to share his grief rather than to close it away.

She had said none of it. She had allowed him all the time and the privacy he had wanted, simply watching and grieving for him. She had set aside her own hurt at being excluded, her confusion as to what he had felt for Elissa that he had deceived by silence as to what she was like.

Then she had begun to doubt herself. She had to remember

more clearly the long hours they had spent together in the fever hospital in Limehouse, working all day and so often all night with the one passionate aim of saving lives, containing the infection. Had she deluded herself that their bond was personal, when it was only the shared understanding of suffering? Was it compassion for the sick which had warmed his eyes, and the knowledge that she felt it, devoted herself to it as he did, that had made him reach out to her?

He had never betrayed his marriage even by a word. Was that honor that had bound him, and for which she had so profoundly admired him? Or was there nothing in his silence that concerned her? Not unspoken loneliness at all?

She looked in the glass and saw herself as she had always been, a little short, definitely too broad, a face which her friends would have said was intelligent and full of character. Those indifferent to her would have described it with condescension as agreeable but plain. She had good skin, and good teeth even now, but she lacked prettiness, and the blemishes of age were all too apparent. How could she have been vain enough or silly enough to imagine any man married to Elissa would have felt anything but professional regard for her, a shared desire to heal some small portion of the world's pain?

At least she had not ever spoken aloud. Although that was decency, not lack of emotion. But Kristian would never know that.

Today personal pride and emotions of any sort must be set aside. There was practical work to do, and the truth to be faced. She would go to the prison and visit Kristian, inform him of Fuller Pendreigh's offer and Monk's willingness to continue searching for some alternative theory to suggest to the jury. She already had a plan in mind, but for it to have even the faintest chance of success, she needed Kristian's cooperation. She might have been useless at the arts of romance, but she was an excellent practical organizer, and she had never lacked courage.

By the time she reached the police station, she had decided to speak to Runcorn first, if he was in and would see her, although she intended to insist.

As it happened, no pressure was necessary, and she was conducted with some awe up the narrow stairs to a room rather obviously tidied up for her. Piles of papers with no connection to each other rested on the corner of the shelf, and pencils and quills had been gathered together and pushed into a cup to keep them from rolling. A clean sheet of blotting paper lay over the scratches and marks in the desk. On any other occasion she might have been gently amused.

Runcorn himself was standing up, almost to attention. "Good morning, Lady Callandra," he said self-consciously. "What can I do for you? Please . . . please sit down." He indicated the rather worn chair opposite his desk, and waited carefully until she was seated before he sat down himself. He looked uncomfortable, as if he wished to say something but had no idea how to begin.

"Good morning, Mr. Runcorn," she replied. "Thank you for sparing me your time. I appreciate that you must be very busy, so I shall come to the point immediately. Mr. Monk told me that you were enquiring into Mr. Max Niemann's visits to London, whether he was here at the time of Mrs. Beck's death, and if he had come here on any other occasion recently. Is that correct?"

"Yes, it is, ma'am." Runcorn was not quite certain how to address her, and it showed in his hesitation.

"And was he here?" There was no purpose in prevaricating. She found her heart was knocking in her chest as the seconds hung before he answered. She had no right to know. Please God, Niemann had been here! There had to be someone else to suspect, some other answer. A week ago she needed to find someone else guilty, now she would be grateful simply for the possibility, any belief to cling to.

"Yes," Runcorn replied. "He has been here three times this last year that we know of." He looked deeply unhappy. "But nobody saw him quarrel with Mrs. Beck, ma'am. They were old friends from her time in Vienna. It makes no difference to the case. It would be very nice for us all if we could blame a foreign gentleman, but there isn't any sense in it."

She could not bring herself to argue with him. The hope was too slender, and she was frightened of trying to keep control of herself without it. She stood up very straight. "Thank you for your candor, Mr. Runcorn. I am obliged to you. I believe I am permitted to visit Dr. Beck, since he is not yet proven guilty." It was a statement.

"Yes, ma'am. Of course. Shall I . . ."

"No, thank you. I have taken up enough of your time. I can find my own way downstairs again, and no doubt the sergeant at the desk will direct me where to go after that. Good day, Mr. Runcorn."

He scrambled to open the door for her, only just reaching it before she did. "Good day, ma'am," he said, jerking the door open and banging it against his feet without making the slightest sign that it had caught the corn in his little toe, except a quick intake of breath and the slow letting out of it again.

Downstairs, Callandra spoke to the desk sergeant, and was conducted to the cells. She had composed in her mind what she was going to say, but nothing could prepare her emotions. She stood on the stone floor in the closed-in space, the smell of iron and dust, the strange mixture of coldness and human sweat clogging her throat. This was a time for courage. It was not the place which frightened her, it was meeting Kristian's eyes, and what she might see in them. In the night, she had always found that to name the fear made it more manageable. Was it rejection, her own foolishness exposed and the ensuing embarrassment, that she was afraid of? Or the struggle to keep up the charade that it was all going to be all right—he was not guilty, and even if it took a while, they would prove it. Or was it the acknowledgment at last that perhaps they would not?

Could she cope with that, survive it and go on? She was not sure.

The constable had already spoken to her twice, and she had not responded. He was beginning to fear that she was unwell.

"Of course," she said briskly, swallowing hard. She did not know what he had said, but that seemed a satisfactory response. He led the way down a narrow, echoing passage, her footsteps sounding as if she were shod with iron. He produced a huge key and let her into a cell where Kristian was standing in the middle. He was wearing a collarless shirt and plain, dark trousers. He looked exhausted, and there was a grayish tinge to his skin, even though he appeared to have shaved very recently.

A flicker of surprise crossed his face, pleasure, and then a guardedness. He had had too many shocks, and he looked at nothing without suspicion. He smiled very slightly. It did not touch his eyes.

She realized with a jolt, as if she had missed a step, that he did not know what to expect from her. Somehow that surprised her, even though it was totally reasonable. After all, she had not known what to expect of herself.

Was the constable going to stand there forever? She turned to him. "You may go now," she said briskly. "Lock me in, if it pleases you, or your instructions require it. I shall be perfectly safe. You may take my reticule, if you fear I have some weapon in it. I shall be ready to leave again in an hour."

"Sorry, Miss, you can't stay that long," the sergeant replied. " 'Alf an hour."

"I am not 'Miss,' I am Lady Callandra Daviot," she corrected him firmly. "Then be so good as to return in half an hour—not twenty-five minutes. And don't waste the little time I have by standing there eavesdropping. I have nothing secret to say, but it is private, and not your concern."

He looked taken aback, but decided he could not afford to be offended. "Yes, my lady," he said, locking the door sharply behind him as he retreated.

There was a flash of humor in Kristian's face, but it died

immediately. He struggled to find something to say that was not absurd, and discarded each idea as it came to him.

"Stop it!" she said sharply. "Stop trying to be polite. We have to talk about what matters. Half an hour will go by far too quickly as it is." She saw relief in his eyes, and then fear, real and deep, gouging into the heart of her. It shocked her more than anything physical could have. But before she could respond to it, it was masked, gone again by an effort of will.

She tried to swallow, but her mouth was dry.

There was nowhere to sit down but the cot, and she was not going to sit side by side with him on that. It was low and awkward.

"Oliver Rathbone is in Italy, so Pendreigh has offered to conduct your defense," she said abruptly.

He breathed in, surprised, not certain if he had heard correctly, if he should believe it.

"He is certain you are not guilty," she added.

Bitterness filled his face, and he turned away from her. "Not guilty," he repeated the words softly. "Not guilty of what? I didn't put my hands around her neck and break it, certainly. I was with a patient. I may have miscalculated the time, but not the essential facts." His voice dropped still lower, filled with bitterness. "But am I 'not guilty' of ignoring her, allowing her to fall further and further into gambling and debt and the kind of desperate boredom that took her to Allardyce's studio, alone, where she could be killed?"

She wanted to deny it immediately. It was an absurd assumption of responsibility for someone else's weaknesses, but she could hear in the strain of his voice that it was more real to him than the physical imprisonment of his own circumstances. Perhaps it was easier to consider that kind of guilt than the future and the accusations he would have to answer in court.

He straightened his shoulders, but he still did not turn to face her. His voice shook when he spoke again. "She was so full of life in Vienna. She made every other woman look gray in comparison.

She would have stayed there, you know? It was I who was sick to the heart of it and wanted to come to England."

Callandra said nothing. She sensed in him the need to talk; she was only the audience for something he was saying to himself, perhaps putting into words for the first time.

"She would have gone to Paris, Milan, Rome, anywhere that the struggle was still going on. But I brought her here and turned her into a housewife to spend her time ordering groceries and exchanging gossip about the daily trivia of lives she saw as perfectly safe and ordered, and with nothing on earth to fight for."

"What absolute rubbish!" She exploded in real anger. "There is everything to fight for, and you know that, even if she did not. There is ignorance and pain to battle, disease, crime, selfishness, domestic and social violence, prejudice, authority, bigotry and injustice of every kind and color. And when you have conquered all of those, you can always try addressing poverty, madness, and perfectly ordinary dirt. Or, if those seem too large and indeterminate, what about common or garden loneliness and fear of death, hungry children with no one to tell them they are good . . . and lonely old people neglected by the rest of us—in a hurry and too busy to listen anymore. If she didn't find that exciting enough, or glorious . . . that is not your fault!"

He turned slowly to face her. For a moment, surprise was sharper in his face than anything else. "Honest to the last," he said. "You really are angry! Thank you at least for not patronizing me with false comfort. But I did ignore her. I knew her, and if I had thought more of her and less of myself I would not have tried to change her. Her gambling was beyond control, and I didn't do anything about it. I argued with her, of course. I pleaded, I threatened, reasoned. But I didn't look at the cause, because that would have meant I would have to change as well, and I was not prepared to."

"It's too late for that now, Kristian," she replied. "We have only fifteen minutes left at the most before the constable comes back. Pendreigh will defend you in court. I don't know whether he expects to be paid for it or not. He may do it simply out of belief, and because he would naturally prefer that you were shown to be not guilty, because it reflects less badly on his daughter if she were killed by someone outside the family. It raises less unfortunate speculation in the minds of others. And if he is in control of the defense, he can exercise some restraint over the exploration of her character by the counsel for the prosecution. At least he can do all that anyone could."

"I can't pay him," Kristian said ruefully. "Surely he is as aware of that as I am?"

"I imagine so. But if the matter arises, I shall take care of it. . . ." She saw his embarrassment, but there was no time to be sensitive to it now. "I think money is the last thing that concerns him at the moment," she said honestly. "He is simply a proud man trying with every skill he has to rescue what is left of his family—the truth of how his daughter died, assurance that the wrong man is not punished for it, and some remnant of her reputation preserved as the brave and vital woman she was."

He blinked suddenly, and his marvelous eyes flooded with tears. He turned sharply away from her. "She was . . ." His voice choked.

Callandra felt awkward, lumpy and ordinary, and bitterly alone. But she could not afford the self-indulgence of her own hurt. There would be plenty of time for that later, perhaps years.

"Kristian—someone killed her." She had not intended it to sound as brutal as it did, at least most of her had not. "The best defense would be to find out who it is."

He kept his back to her. "Do you not think that if I knew I would have told you? Told everyone?"

"If you were aware that you knew, yes, of course," she agreed. "But it was nothing to do with Sarah Mackeson, except that she was unfortunate enough to be there, and it was not Argo Allardyce.

We have exhausted the likelihood of it being anyone who wanted to collect money she owed and make an example of her so others would be more in dread not to pay their debts."

"Have you?"

"Yes. William assures me that gamblers will injure people to make them pay, or even murder those whose deaths would become known among other gamblers, but not to cause a major police investigation like this. It draws far too much attention to them. Gambling houses get closed down. Anywhere she had been is likely to face a lot of trouble. It would be stupid. They are not at all happy that she was killed. They have lost business because of it, and no doubt Runcorn will close the house when he is ready."

"Good!"

"Not permanently." She responded with the truth, and then wished she had not.

"Not permanently?" He looked back at her slowly.

"No. They'll simply open up somewhere else, behind an apothecary's shop, or a milliner's, or whatever. It will cost them a little outlay, a little profit, that's all."

He was too weary to be angry. "Of course. It's a hydra."

"It has to have been someone else," she repeated. "Someone personal."

He did not answer.

There was silence in the cell, but it was as if she could hear a clock ticking away the seconds. "I am going to ask William to go to Vienna and find Max Niemann."

He stared at her. "That's absurd! Max would never have hurt her, let alone killed her! If you knew him you wouldn't even entertain the thought for an instant."

"Then who did?" She stared straight back at him, meeting his eyes unrelentingly. It hurt to see the fear deep in them, the loyalties struggling, the pain. But she had seen death often when she had accompanied her husband abroad on his duties. As an army surgeon's wife she had mixed with other military wives on various postings in Europe, and often she had lent what assistance she could to those who were injured or ill. She had no practical training, as Hester had, but intelligence served for much, and experience had taught her more. Her husband had died before the Crimean War, or she would have seen that terrible conflict, too.

"Not Max," Kristian insisted, but there was less certainty in his eyes, and he knew that she had seen it. "He loved her," he repeated. "Callandra . . ."

She could not wait. The constable would be back any moment now. "What was she meeting him for?" she asked.

He winced. His voice was very quiet. "I don't know. I didn't know he was in London until the funeral."

"And I imagine you did not know the other times he was in London this year, either?"

He started to deny it and then stopped, seeing the truth in her face.

"He was here at least twice before," she told him. "He saw Elissa, and not you. Doesn't that call for some explanation?"

His face was ashen gray. She could only guess how much the thought of Max's guilt hurt him. It was a double betrayal on top of the loss, but turning from it now altered nothing, except that it placed the truth one step further away, and his own life in even greater danger. Those were words she could say while still refusing to picture their meaning. At least while she was talking, thinking of what to do, she could keep it at bay. "If not Max Niemann, who else?" she demanded. Her voice sounded peremptory, even hostile. "Kristian! There is no time to be keeping secrets!"

His eyes opened wide. "I don't know! For God's sake, Callandra, I have no idea. She came and went and I barely saw her. We used to be allies in a great cause, friends and lovers once. The last two or three years we've been strangers meeting in the same house and exchanging empty words. I was consumed in my own causes, and I knew hers were demons, taking us both to destruction, but I didn't know what to do about it and I didn't alter my own cause enough to find out."

Guilt was naked in him. She saw it and could not argue. Perhaps he had deliberately not tackled something which was demanding and dangerous, and which he feared was going to eat away a part of him he needed to keep. Perhaps Elissa had been every bit as lonely as he, and equally unable to do anything about it.

No, that was an excuse. She would have been more so. She had no occupation to use her passion and her intellect to fill her time. Even an hour ago Callandra could not have imagined feeling deep and hurting pity for Elissa Beck, however much she had wasted her talents and ignored all the causes Callandra could name. But now she could not escape pity, nor could she wholly excuse Kristian, for all her furious words.

He saw it in her face. He did not try to evade it, but accepted the unspoken change.

"I'll ask William to go to Vienna," she said again.

He was about to speak when they both heard the constable's footsteps loud and sharp along the corridor. There was no time for anything except the briefest of good-byes before she was escorted out and back up the steps to the entrance, gulping in the tainted air of the street, the sunlight and the everyday noises of horses and wheels and people shouting and jostling, exactly as if life were as always.

She found her carriage and gave orders to go straight to Monk's house in Grafton Street.

She found him in, as she had expected. It was still only early afternoon, and they had no plan to follow yet, no ideas to pursue.

Again she did not pretend to the usual courtesies. As soon as the door was closed she began. "I can think of nothing we can do except pursue Max Niemann," she told Monk and Hester. "Kristian says he is certain Niemann could not be guilty, but I think that is loyalty speaking rather than realism." She ignored the sudden widening of Monk's eyes. "It seems from the evidence that Mrs.

Beck was bored and hungering for excitement such as she had known in the past," she continued relentlessly. "Perhaps she was remembering her days in Vienna with regret compared with the present. Niemann turns up in London, still in love with her, remembering her as she was." She took a deep breath, avoiding Monk's eyes, and Hester's also. "She may have led him to suppose she returned his feelings, and then realized what she was doing and changed her mind. We will probably never know what was said, or quite what emotions drew him. People in love can do things they would be incapable of in other circumstances."

What an idiotically facile understatement. She dared not even guess what lunacy she herself could commit. Friends of a lifetime would think she had lost her wits, and probably they would be right.

"He will have gone back to Vienna now," Monk was saying reasonably. Was that pity in his voice?

It stung her. She felt peculiarly naked in his gaze, which saw so much. His own vulnerability had made him attuned to the weaknesses of others, even those he cared for, and on whose grief or foolishness he would rather not have trespassed.

"I assumed he had," she said crisply. "If not, then I have very little idea where to look for him. Also I know of no one in London, except for Kristian, who will hear no ill of him, who can tell us anything of what manner of man he is."

"Vienna?" Hester said in surprise, looking from Callandra to Monk.

"Can you think of anything better?" Callandra asked. She sounded more defiant than she had intended, but she did not apologize.

"I don't know Vienna," Monk said hesitantly. "And I have no German at all." He gave a slight, embarrassed shrug. "I should be no use. Perhaps I could find someone who would?"

"I need a detective, not an errand boy!" Callandra said, fear eating away at her self-control. "If we don't succeed, Kristian could hang." She had put it into words at last. Only anger gave her any semblance of dignity.

"I'll find someone to translate for me," he said with sudden gentleness. "And to guide me around the city. Perhaps the British Embassy can help. I'm perfectly happy to lie to them. Kristian is not British, but Elissa was, and Pendreigh's name might help. From what you say, he has friends in powerful places."

The relief in Callandra was visible, like color returning. "Yes . . . I'll write letters. There's bound to be someone who can spare the time to go with you. You'll have to be discreet about considering an Austrian subject possibly responsible for murder." Her face darkened again. "I don't know how you will be able to bring him back to London. Perhaps it doesn't matter, if you could show that he is guilty—or even that it is extremely likely . . ." She stopped. They all knew that an acquittal for lack of proof would ruin Kristian. He would be free, but only physically. Emotionally, he would be imprisoned in suspicion for the rest of his life. It was a mark of how desperate they were that they even considered it.

Hester glanced at Callandra and then away again. Monk saw her do it, and knew how intrusive and helpless she felt. And yet he had racked his mind over what they might do, even the most ridiculous things, and nothing was better than this.

"I'll go as soon as I've spoken to Kristian and you've written some letters of introduction for me," he promised. "And if Pendreigh knows anyone, you are right, it might help."

"You'll ask about Niemann, his character, his reputation, especially with women, won't you?" Callandra urged. "Someone is bound to know if he had a temper, if he was obsessive about Elissa. There may be stories about the past that someone will know." Her voice was gathering speed, a semblance of conviction in her face. "If he really loved her all that time, as Kristian says, then his closest friends will be aware of it. You'll have to be careful, of course. They won't want to believe ill of him, and certainly not to—"

"Callandra!" he interrupted her. "I know what is necessary. I'll do all that. I'll even bring people back to testify, if I find anything worth telling the court. I promise."

She colored very faintly, but she was not ashamed. The slight treading on someone else's feelings was not even noticeable, far less did it matter. She could think of only one thing—proving that Kristian could be innocent. "I'm sorry," she said briefly. "I wish I were coming with you, but someone must be here, apart from Pendreigh, to see to all that must be done." She did not add "and to pay," but they all knew it was so.

"It is very well you are not," Monk said crisply. "I don't need my elbow jogged every time I open my mouth."

She gave him a sharp look, but there was a vestige of the old humor in it, which was what he had intended to draw from her, even though he meant every word of the remark.

They parted, Hester to make enquiries as to the best way to travel to Vienna and, with money from Callandra, to make the necessary bookings. Monk himself went to see Kristian and ask for as much guidance as he could obtain, and Callandra left to see Pendreigh and secure all the assistance he could offer.

It was now late afternoon and the fog was returning, but she was perfectly prepared to wait for him as long as necessary.

She was received by the footman with civility and told with exaggerated patience that Mr. Pendreigh was unable to receive her without an appointment. He was engaged on a case of great importance and could not be interrupted.

Callandra forced herself to be courteous, putting a smile on her face which felt like something painted on a mask. "Naturally. However, if you give him a note, which I will write, if you are good enough to lend me a pen and paper, I believe that he will wish to make time for me."

"Madam . . ."

"Are you empowered to make family decisions for Mr. Pendreigh?" she asked, her politeness suddenly icy.

"Well . . ."

"I thought not. Be so good as to oblige me and I shall write to him, and he can decide as he will."

The pen and paper were forthcoming, and she wrote a brief note:

My dear Mr. Pendreigh,

I am about to dispatch William Monk to Vienna to trace all possible leads in the matter which concerns us both. This must be done with the greatest haste, for reasons you will appreciate as well as I.

Unfortunately, I have no friends in that city, and am therefore unable to call upon assistance for him myself. Therefore, if you have any advice or practical help to offer, I should be most profoundly grateful for it. I am in the outer room of your offices, and await your reply, in order to carry it to Monk before he departs tonight.

Yours most sincerely,
Callandra Daviot

The response was immediate. A very startled footman returned and conducted her to the study, where Pendreigh rose to his feet, coming around the desk to greet her. He had obviously dismissed another matter in order to see her again. There were papers all over his magnificent walnut desk. The room smelled of cigar smoke, almost dizzying Callandra with old memories of her husband and his friends, long evenings of argument and conversation, talk of war and medicine and the lunacy of politicians.

But that was the past. The present crowded in, dismissing everything else.

"So, Monk has agreed to go to Vienna?" he said eagerly. "That is the best news I have heard in . . . days! I am loath to think it could be Niemann, but what other explanation is there? Runcorn assures me it is not debt," he said, glossing over the euphemism. "And since apparently it cannot be Allardyce, it seems the only explanation left." His face was tense, his eyes hot blue, as if emotions burned behind them he could neither hide nor share, but they seemed to consume him from within. "Lady Callandra, my daughter was an extraordinary woman." His voice shook a little. "If Monk can learn the details of her time in Vienna, of those who loved her, and perhaps envied her, he may well find the key to what happened in Acton Street. She was a woman of the kind of brilliance, a fire that arouses—"

"He will need help." She cut across his emotions gently, and only because time did not allow them. "Someone who knows the city and can interpret for him so that he can find the people he needs and ask what he has to in language precise and subtle enough for the answers to have meaning."

"Yes, yes, of course," he agreed with slight self-consciousness for his emotion. "Naturally. I shall write to the British ambassador. He is a friend of mine, not close, but we have done each other favors in the past. He will not hesitate to provide someone to assist. I daresay he will have friends who were there thirteen years ago and will be familiar with the circumstances of the uprising. Monk will not find it difficult. Elissa will never be forgotten." His eyes shone, and for a moment the last few weeks were washed away. His voice was soft. "If he could bring back an account of how she was then, of her courage, her love of the people and how she inspired them to fight, to sacrifice anything for the cause of freedom, that may explain Niemann's behavior."

He blinked rapidly. "Tell Monk to find someone who will describe the fighting at the barricades, the camaraderie of danger, how they lived, their passions and loyalties. Make the court here see what she was truly like; it will be the best epitaph for her. She deserves that." His voice cracked and he looked away. "Not the woman they will try to present who owed money to sordid little men who never knew anything of her as she really was, men who never had a cause to fight for but their own greed."

He raised his eyes to look at her fully, intensely. "Bring back something that will make them understand how a man could lose his senses over her so that he never forgot her, even thirteen years later, when she was married to his friend, and how he could still feel for her so overwhelmingly that he lost all judgment and morality, so that her rejection of him made him feel as if his whole life were slipping out of his grasp. She was unique, irreplaceable by anyone else." He stopped abruptly, recalling himself to the present only with the severest effort of will. His hands were trembling. He took a deep breath and steadied his voice. "I wish I could go myself, see the places, speak to the people, but I must stay here and prepare the case. I have been advised that it will be very soon. The Crown believe that they have all the evidence they require to proceed."

He lifted one shoulder very slightly, barely a shrug. "I . . . I hardly know where to begin. Kristian is a fine man, but opinionated. He has made many enemies among those in power in the hospital authorities, and very few friends. Those he has served are the poor and the sick, and in many cases, I'm afraid, those already dead. No doubt they would swear he had the patience of a saint and limitless compassion, but they are beyond our reach."

He stared at her steadily. "Impress upon Monk the utmost importance of his errand, Lady Callandra. And please permit me to assist in the cost of it." He returned to the desk and opened one of the drawers. He produced several gold coins and a treasury note. He held them all out. "I shall transfer to your bank a hundred pounds, but in the meantime, take this for his immediate needs, with my deepest gratitude."

She did not require it—her own funds were ample, and she would have given everything she possessed to defend Kristian—but she sensed his need to give as well, and she accepted it.

He returned to the desk and sat down, pulling pen and paper towards him to begin to write in a large, generous scrawl.

She waited, with the first lift of hope she had felt in days. Perhaps in Vienna, Monk would find the truth and prove Kristian's innocence. Afterwards, when Kristian was free, she would bear the confusion of discovering Elissa Beck was a heroine, brave and beautiful, funny and kind.

"Thank you," she said, taking the letter when it was finished. "Thank you very much."

Monk went to see Kristian in prison to learn from him any information at all which might help, no matter how painful or how irrelevant it might seem.

He was not surprised to see him looking haggard, almost shrunken, as if the shock of Elissa's murder and his own arrest had drained the heart out of him, and even something of the physical substance. Monk had seen it before in other men.

"I'm going to Vienna," he said quickly, knowing they had only minutes. "I need all the help you can give me."

Kristian shook his head. "I can't believe Max would have killed her," he said quietly. "Quarreled, perhaps, lost his temper with her for what she was doing, that she was . . . wasting herself." The pain in his voice was like a razor edge. "And even what she was costing me, and the work I believe in. But he wouldn't have hurt her!"

It was brutal to discuss it, but neither of them could afford to be gentle at the expense of reality.

"He came over here to see Elissa . . . not you," Monk said. "Several times." He saw Kristian wince, and noted the confusion in his face.

Kristian shook his head. "He wouldn't have hurt her," he repeated, his voice hoarse.

"Her neck was broken in one movement," Monk reminded him. "It was probably like this." He put his arm in front of him, as if he were holding one hand over someone's mouth, and crushing that person's body to his chest with the other. He made a swift movement. "As if they had struggled and he had tried to hold her, wrenching around, perhaps one foot on hers."

Kristian shuddered, and his mouth pulled strangely twisted.

"He probably didn't mean to kill her," Monk went on. "Perhaps only to stop her from crying out."

Kristian closed his eyes. "And Sarah Mackeson?" he said in a whisper. "Whoever killed her meant to!" He shuddered convulsively. Imagination, or a memory too hideous to bear? Or the realization that Max Niemann could be guilty after all?

"Tell me about him," Monk demanded tensely. "Kristian, for God's sake, give me all you can! I need to find the truth. If it isn't Niemann, then I need to know that. But someone killed them . . . both!"

Kristian made an effort to regain his composure and appeared to concentrate, but still he said nothing, as if the past enclosed him in its reality and the present ceased to be.

"Somebody's going to the rope for it!" Monk said brutally. "If you didn't kill them, don't let it be you! Are you protecting someone?" He had no idea who. Why should Kristian die to save Max Niemann? Or to hide something that had happened in Vienna thirteen years ago? He couldn't possibly think Callandra had any part in it. Did he even know how much she loved him? Monk doubted it.

"I'm not defending anyone!" Kristian said with startling force, almost anger. "I just don't know what to tell you. I haven't any idea who killed them, or why. Do you think I want to hang—or that I don't realize that I almost certainly will?" He managed to say the words with superb control, but looking at his eyes, Monk saw the fear in them, black and bottomless, without faith to build a bridge over the void, nothing but courage. And when at the very last he was utterly alone, with his pain, and oblivion in front of him, all love and friendship and pity left behind, there would be nothing to hold on to.

"Tell me where to look," Monk said, horrified by the vision himself, aware that the similarity between them was far more profound than any difference. "Where did you live? Who were your friends? Who do I look for to ask?"

Reluctantly, each one an effort, Kristian gave him half a dozen names and addresses in three different streets. There was no lift of hope in his voice, no belief. "She was beautiful," he said softly.

"They'll all say that. I don't mean her face." He dismissed it as trivial, but Monk could not. He saw in his mind the haunting loveliness of the woman on Allardyce's canvas. That face was full of passion, dreaming just beyond the grasp, inviting the onlooker to dare anything, imagine the impossible and love it, need it enough to follow her to the ends of the earth.

"I mean the heart of her," Kristian went on. "The will to live, the courage to meet anything. She lit the fire that warmed us all."

Was it memory speaking, or wish, or the kind of emotion that gilds the recollection of people who are loved and lost? Or was it guilt trying to make up for the gulf that had grown between them since then? Would Monk find in Vienna the truth about Kristian as well?

He wrote down what Kristian gave him, then tried to think of something to say in parting which would convey what he wanted to. It was impossible. Frustration. The hunger to believe that Kristian was innocent, not only for his sake but for Callandra's, because she was in love with him, and Monk knew what it was to be in love. He had not wished to be; it laid one open to pain far out of any control.

He wanted Kristian's innocence for Hester, because she believed in him, and would be so hurt for them all. Even for Pendreigh, because he would not be able to contain the disillusion about his daughter if it had been a tragic domestic crime after all. Perhaps also for the woman who stared out of Allardyce's canvas, and surely deserved better than to end a crumpled heap on a studio floor, killed by accident or on purpose by a husband she had destroyed in her crazy compulsion, throwing away everything on the turn of a card or the roll of dice—not after she had fought for everything that mattered infinitely, known freedom and dignity, the right of strangers to govern their own destiny.

"I'll do all I can," he said to Kristian. "We all will."

Kristian nodded, not trusting himself to speak.

CHAPTER
TEN

———

Monk left London on the last train to Dover, so he could catch the first boat of the morning across to Calais and on through Paris to Vienna. It was a journey which would take him three days and eight hours, assuming all went well and he at no time got lost or met with any delays or mechanical faults. A second-class ticket cost eight pounds, five shillings, six pence.

At any other time the journey would have fascinated him. He would have been absorbed by the countryside, the towns he passed, the architecture of the buildings, and the dress and manners of the people. His fellow passengers would have interested him particularly, even though he did not understand their conversation and could deduce only what observation and knowledge of human nature told him. But his mind was intent upon what he would find in Vienna, and upon trying to formulate the questions he should ask in order to learn some truth through the mist of heroic memory.

The journey seemed endless, and he lost the sense of time and place. He was imprisoned with strangers in a padded iron room which swayed and jolted through alternate gray daylight and intense darkness as the late autumn evenings closed in. Sometimes it was clear, sometimes rain pattered against the windows, blurring the view of farmland, villages, bare forests.

He slept fitfully. He found it difficult because there was no space to lie, and after the first night and day his muscles protested against the constant inactivity. He could speak to no one because it seemed all the other passengers in his coach understood only French or German. He exchanged polite nods and smiles, but it did little to break the monotony.

His mind raced over possibilities of success and failure, all the difficulties that might arise to prevent his learning anything of use, above all that he was ignorant not only of the language but of the culture of the people.

And what would success be? That he could prove Niemann guilty? That he could find and take back to London something at least to raise a reasonable doubt? What, for example? No one was going to confess, not in any form that could be used. Sworn testimony of a quarrel, money, or revenge? Would that be sufficient, along with the evidence that Niemann had been in London?

And was Monk taking the chance of accusing and perhaps slandering a man who was innocent?

All that turned over and over in his mind during the long days and interrupted nights as the train crossed France and made its way over the border into Austria, and finally through the city outskirts into the heart of Vienna.

Monk climbed to his feet and retrieved his luggage. His back and legs ached, his mouth was dry and his head pounded with weariness. He longed to smell fresh air and to be able to walk more than a few swaying steps without bumping into everything and having to stand aside as someone passed him.

He alighted onto the platform amid clouds of steam and the rattle and clang of doors, shouted orders, greetings, demands for porters and assistance, little of which he could understand. He grasped his single case and, feeling profoundly lost, he started to walk along the platform, patting his inside pocket again to assure himself his money and letters from Callandra and Pendreigh were still there. He looked for the way out to the street, to begin the struggle to find a cab of some sort with a driver who would understand his request to be taken to the British Embassy.

He was crumpled and dirty, which he loathed, and tired beyond the point of thinking clearly, when at last he was deposited on the steps of Her Britannic Majesty's Embassy to the Court of the Emperor Franz Josef of Austro-Hungaria. He paid the driver in Austrian shillings; from the startled look on his face, Monk gave him far more than he deserved. He climbed up the steps, his case in his hand, knowing he looked like some desperate Englishman fallen on hard times and begging for assistance. It galled his pride.

It was another hour and a half before his letters gained him an audience with a senior aide to the ambassador, who explained that His Excellency was heavily engaged in matters of state for the next two days at the least. However, if a guide and interpreter were all Monk required, no doubt something could be done. He looked down at Pendreigh's letter, spread open on the desk in front of him, and Monk thought he saw more respect in the man's face than affection. It did not surprise him. Pendreigh was a formidable man, a good friend perhaps, but a bad enemy for certain. But then, no doubt the same would have been said of Monk himself. He recognized the impatience, the ambition to assess and to judge.

"Thank you," he accepted stiffly.

"I will send someone in the morning," the aide replied. "Where are you staying?"

Monk glanced down at his suitcase and then at the man, his eyebrows raised very slightly. The question had been intended as patronizing, and they both knew it.

The aide blushed very slightly. "The Hotel Bristol is very good. It is not inspiring from the outside, but it is beautiful inside, especially if you like marble. The food is excellent. It is first in the Karntner Ring. They speak excellent English, and will be delighted to help you."

"Thank you," Monk said graciously, relieved to have Callandra's money, and Pendreigh's, so that the charge was immaterial to him. "I shall be obliged if whoever is good enough to assist me would present themselves there at nine o'clock at the latest, so I can begin this extremely urgent matter as soon as possible. You are no doubt aware of the tragic death of Mr. Pendreigh's daughter, Elissa von Leibnitz, who was something of a heroine in this city." He was highly satisfied to see from the man's blush that he was not.

"Of course," the aide said soberly. "Please convey my condolences to the family."

"Of course," Monk muttered, picking up his case and going out into the distinctly chilly night air, aware of the sharp east wind like a slap on his skin.

He was up and breakfasted early the next morning, and was waiting, his temper already raw, when a fair-haired youth of no more than fourteen or fifteen approached him in the magnificent marble lobby of the hotel. He was slender, and his face had a freshly scrubbed look, probably occasioned by the weather outside. He looked more like a schoolboy than a servant on an errand.

"Mr. Monk?" he asked with a certain eagerness which instantly confirmed Monk's impression. He had probably come from the embassy to say that his father, or brother, could assist Monk in the afternoon, or worse still, tomorrow.

Monk answered him rather curtly. "Yes? Have you a message for me?"

"Not exactly, sir." His blue eyes were bright but he maintained his self-possession. "My name is Ferdinand Gerhardt, sir. The British ambassador is my uncle. I believe you would like someone to guide you around Vienna and interpret for you on occasion. I should be glad to offer my services." He stood to attention, polite, eager, a curious mixture of English schoolboy and young Austrian aristocrat. He did not quite click his heels.

Monk was furious. They had sent him a child, as if he wished to while away a week or so seeing the sights. It would be inexcusable to be rude, but he could not waste either time or Callandra's money in evasion.

"I am not sure what you were told," he said with as much good grace as he could manage. "But I am not here on holiday. A woman has been murdered in London, and I am seeking information about her past here in Vienna, and friends of hers who may be able to lead me to the truth of what happened. If I fail, an innocent man may be hanged, and soon."

The boy's eyes widened, but he did his best to maintain the sort of calm his imagination told him was dignified. "I'm very sorry, sir. That sounds a terrible thing. Where would you like to begin?"

"How old are you?" Monk said, trying to conceal his mounting anger and sense of desperation.

A couple of very pretty women walked past them, giving them a curious glance.

Ferdinand stood very straight. "Fifteen, sir," he said softly. "But I speak excellent English. I can translate anything you wish. And I know Vienna very well." There was a definite touch of pink in his cheeks.

Monk had no memory whatever of having been fifteen. He was embarrassed and angry, and he had no idea where to begin. "The events I need to enquire about took place when you were two years old!" he said between clenched teeth. "Which is going to limit your abilities considerably, no matter how excellent your English."

Ferdinand was embarrassed also, but he did not give up easily. He had been handed an adult job to do, and he intended to discharge it with honor. His eyes did not waver from Monk's, even though Monk's were distinctly challenging and unhappy. "What year exactly, sir?"

"Eighteen forty-eight," Monk replied. "I expect you learned about it in school." It was not a question, simply a rather tart observation.

"Actually, not very much," Ferdinand admitted with a slight tightening of his lips. "Everybody says something different. I'd jolly well like to know the truth! Or rather more of it, anyway." He glanced around at the marble-faced hotel lobby where a small group of well-dressed gentlemen had come in and were talking. Two ladies seated on well-upholstered chairs exchanged a piece of entertaining gossip, bending towards each other very slightly to bridge the gap between them created by the billowing of their skirts.

"Are you going to stay in Vienna for a while?" Ferdinand asked. "If you are, maybe you'd be better to find rooms over in the Josefstadt, or somewhere like that. Cheaper, too. That's where people sit around in cafés and talk about ideas and . . . and plan sedition. At least, so I've heard," he added quickly.

There was no better alternative offering, except wandering around alone, unable to understand more than a few words, so with as much gratitude as he could assume, Monk accepted. He checked out of his room, settled the bill, and with his case in his hand, followed Ferdinand down the steps of the hotel and into the busy street of a strange city with very little idea of what to do or where to begin in what was looking like an increasingly hopeless task.

"You may call me Ferdi, if you don't mind, sir," the boy said, watching carefully as if Monk had been not only a stranger in the city but one lacking in the ordinary skills of survival, such as watching for traffic before crossing the road, or paying attention so as not to become separated from his guide and thus getting lost. Perhaps he had younger brothers or sisters and was occasionally put in charge of them. With a considerable effort, Monk schooled himself to be amused rather than angry.

Most of the morning was taken up in finding a more suitable accommodation in a very small guest house in the less-expensive quarter, where it seemed students and artists lived. "Revolutionaries," Ferdi informed Monk in a discreet manner, making sure he was not overheard.

"Are you hungry?" Monk asked him.

"Yes sir!" Ferdi responded instantly, then looked uncomfortable. Perhaps a gentleman did not so readily admit to such needs, but it was too late to take it back. "But of course I can wait a while, if you prefer to ask questions first," he added.

"No, we'll eat," Monk said unhappily. This whole thing was abortive. He had made Callandra believe he could learn something of use when it was beyond his capabilities even to ask for a slice of bread or a cup of tea—or, as it was far more likely to be, coffee.

"Very good," Ferdi said cheerfully. "I suppose you have some money?" he added as an afterthought. "I'm afraid I haven't much."

"Yes, I have plenty," Monk said without relish. "I think it is perfectly fair that the least I do is offer you dinner."

Ferdi duly found a small café, and with his mouth full of excellent steak, he asked Monk who, precisely, it was that he was looking for.

"A man named Max Niemann," Monk replied, also with his mouth full. "But I need to learn as much as possible about him before he is aware that I am looking for him." He had decided to trust Ferdi with a reasonable portion of the truth. He had very little to lose. "It is possible that it was he who killed the woman in London." Then, seeing Ferdi's face, he realized that he had no right whatever to endanger him, even slightly. Perhaps his parents would prefer that he did not even know about such subjects as murder. Although that consideration was rather late. "If you are to help me, you must do exactly what I say," he said sternly. "If I allow any harm to come to you, I daresay the Viennese police will throw me in prison and I shall never find my way out."

"That would be very unfortunate," Ferdi agreed gravely. "I gather what we are about to do is a trifle dangerous."

It was completely idiotic. Monk was foundering out of his depth and trying very hard not to let despair drown him.

Ferdi looked keen and attentive. "What would you like me to ask someone, sir? What is it you really need to know, other than who killed this poor lady?"

There was nothing to lose. "Say that I am an English novelist, writing a book about the uprising in '48," he began, the ideas form-ing in his head as he spoke. "Ask for as many firsthand stories as you can find. The names I am concerned with are Max Niemann, Kris-tian Beck and Elissa von Leibnitz."

"Absolutely!" Ferdi said fervently, his eyes bright with admiration.

The rest of that day was largely a matter of asking people tenta-tively and being more or less dismissed. By the time Monk went to bed in his new lodgings, saying thank-you in some approximation of German, he felt lost and inadequate. He lay in the dark, acutely conscious that Hester was not beside him. She was in London, trusting that he would bring back weapons of truth to defend Kris-tian. And Kristian would be lying awake in a narrow prison cot. Was he also trusting Monk to find some element which would be a key to make sense of tragedy? Or did he know it already, and trusted with just as much passion that Monk would wander pointlessly around a strange city where all speech was a jumble of noise, every-body else was rushing about their business, or strolling in fashion-able idleness, but belonging, understanding?

Damn them! He would seek out the past! He would find it, whether it meant anything or not. If nothing else, Max Niemann would be able to tell him about Kristian as he had been then. But before he approached him, he would hear the same stories from other people, so he could judge the truth of Niemann's account. What he needed was another member of that group from sixteen years ago, from Kristian's list.

He finally drifted off to sleep with a firmer plan in mind, and did not waken until it was broad daylight. He was extremely hungry.

With much nodding and smiling, his hostess gave him an ex-cellent breakfast with rather more rich, sweet pastry than he cared for, but the best coffee he had ever tasted. Repeating *Danke schön* over and over, he smiled back, and then set out with a freshly scrubbed and very eager Ferdi, who had spent all evening and a good part of the night reading accounts of the '48 rising. He was full of a jumble of facts and stories that had gathered the patina and exaggeration of legend already. He relayed them with great enthusiasm as they walked along the street side by side towards the magnificence of the Parliament and the gardens beyond, now winter bare.

"It actually sort of began in the middle of March," Ferdi told him. "There was an uprising in Hungary already, and it spread here. Of course, Hungary is vast, you know? About six or seven times as big as Austria. All the nobles and senior clergy were due to meet in the Landhaus. That's on the Herrengasse." He pointed ahead of them. "That's over there. I can take you if you want. Anyway, it seems they were asking for all sorts of reforms, particularly freedom of the press and to get rid of Prince Metternich. Students, artisans, and workers, mostly, forced their way into the building. About one o'clock a whole lot of Italian grenadiers shot into the crowd and killed thirty or more ordinary people—I mean, they weren't criminals or the very poor, or lunatics like the French revolutionaries were in '89, last century."

He stared at Monk as they came to the Auerstrasse and were obliged to wait several moments for a break in the traffic to cross.

"That was the really big one," he went on. "Ours was over within the year." He smiled almost apologetically. "Pretty much everything is back as it was. Of course, Prince Metternich is gone, but he was seventy-four anyway, and he'd been around since before Waterloo!" His voice rose in incredulity as if he could barely grasp anyone having been alive so long.

Monk hid a smile.

"Then the barricades went up all over the city," Ferdi went on, matching his stride to Monk's. "But it was killing the people that really drove them to send Metternich into exile." A flash of pity lit his young face. "I suppose that's a bit hard, when you're that old.

Anyway," he resumed, "in May they drove the whole court out of Vienna, Emperor Ferdinand and everyone. They all went to Innsbruck. Actually, you know, there was trouble just about everywhere that year." He checked to make sure Monk was listening. "In Milan and Venice, too, which gave us a lot of bother. They are ours as well, even though they're Italian. Did you know that?"

"Yes," Monk answered, remembering his own trip to Venice, and how the proud Venetians had hated the Austrian yoke on their shoulders. "Yes, I did know."

"We've sort of got the German Empire to the northwest, and the Russian Empire to the northeast, and us in the middle," Ferdi went on, increasing his pace to keep up with Monk's longer legs. "Anyway, in May they formed a committee of public safety— sounds just like the French, doesn't it? But we didn't have a guillotine, and we didn't kill many people at all."

Monk was not certain if that was pride or a slight sense of anticlimax.

"You must have killed some," he responded.

Ferdi nodded. "Oh, we did! We made rather a good job of it, actually, in October. They hanged the war minister, Count Baillat de Latour—from a lamppost. The mob did. Then they forced the government and the Parliament to go to Olmutz, which is in Moravia— that's north of here, in Hungary." He heaved a great sigh. "But it all came to nothing. The aristocracy and the middle classes—which is us, I suppose—supported Field Marshal Prince Windischgrätz, and it was all put down. I expect that was when your friends were very brave, and did whatever it was you need to find out about."

"Yes," Monk agreed, looking about him at the busy, prosperous streets with their magnificent architecture, and trying to imagine Kristian here, and Elissa, battling for reform of such a vast, seemingly untouchable force of government. He had seen in every direction the superb facades of the state and government buildings, the mansions and theaters, museums, opera houses and galleries. What fire of reform had burned inside them that they dared attempt to overthrow such power? They must have cared passionately, more than most people care about anything. Where would you ever begin to shake the foundations of such monolithic control?

He could see in Ferdi's young face that something of it had caught him also.

"I need to find the people on my list," he said aloud. "The people who were there then, and knew my friends."

"Right-oh!" Ferdi answered, blushing with happiness and enthusiasm, striding out even more rapidly so Monk was now obliged to lengthen his own step to keep up. "Have you got money for a carriage?"

That afternoon they saw streets where the barricades had been, even chips out of stone walls where bullets had struck and ricocheted. They had supper in one of the cafés in which young men and women had sat huddled over the same tables, planning revolution by candlelight, a new world of liberty on the horizon, or mourned the loss of friends, perhaps in silence but for the rain on the windows and the occasional tramp of passing feet on the pavement outside.

Monk and Ferdi ate soup and bread in silence, each lost in thoughts which might have been surprisingly similar. Monk wondered about the bond between people who shared the hope and the sacrifice of such times. Could anything that came in the pedestrian life afterwards break such a bonding? Could anyone who had not been in that danger and hope enter into the circle or be anything but an onlooker?

In the flickering candlelight, with the murmur of conversation at the little tables around them, it could have been thirteen years ago. Ferdi's young face, flushed and lit golden by the candle in an upright wine bottle, could have been one of theirs. The smells of coffee and pastry and wet clothes from the rain outside would be the same, the water streaking the windows, wavering the reflecting street lamps, and as the door opened and closed, the splash of water, the brief hiss of carriage wheels. Except that the dreams were gone, the air was no longer one of excitement, danger and sacrifice; it was comfortable, rigidly set prosperity and law in the old way, with the old rules and the old exclusions. The powerful were still powerful, and the poor were still voiceless.

In spite of the defeat, Monk envied Kristian and Max their past. He had no memory of belonging, of being part of a great drive for his own people, any cause fought for or even believed in. He had no idea if he had ever cared about an issue passionately enough to fight for it, die for it, enough to bond him to others in that friendship that is the deepest trust, and goes through life and death in a unity greater than common birth and blood, education or ambition, and makes you one of a whole that outlasts all its parts.

The closest he had ever come to that was fighting a cause for justice, with Hester, and then with Oliver Rathbone and Callandra. That was the same feeling, the will to succeed because it mattered beyond individual pain or cost, exhaustion or pride. It was a kind of love that enlarged them all.

How could it possibly be that Kristian or Max Niemann could have murdered Elissa, no matter how she had changed in the years since?

He pushed his empty cup away and stood up. "Tomorrow we must find people who fought in May, and in October," he said as Ferdi stood up, too. "The ones on my list. I can't wait any longer. Begin asking. Say it is for anything you like, but find them."

The first successful conversation was stilted because it was translated with great enthusiasm by Ferdi, but of necessity went backwards and forwards far more slowly than it would have had Monk understood a word of German.

"What days!" the old man said, sipping appreciatively at the wine Monk had bought for them, although he insisted on water for Ferdi, to the boy's disgust. "Yes, of course I remember them. Wasn't so long ago, although it seems like it now. Except for the dead, you'd think they never happened."

"Did you know many of the people?" Ferdi asked eagerly. He had no need to pretend his ardor; it shone in his eyes and quivered in the edge to his voice.

"Of course I did! Knew lots of them. Saw the best—those that lived through it, and those that didn't." He reeled off half a dozen names. "Max Niemann, Kristian Beck, Hanna Jakob, Ernst Stifter, Elissa von Leibnitz. Never forget her. Most beautiful woman in Vienna, she was. Like a dream, a flame in the darkness of those days. As much courage as any man . . . more!"

Ferdi's eyes shone. He was leaning forward, lips parted.

Monk tried to look skeptical, but he had seen Allardyce's painting of her, and he knew what the old man meant. It was not a perfection of form, or even a delicacy of feature, it was the passion inside her, the force of her vision, which made her unique. She had had the power to carry others into her dreams.

The old man was frowning at him. He spoke to Ferdi, and Ferdi smiled at Monk. "He says I'm to tell you that if you don't believe him, you should go and ask others. Shall I tell him you'd like to do that?"

"Yes," Monk agreed quickly. "Ask him about Niemann and Beck, but don't sound too keen." He must find something relevant to the personal passions and envies, more than a history lesson, however ardent.

Ferdi ignored the warning with great dignity. He turned to the old man, and Monk was obliged to listen to a quarter of an hour of animated conversation, mostly from the old man, but with Ferdi putting in increasingly excited questions. Ferdi kept glancing at Monk, willing him not to interrupt.

As soon as they were outside again in the rain and the shifting pattern of gas lamps, the wind sharp-edged and cold in their faces, Ferdi began. "Max Niemann was one of the heroes," he said excitedly. "He came out for the reforms straightaway, not like some people, who waited to see the chances of success or what their friends or family would think of them."

They came to the corner of the street and a carriage swished by, spraying mud and water. Monk leaped backwards but Ferdi was too absorbed in his story to notice. He was wet up to the knees, and oblivious of it. As soon as the street was clear, he set out across the roadway and Monk hastened to keep up with him.

"He was brave as well," Ferdi went on. "He was right out there on the barricades when the real fighting began. So was Elissa von Leibnitz. He told me one story of how when the fighting was really awful in October, after they'd hanged the minister and the army just charged in, several young men were shot and fell in the street. She took a gun herself and went out, shouting and waving, firing the gun at the soldiers. She knew how to and she wasn't scared. All by herself, she drove them back until others could crawl out and get the wounded men back behind the barricades."

"Where was Kristian?" Monk asked. "Or Max?"

"Max was one of the ones hurt," Ferdi replied, glancing sideways to make sure Monk was keeping up with him in the dark. "Kristian was trying to stop a man from bleeding to death from a terrible wound. He had one hand holding a pad on the man's shoulder, and he was shouting to Elissa to stop, or someone to help her, and waving his other arm."

"But Elissa wasn't hurt?"

"Apparently not. There was one woman called Hanna who was with them. She went right out in front, too. She was one of those who dragged the wounded men back. And she used to carry messages, too, right through where the army had taken the city back, to where their own revolutionaries were cut off at the far side. And carry messages to their allies in the government as well."

"Can we speak to her?" Monk asked eagerly. It would be a first-hand account from another person who knew them well. She might have noticed more of relationships, the undercurrents of envy or passion between Kristian and Max.

"I asked," Ferdi agreed, his face suddenly very sober. "But he thinks she is one of those killed in the uprising. He told me roughly where Max Niemann still lives. He's very respectable now. The government hasn't forgotten which side he was on when it mattered, and they just can't afford to punish everybody, or it would all get out of hand again. Too many people think highly of Herr Niemann." He waved his hands excitedly. "But that's not all. It seems that your friend Herr Beck was a pretty good hero too, a real fighter. Not only brave, but pretty clever, a sort of natural leader. He had the courage to face the enemy down. Could read people rather well, and knew when to call a bluff, and just how far to go. He was tougher than Niemann, and prepared to take the risks."

"Are you sure?" It did not sound like the man Monk had seen. Surely Ferdi had it the wrong way around. "Beck is a doctor."

"Well, he could have it wrong, I suppose, but he seemed absolutely sure."

Monk did not argue. His feet ached and he was exhausted. He felt cold through to the bone, and it was still more than a mile back to his room in the Josefstadt. Before he could even think of that he must make certain he found a carriage to take Ferdi safely home. This was the boy's city, but Monk still felt responsible for him. "We'll start again tomorrow," he said decisively. "Speak to some more of the people on the list."

"Right!" Ferdi agreed. "We're not finding anything very helpful . . . are we?" He looked anxiously at Monk.

Monk had his own feelings. "Not yet. But we will. Perhaps tomorrow."

Ferdi was prompt in the morning, and with renewed zeal they planned where to continue their search. This time they found a charming woman who must have been in her twenties thirteen years ago, and now was comfortably plump and prosperous.

"Of course I knew Kristian," she said with a smile as she admitted them to her sitting room and offered them a choice of three kinds of coffee, and melting, delicious cake, even though it was barely half past ten in the morning. "And Max. What a lovely man!"

"Kristian?" Monk asked quickly, by now catching from Ferdi a large part of the sense of the conversation. "Is she speaking of Kristian?"

But apparently it was Max she considered lovely.

"Not Kristian?" Monk persisted.

Little by little, Ferdi drew from her a picture of Max as quieter than Kristian, with a wry sense of humor and an intense loyalty. Yes, of course he was in love with Elissa, anyone could see that! But she fell in love with Kristian, and that was the end of the matter.

Was there jealousy? She shrugged her shoulders and smiled across at Monk with a little laugh, sad and rueful. Of course there was, but only a fool fights the inevitable. Kristian was the leader, the man with the courage of his dreams and the nerve to make the decisions and pay the price. But it was all a long time ago now. She was married with four children. Kristian and Elissa had gone to England. Max lived very well, somewhere in the Neubau District, she thought. Was Monk staying long in Vienna? Did he know that Herr Strauss the younger had been appointed Keppelmeister to the National Guard during the uprising? No? Well, he had. Mr. Monk could not visit Vienna and not listen to Herr Strauss. It would be like being a fish and not swimming. It was to deny nature and insult the good God who created happiness.

Monk promised that he would, thanked her for her hospitality, and urged Ferdi to leave.

They saw two more people on Kristian's list, and they confirmed all that they had heard so far. According to them both, the revolutionaries had worked largely in groups, and the group of which Kristian Beck had been the leader consisted of seven or eight people. Max Niemann, Elissa, and Hanna Jakob had been in it from the beginning. Another half dozen or so had come and gone. Four had been killed, two at the barricades, one in prison, and Hanna Jakob tortured and shot in one of the back streets when she would not betray her fellows.

Monk felt sick, forced to listen to a shocked and white-faced Ferdi recounting the story in the comfortable surroundings of Monk's guest house, where they had returned, hands frozen from a hard wind out of a clear sky smelling like snow.

They sat in front of the fire with the remains of cakes and beer on the table between them and the last of the fading sunlight high in the windows as the early evening closed in. He tried to imagine how Kristian had felt when he heard it sharp with the shock of immediacy thirteen years ago. Hanna had been one of them, alive only hours ago, her pain barely over, her life as precious and urgent as their own. Had he sat in a quiet room somewhere, about this time of year, with the wind cold outside, and thought of Hanna dying in an alley among enemies, silent to save the rest of them? What guilt did he feel simply because he was alive? What had they done to try to rescue her? Or had they known nothing about it until it was too late?

"It seems Dr. Beck was a real firebrand," Ferdi said, blinking hard and swallowing. "They respected him like mad, because he never told anybody else to do things he wasn't prepared to do himself. And he saw several steps ahead, thinking what his decisions would do, what they might cost." He looked down at the table, his voice soft. "He really hated the commander of one of the divisions of police, Count von Waldmuller. There was sort of . . . a feud between them, because this Count von Waldmuller was a great believer in military discipline, and certain people being fit to rule, and others not. He was pretty rigid, and he and Dr. Beck got across each other, and every new thing made it worse."

"What happened to him?" Monk asked.

"He got shot during the fighting in October," Ferdi replied with satisfaction. "In the streets, actually. He led the army against the barricades and Dr. Beck led the resistance." He pulled a rueful face. "The revolutionaries lost, of course, but at least they got Count Waldmuller. I'd love to have been there to see that! It was one of the count's lieutenants who found out where that group were all going to be, and brought the troops up behind them." He shivered and reached for another cake. "But he did it too late. Elissa von Leibnitz had taken a message to one of the other groups, and reinforcements came. Dr. Beck led them out to fight and they were so brave, and acted as if they knew they'd win, that Count Waldmuller fell back, and got shot. Lost his leg, apparently." He grinned suddenly. "Has a wooden one now. They said it was Dr. Beck who shot him! I know where Max Niemann lives. Shall we go to see tomorrow?"

"Not yet," Monk said thoughtfully. He was aware of Ferdi's acute disappointment, and also rather surprised that his father had not curtailed his time spent assisting someone of whom they had no personal knowledge whatever. Were Pendreigh's and Callandra's letters really of such force as to allay all anxieties?

"But you know everything about him," Ferdi urged, leaning forward and demanding Monk's attention. "What else can I find out? Dr. Beck lives in England now. He and Elissa von Leibnitz fell in love and married." His face was bleak for a moment. "The others are dead. What's wrong, Mr. Monk? Isn't it what you needed?"

"I don't know. It certainly isn't what I expected." It had given him nothing to indicate that Max Niemann had gone to London seeking to rebuild an old love affair, and when rejected had lost control of himself and murdered two women. Every one of the stories Ferdi had told him only emphasized the bonds of loyalty among them all, and it seemed very clear that Elissa had chosen Kristian from the beginning, and married him before they left Vienna. If Niemann had come imagining a change in love or loyalty, then

Monk would have to find irrefutable proof of it before it would be of any use to Pendreigh in court.

"What about Beck's friends who weren't revolutionaries?" he asked. "He must have known other people. What about his family?"

Ferdi sat up. "I'll find them! That should be very easy. I know just where to ask. My mother's brother knows everyone, or if he doesn't, he can find out. He is in the government."

Monk winced, but he had already been away from London for almost a week. He could not afford the luxury of being careful. He accepted.

It took another exhausting, precious two days to engineer the meeting, and since they apparently spoke excellent English, to his chagrin, Ferdi was not required. Monk promised to report to him anything that was of interest, wording his pledge carefully so that it allowed him to exclude bits at his own judgment, and saw Ferdi's face light up with belief. Then he felt a sharp and totally unexpected stab of guilt. Ferdi was not listening to his precisely chosen words, but to the honest intent he believed in. Monk realized with surprise that he would fulfill the boy's expectation. Ferdi's opinion mattered to him more than the guarding of the case, or the trouble it would take him to explain to anybody . . . except Hester. She had earned that right, and it was also comfortable and often very productive to share his thoughts, even when they were half formed or mistaken, with her. It clarified his own mind, and she frequently added to his perception. He realized with sudden misery how much he missed her now.

Fifteen-year-old Ferdi, whom he barely knew, was a totally different matter. Nevertheless, he would do it.

Kristian's elder brother and his wife lived in Margareten, a discreet but obviously well-to-do residential area to the south of the city. Monk had the address, and had picked up enough German from experience with Ferdi to acquire a cab and arrive there at five o'clock in the darkening afternoon, as had been arranged.

He was admitted by a footman, much as he might have been in England, and then to a beautiful, rather ornate withdrawing room, although he hesitated to think of it by that term. It was far too formal to give the feeling of a place where one withdrew for comfort and privacy after a meal, to talk to guests or one's family, and to relax at the end of the day.

Within minutes he was joined by Josef and Magda Beck. Monk was intrigued by how like Kristian his brother was. He had the same build—the average height, slender but strong body, good breadth of chest, neat well-manicured hands which he moved very slightly when he spoke. His hair was also very dark, and good, but his eyes had not the extraordinary, luminous beauty of Kristian's. Nor had his features the passion or the sensuality of the mouth.

His wife, Magda, was fairer, although her skin had an olive warmth to it, and her eyes were golden brown. She was not so much pretty as pleasing.

"How do you do, Mr. Monk," Josef said stiffly. "I understand from your letter that you have some serious news about my brother." He did not sound startled or afraid, but perhaps those were private emotions he would not have betrayed in front of a stranger. If Magda felt differently within herself, she was too dutiful not to follow his example.

Monk had already decided that directness, up to a point, was the tactic most likely to be productive, and therefore to help Kristian, if that were possible. His hope for that was dwindling day by day.

"Yes," he said gravely. "I am not sure if you are aware that his wife was killed about three weeks ago . . ." He saw from the horror in their faces that they were not. "I'm sorry to have to tell you such tragic news."

Magda was clearly distressed. "That's terrible." Her voice was charged with emotion. "How is Kristian? I know he loved her very deeply."

He searched her face to read what her own emotions were. How well had she known Elissa? Was her sorrow only for Kristian, or for her sister-in-law as well? He decided to keep back the rest of the story until he was more certain of their reactions. "He is very shocked, of course," he replied. "It was sudden and profoundly distressing."

"I'm sorry," Josef said rather formally. "I must write to him. It is good of you to have told us." He made no remark of surprise that Kristian had not told them himself. The omission gave Monk a feeling of unease. In his mind's eye, he saw Hester's turmoil of distress over Charles's pain, and it gave him a sharp sense of loneliness for Hester. He thought of his own sister, Beth, in Northumberland, and how seldom he wrote to her. He was the one who had broken the bond, first by leaving the north, then by answering her letters only perfunctorily, giving nothing of himself but bare facts, no feelings, no sharing of laughter or pain, none of the details that make a picture of life. He had done it for so long that Beth wrote only at Christmas and birthdays now, like someone who has had the door closed in her face too often.

The conversation seemed to have died. They assumed he had called merely to inform them of Elissa's death. In a moment they would politely wish him good-bye. He must say more, just to jolt them into reaction. "It is not so simple as that," he said a trifle abruptly. "Mrs. Beck was murdered, and the police have arrested Kristian."

That certainly provoked all the emotional reaction he could have wished. Magda buckled at the knees and sank onto the sofa behind her, gasping for breath. Josef went absolutely white and swayed on his feet, ignoring his wife.

"God in heaven!" he said sharply. "This is terrible!"

"Poor Kristian," Magda whispered, pressing her hands up to her face. "Do you know what happened?"

"No," Monk replied with less than the truth. "I think the beginning of it, and perhaps even the end, may be here in Vienna."

Josef jerked up his head. "Here? But Elissa was English, and they both lived there since '49. Why should it be here? That makes no sense at all."

Magda looked at Monk. "But Kristian didn't do it, did he!" It was an exclamation, almost a challenge. "I know he is very passionate about things, but fighting at the barricades, even killing people— strangers . . . for the cause of greater freedom . . . is quite different from murdering someone you know. I can't say we ever understood Kristian. He was always . . ." She gave a tiny shrug of her shoulders. "I'm not sure how to explain it without giving a false impression. He made quick decisions, he knew his own mind; he was a natural leader, and other men looked to him because he never never showed his fear."

"He was hotheaded," Josef said simply, looking at Monk, not at Magda. "He didn't always listen to reason, and he had no patience. But what my wife is trying to say is that he was a good man. The things he did which were violent were for ideals, not out of anger or desire for himself. If he killed Elissa, then there was a cause for it, one which would surely act as mitigation. I assume that is what you are looking for, although I doubt it is actually here in Vienna. It is all too long ago. Whatever occurred here is long since resolved, or forgotten." He was looking at Monk and did not notice the shadow pass across Magda's face.

"Did you know a man named Max Niemann?" Monk asked them both.

"I've heard of him, of course," Josef replied. "He was very active in the uprisings, but I believe he has made a good life for himself since then. There were reprisals, naturally, but not long, drawn-out reprisals. Niemann survived quite well. It was wise of Kristian to have left Austria, and certainly for his wife to have. She became . . ." He hesitated. "She was quite famous among a certain group. But all the same, I don't find it easy to imagine that someone held on to a hunger for revenge for her part in the uprisings all those years, and went all the way to England to kill her." He frowned. "I wish I could be of assistance to you, but I assure you, that really is too unlikely to waste your time with." He made a slight gesture with his hands. "But, of course, we will do anything we can. Do you have names, anyone you wish to meet or to make enquiries about? I know several people in government and in the police who would assist, if I asked them. It might be wiser not to mention that Kristian himself is suspected."

"It would be helpful to hear other stories of his part in the uprising," Monk said, trying to keep the confusion and disappointment out of his voice. "Even other opinions of Kristian himself."

"You want witnesses for his character?" Magda asked quickly. She glanced up at Josef, then back at Monk. "I'm sure Father Geissner would be willing to do that, even to travel to London, if that would help."

"Father Geissner?" For a moment Monk was lost.

"Our priest," she explained. "He is very highly regarded, even though he supported the uprisings, and actually ministered to the wounded at the barricades. He would be the best advocate I can think of, and—"

"Absolutely!" Josef agreed instantly and with enthusiasm. "Well done, my dear. I don't know why I didn't think of him. I shall introduce you—tomorrow, if you wish?"

"Thank you." Monk grasped the unlikely thought immediately. Perhaps the priest would give him a clearer picture of Niemann. He might have observed subtler emotions than the rather colorful stories that had grown up in the thirteen intervening years, mostly of the acts of courage and loyalty or betrayal, death and the closing in of the old oppressions again. The human jealousies or wounds were lost in the political needs.

"We must see him anyway, to have a mass said for Elissa's soul," Magda added, making the sign of the cross.

Josef hastily did the same, and bowed his head for a moment.

Monk was taken by surprise. He had not realized that Kristian was Catholic. It was another dimension he had not considered. For that matter, he did not know what his own religious background was. What had his parents believed? He had no memory whatever of having gone to church as a child. But then he had only the barest snatches of anything at all from that part of his life. It was all gone, as if dreamed long ago. Surely if faith was worth anything it should inform a person's entire life. It should be the rock upon which everything was built, guide all moral decision, and in time of distress give the comfort to sustain, to heal, to give meaning to conflict and make tragedy bearable.

He looked again at Magda Beck's round, serious face, and saw a flicker of some inner certainty in it, or at least the knowledge of where to reach for it.

When he got home he must make sure that Kristian had a priest to visit him as often as he wished and it was allowed.

"Thank you very much," he said with more confidence. "I should like very much to speak with Father Geissner."

"Of course." Josef looked happier. He had been able to do something to help.

Monk was about to ask where and when they should meet, and then take his leave, when the footman came to announce the arrival of Herr and Frau von Arpels, and Josef told him to show them in.

Von Arpels was slender, with wispy fair hair and a lean, rather sharp face. His wife was plain, but when she spoke her voice was surprisingly attractive, very low and a little husky.

Introductions were made, and Josef immediately told them of Elissa's death, although not the cause of it. Suitable distress was expressed, and both of them offered to pray for her soul and to attend mass for her.

Von Arpels turned to Monk. "Are you staying in Vienna long, Herr Monk? There are many sights for you to see. Have you been to the opera yet? Or the concert hall? There is an excellent season of Beethoven and Mozart. Or a cruise on the river, perhaps? Although it is a little late for that. Too cold by far. The wind comes from the east and can be rather biting at this time of year."

Frau von Arpels smiled at him. "Perhaps you prefer something a little lighter? Café society? We can tell you all the best and most fashionable places to go . . . or even some of those which are less fashionable but rather more fun? Do you dance, Herr Monk?" Her voice lifted with enthusiasm. "You must waltz! You cannot be in Vienna and not waltz. Herr Johann Strauss has made us the capital of the world. Until you have heard him conduct . . . and danced till you drop, you have been only half alive!"

"Helga . . . please!" Von Arpels said quickly. "Herr Monk may find that too frivolous."

Monk thought it sounded wonderful. His imagination raced far ahead of anything of which his feet were capable. But he remembered from Venice that, surprisingly, he could dance . . . rather well. "I should love to," he said honestly. "But I know no one, and unfortunately I have to return to London as soon as my business here is completed."

"Oh, I can introduce you to someone," Helga von Arpels offered easily. "I am sure I can even get you an introduction to Herr Strauss himself, if you like?"

"Helga! For heaven's sake!" Von Arpels was brisk to the point of rudeness. "Herr Monk will not wish to meet Strauss socially. The man's an excellent musician, but he's a Jew! I've warned you before about making unfortunate friendships. One must be civil, but one must also be careful not to be misunderstood as to one's loyalties and one's identity. Look what happened to Irma Brandt! She had only herself to blame."

The air in the room seemed suddenly brighter and colder. A dozen questions poured into Monk's mind, but these were not the people to ask. Helga von Arpels looked angry. She had been embarrassed in front of her friends and a stranger, but there was nothing she could do about it. She had strayed into forbidden territory, and apparently it was so by mutual agreement. Monk was sorry for her, and angry on her behalf, but also totally helpless.

"Thank you for your generosity, Frau von Arpels," he said to her. "I shall endeavor to hear Herr Strauss conduct, even if I am alone and cannot dance. Then my imagination can store the memory."

She made an effort to smile, and there was a flicker of light in her eyes, and recognition of his feeling.

He thanked Josef and Magda again, getting from them the address of the priest, Father Geissner, and Magda accompanied him to the door. Out in the hall, she dismissed the maid and went to the step with him herself.

"Mr. Monk, is there anything else we can do to help Kristian?"

Was that really what she wanted to say that she had followed him to speak privately? There would only be a few moments before Josef would miss her.

"Yes," He decided without hesitation. "Tell me what you know of the feelings between Kristian and Elissa, and Max Niemann. He has visited London at least three times this year, and seen Elissa secretly, and not Kristian at all."

She looked only slightly surprised. "He was always in love with her," she answered very quietly. "But as far as I know, she never looked at anyone but Kristian."

"She was really in love with Kristian?" Monk wanted it to be true, even if it did not help.

"Oh, yes," she said vehemently. A tiny, sad smile linked her lips. "She was jealous of that Jewish girl, Hanna Jakob, because she was brave as well, and full of character. And Hanna was in love with Kristian, too. I saw it in her face . . . and her voice. Max was too easy for Elissa. She had to do no work to win his love." She gave a tiny shrug. "Very often we don't want what we are given without an effort. If you don't pay, perhaps it isn't worth a lot. At least, that is what we think."

There was a noise of doors opening and closing.

"Thank you for coming to tell us personally, Mr. Monk," she said quickly. "It was most courteous of you. Good-bye."

"Good-bye, Frau Beck," he answered, stepping outside into the wind and walking away, new thoughts filling his mind.

* * *

Ferdi was not the person to ask about the sudden ugliness he had seen in the Beck house, and it was almost entirely irrelevant to Kristian and Elissa, and to Max Niemann. However, Ferdi was burning with curiosity as to everything that Monk had learned and where it might fit in to form a clearer picture of the people who were already heroes to him. He asked question after question about Josef and Magda as he and Monk sat over hot chocolate and watched the lights come on as the streets grew darker and the cafés filled with chattering people. Without intending to, Monk let slip von Arpels's comment about Strauss. He saw no discernible reaction in Ferdi's young face.

"Do many people feel like that about Jews?" Monk asked.

"Yes, of course. Don't they in England?" Ferdi looked puzzled.

Monk had to think about it a moment. He had not moved in any area of society where he would have experienced such a thing. He realized with a jolt of surprise how few people he knew in a way of friendship rather than professionally. It was really only Rathbone, Callandra and, of course, Kristian. Those relationships were intense, built in extraordinary circumstances, the kind of trust most people are never called upon to exercise. But the lighter sides of friendship, the shared trivia, were missing.

"I haven't come across it," he said evasively. He did not want Ferdi to know that his life lacked such ordinary solidity. He did not really want him even to know that he had been a policeman. Ferdi might regard it as having a friend of excitement, but it would make Monk unquestionably socially inferior. One called the police when they were required; one did not invite them to dinner. One certainly did not allow one's daughter to marry them.

Ferdi was puzzled. "Don't you have Jews in England?"

"Yes, of course we do." He struggled for an acceptable answer. "One of our leading politicians is a Jew—Benjamin Disraeli. I'm just not sure that I know any myself."

"We don't, either," Ferdi agreed. "But I've seen them, of course."

"How do you know?" Monk said quickly.

"What?"

"How do you know they were Jews?"

Ferdi was perplexed. "Well, people do know, don't they?"

"I don't."

Ferdi blushed. "Don't you? My parents do. I mean, you have to be polite, but there are certain things you don't do."

"For example?"

"Well . . ." Ferdi was a little unhappy, and he looked down at the remains of his coffee. "You'd do business, of course. Lots of bankers are Jews. But you wouldn't have them in your house, or at your club, or anything like that."

"Why not?"

"Why not? Well . . . we're Christians. They don't believe in Christ. They crucified Him."

"Eighteen hundred years ago," Monk pointed out. "Nobody did it who's alive today, Jew or otherwise." He knew he was being unkind as he said it. Ferdi was only repeating what he had been taught. He was not equipped to find reasons for it, even to know where to look in the history of society, or the need for belief and justification to rationalize such a thing. The boy felt a stab of shame, and yet he kept on doing it. "Do a lot of people feel like that?" Monk asked.

"Everybody does that I know," Ferdi replied, screwing up his face. "Or they say they do. I suppose it's the same thing . . . isn't it?"

Monk had no answer, and it probably had nothing to do with Elissa Beck's death anyway. It was just another facet of Kristian he had not expected, and could not fit in with the man he had known, or thought he had. He ordered coffee for both of them, forgetting it was chocolate they had had before.

Ferdi smiled, but said nothing.

CHAPTER
ELEVEN

The upcoming trial of Kristian Beck caused a certain amount of public interest. It was not exactly a cause célèbre. He was not famous, and certainly far from the first man to have been accused of killing his wife. That was a charge with which everyone was familiar, and not a few felt a certain sympathy. At least they withheld their judgment until they should hear what she had done to prompt such an act. The charge of killing Sarah Mackeson as well was another matter. Opinion as to her style of life, her values or morality, varied from one person to another. There were those who considered she might have been little better than a prostitute, but even so, the brutality of her death filled them with revulsion.

The first picture of Elissa, taken from one of Allardyce's best sketches, that was published in the newspapers changed almost everyone's view, and any tolerance or compassion for Kristian vanished. The beauty of her face, with its ethereal sense of tragedy, moved men and women alike. Anyone who killed such a creature must be a monster.

Hester was with Charles when she saw the newspaper. She had heard Monk's description of Elissa, but she was still unprepared for the reality.

They were standing in her front room, which was robbed of its life for her because Monk was in Vienna and not returning tonight, or tomorrow, or any date that had been set. She was disconcerted by how profoundly she missed him. There was no point to the small chores she had to perform daily, no one with whom to share her thoughts, good and bad.

Charles had come because he was still desperately worried about Imogen, but he was also concerned for Kristian, and for her, too.

"I was uncertain whether to bring the newspaper," he said, glancing at it where it lay open on the table. "But I felt sure you would see it sometime . . . and I thought it might be easier if it were here. . . ." He still looked uncomfortable at his assumption. "And if you had someone with you."

"Thank you," she said sincerely. She found she was quite suddenly moved by his care. He was trying so hard to reach across the gulf they had allowed to grow between them. "Yes, I am glad you are here." Her eyes moved to the picture of Elissa again. "William tried to describe her to me, but I was still unprepared for a face that would touch me so closely." She looked across at him. "I never met her, and I suppose I imagined someone I would dislike, because in my mind she . . ." She stopped. She should not expose Callandra's vulnerability to anyone at all. She ignored his look of confusion. "But when I see her, I feel as if I have lost someone I knew." She went on as if no explanation were necessary. "I wonder if other people feel like that? It's going to make it far worse for Kristian, isn't it?"

His face pinched a little. "I think so. I'm sorry. I know you admire him a great deal. But . . ." He hesitated, obviously uncertain how to say what he was thinking, perhaps even if he should say it at all. And yet it was equally plainly something he believed to be true.

She helped him. "You are trying to tell me he might be guilty, and I must be prepared for that."

"No, actually I was thinking that one can never know another person as well as one thinks one does," he replied gently. "Perhaps one cannot even know oneself."

"Are you being kind to me?" she asked. "Or are you equivocating the way you always do?"

He looked a little taken aback. "I was saying what I thought.

Do you think I always equivocate?" There was a thread of hurt in the question.

"I'm sorry," she answered quickly, ashamed of herself. "No, you are just careful not to overstate things."

"You mean I am unemotional?" he pressed.

She could hear Imogen's accusation in that, and unreasonably it angered her. She would not have been happy married to a man as careful and as guarded of his inner life as Charles was, but he was her brother, and to defend him was as instinctive as recoiling when you are struck. If she sensed capacity to be hurt, she tried to shield it. If she sensed failure, and she hardly admitted even the word, then she lashed out to deny it, and to cover it from anyone else's sight.

"Being self-controlled is not the same thing as having no emotions," she said with something approaching anger, as if she were speaking through him to Imogen.

"No . . . no." He was watching her closely. "Hester . . . don't . . ."

"What?"

"I don't know. I wish I could help, but . . ."

She smiled at him. "I know. There is nothing. But thank you for coming."

He leaned forward and gave her a quick peck on the cheek, then suddenly put his arms around her and hugged her properly, holding her closely for a moment before letting her go, coughing to clear his throat, and muttering good-bye before he turned to leave.

Sitting alone at the breakfast table, Callandra also was deeply shaken by the picture of Elissa in the newspaper. Her first thought was not how it might affect the jury in the court, but her own amazement that Elissa should look so vulnerable. She had found it difficult enough when Hester had told her that she was beautiful, and then that her actions in Vienna had been passionate and brave.

Callandra had created in her mind the picture of a hard and brittle loveliness, something dazzling, but a matter of perfect bones and skin, dramatic coloring, perhaps handsome eyes. She was not prepared for a face where the heart showed through, where the dreams were naked and the pain of disillusion clear for anyone to see. How could Kristian have stopped loving her?

Why do people stop loving? Could it be anything but a weakness within themselves, an incapacity to give and go on giving, somewhere a selfishness? Her mind raced back over all she could remember of Kristian, every time they had met in the hospital, and before that the long hours they had spent during the typhoid outbreak in Limehouse. Every picture, every conversation, seemed to her tirelessly generous. She could see, as if it were before her now, his face in the flickering lights of the makeshift ward, exhausted, lined with anxiety, his eyes dark and shadowed around the sockets. But he had never lost his temper or his hope. He had tried to ease the distress of the dying, not only their physical pain but their fear and grief.

Or was she recalling it as she wished it to have been? It was so easy to do. She thought she was clear-sighted, a realist, but then perhaps everyone thought he was.

And even if Kristian were all she believed in, his work with the sick, that did not mean he was capable of the kind of love that binds individuals. Sometimes it is easier to love a cause than a person. The demands are different. With a blinding clarity like the clean cut of a razor, so sharp at first you barely feel it, she saw the inner vanity of experiencing the uncritical dependence of someone profoundly ill who needs your help, whose very survival depends upon you. You have the power to ease immediate, terrible physical pain.

The needs of a wife are nothing like that. A close human bond demands a tolerance, an ability to adjust, to moderate one's own actions and to accept criticism, even unreasonable behavior at times, to listen to all kinds of chatter and hear the real message behind the words. Above all, it needs the sharing of self, the dreams and the fears, the laughter and the pain. It means taking down the defenses, knowing that sooner or later you will be hurt. It means tempering ideals and acknowledging the vulnerable and flawed reality of human beings.

Perhaps, after all, Kristian was not capable of that, or simply not willing. She thought back to earlier in the year, to the men from America who had come to buy guns for the Civil War which was even now tearing that country apart. They had been idealists, and one at least had permitted the general passion to exclude the particular. Hester had told her of it in one of their many long hours together, of the slow realization, and the grief. It was a consuming thing, and allowed room for nothing and no one else. It sprang not from the justice of the cause but from the nature of the man. Was Kristian like that, too, a man who could love an idea but not a woman? It was possible.

And perhaps she herself had been guilty of falling in love with an ideal, not a real man, with his passions that were less bright, and his weaknesses?

Then it would not matter what Elissa was like, how brave and beautiful, how generous or how kind, or funny, or anything else. It could have been she who was trapped in the marriage, and sought her way out through the lunacy of gambling.

And all the thoughts filling her mind did not succeed in driving out the image of the other murdered woman, the artists' model whose only sin had been seeing who had killed Elissa. No rationalization could excuse her death. The thought that Kristian might have killed her was intolerable, and she thrust it away, refusing even to allow the words into her mind.

There were things to be done. She closed the newspaper, ate the last of her toast and ignored the cold tea in her cup. Before the trial opened she had one visit to make which was going to require all her concentration and self-control. She had no status whatever in the matter. She was not a relative, employer or representative of anyone. To attend every day with no duty, no reason beyond friendship, and to be obliged to be nothing but a helpless onlooker would be excruciating. If she were there representing the hospital governors, who very naturally had a concern for Kristian as his employers, and for their own reputation because of that, then her presence was explained, even her intervention, if any opportunity presented itself.

To do this she must go and see Fermin Thorpe, and persuade him of the necessity. It was an interview she dreaded. She loathed the man, and now she had not her usual armor of assurance, or the indifference to what he thought which her social position normally provided. She needed something only he could grant her. How could she ask him for it while hiding her vulnerability so he did not sense it and take his chance to be revenged for years of imagined affront?

The longer she thought about it the more daunting it became. She had no time to waste, the trial would begin tomorrow. Better she go now, before too much imagination robbed her of what courage she had left.

She walked out of the dining room across the hall and went upstairs to prepare herself, collect her costume jacket and the right hat.

The journey out to Hampstead took her over an hour. Progress was sporadic because of the traffic and the drifting fog, and she had far too much time to think and play the scene in her mind a dozen times, none of them less than painful.

When she arrived at the hospital, she told her coachman to wait for her as she did not intend to remain, then was obliged to sit for nearly an hour while Fermin Thorpe interviewed a new young doctor with, apparently, a view to employing him. She kept her temper because she needed to. On another occasion, as a governor herself, she could simply have interrupted. Today she could not afford to antagonize him.

When Thorpe finally showed the young doctor out, smiling and sharing a joke, he turned to her with satisfaction shining in his face. He hated Kristian, because Kristian was a better doctor than he, and they both knew it. Kristian did not defer to him. If he thought differently—which he often did in moral and social matters—he said so, and Thorpe had lost the issue, for which, in his stiff, frightened mind, there was no forgiveness. Now he was on the brink of getting rid of Kristian forever, and the taste of victory was sweet on his lips. He was going to be proved right before the world in every bitter or critical thing he had ever said about Kristian, beyond even his most far-fetched dreams.

"Good morning, Lady Callandra," he said cheerfully. He was almost friendly; he could afford to be. "A bit chilly this morning, but I hope you are well?"

She must playact as never before. "Very," she said, forcing herself to smile. "The cold does not trouble me. I hope you are well also, Mr. Thorpe, in spite of the burden of responsibility upon you?"

"Oh, very well," he said forcefully, opening his office door for her and standing aside for her to enter. "I believe we will rise above our temporary difficulties. Young Dr. Larkmont looks very promising. Good surgical experience, nice manner, keen." He met her eyes boldly.

"Good," she responded. "I am sure your judgment is excellent. It always has been. You have never allowed an incompetent man to practice here."

"Ah . . . well . . ." He was not sure whether to mention Kristian or not, to argue with her and let himself down, or agree with her and box himself into a corner of approving Kristian, even implicitly. "Yes," he finished. "My task . . . my . . ."

"Responsibility," she finished for him. "The reputation of the Hampstead Hospital rests largely upon the excellence of our doctors."

"Of course," he agreed, moving around behind his desk and waiting until she had taken the seat opposite, then he sat down also. "And, of course, discipline and organization, and the highest moral standards." He emphasized the word *moral* with a very slight smile.

She inclined her head, too angry for a moment to control her voice. She breathed in and out, telling herself that Kristian's life might depend upon this. What was her pride worth? Nothing! Nothing at all. "Yes," she agreed. "That is one of our highest assets. We must do everything we can to see that it is not taken from us. The damage that could do would be tragic, and perhaps irretrievable." She saw the shadow in his eyes and felt a tiny lift of confidence. "It is our duty . . . well, yours. I do not wish to presume, but I would offer all the assistance I can."

Now he was confused, uncertain what she meant. "Thank you, but I am not at all sure what you could do. We are about to suffer a very serious blow, if Dr. Beck is found guilty, and it looks as if that is now inevitable." He ironed out the satisfaction from his face and composed it into lines of suitable gravity. "Of course, we must hope it is not so. But if it is, Lady Callandra, for the sake of the hospital, which is our principal responsibility, regardless of our personal distress or the loyalties we would wish to honor, we must act wisely."

The words nearly choked her, but she said them steadily, as if she meant it. "That is exactly my point, Mr. Thorpe. We must do all we can to preserve the reputation of the hospital, which, as you say, is more important than any of our individual likes or affections." She did not say "dislikes," still less "jealousies." "We must be aware hour by hour of exactly what the evidence is, and do all we can to make sure we respond the best way possible—for our reputation's sake."

It was clear in his face that he did not know what she meant, and the possibility that he might make a wrong judgment made him distinctly uneasy. "Yes . . . yes, of course we must be . . . right," he said awkwardly. "We would not wish to be misunderstood."

She smiled at his puzzled expression as if he had been totally lucid. "I know how extremely busy you must be in these appalling circumstances, with decisions to make, more doctors to interview. Would you like me to attend the court on behalf of the Hospital Governors, and keep you informed?" She could feel her heart beating as the seconds passed while he weighed the repercussions of his answer. What did he want? What was safe? Could he trust her? The hospital's reputation was inextricably bound with his own.

She dared not prompt him.

"Well . . ." He breathed out slowly, staring at her, trying to gauge what she wanted and why.

"I would not speak on the hospital's behalf, of course," she said, hoping it was not too subservient. Would he suspect her meekness? "Except as you directed me. I think extreme discretion is the best role at the moment." It was a promise she had no intention of keeping if Kristian's freedom or his life hung in the balance. She gave the lie no thought now.

"Yes, I . . . I think it would be wise for me to be as fully informed as possible," he agreed cautiously. "If you would report to me, that would save me a great deal of time. Forewarned is forearmed. Thank you, Lady Callandra. Most dutiful of you." He made as if to rise, in order to signify to her that the interview was over.

She stood up, taking the cue so that he did not appear to have hurried her, and she saw the flash of satisfaction in his face. In every other circumstance she would have sat down again simply to annoy him. Now she was eager to escape while she still had what she wanted. "Then I shall not take up more of your time, Mr. Thorpe," she said. "Good day." She went out without looking back. If she were too civil it would cause him to think the matter over, and perhaps change his mind.

She was not certain whether she wished to go to the trial with Hester or alone. She did not consider her emotions to be transparent generally, but she did not delude herself that Hester would be unaware of the turmoil inside her. Still, it might be too hard to find an excuse not to go together. And whether she wished it or not, they might need each other deeply before it was over.

* * *

She and Hester were in court side by side when the trial opened and the two protagonists faced each other. Pendreigh was magnificent merely in his presence, even before he needed to speak. He was a most striking figure with his height and his elegance of movement. His mane of shining hair was largely concealed by his wig, but the light still caught the golden edges of it. To those who knew he was the victim's father, and thus the father-in-law of the accused, his presence was like the charge of electricity in the air before a storm.

Up in the dock, which was set at a height and quite separate from the body of the court, Kristian was white-faced, his eyes hollow, looking dark and very un-English. Would that tell against him? She looked again at the jury. To a man they were concentrating on the counsel for the prosecution, a diminutive man with a quite ordinary face of intense sincerity. When he spoke briefly his voice was gentle, well-modulated, the kind that almost immediately sounds familiar, as if you must know him but simply have forgotten where and how.

The indictment was read. Callandra had been to trials before, but there was a reality about this one that was almost physical in its impact. When she heard the word *murder*, not once but twice, she could feel the sweat break out on her body, and the packed room seemed to swim in her vision as if she were going to faint. Dimly, she felt Hester's fingers grasp her arm and the strength of it steadied her.

The witnesses were brought on one by one, starting with the police constable who had first found the bodies. The shock and sense of tragedy were still clear in him, and Callandra could feel the response to it in the room.

There was nothing Pendreigh or anyone else could have done to alter either the facts or the compassion. At least he was wise enough not to try.

The constable was followed by Runcorn, looking unhappy but perfectly certain of himself, and suitably respectful both of the court and of the subjects of passion and death. Callandra was startled at the anger in him when he spoke of Sarah Mackeson, as if in some way he did not understand himself and it outraged him. There was a gulf of every kind of difference between her and this relatively uneducated, certainly unpolished, policeman with his prejudices and ambitions. He had been an enemy to Monk all the time she had known him, and long before that, and she thought him pompous, self-absorbed and thoroughly tiresome.

And yet looking at him now, she could see that his anger was honest, and cleaner than any of the ritual words of the legal procedure being played out. He would have hated anyone to know it, but he cared.

The jury heard it, and Callandra saw with cold fear how an answering anger was born in them. Because Sarah was real to Runcorn, with a life that mattered, she became more real to them also, and their determination to punish someone for her death the greater.

She knew it would go on like this, day after day. For all his sharpness of intellect, the legion of words at his command, and his understanding of the law, there was nothing Fuller Pendreigh could do against the facts which would be displayed one by one. Where was Monk? What had he learned in Vienna? There must be some other explanation, and please heaven he would find it. Please heaven it would be soon enough.

She sat sick and shivering as the trial went on around her as relentlessly as if it were a play being acted from a script already written and there was no avoiding the climax at the end, or the tragedy.

Monk went to see Father Geissner in his home as Magda Beck had suggested. The first time, the housekeeper told him that the Father was occupied, but he made an appointment for the following day.

Fretting at the time lost, he spent the remaining hours of daylight wandering around the city looking at the areas which had featured most heavily in the uprising, trying to picture it in his mind, event by event, as he had been told it.

Nothing in the calm, prosperous streets told him that the cafés and shops, the comfortable houses, had witnessed desperation and violence, nor was there anything reflected in the faces of people hurrying about their business, buying and selling, gossiping, calling out greetings in the sharp, cold air.

In the evening, Monk did as everyone had been so keen to suggest to him, and went to hear the young Johann Strauss conduct his orchestra. The gay, lyrical music had caught Europe by storm, delighting even the rather staid and unimaginative Queen Victoria, and set all London dancing the waltz.

Here in its own city it had a magic, a laughter and a speed that forgot politics, the cold wind across Hungary from the east beyond, or the losses and mistakes of the past. For three hours Monk saw the heart of Vienna, and past and future were of no importance, swallowed in the delight of the moment. He would never again hear three-quarter time without a lurch of memory and a sweetness.

He returned to his hotel long after midnight, and at ten o'clock the next morning, after an excellent cup of coffee, he set out to keep his appointment with Father Geissner.

This time he was shown in immediately, and the housekeeper left them alone.

Father Geissner was a quiet, elderly man with an ascetic face, which was almost beautiful in its inner peace.

"What can I do for you, Mr. Monk?" he asked in excellent English, inviting him with a wave of his hand to be seated.

Monk had already considered any possible advantage it might give him to approach the subject obliquely, and had discarded it as more likely to lose him the priest's trust if he were discovered. This man spent his professional life listening to people's secrets. Like

Monk, he must have learned to tell truth from lies and to understand the reasons why people concealed their acts and often their motives. "You were recommended to me by Frau Magda Beck," Monk answered, barely glancing around the comfortable, book-lined office where he had been received. "She told me that you knew her brother-in-law, Kristian Beck, when he lived here, especially during the uprising in '48."

"I did," Geissner agreed, but his expression was guarded, even though he looked directly at Monk and his blue eyes were candid. "Why is that of interest to you?"

"Because Elissa Beck has been murdered in London, where they lived, and Kristian has been charged with the crime." He ignored the startled look in Geissner's face. "He is a friend of my wife, who is a nurse." Then he added quickly, "She was in the Crimea with Miss Nightingale," in case Geissner's opinion of nurses was founded upon the general perception of them as domestic servants whose moral character precluded their obtaining an ordinary domestic position. "And he is also a friend of Lady Callandra Daviot, whom I have known for many years. We all feel that there is another explanation for what happened, and I have come to Vienna to see if it may lie in the past."

A brief flash of pity crossed Geissner's face, but there was no way to tell whether it was for Elissa because she was dead, Kristian for his present situation, or even for Monk because he had set out on a task in which he could not succeed.

"I used to be in the police force," Monk explained, then realized instantly that that also might be little recommendation. "Now I investigate matters privately, for people who have problems beyond the police's interest or on which they have given up."

Geissner raised white eyebrows. "Or have an answer which they find unacceptable?"

"They might be forced to accept it," Monk said carefully, watching Geissner's face and seeing no reaction. "But not easily, not as long as there is any possibility at all of a different one. Those who know Dr. Beck now cannot believe he would do such a thing. He is a man of remarkable self-discipline, dedication and compassion."

"That sounds like the man I knew," Geissner agreed with a faint smile which looked to be more sorrow than any reluctance to feel admiration.

Monk struggled to read his emotions, and knew he failed. There was a world of knowledge behind his words, far more subtle than merely the passage of events.

"Did you know Max Niemann also?" he asked.

"Of course."

"And Elissa von Leibnitz?"

"Naturally." Was that a shadow in his voice or not? The priest was too used to hiding his feelings, keeping the perfect mask over his response to all manner of human passions and failings.

"And Hanna Jakob?" Monk persisted.

At last there was a change in Geissner's eyes, in his mouth. It was slight, but an unmistakable sadness that also held regret, even guilt. Was it because she was dead, or more than that?

"How did she die?" Monk asked, expecting Geissner to tell him it could not have any connection with Elissa's murder. But there was the slightest tightening in the muscles of his neck, a hesitation.

"It was during the uprising," he answered. "But I imagine you know that already. Both she and Elissa were remarkably brave. I suppose Elissa was the more obvious heroine. She was the one who risked her life over and over again, first exhorting people to have the courage to fight for what they believed in, then going to the authorities quite openly, pleading for reform, for any yielding of the restrictions. Finally, when real violence erupted, she stood at the barricades like any of the men. In fact, she was frequently at the front, as if she felt no fear. She was far from being a stupid woman; she must have been aware of the dangers as well as anyone."

He smiled, and there was a terrible sadness in him. When he spoke his voice was rough-edged, as if the pain still tore at him. "I remember once when a young man fell before the rifle fire, far out in front of the piled-up wagons, chairs and boxes that had been set across the street. It was Elissa who called out for them to climb to the top and hold the soldiers at bay while she ran out to try to save him, pull him back to where they could treat his wounds. The army were advancing towards them, about twenty hussars with rifles at the ready, even though they were reluctant to slaughter their own people." He shrugged very slightly. "Of course, the army lived in barracks, and didn't even know their neighbors. But it is still different from attacking foreigners who speak another language and are soldiers like yourself."

Monk wondered for an instant, a flash there and then gone again, how many times Geissner had heard the confessions of soldiers, perhaps trying to justify to themselves the unarmed civilians they had shot, trying to live with the nightmares, make sense of duty and guilt. But he had no time to spare for that now. He needed to understand Kristian, and to know if he could have killed Elissa—or if Max Niemann could have. "Yes?" he said sharply.

Geissner smiled. "Kristian went to the top of the barricade and fired at the advancing soldiers," he answered.

Monk was surprised, and perhaps saddened. "He didn't try to stop Elissa from going?"

Geissner was watching him closely. "You don't understand, Mr. Monk. It was a great cause. Austria labored under a highly repressive regime. For thirteen years before we had been effectively ruled by the aging Prince Metternich. He was conservative, reactionary, and used the vast civil service to stifle all reform. Intellectual life was suffocated by the secret police and their informers. Censorship stifled art and ideas. There was much to fight for."

He sighed. "But as you know, the uprising was crushed, and most of our burden was left still upon us. But then we had hope. Kristian was the leader of his group. Personal feelings of love or tenderness had no place. Where is an army's discipline if each man will make special allowances for a friend or a lover? It is dishonorable, but above all it is ineffective. How could anyone trust you, or believe that you, too, set the cause above life or safety? Kristian did as he should have done. So far as I know, he never failed to, even afterwards." There was a catch in his voice, and again the moment of darkness in his eyes.

"Afterwards?" Monk said quickly, trying to retrieve and catch the nuance of something more.

Geissner took a deep breath and let it out in a sigh. "After Hanna's death," he said softly.

"Why do you say that? Did something change?" Monk's voice fell into a charged silence.

"Yes." Geissner did not look at him. "Something changed, one way or another, but . . . but I can tell you little of it. They all made their confessions, as good Catholics, but some troubles were spoken of, others lay deeper than words, I think deeper than their own understanding. Knowledge of such things sometimes comes slowly, if at all."

Monk strained to keep his manner calm and the first leap of real hope from betraying him, and perhaps breaking the priest's train of recollection. "What things?" he said gently.

"Regret for what was not done, for perceptions too late," Geissner replied. "For seeing something ugly in others, and realizing that perhaps it was in yourself also."

Monk felt warning like a prickling on the skin. He must speak slowly, indirectly. This man held confidences dearer than life. Even to ask that he break one would be an insult which would slash the understanding between them as with a sword.

"How did she die?" Monk asked instead.

Geissner looked up at him. "As well as fighting on the barricades, she was the one who took messages to other groups in different parts of the city. It was difficult, and became more and more dangerous. I don't know if she was afraid. Naturally, I didn't know her as I did the others. They were all Catholic, and she was Jewish."

"Are there many Jews in Vienna?"

"Oh, yes. We have had Jews here for about a thousand years, but we have tolerated them only when it suited us. Twice we have driven them all out and confiscated their goods and property, of course, and burned at the stake those who remained. Although that is several hundred years ago now. We let them back in again when we needed their financial skills. Many of them have changed their names to make them sound more Christian, and hidden their faith. Some have even become Catholic, in self-defense."

Monk searched Geissner's face but could see nothing in it to betray his feelings, either about someone who denied his faith and converted to that of his persecutors, leaving his roots and his heritage behind, or about the society which drove him to do it in order to survive. Did Father Geissner feel any guilt in that? Or was his own faith such that it held every means acceptable to bring more people to what was for him the truth? Monk found the thought repellent. But then he was not Catholic, at least not as far as he knew. In fact, he was not anything at all. But was there any truth he felt so passionately—a truth of mind, an honor, courage, pity or any other virtue—that he strove to share it with others, to preserve and pass it on at any cost to himself? Shouldn't there be? If he had any beliefs at all, were they not to be shared, strengthened, widened with all men?

Why was this occurring to him only now? He should surely have been conscious of the gap in his life, in his thought, where some kind of faith should have been.

He forced his mind from himself back to the present, and the need for justice. "How did Hanna Jakob die?" he said again.

If Geissner sensed the anger or the urgency in him there was nothing in his face to show it. "She was carrying a message of warning," he replied. "She was captured by the army and tortured to tell them where part of Kristian's group was and what they were planning. She would not reveal it, and she was killed."

"Was she betrayed?" Monk asked harshly. He wanted both the possible answers, and neither. If she had been, it might somehow explain Elissa's murder, and yet it would be so repellent, so hideous a sin in his mind, that for Hanna's sake, he could hardly bear it. And even more for the sake of whoever had done it. Surely the brave, idealistic Elissa could not have soiled herself with such an act of jealousy?

"You know I cannot answer you with what I know from the confessional, Herr Monk," Geissner said softly. "All that Hanna did was always a risk. She knew it, but she still went."

"They still sent her!" Monk challenged, his voice catching in his throat. He had expected Geissner to deny even the possibility of betrayal, firmly and with anger, and he had not. That was almost a confirmation in itself. Suddenly he was cold, shivery, sick inside.

"Yes." Geissner went on, breathing softly, his eyes down, away from Monk's. "It was important, and she was the best at finding her way through the back streets, especially of Leopoldstadt, the old Jewish quarter. Had she been able to get through and warn the others, she believed it would have saved their lives . . . at least until next time."

"Believed?" Monk seized on the word. "Was it not true?"

"Someone else warned them also." The answer was so quiet Monk barely caught it.

"So her death was unnecessary!" Monk found his fury choking him so he could not speak the sentence clearly.

Geissner looked up, his eyes pleading not to be asked, and yet to be understood, so Monk might share with him a terrible truth without his betraying anyone by speaking it aloud.

Monk stumbled towards it in growing horror. "She was in love with Kristian?" he said, repeating what Magda Beck had told him.

"Yes." Geissner said only the one word.

"And could he have felt more deeply for her than only friendship and loyalty?" Monk asked him.

"He did not say so to me," Geissner replied, gazing at Monk steadily.

Was that a deliberate omission, to imply that it had been so?

For a long moment Monk allowed the silence to remain, and Geissner did not interrupt it. The certainty settled with Monk, heavy as stone.

"Did Elissa believe that he did?" Monk asked finally.

"Mr. Monk, you are asking questions I cannot answer."

Why? Because he did not know, or because the confessional bound him? He had very carefully refrained from saying that he did not know. Or was that his way with English? Monk studied his face and saw pain in it, pity, and silence. What could he ask that Geissner could answer?

"You were there yourself?" he said. "With them at the barricades, and in the times before . . . and after?"

Geissner smiled, a wry twitch of the lips. "Yes, Mr. Monk, I was. Being a priest does not prevent me from believing in the greater freedom of my people. I did not hold a gun, but I carried messages, tried to argue and persuade, and I tended the troubled and the injured, and heard confession from those who had done physical harm to others in the cause they believed in."

"And those who from their own passions had done things, or omitted them, which gravely harmed others?" Monk urged, this time directly looking into Geissner's eyes.

"I know what you are asking me, Herr Monk," Geissner said very quietly. "And you know that my oath as a priest prevents me from answering you. I would give a great deal to be able to help you learn the truth as to what happened to Elissa von Leibnitz. I grieve for her, for the bright flame that has been quenched. I grieve still more for Kristian. As I knew him, he was a man of remarkable inner courage, an honesty to look at himself and measure his failings against his dreams. He did not run away from truth, even when it hurt him profoundly."

"You are speaking of Hanna's death?" Monk said quickly.

Geissner blinked and drew in his breath slowly. "Do not misunderstand me, I am speaking of the regret he felt afterwards, the self-doubt he suffered because they had chosen Hanna for the errand.

He came to believe that they had done so because she was Jewish, and therefore, in some way deeper than conscious thought, not entirely one of them. I don't know if that was true, but he feared it was, and he was horrified with himself for it."

"And the others? Elissa? Max?"

He shook his head. Fractionally. "No. That was the beginning of a subtle difference between them, a divergence of inner paths, but not outer. Kristian married Elissa. Max Niemann remained his friend. I think Kristian only ever spoke of it to me. I tell you because it reflects on the kind of man he was, and I believe will always be. It was that core of strength in him that Elissa saw, and loved."

"And Hanna?" Monk asked. He was not certain how far he could push Geissner, but he could not leave it as it was. He was almost certain that Elissa had betrayed Hanna, but almost was not enough. "Was that what she loved in him, too, and trusted?"

Something shivered inside Geissner. "She was not my parishioner, Herr Monk. She did not confide such things in me."

Monk chose his words very carefully. "Father, if someone had betrayed Hanna Jakob to the authorities, would they have expected that she would be tortured to death and yet keep silent? That seems a very terrible thing. Is there any alternative, other than that the people whose whereabouts she kept secret would have been killed?"

Geissner was silent for so long Monk thought he was not going to reply, then at last he spoke. "I think it would be possible that they had made provision that the people concerned were warned, and were safe, so that if Hanna should break, to save herself, she would not, in fact, have betrayed anyone, except in her own mind." He bit his lip, as if the cruelty of it only just came fully to him as he spoke the words aloud and heard them. "It was a time of great passions, Herr Monk. Perhaps we should not judge people for acts committed then by the calmer and colder light of today, when we sit here comfortably talking together of things we know only partially."

"And you cannot tell me if this thing even happened. Does

anyone else know of it? Max Niemann, for example? Or Kristian himself?"

"No. There is no one you can ask, because no one else knows of it, and I cannot speak of it any further. I am sorry." He lifted his chin a little. "But if you imagine it has to do with Elissa's death, I believe you are wrong. I alone know what happened, and I have told no one." A little smile touched his lips. "Nor does anyone else ever come to me with guesses, such as you have."

Monk waited.

Geissner leaned forward a little. "Kristian's guilt was for himself. He did not hold anyone else responsible. He understood not only what he had done in sending Hanna, but why. They did not. The difference was one of understanding, and he did not expect it of Elissa or of Max." He looked at Monk with intensity. "One does not have to imagine people perfect in order to love them, Mr. Monk. Love acknowledges faults, weaknesses, even the need now and again for forgiveness where there is no repentance and no understanding of fault. We learn at different speeds. Elissa had many strengths, many virtues, and she was unflinchingly brave. I think she was the bravest woman I ever knew. I am truly sorry she is dead, but I cannot believe Kristian killed her, unless he has changed beyond all recognition from the man I knew."

"I think he has," Monk said slowly. "But to someone even less likely to have killed anyone at all . . . even a soldier of the Hapsburg army."

"That does not surprise me."

"What about Max Niemann?"

"Max? He was in love with Elissa. I am not telling you anything that is a confidence. It was no secret then, or now. He never married. I think no one could take her place in his mind. No other woman could be as brave, as beautiful, or as passionate in her ideals. She was so intensely alive that beside her anyone else would seem gray."

"Did Hanna Jakob have family?"

Geissner looked surprised. "You think one of them might have traveled to London after all these years and exacted some kind of revenge?"

"I'm looking for anything," Monk admitted.

"Her parents still live here, in Leopoldstadt. On Heinestrasse, I believe. You could ask."

"Thank you." Monk rose to his feet. "Thank you for your frankness, Father Geissner."

Geissner stood also. "If there is anything I can do to help Kristian, please let me know. I shall pray for him, and say a mass for Elissa's soul, and her abiding peace at last. There will be many who revere her memory and would wish to come. Godspeed to you, Herr Monk."

Monk went out into the street, deep in troubled and painful thought.

In London, the trial of Kristian Beck continued, each day seeming worse than the last, and more damning. Mills was spending less time with his witnesses for the prosecution, sensing that Pendreigh was desperate to stretch out the evidence.

Sitting in the seats reserved for the general public, not daring to look at Callandra in case she should read her growing sense of despair, Hester tried to tell herself that that was ridiculous. Mills could not know that Monk was in Vienna. He was amply experienced and intelligent enough to have read the signs that the defense had no case, no disproof, not even a serious doubt to raise that any jury would be obliged to consider. One did not need any more than observation of human nature to know that; an eye to see Pendreigh's face, the concentration, the slightly exaggerated gestures as he strove to keep the jury's attention, the increasing sharpness in his voice as his questions grew longer and more abstruse.

Mills had already called all the police and medical evidence, and Pendreigh had argued anything that was even remotely debatable, and several things that were not. Mills had called witnesses who said that Kristian had originally told the police he had been with patients at the time that Elissa and Sarah had been killed, then more witnesses to prove that he had lied.

Pendreigh had tried to show that it was an error, the mistake of a man hurrying from one sick person to another, preoccupied with suffering and the need to alleviate it.

Hester had looked at the faces of the jurors. For a moment she convinced herself she saw genuine doubt. She looked up to Kristian. He was so pale he appeared ghostly. Even the full curve of his cheek, the sensuous line of his lips, could not give his face life. He may have known that what Pendreigh said was true, but there was no hope in his eyes that the jury would believe it.

She could not look at Callandra. Perhaps it was cowardly of her, possibly it was a discretion not to intrude on what must be a double agony. No matter what courage she had, she could not deny the possibility—the probability—that Kristian would be found guilty, unless Monk returned with a miracle. Did she also now begin to wonder in her shivering, darkest fears if perhaps he was? Who could say what emotions had filled Kristian when he was faced with ruin, not only personally, but of all the good he could do for those who suffered poverty and disease, pain, loneliness and bereavement? He had done so much, and it would all come to an end if he were ruined by debt.

Of course, killing Elissa was no sensible solution. He could not ever, in a sane, rational moment, have thought it was. But in the heat of desperation, knowing what she was doing, perhaps being told of a new and even more crippling loss, that the gamblers were after her and perhaps even the house would have to go, maybe he had finally lost control, and his violent, revolutionary past had swept back to him. One quick grasp, a twist of the arms, and her neck was broken.

And then Sarah the same?

No! Nothing made that understandable. She shivered convulsively, even though in the press of bodies the courtroom was warm. Kristian could surely never have done that!

Pendreigh's voice filled her ears as he called yet another witness as to Kristian's character, and the jury were already bored. They knew he was a good doctor. They had heard a dozen witnesses say so, and they had believed them. It was irrelevant. The defense was fumbling, and they saw it. It was in the air like the echo of a sound just died away.

Hester sat through day after day longing for Monk to return, wondering what he was doing, even if he was safe. She tried to imagine where he was, what kind of rooms he had, if he was well cared for, if he was cold or ill-fed, if Callandra had given him sufficient money. It was all only a way of avoiding thinking about the real issue: what he was learning about Kristian. Even the loneliness of missing him with an almost physical pain was better than the fear and the bitter disillusion, the inability to offer any help at all.

She tried not to turn and stare up at the dock, and felt intrusive. What would Kristian see in her face if he looked? Doubt. Fear for him, and for Callandra. She was terrified of the hurt Callandra would feel if he were found guilty. Would she go on believing in his innocence, make herself believe it no matter what happened? Or would she finally yield and accept that he could have been guilty, with all the terrible shattering of faith that that would bring?

Then would she ever be the same again? Or would something inside her be broken, some hope, an ability to trust not only people, but life itself?

Hester sat on the hard seat, pressed in on either side by the curious and critical, aware of their breathing, of their slight movement, the creak of corsets and faint rustle of fabric, the smell of damp wool and the sweat of tension and excitement.

She looked across at Callandra and saw the exhaustion in her face. Her skin was papery and without any color, gray, almost as if it were dirty. The lines between nose and mouth were deeply etched.

As almost always, her hair was escaping its pins. She looked every day of her years.

Hester ached to be able to comfort her, to offer anything at all that would help, but there was nothing. She knew the bruising and terrible pain she had felt when she believed it could have been Charles. She was almost ashamed of her relief to know that it was not, no matter how humiliating the truth. Platitudes would only make it seem that she did not understand, and it was not the time to reach out and touch, even take a hand. She thought about it, and once she moved as if to lean across, then changed her mind. What might be read into it that she did not mean? Hope, a false importance to what was being said at that instant, even a despair she did not intend.

Pendreigh was still calling character witnesses, but he was now reduced to Fermin Thorpe. They had debated whether to call him or not. He hated Kristian, but he would occupy time, which was now their only hope. He loved to talk, reveling in the sound of his own voice. He was a conserver, frightened of change, frightened of losing his power and position. Kristian was an innovator who challenged him, questioned things, jeopardized his authority. There had been particular instances, not long enough ago to forget, when Thorpe had lost. The memory and the resentment were there in his face as he took the stand. Pendreigh had known it; both Hester and Callandra had made certain he had no illusions. They had even told him the story in detail. But the only alternative was to end the defense with Monk still not here, and that they could not do.

So, Fermin Thorpe stood in the high witness box, smiling, a tight, narrow little grimace, staring down at Pendreigh in the middle of the floor, and the judge and jury waited for them to begin; impatiently, it was time-wasting.

Pendreigh smiled. He understood vanity and he knew his own power.

"Mr. Thorpe," he said cautiously. "So the court can understand the value of your testimony, the years of experience you have had upon which to base any judgment, both of men and of medicine, perhaps you would tell me the details of your career?"

There was a sigh of impatience from the judge, and Mills half rose to his feet, but it would be pointless to object, and he knew it. Pendreigh had every right to establish his witness, to give every ounce of weight to his testimony that he could.

Thorpe was grateful. It showed in the easing of his body, the way he relaxed his shoulders and began to speak, at some length, of his achievements.

Pendreigh nodded without once interrupting him or hastening him on. Finally, when they came to the point of his offering an opinion on Kristian's character, Hester found herself aching with the tension in her body. Her shoulders were stiff, her hands knotted so tightly her nails hurt her palms. There had been no alternative, but still she was sick with fear. This was Thorpe's chance to savor revenge. Had Pendreigh the skill to control him? She dared not look at Callandra.

"So you have worked with many physicians and surgeons and had the responsibility for their behavior, their skill, ultimately even their employment by the hospital?" Pendreigh said graciously.

"Yes. Yes, I have," Thorpe answered with satisfaction. "I suppose you could say that in the end it was all my responsibility."

"An extraordinary burden for one man," Pendreigh agreed deferentially. "And yet you never flinched from it."

Mills stood up. "My lord, I think we are all agreed that Mr. Thorpe has a great responsibility, and that he has discharged it with skill and conscience. I feel we are now wasting the court's time by going over that which is already established."

"I have to agree, Mr. Pendreigh," the judge said a trifle sharply. "Please ask your questions regarding Mr. Thorpe's estimate of Dr. Beck's character, not his medical skills. We have no doubt of them. You have given them to us abundantly over the last few days." His impatience and lack of sympathy were only too apparent.

"Yes, my lord, of course," Pendreigh conceded. He turned to

Thorpe. "You have always selected your staff with the utmost care, not only for their medical skill but for their moral character as well, as is your charge. May the court assume that in keeping Dr. Beck you did not alter those high standards, or make any exception?"

Thorpe was caught. He had been planning to damn Kristian, to taste a very public revenge for past defeats, but he could not do so now without ruining himself. The anger of it, the momentary indecision even at this date, as he saw his victory sliding away, was all so clear in his face Hester could have spoken his thoughts aloud for him.

"Mr. Thorpe?" Pendreigh frowned. "It is surely an easy question. Did you maintain the same high standards as you always have in keeping Dr. Beck in your employ and allowing him to operate on the sick and vulnerable men and women who came to your hospital for help . . . or did you, for some personal reason, allow a man you did not trust to keep such a position?"

"No! Of course I didn't!" Thorpe said, then instantly realized he had been forced into committing himself. He flushed dark red.

"Thank you," Pendreigh accepted, moving backwards and indicating that Mills might now question the witness.

Mills stood up, dapper and confident. He opened his mouth to speak to Thorpe.

Hester froze. Thorpe was bursting to undo what he had said, his eyes pleading with Mills somehow to create the chance for him.

The entire room was silent. If only it mattered as much as it seemed to. Whatever Thorpe said would make little real difference. It was emotional; the facts were not touched.

"Mr. Thorpe," Mills began.

"Yes?" Thorpe leaned a little forward over the rail of the witness box, staring down at Mills below him.

"Thank you for sparing us your time," Mills said flatly. "I don't think I can ask you to add to what you have said. Your loyalty does you credit."

It was sarcastic. It was also a tactical error.

"It is not loyalty!" Thorpe said furiously. "I loathe the man! But personal feelings did not alter my judgment that he is an excellent and dedicated surgeon, and a man of high moral character. Otherwise I would not have kept him in the hospital." He did not have to add that if he could have found an excuse to dismiss him he would have taken it; it was only too unpleasantly evident in his furious bright eyes and snarling mouth.

"Thank you," Mills murmured, returning to his seat. "I have no further questions, my lord."

CHAPTER
TWELVE

———

"What did you learn from the Father?" Ferdi asked Monk eagerly on the following morning as they sat over coffee in one of the numerous cafés. Vienna served more kinds of coffee than Monk knew existed, with or without chocolate added, with or without cream, sometimes whipped cream, or hot milk, or laced with rum. This morning the wind scythed in from the Hungarian plains, touching his skin like a knife, and Monk felt an even deeper coldness inside him. He had ordered coffee with chocolate and thick cream for both of them.

Ferdi was waiting for an answer. Monk had wrestled long into the night, much of it when he should have been asleep, worrying how much to tell the boy of the truth he was now certain of, even though he had no proof and no one who would testify. Did it really have anything to do with Elissa's death?

"Mr. Monk?" Ferdi prompted, putting down his coffee and staring across the table.

He needed Ferdi's help. "He didn't exactly tell me," Monk answered slowly. "He knew many things about the time, the people, but some of them were told to him under the seal of the confessional."

"So you learned nothing?" Ferdi said, his young face filling with disappointment. "I . . . I was sure you had discovered something terrible. You seem . . . different, as if all kinds of things had changed . . . feelings . . . ." He stopped, confused and a little embarrassed that he had intruded on inner pain without thinking.

Monk smiled very slightly and stared at the cream slowly melting into his coffee. "You can guess this much from my face, and my manner?"

Ferdi hesitated. "Well . . . I thought I could."

"You can," Monk agreed. "And if I did not deny it, and you asked me questions, made good guesses as to what it was I know, would you say that I had told you anything?" He looked up and met Ferdi's eyes.

"Oh!" Ferdi's face filled with understanding. "You mean the Father couldn't tell you, but you know from his manner, his feelings, that you were right. I see." His eyes clouded. "And what was it? It was hard, wasn't it? Something terrible about your friend, Dr. Beck?"

"No, only slightly shabby, and he knew it and was ashamed. What was tragic and destructive"—he could not find a word powerful enough for the darkness he felt—"was about Elissa von Leibnitz. We didn't live here in those days, we haven't stood in her place, so we shouldn't judge easily, and God knows, I have done many things of which I am ashamed . . ."

"What?" Ferdi sounded almost frightened. "What did she do?"

Monk looked at him very steadily. "She was in love with Dr. Beck, and she knew that the Jewish girl Hanna Jakob was in love with him also, and she too was brave and generous . . . and perhaps she was funny or kind . . . I don't know. Elissa betrayed her to the authorities, who tortured her to death." He saw the color drain from Ferdi's skin, leaving his face ashen and his eyes hollow. "She expected Hanna to break, to tell them where the others were, and she saw to it that they escaped long before they could have been caught," he went on. "She believed Hanna would crack, and only be hurt, not killed. I don't think she wanted anyone killed . . . just broken . . . shamed."

Ferdi stared at him, tears suddenly brimming and sliding down his cheeks. He stumbled for words, and lost them.

"We all do bad things," Monk said slowly, pushing his fingers through his hair. "She may have repented of it, or found it impossible to live except with terrible pain. It seems that after that no risk was too great for her, no mission too dangerous. We can't say whether it was glory or redemption she was looking for . . . or simply a way out."

"What are you going to do?" Ferdi asked, his voice a whisper.

"Finish my coffee," Monk replied. "Then I'm going to look for Hanna Jakob's family. Father Geissner said they live somewhere in Leopoldstadt—he thinks, on Heinestrasse."

Ferdi straightened himself up. "It shouldn't be too difficult. At least we know where to start."

Monk had already considered whether to send a letter introducing himself once they found the address, but he had already been in Vienna for several days, and he had no idea what had been happening in London. He could not afford the delay. Also, it would give Herr Jakob the opportunity to refuse to see him, and he could not afford that, either. He drank the last of his coffee and stood up. Ferdi left his and stood up also, facing the door and the wind outside.

It took them a surprisingly long time to trace the Jakob family. They had moved, and it was afternoon, the lamplighters out in the streets, the lights flickering on like a ribbon of jewels in the windy darkness, when they finally arrived at the right house on the Malzgasse.

The house itself was inconspicuous in an area of very similar several-story dwellings. A smartly uniformed maid answered the door, and Monk gave her the speech already prepared in his mind. Through Ferdi he told her that he was a friend of someone who had fought with their daughter Hanna in the uprising thirteen years ago and whose admiration for her had altered his life. Since Monk was in Vienna he wished to call and carry greetings, and if possible take news of them back to London. Not speaking German, he had brought a young friend to interpret for him. He hoped it did not sound as stiff as he felt.

The maid looked a trifle startled, as if he had come at an

inappropriate time, but she did not rebuff him. He had thought that half past four on a weekday afternoon was quite suitable for visiting. Certainly it would have been in London. It was an hour when women would be receiving, and he thought Hanna's mother might be the one to have observed more of Kristian, and certainly more of the relationships between people. She might well invite him to stay until Herr Jakob returned. It was far too early to disturb anyone at their evening meal.

He looked around the room where they had been asked to wait. It was warm and comfortable, decorated in excellent taste, a little old-fashioned, but the furniture was of fine quality, and his police-man's eye estimated the value of the miniatures on the walls to be higher than one would find in most private houses, even of the well-to-do. The larger pictures over the fireplace he thought to be very pleasant but of less worth, either artistically or intrinsically.

The maid returned and said that Mr. and Mrs. Jakob would see them both, if they would follow her.

Going into the parlor, Monk had a sudden and sharp awareness of being in a different culture. This was not Austria as he had seen it; it was something intimate and far older. He glanced at Ferdi and saw the same look in his face, surprise and slight discomfort. It was a timeless room for family, not strangers. There were two beautiful, tall candles burning. Herr Jakob was a slender man with dark, shin-ing eyes, a black cap on the crown of his head.

With a jolt of embarrassment, scraps of memory came back to Monk, and he realized why his visit had occasioned such surprise. This was Friday evening, near sundown, the beginning of the Jew-ish Sabbath. He could hardly have chosen a worse time to interrupt a family meal—and a religious celebration. It was an act of the greatest courtesy that they had received him at all.

"I'm sorry . . ." he said awkwardly. "I have been traveling and I forgot what day it is. I am sorry, Frau Jakob. This is an intrusion. I can return tomorrow . . . or . . . or is that even worse?" How could he explain to them his urgency without prejudicing anything they might tell him?

Herr Jakob looked at him very directly, his eyes unflinching, but his deep emotion was impossible to miss. "You said that you are here on behalf of a friend of my daughter, Hanna. If that is true, Herr Monk, then you are welcome at any time, even on Shabbat." He had replied in English, heavily accented but easily understandable. Monk need not have brought Ferdi after all.

Monk framed his answer carefully. "It is true, sir." Only afterwards did he even realize he had deferred to this man by using the word *sir*. It had come naturally. "I am a friend of Kristian Beck, who is at present in serious difficulty, and I am in Vienna to see if I can be of some help to him. It is urgent, or I would more willingly delay disturbing you."

"I am sorry to hear he is in difficulties," Herr Jakob replied. "He is a brave man who was willing to risk all for his beliefs, which is the most any of us can do."

"But his beliefs were different from yours?" Monk said quickly, then wondered why he had.

"No," Herr Jakob replied with a faint smile. "Politically at least, they were the same."

Monk did not need to ask about the other side of ethical values. He had met Josef and Magda Beck, and seen the depth and fervor of their Catholicism. He had also seen that, for whatever reason, they countenanced in their house friends who were profoundly anti-Jewish. Whatever their beliefs, their words tipped over from discrimination into persecution. The first allowed the second, and therefore was party to it, even if only by silence. A sudden memory flashed into his mind, sharp as spring sunlight in the rectory front room, the vicar himself standing quoting John Milton to a twelve-year-old Monk, teaching him great English literature. "They also serve who only stand and wait." But now it came differently to his mind: "They also sin who only stand and watch."

He came back to the present candlelit room in Vienna with the daylight fading rapidly beyond the windows, and this quiet couple waiting for him to say something to make sense of his visit here, and their courtesy in receiving both him and Ferdi, and welcoming them on this of all days. Anything but the truth would insult them all, he as much as they, and perhaps Kristian and Hanna as well.

"Did you know Elissa von Leibnitz?" he asked.

"Yes," Jakob answered. There was profound feeling in his face and in the timbre of his voice, but Monk was unable to read it. Had they resented her, known that their daughter had been picked for the errand that cost her life, rather than Elissa, because Elissa, the Aryan Catholic, was valued more, her life held more important than that of Hanna, the Jewess? Immeasurably worse than that, did they know or guess that she had betrayed their daughter to a pointless death? But he had left himself no way to retreat.

"Did you know that Kristian married her?"

"Yes, I knew that."

Monk could feel the heat burning his face. He was ashamed for people he had not even known, far less shared acts or judgments with, and yet he felt tarred with the same brush. He was aware of Ferdi next to him and that perhaps he felt the same embarrassment.

"Will you eat with us?" Frau Jakob asked softly, also in English. "The meal is nearly ready."

Monk was touched, and oddly, he was also afraid. There was a sense of tradition, of belonging, in this quiet room, which attracted him more than he was able to cope with, or to dismiss as irrelevant to him. He wanted to refuse, to make some excuse to come back at another time, but there was no other time. Kristian's trial would begin any day, or might already have begun, and he was no real step nearer to the truth of who had killed Elissa, or why. Certainly he had nothing to take back to Callandra.

He glanced at Ferdi, then back at Frau Jakob. "Thank you," he said.

She smiled and excused herself to attend to matters in the kitchen.

The meal was brought in, a slow-cooked stew in a deep, earthenware pot, and served with prayers and thanksgiving, which included the servants, who seemed to join as a matter of custom. Only after that was the conversation resumed. A peace had settled in the room, a sense of timelessness, a continuity of belief which spanned the millennia. Some of these same words must have been spoken over the breaking of bread centuries before the birth of Christ, with the same reverence for the creation of the earth, for the release of a nation from bondage, and above all the same certainty of the God who presided over all things. These people knew who they were and understood their identity. Monk envied them that, and it frightened him. He noticed that Ferdi also was moved by it—and disturbed, because it reached something in him older than conscious thought or teaching.

"What is it that we can do for Kristian, or Elissa?" Herr Jakob asked.

Monk spoke the truth without even considering otherwise. "Elissa was killed ... murdered ..." He disregarded their shock. "Kristian has been charged, because he appears to have had motive, and he cannot prove that he was elsewhere. I don't believe he would have done such a thing, no matter what the provocation, but I have no evidence to put forward in his defense."

Herr Jakob frowned. "You say 'provocation,' Herr Monk. What is it that you refer to?"

"She was gambling, and losing far more than he could afford," Monk answered.

Herr Jakob did not look surprised. "That is sad, and dangerous, but perhaps not impossible to understand in a woman who had known the passion and danger of revolution, and exchanged it for the tranquillity of domestic life."

"Domestic life should be enough." Frau Jakob spoke for the first time. "To give of yourself is sufficient for the deepest happiness. There are always those who need. There is the community . . . and of course, no matter what age they are, your children always need you, even if they pretend otherwise." The sadness was only momentary in her face, the memory of her daughter who was beyond her help.

"Elissa had no children," Monk explained.

"And she was not one of us," Herr Jakob added gently. "Perhaps in England they do not have a community like ours." He turned to Monk. "But I agree with you. I cannot imagine Kristian meaning to harm her."

The nature of the killing sprang sharply to Monk's mind. Elissa's death, at least, could have been accidental, a man who had not realized his own strength. But Sarah Mackeson's had been a deliberate act of murder. Quickly, he explained it to them, seeing the revulsion and the grief in their faces. He heard Ferdi's sharply indrawn breath, but did not look at him.

Frau Jakob glanced at her husband.

He shook his head. "Even so," he said grimly, "I cannot believe it. Not the second woman."

"What?" Monk demanded, fear biting inside him. "What is it?"

Frau Jakob looked to her husband, and he to her.

"For God's sake, his life could depend on it!" Monk said with rising panic, knowing he was failing and seeing his last chance slip away. "What do you know?" Was it the betrayal? Had it, after all, not been the secret Father Geissner had believed?

"I cannot see if it will help, and perhaps it will make things worse," Herr Jakob said at last, his eyes filled with a sorrow that seemed too harsh and too deep for what Monk had told him, even the murder of a woman he might have admired, and the possibility that a man he had most certainly regarded highly could have been responsible.

"I need to know it anyway," Monk said in the heavy silence. "Tell me."

Beside him, Ferdi gulped. Herr Jakob sighed. "The history of our race is full of seeking, of homecoming, and of expulsion," he said, looking not at Monk but at some point in the white linen tablecloth, and some vast arena of the world in his vision. "Again and again we find ourselves strangers in a land that fears us, and in the end hates us. We are permanent exiles. In Egypt, in Babylon, and across the world."

Monk held his patience with difficulty. It was the passion of feeling that stilled his interruption rather than any regard for the words.

"We have been strangers in Europe for more than a thousand years," Jakob went on. "And still we are strangers today, hated by many, even behind their smiling faces and their courtesy. We have lost some of our people to the fear, the exclusion, the unspoken dislike."

Frau Jakob leaned forward a little as if to interrupt.

"I know," he said, looking at her and shaking his head a little. "Herr Monk does not want a lesson in our history, but it is necessary to understand." He turned to Monk. "You see, many families have changed their names, their way of life, even abandoned the knowledge of our fathers and embraced the Catholic faith, sometimes in order to survive, at other times simply to be accepted, to give their children a better chance."

In spite of himself, Monk understood that, even if he did not admire it.

Jakob saw that in his eyes, and nodded. "The Baruch family was one such."

"Baruch?" Monk repeated, not knowing what he meant.

"Almost three generations ago," Jakob said.

Suddenly, Monk had a terrible premonition what Jakob was going to say.

Jakob saw it in his eyes. "Yes," he said softly. "They changed their name to Beck, and became Roman Catholic."

Monk was stunned. It was almost too difficult to believe, and yet not for an instant could he doubt it. It was monstrous, farcical, and it all made a hideous sense. It was a denial of identity, of birthright, of the faith that had endured for thousands of years, given up not for a change of conviction but for survival, to accommodate their persecutors and become one of them.

And yet had he been in the same circumstances, with a wife and children to protect, honesty told him he could not swear he would have acted differently. For oneself . . . perhaps . . . but for the parent who had grown old and frightened, desperately vulnerable, for the child who trusted you and for whom you had to make the decisions, with life or death as a result . . . that was different.

One question beat in his brain above all others. "Did Kristian know?" he demanded.

"No," Jakob said with a rueful smile. "Elissa knew. Hanna was the one who told her. She had a friend whose grandfather was a rabbi, and interested in all the old records. I think she wanted Elissa to know that it was she who was the one who did not belong, not Hanna. But no one told Kristian. Elissa protected him more than once. She was a remarkable woman. I am very sorry indeed to hear that she is dead . . . still more that it was the result of murder, not accident. But I do not believe that Kristian would do such a thing."

Monk took a deep breath. Hanna's family did not know of the betrayal. His throat was suddenly tight with relief and his next words were hoarse. "Not even if she told him this now, without warning, perhaps to heighten the obligation to her?"

Jakob's face darkened. "I don't know," he said softly. "I think not. But people do strange things when they are deeply distressed, out of the character we know, even that they know of themselves. I hope not."

Monk stayed a little longer, enjoying the comfort and the strange, alien certainty of the room with its millennia-old rituals and memories of history which was to him only faint, from old Bible stories. It was like a step outside the daily world into another reality. He envied Herr Jakob his belief, dearly as it had been bought.

Then, at about nine o'clock, he thanked them and he and Ferdi excused themselves. Tomorrow, Monk must face Max Niemann.

Outside in the street, it was freezing. The pavements glistened with a film of ice in the pools of light from the street lamps. Monk glanced sideways at Ferdi and saw the emotion raw in him. In a few hours he had been hurled through a torrent of passion and loss beyond anything his life had prepared him for, and seen it in a people he had been taught to despise. It had been installed in him that they were different, in some indescribably way less. And he had been touched by their dignity and their pain more deeply than he could control. Even if he could not have put it into such simple words, he was inwardly aware that their culture was the fount of his own. It stirred a knowledge in him too fundamental to be ignored.

Monk wanted to comfort him, assure him. But more than that, he wanted Ferdi to remember what he felt this moment as they walked, heads down in the darkened street, feeling the ice of the wind on their faces. He wanted him never to deny it within himself, or bend or turn it to suit society. It would be yet another betrayal. He had not the excuse of ignorance anymore.

He remained silent because he did not know what to say.

By the time Monk was face-to-face with Max Niemann at last, he had decided exactly what he was going to ask him. He already knew a great deal about Niemann, his heroism during the uprising, his love for Elissa, and how generously he had reacted when she married Kristian instead. From his outward behavior it was not difficult to believe he had largely got over his own passion for her and it had resolved into a genuine friendship for both Elissa and Kristian. He had never married, but that could have been due to a number of reasons. It was not so long ago that Monk himself had been quite sure that he would never marry, or if he did it would be someone quite unlike Hester. He had been certain he wanted a gentle, feminine woman who would comfort him, yield to him, admire his strength and be blind to his weaknesses. That memory prompted in him a wry laughter now. How little he had known himself. How desperately lonely that would have made him, like a man staring into a looking glass, and seeing only his own reflection.

But then he did know himself little, only five years, and those were strands worked out by deduction and sharp, sometimes ugly, flashes of disconnected memory.

He followed Max Niemann from his work as he strolled along the Canovagasse towards the open stretch of the Karlsplatz. It was not an ideal place for the conversation he needed to have, but he could not afford to wait any longer. In London, the trial might already have started. It was that urgency which impelled him to approach Max Niemann in the café where he sat listening to the chatter, and the clink of glasses.

It was discourteous, at the least, to pull up a chair opposite a man who was obviously intent upon being alone, but there was no alternative.

"Excuse me," he said in English. "I know you are Max Niemann, and I need to speak to you on a matter which cannot wait for a proper introduction."

Niemann looked only momentarily startled, his face set in lines of mild irritation.

Before he could protest, Monk went on. "My name is William Monk. I saw you in London at the funeral of Elissa Beck, but you may not remember me. I am a friend of Kristian's, and it is in his interest that I am here."

He saw Niemann's expression ease a little.

"Did you know that Kristian has been charged with the murder, and is due to stand—" He stopped. It was apparent from Niemann's wide eyes and slack mouth that he had not known, and that the news distressed him profoundly. "I'm sorry to tell you so abruptly," Monk apologized. "I don't believe it can be true, but there seems to be no other explanation for which there is any evidence, and I hoped I might find something here. Perhaps an enemy from the days of the uprising."

A look of irony and grief crossed Niemann's face. "Who waited thirteen years?" he said incredulously. "Why?"

A waiter came by, and Monk asked Niemann's permission, then ordered coffee with cream and chocolate in it, and Niemann ordered a second coffee with hot milk.

"Of course we had quarrels then, loves and hates like any other group of people. But they were all over in hours. There were far bigger issues to care about." His eyes were bright, his brow furrowed a little. The noises of crockery and voices around him seemed far away. "It was passionate, life and death, but it was political. We were fighting for freedom from Hapsburg tyranny, laws that crushed people and prevented us from having any say in our own destiny. The petty things were forgotten. We didn't wait to murder our enemies in London thirteen years later; we shot them openly at the time." He smiled, and his eyes were bright. "If there was anything on earth Elissa hated it was a hypocrite, anyone, man or woman, who pretended to be what they were not. It was the whole charade of the court, the double standards, that drew her into the revolution in the first place."

"Do you believe Kristian could have killed Elissa, even unintentionally, in a quarrel that got out of control?" Monk asked bluntly.

Niemann appeared to consider it. "No," he said at length. "If you had asked me if he would have during the uprising, if she had betrayed us, I might have thought so, but he would not have lied, and he would not have killed the second woman, the artists' model." He looked directly at Monk without a shadow across his face. There was no guard in him, no withholding of the deeper, more terrible secret. He had used the word betrayed quite easily, because as far as he knew it had no meaning in connection with Elissa.

Monk hated the knowledge that he would have to tell him, and see the disbelief, the anger, the denial, and at last the acceptance.

"You know him well." Monk made it half a statement, half a question.

Niemann looked up. "Yes, we fought side by side. But you know that."

"People change sometimes, over years, or all at once because of some event—for example, the death of someone they are close to." He watched Niemann's face.

Niemann fiddled with his coffee cup, turning it around and around in his fingers. "Kristian changed after Hanna Jakob's death," he said at last. "I don't know why. He never spoke about it. But he was quieter, much more . . . solitary, as if he needed to consider his beliefs more deeply. Something changed in his ability to lead. Decisions became more difficult for him. He grieved more over our losses. I don't think after that he could have killed someone, even if he or she was a liability to the cause. He would have hesitated, looked for another way . . . possibly even lost the moment."

"And you didn't know why?" Monk said, compelled to press again to see if Niemann had any idea of the betrayal, or if all he knew was the subtle guilt in Kristian, the perception of his own bigotry which troubled him ever after that.

"No," Niemann answered. "He couldn't talk about it. I never knew what it was."

"Do you think Elissa knew?" The question was a double irony.

Niemann thought for quite some time, then eventually answered with sadness edged in his voice. "No. I think she wanted to, and was afraid of it. I don't think she asked him."

Monk leaned forward a little over the table. "You went to London three times this last year. Each time you saw Elissa, but not Kristian. You did not even let him know you were in England. What happened to your friendship that you would do that?"

Niemann looked up at him, then away. "How did you know that?"

"Are you saying it is untrue?" Monk challenged.

"No." There was weariness in Niemann's voice, and a slump to his shoulders. "No, I did not tell Kristian because I did not want him to know. Elissa wrote to me. She was badly in debt and she knew Kristian had no more money to give her. She needed help. I went and did what I could for her, paid her debts. They were not so very great, and I have done well." He smiled very slightly. "I did not tell Kristian. Sometimes the best way to help a friend is not to let him know that you have seen that he needs help."

He looked up from his cup. "But surely it was the artist who killed her? What was his name . . . Allardyce? He was utterly in love with her, you know. Sarah Mackeson must have known it, and she had enough imagination to fear that Elissa would supplant her not only in Allardyce's affections, but more importantly, on canvas, and she would be without the means of support. She must have been frightened and jealous. What if she killed Elissa? She was a stronger and heavier woman. And when Allardyce came home he found Elissa's body and knew what had happened, and in his own rage and grief, he killed Sarah."

"Possibly," Monk agreed with a shrug. "But he wasn't there that evening. He was in Southwark, and didn't return until the morning."

Niemann looked startled, staring at Monk with slow incredulity. "Yes he was! I saw him myself. He was coming out of the gambling house with paper and pencils and things under his arm. He'd been drawing the people at the tables—he often did. There were several people in the street, men and women, but he's highly individual to look at with that broad brow and black hair falling over it. Besides that, I knew him. I spoke to him."

Hope surged up in Monk, making him almost dizzy. "Allardyce was there? You're sure it was that night?"

"Yes. He was in Swinton Street. Whether he went back to the studio or not I don't know, but he certainly wasn't all evening in Southwark. If he said he was, then he lied." He watched Monk closely.

"Are you prepared to come back to London and swear to that?" Monk asked.

"Of course. And you'll find others who saw him, but they may have their own reasons for not being willing to say so."

"Thank you. We had better hurry. Can you, leave tomorrow? I know that is almost without notice, and . . ."

"Of course I can." Niemann finished his coffee and stood up. "It's a murder trial. Once the verdict is in, nothing I say can help, unless I knew who did kill poor Elissa, and could prove it. Unfortunately, I don't, nor can I swear that Kristian was somewhere else. Through Cologne is the best way. The train leaves at half past eight. I'll meet you in the morning at the ticket office at the station at eight o'clock. Now you must excuse me. I need to make some arrangements, and pack my suitcase."

Hester and Callandra sat opposite each other in the quiet, comfortable sitting room in Callandra's house. They had been back from the trial for nearly an hour. It was dark outside but not particularly cold, and the fire blazed up in the grate, yet both were shivering. They had spoken of events during the evidence of the day, but neither had said what Hester knew they were both thinking. Kristian looked haggard and without hope as one witness after another built up a picture of Elissa's gambling, her desperation, her total inability to exercise any control over her compulsion. Pendreigh's skill was remarkable in that he had been able to drag out the proceedings this far. It was perhaps the greatest testament to Kristian's innocence that the victim's father so obviously believed it.

"It's going badly, isn't it?" Callandra said at last. "I can see it in the jury's faces. They are beginning to realize that all Pendreigh's tactics mean nothing except to spin out time." She did not ask when Monk would be home, but the question hung heavily in the air between them. If he had found something easily he would have returned by now, or at least have sent word. Hester had received a couple of short letters, but they had been only personal, a desire to speak to her that could be partially satisfied on paper, and to let her know that he was well and still searching. He had asked her to tell Callandra so on his behalf.

The fire roared in the grate and the coals collapsed inward with a shower of sparks. It seemed the only brightness in the room.

"Yes," Hester said aloud. There was no point in lying, and she could think of nothing to say to offer any comfort. "The trouble is we have no alternative they could believe." Even a day ago she might have added that there must be one; today it seemed hollow. Then she looked across at Callandra. "But I have an idea where to look for one," she said, pity wrenching inside her. Perhaps she was only putting off the inevitable, but she could see no farther than tonight. Tomorrow would have to bring whatever it would, and she would deal with it then.

"Have you?" Callandra asked, struggling to grasp hope and feeling it almost impossible. Her eyes asked not to be told, so she could imagine it was real, just for a while.

Hester stood up. She was astonished by how physically tired she was, and yet she had done nothing but sit in the courtroom all day, her body locked in the aching tension of hope and fear. "I shall begin to seek proof of it tomorrow, so I shall not be in court. Will you be all right?"

"Of course." Callandra rose to her feet also, a lift in her voice as if real, tangible alternatives were suddenly there in plain sight. If Hester had a clear intention, it must be something capable of proof. "Do you want my carriage?" she said hastily. "It would be quicker for you." She did not add "and cheaper," but that was a consideration also. She had not thought to get actual money to give Hester for the expenses of hansoms, and to wait for it tomorrow would be another delay.

"Thank you," Hester accepted. "That is a good idea." She gave

Callandra a quick, hard hug, then took her leave, her mind already planning ahead. There was no time to wonder about tactics, if she were offering false hope, or if it were wise or safe. She knew of no other course towards anything but defeat.

She slept only fitfully, waking every hour or two, her mind still racing over what she should do, mistakes to avoid, how to get around lies she might be told. And always at the back, spreading across everything like a coming nightfall drawing closer every time she looked, having to tell Callandra that she had failed.

She missed Monk with a constant hunger. Sometimes she could forget it, only to be reminded by the ache inside her. He would have known how to do this properly; success would not have eluded him if there were any chance of it whatever.

She rose early, and ate two pieces of toast. She had learned long ago that no matter how busy your mind or clenched up your stomach, if you had work to do then you must eat. To say you were too excited or too worried was a self-indulgence and highly impractical. To be of any use to others you must maintain your own strength.

Then she set out in Callandra's carriage, whose driver had stayed around the corner at a suitable lodging house and was ready and waiting for her by half past seven. She requested to be driven straight to the police station, where she presented herself at the desk and asked for Superintendent Runcorn, telling the sergeant that it was a matter of urgency. The hour of the day and her name were sufficient to impress him, and he took the message straightaway. He returned with the answer that if she were to wait ten minutes, Mr. Runcorn would see her, and would she like a cup of tea. She declined the tea with thanks, and sat down, grateful that he was there and she could gain his attention.

In ten minutes she was duly shown up to a freshly shaven Runcorn sitting behind a tidy desk. The shaving had obviously not been for her, but she thought the clearing of the desk might have been.

"Good morning, Mr. Runcorn," she said, swallowing down her nervousness. "Thank you for seeing me so rapidly. As you know, the trial of Dr. Beck is going badly for him. I have worked beside him for several years, and I believe there must be more to know than we have yet learned, and that the artist Argo Allardyce may be the source of at least some of it. William is in Vienna seeking knowledge of Max Niemann. I should like to pursue Argo Allardyce." She had spoken too rapidly to allow him time to interrupt her, but she was aware that he had not attempted to, and it surprised her. His face looked sad, as if the way the evidence had gone distressed him also. He had not wished Kristian to be guilty, he had simply found it unavoidable.

"Allardyce was in Southwark all that evening, Mrs. Monk," Runcorn said ruefully. "Got a picture that proves it, much as I'd like it not to."

She must be very careful exactly what she said. A month ago she would have been delighted to dupe him in any way. Now she hated the necessity. She frowned, looking puzzled. "Does it really?"

"Oh it's him, plain as day," he replied. "And it's the Bull and Half Moon for sure. Landlord recalls Allardyce there, knows him quite well."

She managed to look doubtful. "I still believe he had something to do with it," she insisted. "One way or another. If Dr. Beck wanted to kill her, he would hardly do it in another man's house."

"Murder isn't often very sensible," he said sadly.

She remained sitting. "Your sergeant was good enough to offer me a cup of tea, and I am afraid I was so eager to see you that I refused. I wonder . . ."

He was glad of the chance to do something for her. "Of course." He stood up immediately. "Just sit there, and I'll have him bring one up."

"Thank you," she accepted with a slight smile.

He went out, and instantly she darted around his desk and opened the first drawer. There was nothing in it but pencils and blank paper. The second had neatly written reports. She was desperate, trying to keep her fingers from fumbling. He had spoken of the picture. Which way had he been looking? She had only moments before he came back.

Third drawer . . . nothing. She turned to the shelf beside the desk. She moved two books lying flat. There it was! An artist's sketch of a group of men sitting around a table. She snatched it and pushed it down inside her jacket just as she heard his hand on the door. She had no time to sit again. Instead, she moved towards him as if she had risen to take the cup from him.

"Thank you!" she said with gratitude more for the escape than the tea. "I hadn't realized I was so cold, or so thirsty. That is very good of you."

He colored very slightly. "I'm sorry it's going badly for Dr. Beck. I wish there were . . ."

"Of course," she agreed, sitting down again and sipping the tea. "But you can't alter the evidence, I know that. I was just hoping. I daresay it was foolish." Since she had asked for the tea, she was obliged to stay long enough to finish it. She was terrified in case he decided to get the picture out just to prove to her that Allardyce was really in it. "I mustn't take up your time," she said, swallowing hastily. "You have been very patient. I suppose there is no possibility it had to do with gambling?"

"Doesn't make any sense, Mrs. Monk," he said regretfully. "Nothing I'd like more than to string a few of them up, but I've got no excuse to. They kill slowly, not by breaking a neck."

She put the teacup down.

"I'm sorry," he apologized, his face flooding with color.

"Please don't be," she said quickly. "It is only the truth." She stood up. "I appreciate candor, Mr. Runcorn. Too many evils are tolerated because we give them harmless-sounding names. Thank you for your courtesy." She did not hold out her hand in case the paper under her jacket crackled. "I can find my way downstairs. Good day."

"Good day, Mrs. Monk." He had risen also, and came around the desk to open the door for her.

She escaped with a pounding heart, and an acute sense of guilt, but she had the drawing.

She spent a useless morning and early afternoon around the area of Allardyce's studio, and came to the conclusion that in this type of detective work she lacked a skill. By the middle of the afternoon she had decided to follow Allardyce's friends more directly, and if she took the carriage south of the river Southwark she would find some of them at least already in the Bull and Half Moon. The light was fading, and no one would be able to paint by it at four o'clock or later.

It was nearly dark and the lamps were lit by the time she went through the tavern door. The warm, smoky, ale-smelling interior was already filled with the babble of conversation. The yellow light of a dozen lamps shone on all manner of faces, but entirely masculine. It was too early for street women to be seeking custom, and more respectable women had work to do: dinners to cook, laundry to iron, children to care for. She took a deep breath and went in anyway.

One or two bawdy remarks, which she ignored, were hurled at her. She was too eager to find anyone who might be a friend or associate of Allardyce to have time for offense. Then she saw a man with an arm amputated above the elbow and a scar on one lean cheek. Her spirits leapt at the thought that he might be a soldier. If he were, that would be at least one person whom she could talk to, perhaps find an ally.

There was no time for delicacy. She smiled at him, coolly, not an invitation. "Where did you serve?" she asked, hoping she was right.

Something in the tone of her voice, an expectation of friendship, even equality, startled any misunderstanding he might have had. He glanced momentarily at his empty sleeve, then up at her. "Alma," he answered, a slight curiosity in his voice. He was waiting to see if the name of that dreadful battle had any meaning for her.

"You were lucky," she said quietly. "Many fared a lot worse."

Something lit in his eyes. "How do you know that, Miss? You lose somebody?"

"A lot of friends," she replied. "I was in Sebastopol and Scutari."

"Widow?" He raised his eyebrows, pity in his face.

She smiled. "No, nurse."

"Let me buy you a drink," he offered. "Anything you want. I'd get you French champagne if I could."

"Cider will do fine," she accepted, sitting down opposite him. She knew better than to say she would get it herself, and rob him of his generosity, or the feeling that he was in control and did not need anyone else to fetch or carry for him.

"What you doing here?" he asked after they were settled and she was sipping her drink. "You've not been here before."

She had already decided that candor was the only way. She told him that she was looking for information to help a friend in serious trouble, accused of a crime of which she believed him innocent, if not in fact, then at least under mitigating circumstances. She wanted more knowledge of someone who had been here on the night of the crime, and showed him the picture she had taken from Runcorn's office.

He screwed up his eyes as he looked at it, one face after another. "What night was that, then?" he said at last.

She told him the date.

"That's a while back." He pursed his lips.

"Yes, I know," she admitted. "I should have come sooner. There have been several reasons. We were looking in a different direction. Will anyone remember? It was the night there was a big spill of raw sugar in Drury Lane, if that's any help?"

"Wouldn't know." He shook his head. "Don't have any reason to go up that way." He concentrated on the picture again. "Know that artist fellow." He pointed to one of the men. "And that one." He indicated Allardyce. "He lives up that way, but he comes here every now and then." He stared at the picture of half a dozen men around a table, ale mugs in their hands, the surroundings roughly sketched in, suggesting the tavern, the parallel walls, a couple of hanging tankards and a poster advertising a juggling act at a nearby music hall.

Hester waited with a sinking feeling of disappointment growing inside her.

The soldier still frowned. "There's something wrong," he said with a shake of his head. "Don't know what."

Hester stared around the room, looking for the place where they had been sitting. Perhaps it was not this tavern? It was too slim a thought to offer hope. Almost before it had taken form in her mind she recognized the tables and the chairs, the angles of the paneling on the wall behind them.

Then it struck her. The poster was different. The one on the wall now was for a singer in a red shirt. She hardly dared put words to it. Her heart was hammering inside her chest.

"When did they change the poster?" she asked.

The soldier's eyes widened. "That's it!" he said with a long sigh. "You've got it. That one was up the night you're talking about— not the juggler they've got here. You can check at the music hall, check with anyone, they'll tell you. This wasn't made that night!" He poked his finger at the drawing. "He was here, all right, but not then."

His face shone with triumph. "That help you?"

"Yes!" she said, smiling at him so widely it was a grin. "Yes, it does! Thank you very much. Now, let me get you a cider, and maybe something to eat. I could certainly do with a pie. Then I'll go and make sure the music hall will swear to it, if necessary."

"Thank you," he accepted graciously. "I'll have a mutton pie with mine, if you please. You'd like that, too. Real tasty, they are. Fill you up."

She left the Bull and Half Moon and was startled as she stepped out into the street to see how the fog had surrounded everything with a dark shroud so thick she could barely see five or six yards in front of her. She had intended to go to the music hall and check to be absolutely certain about the dates of the juggler and the singer, and that they had actually changed the bill, but in this murk that had blown up from the river it would be almost impossible. She could not even see the other side of the street. Where was the carriage? It was not where she had left it, but the driver would not have been able to wait there. No doubt he was in the next side street.

She started to walk, and was aware of footsteps behind her, or was it an echo of her own? Fog distorted sound. But it muffled rather than magnified.

She whirled around, and saw a figure darkening the white vapor that islanded her in every direction. She stepped back, but he came forward. She went back again until she was under the street lamp and the light filtered down pale and patchy as the mist moved, and she saw Argo Allardyce's ashen face and black hair. Her breath caught in her throat, and for a moment she choked with blind terror. There was no point whatever in trying to deny what she had been doing. He must have followed her from the Bull and Half Moon, though she hadn't seen him there. She still had the picture with her. Where was the carriage? How far away? Could she turn and run? Was she even going in the right direction?

She took another step back, and another. The fog thickened, then a gust of cold air blew it away again and he looked only feet from her. He must see in her face that she knew he had lied.

"Who are you?" he demanded, his voice hard and angry, or was it frightened because in a way he, too, was cornered? "Why are you asking questions about me? I didn't kill Elissa or Sarah!"

"You lied!" she accused. "You said you were here that night, but you weren't. If you didn't kill them, why didn't you tell the truth?" She was still moving away from him, and he was following.

"Because I was afraid they'd blame me anyway!" His voice was sharp and brittle. "I was in Acton Street at the gambling house, and one of the women I drew was furious about it. Her husband made a terrible scene and they knocked him senseless. She followed me out and practically tore the pictures of her away from me."

With a wild mixture of misery and elation, Hester realized he was talking about Charles and Imogen. It wasn't proof of his innocence, but that much at least was honest.

She gulped. "What was she like, the woman?"

He was incredulous. "What?"

"What was she like?" she all but shouted at him.

The cold mist swirled around in heavier wreaths, and the boom of a foghorn drifted up from the river, followed almost immediately by another.

"Dark," he said. "Pretty. Soft features."

It was enough. Imogen. "Then where did you go?" she demanded, taking another step back. Now she was in the gloom and he was under the light. She could see the droplets of moisture clinging to his hair and skin.

"Not to Acton Street!" he shouted back at her. "I got a hansom and went all the way to Canning Town. I never came back until morning."

"If you can prove that, why did you lie?" she charged him. He was still coming towards her. Were all his words only a distraction, and when he was close enough and she was off guard, would he lunge for her, and with a swift movement, a wrenching pain, a crack, her neck would be broken, too? She wheeled around, picked up her skirts, and ran as fast as she could in the blind, clinging fog, her heart beating so violently it almost stopped her breathing, the sound of her footsteps muffled. She had no idea where she was going. She tripped over the curb of the cross street and lurched forward, almost losing her balance, flinging her arms wide to stop from pitching over.

There was a snort beside her, a blowing of air, and she stifled a scream. She shot forward and ran straight into the side of a horse. It jerked up and backwards, and the next moment a man's voice called out angrily.

"Albert!" she yelled as loudly as she could.

"Yes, Miss! Where are you?"

"Here! I'm here!" she sobbed, scrambling back past the horse to feel for the dark bulk of the carriage and fumble to open the door. "Drive me home! If you can see your way, get me back to Grafton Street, but hurry out of here, please!"

"Yes, Miss, don't worry," he said calmly. "It'll not be this bad once we're away from the river."

She collapsed inside the coach and slammed the door shut.

They were over the bridge and climbing into clearer air before she thought to tell the coachman to go past the police station so she could leave a message for Runcorn, and return the picture with an abject apology.

In Vienna, Monk took his leave of Ferdi over a very early breakfast, thanking him for the inestimable help he had been not only in practical terms but also for his friendship.

"Oh, it was nothing," Ferdi said quite casually, but his eyes never left Monk's face, and there was a deep flush in his fair cheeks. "It was all rather important, wasn't it?"

"Yes," Monk agreed. "Very important indeed."

"Will you . . . will you write and tell me what happens to Dr. Beck?" Ferdi asked. "I . . . I'd like to know."

"Yes, I will," Monk promised, fearing already that it would be hard news, and he would have to struggle to find a way of wording it so it would not wound the boy more than it had to.

Ferdi smiled. "Thank you. I don't have a card, but I borrowed one of my father's. The name is the same, so you could get in touch with me here. If you come to Vienna again . . ." He left it, suddenly self-conscious.

"I shall write you, of course," Monk finished for him. "And most certainly I shall call."

"Oh . . . good." A smile lit Ferdi's face, and he shot out his hand to clasp Monk's, and then as suddenly let it go and bowed very formally, clicking his heels. *"Auf Wiedersehen,"* he said, looking at Monk through his lashes.

"Auf Wiedersehen, Herr Gerhardt," Monk replied. "Now I must hurry, or I shall miss the train!"

Monk met Max Niemann at the railway station as arranged; half an hour later they were settled on the train as it pulled out. He was impatient to be home and to tell Hester what he had found. It was not the absolute solution he had hoped for, one which would save Beck, but it was as much as he could find, and he had run out of places to look.

Suddenly the burden of it was almost insupportable. Elissa had betrayed another woman to her death. Max Niemann had not known it, nor had Kristian. Assuredly, Fuller Pendreigh would not have, either. The truth he brought with him would shatter all of them.

He looked at Niemann, sitting opposite him in the carriage as they rattled and jolted, picking up speed into the dark countryside. If he knew, would he even be coming to London? What would he have paid for it not to be true? It would shatter an image he had loved and believed for years.

And what would Kristian feel? Had he ever guessed any of it? Hanna's love for him, her knowledge that he was of her own people, even though he did not know it himself. Elissa's single act of unbearable destruction . . .

Or did he know? That was the darkness greater and deeper than the night which lay beyond the carriage windows, ice-cold in the wind off the plains stretching north to the bounds of Russia. Had something happened which had told him of that awful betrayal, and had he exacted revenge for it?

Could any of it help, except possibly Max Niemann's testimony that Allardyce had been in the neighborhood of the studio, not on the south side of the river, as he had sworn. Would Niemann's testimony be believed? He was a foreigner, a longtime friend of Kristian's. Might the jury think it was no more than old loyalties that prompted him now?

Of course, Monk would say nothing to Pendreigh or to Callandra about what had happened to Kristian years ago. It would be better for everyone if the tragedies and the guilt could be buried.

Unless Kristian already knew? If so, it seemed he was prepared to go to the grave keeping Elissa's secret, and his own.

There were too many decisions to make now, without Hester.

He settled down a little further into the seat and prepared to sleep as much as he could during the long journey home, rattling and lurching through the darkness, troubled by dreams, permanently uncomfortable.

He had not intended to, but in the morning he found himself sharing the trials and wry amusements, the interest and the tribulation of travel, with Max Niemann. The Austrian was an intelligent man with quirks of character which were both unusual and pleasing. Talking with him made the time pass far more rapidly, and as long as they did not speak of Kristian, Elissa, or the uprising, there was no difficulty in avoiding the emotional traps of the knowledge he could not share.

They passed through Cologne and moved onward towards Calais. Time dragged by interminably, but they were mile by mile getting closer to England.

The Channel crossing was rough and cold, and docking seemed

to take ages. The London train was delayed, and they had to go up and down looking for seats, but eventually, in the evening of the third day, at last they pulled in. Doors were flying open and people were shouting; cases were heaved out, and the scramble began to find hansoms.

Monk was tired beyond any sharpness of sense. He walked as if in a dream. Every part of his body ached, and he felt as if his muscles would never move easily again. He wanted to see Hester so intensely he half imagined her in the back of every slender woman he saw. He began to wonder if he were awake or asleep.

Max Niemann said he would stay at his usual hotel. They always found a room for him, regardless of the lack of notice, and he would report to Monk at Grafton Street in the morning.

Monk bade him good-night and began to relax at last as his cab made for the Tottenham Court Road, and Grafton Street. He was almost asleep when it jerked to a halt and the driver informed him that he had arrived. He was startled, falling half forward as he staggered out, paid him, and pulled out his door key so that he might surprise Hester and see the delight in her face, feel the warmth of the house, the familiar smells of polish, burning coal, winter leaves in the vase, and above all feel her in his arms.

But it was dark, and there was no one there. He dropped his cases, then fumbled in the gloom to find the gas knobs. There was no fire lit. There had not been all day. He was so stunned with disappointment it was as if someone had struck him physically, bruising his flesh and driving the breath out of his lungs. Exhaustion took hold of him and he began to shiver uncontrollably.

He went to the kitchen and filled the kettle. It took him half an hour to light the stove and for it to burn up heat enough to boil the water. He was about to make tea when he heard the front door open. Still with the caddy in his hand, he strode through to the front room.

Hester was just inside the front door, her coat still on. Her face was white and there was a bruise on her cheek. Her hair was coming undone and her clothes were disheveled.

"Where the hell have you been?" he shouted at her. "Do you know what time it is?"

She looked astonished, then angry. "No! Nor do I care!" she retorted.

"Where were you?" he repeated, his voice shaking with emotion he could not conceal. He could not take his eyes from her face, drawing into himself every detail of her, furious that he cared more than he could control, or hide. He wished to hold her and never let her go, not all night, not tomorrow, not ever. The power of it frightened him. "Don't stand there! Where were you?" he demanded.

"Are you saying that you may go halfway around Europe and I may not go around the corner to the police station?" she asked with a sharp lift to her voice. She stared at him, her eyes brilliant, her face almost colorless except for the dark bruise.

"The police station? Why?" he demanded. "What's happened?"

"I have discovered that Argo Allardyce was not in Southwark on the night Elissa was killed," she replied. "He was in Swinton Street, at least earlier on."

"Yes, Max Niemann saw him," he replied. "How do you know?"

Her eyes widened in surprise. "I detected it," she said icily. "The picture he gave Runcorn wasn't drawn that night; the music hall poster was wrong. He admitted he was in the gambling club."

"Runcorn told you?"

"No, I told him."

"How the devil did you know? Where have you been?" He did not intend to, but his voice had risen until he was once more shouting at her. Fear drove him, fear that she had been in danger and he had not been there to protect her, or prevent her from taking risks. "Damn it, Hester!" He hurled the caddy into the corner and watched the tea fly all over the floor.

Without any warning she began to laugh. Tearing at the ribbons of her hat, she flung it away and walked into his arms. Her laughter turned to weeping and she clung to him so hard it bruised his skin, and he was happy just to feel the strength of her. He closed his own arms around her and held on to her while he lost all sense of time and it really did not matter anymore.

CHAPTER
THIRTEEN

———

Monk could have held Hester in his arms all night, but the trial would resume in the morning and they could not afford to leave seeing Imogen and Pendreigh until then. It might be too late.

Hester pushed away and looked up at him. "The judge's patience is all but ended," she said. "We must prepare everything we can tonight." She reached his eyes, seeing the exhaustion in him. "I'm sorry."

"Have we enough to cast doubt?" he asked. "Allardyce was there, but what if someone can find proof he left before the murders?" His mind was racing over all he had learned in Vienna, and about Max Niemann, who he could not believe had killed Elissa. But deeper and more bitter than anything else was the betrayal of Hanna Jakob. He did not want to tell Hester of it, he wanted to bury it in a silence that would recede into the past until the details blurred and whole months went by without it troubling his mind. Perhaps implicating Allardyce as a suspect would be sufficient, without anything else being said?

"I told Runcorn," she said quietly. "He's bound to look for the cabbie he says picked him up. Of course, he may not find him before the end of the trial. It may not even be true."

He told her Niemann's theory that Sarah killed Elissa, and then Allardyce in turn killed Sarah.

She looked skeptical. "I don't believe it, but I know of no reason why it couldn't be possible. But we must persuade Imogen to testify. That will corroborate what Niemann says about Allardyce definitely being there. If she won't, I suppose we can always oblige her to?"

"Yes . . . but it would be . . . unpleasant."

"I know." She straightened her shoulders. "We need to go tonight." As she said it she turned and went for her coat.

They had to walk in the fine rain down to Tottenham Court Road before they could find a hansom, and directed it to Charles and Imogen's house. They rode in silence. There was no point in planning what to say, there was only the truth, and no time or purpose in dressing it this way or that.

The butler opened the door looking startled and considerably put out. He was obviously about to give a very abrupt answer until he recognized Hester, then his expression turned to alarm. "Is everything all right, Mrs. Monk?" he said nervously.

"There has not been any accident, thank you," she replied. "But we do have a concern which unfortunately cannot wait until morning. Would you be good enough to tell Mr. Latterly that we are here, and Mrs. Latterly also. We need to speak with them as urgently as possible."

"Yes, ma'am." He glanced at Monk. "Sir. If you will come this way, I shall rake the fire in the withdrawing room and get it going again—"

"I can do that," Monk cut across him. "Thank you. If you would be good enough to fetch Mrs. Latterly."

The butler looked startled, but he did not argue.

In the withdrawing room, Monk lit the gas and turned it up until the room was as light as possible, then moved over and worked at the fire until it started to burn again. It was not difficult; the embers were still hot and it only required the riddling away of the clogging ash and a little new coal. He was finished before the door opened and Charles came in.

"What is it?" he asked, turning from Hester to Monk, and back again. He looked tired and drawn, but not as if he had been asleep.

He greeted them only perfunctorily. "What's happened?" No one mentioned the trial; it was unnecessary to say that it was concerning Kristian, and Elissa's death, that they had come. The subject crowded everything else from their thoughts.

Hester answered him, to save Monk the difficulty of trying to word it so as to spare his feelings. There was no time for that. She hated having to tell Charles, to see his fear and embarrassment, but there was no evasion possible.

"Max Niemann saw Imogen leaving the gambling house on the night Elissa was killed." Odd how she spoke of her, even thought of her, by her Christian name, as if she had known her. "Niemann saw Allardyce there, too, meaning that he was not miles away, as he swore. If Imogen also saw him, it could help to raise reasonable doubt enough to acquit Kristian."

Charles was very pale, almost jaundiced-looking in the yellow glare of the gas. "I see," he said slowly. "And you want her to testify."

"Yes!" Thank heaven at least he understood. "I am afraid it is necessary."

Silence almost clogged the air. There was no sound at all but the faint whickering of the flames in the fireplace as they burned up and caught the new coal Monk had placed in there.

"I'm sorry," Hester said gently.

The tiniest of smiles touched Charles's mouth.

The door opened and Imogen came in. She had dressed, but not bothered to pin up her hair. It hung loose in a cloud of dark waves about her head. Just for an instant, before she came into the direct light of the lamp, she could have been one of Allardyce's paintings of Elissa come to life.

"What is it?" she asked, looking straight at Hester. "What's happened?"

It was Charles who answered. It was clear he was torn between swift honesty and trying to soften the blow for her to shield her from embarrassment. He should have known it was impossible. Perhaps he did, but still could not break the habit of a lifetime. "Allardyce was seen near his studio on the night Mrs. Beck was killed," he began. "That means he could be guilty after all. The person who saw him also saw you . . ." He flushed as her body stiffened. "And if you saw him, then that would be additional proof that he was there."

"Why should anyone doubt it?" she said quickly. "If this other person says he saw him, isn't that enough?"

Charles looked at Monk questioningly.

"He is a friend of Kristian Beck's," Monk answered. "They may believe he is saying it simply to defend him. He needs corroboration."

Imogen looked at Charles, her eyes wide. Hester tried to read her expression. It was more than fear alone. Was it shame, even some kind of apology for having to admit publicly where she was and that she had gone without him? It would humiliate him publicly. Had she any idea what else had happened to him at the club that night?

Charles was standing close to her, as if in some way he could physically protect her. She looked at him, but the angle of his shoulders kept a distance between them, a separation.

"It is the only honorable thing to do," Charles said quietly. He looked at Monk. "Describe this man, exactly where he was, and when. Perhaps Imogen should see him in person?"

"No," Monk responded hastily. "If we bring him here we shall be prejudicing her testimony. The prosecution will very quickly point out that we, too, are friends of Kristian's and could have arranged it. It is best the first time she sees him is in court. Pendreigh can call him, and then call Imogen to testify."

Imogen turned to him. She was shivering, her eyes fever-bright. "But I can't help! I have no idea who else was in the street that evening. I wouldn't be able to point to the right man. I think I might only make things worse. I . . . I'm sorry."

Charles stared at her. "Are you sure? Think back. Try to put yourself there again. Think of leaving the . . . the house, stepping—"

"I can't remember!" she interrupted. "I'm sorry. I was simply staring ahead of myself. I could have passed anyone, for all I noticed!" She turned away and smiled apology at Monk, then at Hester, but the refusal in her face was final.

Monk put Hester into the hansom to send her back home to Grafton Street, and he took another to Lamb's Conduit Street, where Runcorn lived. It was after midnight when he woke Runcorn by banging on the door. As he had expected, it was several minutes before Runcorn appeared, rumpled and half asleep, but as soon as he recognized Monk in the eerie glow of the streetlights, his hair plastered to his face in the rain, he opened the door wider to invite him in.

"Well?" he said as soon as they were in the small hallway. "What did you find in Vienna? Anything?"

"Yes." Somehow being with Runcorn in this close, ordinary hallway took Monk back to the facets of police procedure, of the law, of what the realities were, separated from the emotions of love and need. As Runcorn went into the kitchen ahead of him, Monk pulled out one of the kitchen chairs and sat down.

Runcorn turned up the gas and went to riddle the ashes out of the black stove and try to get it burning hot again. "Well?" he said with his back to the room.

"I brought Niemann back," Monk replied. "He's more than willing to testify, both to Kristian's good character . . ."

Runcorn swiveled around on his haunches and glared at Monk.

Monk rubbed his eyes and took a deep breath. For all the years of rivalry and dislike, the petty quarrels between them, they shared more beliefs than he had thought even a month ago, and they knew each other too well to hedge around with half-truths. He looked up at Runcorn, who had risen to his feet. The stove was beginning to draw again, and the heart of the fire burned red.

"Niemann says he was in Swinton Street near the gambling

house just before the murders, and saw Allardyce leaving." Of course, Runcorn knew Allardyce had been there, from Hester. He must also know that she had stolen the picture, although she had returned it.

Runcorn stared at him unblinkingly, only the barest, momentary reflection of that in his eyes. "Go on," he prompted. Absentmindedly, he moved the kettle over onto the hot surface. "There's more to it, or you wouldn't be looking like a wet weekend in Margate. Maybe Allardyce is lying, but maybe he isn't. Is Niemann Dr. Beck's friend, or his enemy? Was he Elissa's lover?"

"Friend. And no, I don't think so."

Runcorn leaned forward over the table. "But you don't know! Have you got time to sit here half the night while I pull out of you whatever it is?"

Monk looked up at him. It was extraordinary how familiar he was, every line of his face, each intonation of his voice. Evidence said that they had known each other since early manhood, over twenty years. And yet there were vast areas of emotion, belief, inner realities Monk was seeing only now. Perhaps he had never cared before?

"There's quite a lot of feeling against Jews in Vienna, in Austria," he said slowly. "They've been persecuted for generations. I suppose centuries would be more accurate."

Runcorn waited patiently, his eyes steady on Monk's face.

"In order to survive, to escape discrimination, even persecution," Monk went on, "some Jews denied their race and their faith and changed their names to German ones. They even became Roman Catholic."

"This must be going to mean something, or you wouldn't be telling me," Runcorn observed.

"Yes. The kettle's boiling."

"Tea can wait. What about people changing their names? What has it to do with the murder of Elissa Beck?"

"I don't know. But Kristian Beck's family was one of those who did that. Elissa knew, but she never told Kristian, and he himself did not know. At least not at the time. She even went out of her way to protect him, knowing that if he were caught, and it became known he was really a Jew, it would be even harder for him." Why was he still telling less than half the truth? To protect Kristian or Pendreigh?

Runcorn's face tightened. There was a flash of pity in his eyes, something that might even have been understanding. He turned away, hiding it from Monk, and began to make tea for both of them, clattering the teapot, spilling a few leaves onto the bench. The silence in the kitchen was heavy as he left the tea to steep. Finally he poured it, putting in milk and passing over two cups onto the table, pushing one across to Monk. He did not need to ask how he liked it.

"And if she told him recently, perhaps in a quarrel over money and her gambling it away," Runcorn said, stirring sugar into his own tea, clicking the spoon against the side of the cup, "that only gives him more reason to kill her."

"The prosecution doesn't know that!" Monk said sharply.

Runcorn raised his eyebrows. "Aren't you going to testify?"

"Yes, but I shan't tell them that. It may have nothing to do with it. It would prejudice them against him . . ."

Runcorn lifted up his tea, decided it was still too hot, and put it down again. "Because he's a Jew?"

"No! For God's sake! Because his family denied it in order to make things easier for themselves. There's nothing wrong with being a Jew—there's everything wrong with being a hypocrite! Neither Christian nor Jew would own the Becks for that."

"You're sure he didn't know?"

Monk had no answer, but as he sat staring at his tea, and the scrubbed boards of the kitchen table in front of him, the possibility was inescapable that Elissa had told Kristian and that it had been the final straw that had broken his self-control. And the jury would see it far more easily than he did. They would not be reluctant, hating the thought, pushing it away with every shred of will and imagination, and finding it returning, stronger each time. And always there was the other, immeasurably worse thought as well, that somehow he had discovered the betrayal of Hanna Jakob. No one would find it difficult to believe he had killed her in revenge for that. Any man might. But always the shadow of Sarah Mackeson robbed it of pity or mitigation.

Runcorn sipped his tea. Monk's steamed fragrantly in front of him, and he ignored it.

"If you'd been her, desperate for money to pay your debts, frightened of the gamblers coming after you," Runcorn said grimly, "and you'd saved him in Vienna, knowing what his family was, wouldn't you have been tempted now to tell him? Especially if he was angry with you, a bit condescending about your bad habits of losing on the tables, perhaps."

"I don't know . . ." Monk was prevaricating. He sipped his tea also, aware of Runcorn staring at him, imagining the disbelief and the contempt in his gray-green eyes.

The silence grew heavier. Monk was damned if he was going to be manipulated by Runcorn, of all people. Runcorn who disliked him, who had spent years resenting him, trying to trip him up. They had watched each other's weaknesses, probing for a place to hurt, to take advantage, always misunderstanding and seeing the worst.

Runcorn who had once been his friend, before ambition and envy eroded that away. That had been a painful discovery, but undeniable. Perhaps he had been the more to blame of the two of them. He was the stronger. Runcorn was full of prejudices, always trying to do the things others would approve of, and yet who had felt pity for Sarah Mackeson, and was embarrassed by it, and defiant. Runcorn half hated Monk, half wanted his approval . . . and wholly expected him to love the truth above all else, no matter what other pain it brought.

"If they find Beck not guilty"—Runcorn's voice cut across the silence—"then we'll have to start again. Somebody killed those women, one maybe accidentally, but not the second. She was on purpose." He did not add anything about her, but the emotion was in his voice, and when Monk looked up at him, the anger, the expression, the defensiveness were in his face as well.

"Yes, I know," Monk agreed. "Niemann will testify anyway, for whatever good that will do. He can at least show them that Kristian was a hero in the uprising."

"And that she was a heroine," Runcorn added relentlessly. "And perhaps that they were in love. That could help. And that she was reckless of her own safety."

"Why was she so drawn to danger?" Monk said, staring not at Runcorn but at the black kitchen stove and the poker sitting upright in the half-empty coke scuttle. "Did she really imagine she could always win?"

"Some people are like that," Runcorn replied, confusion in his voice. He did not even expect to understand. "Even as if they're looking to be . . . I don't know . . . swamped by something bigger than they are. Seen children like it, go on taunting until they get walloped, sometimes black an' blue. Kind of attention. With grown people, I don't know . . . " He put more sugar into his tea and stirred it. "Some people will do anything to survive. Others seem to want to destroy themselves. Pick 'em out of trouble, and they get straight back into it, almost as if they didn't feel alive if they weren't afraid. Always trying to prove something."

Monk picked up his cup. It was not quite hot enough anymore, but he could not be bothered to get the kettle and add to it. "It's a bit late now. I'll go and see Pendreigh in the morning."

Runcorn nodded.

Neither of them said anything about how Callandra would feel, or Hester, about loyalties, or pain, or compromise, but it had already torn dreams apart inside Monk as he walked towards the door, and he could not even imagine the hurt that lay ahead.

At the front door they looked at each other for only a moment, and then Monk stepped out into the rain.

The judge allowed a slight delay for Pendreigh to speak alone to Max Niemann. He had already given the judge notification that he would call Niemann as a witness, in the hope that Monk would be able to bring him back from Vienna. However, he still needed to have a clearer idea of what Niemann could contribute to the defense.

It was nearly half past ten when, in a hushed and crowded courtroom, Max Niemann walked across the empty space of floor, climbed up the steep steps to the witness stand and swore to his name and that he lived in Vienna.

Pendreigh stood below him, picked out as in a spotlight by the sudden blaze of sunlight through the high windows above the jury. Every eye in the room was upon one or the other of them.

"Mr. Niemann," Pendreigh began. "First let us thank you for coming all the way to London in order to testify in this trial. We greatly appreciate it." He acknowledged Niemann's demur, and continued. "How long have you known the accused, Dr. Kristian Beck?"

"About twenty years," Niemann replied. "We met as students."

"And you were friends?"

"Yes. Allies during the uprisings in '48."

"You are speaking of the revolutions which swept Europe in that year?"

"Yes." A strange expression crossed Niemann's face, as if the mere mention of the time brought all kinds of memories sweeping back, bitter and sweet. Hester wondered if the jury saw it as clearly as she did. Monk was not permitted in the room because Pendreigh had reserved the right to call him as witness.

"You fought side by side?" Pendreigh continued.

"Yes, figuratively, not always literally," Niemann answered.

"Most of us in the room"—Pendreigh waved an arm to indicate the crowd—"but principally the jury, have never experienced such a thing. We have not found our government sufficiently oppressive to rise against it. We have not seen barricades in the street, nor had our own armies turned upon us." His voice was outwardly quite calm, but there was an underlying passion in it, not in the tone, but in the timbre. "Would you tell us what it was like?"

Mills rose to his feet, his face puckered with assumed confusion. "My lord, while we sympathize with the Austrian people's desire for greater freedom, and we regret that they did not succeed in their aim, I do not see the relevance of Mr. Niemann's recollections to the murder of Mrs. Beck in London this year. We concede that the accused was involved, and that he fought with courage. Nor do we doubt that Mr. Niemann was his friend, and still is, and is prepared to put himself to considerable trouble and expense to attempt to rescue him from his present predicament. Old loyalties die hard, which is in many ways admirable."

The judge looked at Pendreigh enquiringly.

"Mr. Niemann has a long friendship with the accused *and* the deceased, my lord," Pendreigh explained. "He can tell us much of their feelings for one another. But he was also in London at the time of the murder, and was in Swinton Street immediately before that event—" He was interrupted by a buzz of amazement from the crowd, and the rustle and creak of two hundred people shifting position, sitting more upright, even craning forward.

"Indeed?" the judge said with some surprise. "Then proceed. But do not drag it out with irrelevancies, Mr. Pendreigh. I have already given you a great deal of latitude in that direction."

"Thank you, my lord." Pendreigh bowed very slightly and turned to Niemann again. "Can you tell us, as briefly as possible without sacrificing truth, the parts each of them played in the uprising, and their relationship to each other?"

"I can try," Niemann said thoughtfully. "They were not married then, of course. Elissa was a widow. She was English, but she fought for the Austrian cause with a passion I think greater than many of us who were native had." His voice was soft as he spoke, and both the tenderness and the admiration he felt were apparent. "She was tireless, always encouraging others, trying to think of new ways to confront the authorities and draw the sympathy of more people to make them understand the justice of our cause and believe we could win. It was as if there were a light inside her, a flame from which she would set a spark to burn in the souls of more lukewarm people."

For a moment he was silent, as if needing to regain his self-control so he could go on trying to show these calm-faced Englishmen in their tailored suits what passion and courage had been in the streets of Vienna, facing an overwhelming enemy.

Everyone was watching him. Hester moved fractionally in her seat. She wondered what Callandra was thinking, if this memory of heroism and unity hurt her, or perhaps if all she cared about now was proving Kristian innocent, or even just saving his life. She glanced sideways at her and wished she had not. It was intrusive, looking at a nakedness that should not be seen.

Then, to her surprise, she caught sight of Charles on the other side of the aisle, and Imogen beside him. Since she had refused to testify, saying she had not seen Niemann, why were they here? Was it simply a concern to see the truth of the matter, even a loyalty to Hester, although neither of them had spoken to her? Or was there some deeper cause, some purpose of their own?

Imogen looked haggard, her eyes enormous. Could she know something after all, and if the utmost disaster fell, she would speak?

"She was the bravest person I ever knew." Niemann's voice filled the room again. It was quiet, as if he were talking to himself, and yet the absolute stillness carried the sound of it to every ear.

Hester turned forward again.

"She was not foolish, and God knew, we lost enough of us that she saw death intimately." Niemann's lips tightened, and there was a wince of pain as he spoke. His voice dropped a little. People strained to hear him. "She knew the risks, but she conquered her own fear so completely I never once saw her show it. She was a truly remarkable woman."

"And Kristian Beck?" Pendreigh prompted.

Niemann lifted his head. "He was remarkable also, but in a different way." His voice resumed its strength. He was speaking now of a man who was his friend, and still alive, not of a woman he had only too obviously loved. "He was the leader of our group—"

Pendreigh held up his hand. "Why was he the leader, Mr. Niemann? Why he, and not, for example, you?"

Niemann looked slightly surprised.

"Was it by election, because of superior knowledge, or was he perhaps older than the rest of you?" Pendreigh enquired.

Niemann blinked. "I think it was common assent," he replied. "He had the qualities of decision, courage, the ability to command respect and obedience and loyalty. I don't remember us deciding. It more or less happened."

"But he was a doctor, not a soldier," Pendreigh pointed out. "Would it not have been more natural to put him in some kind of medical duty, rather than in command of what was essentially a fighting unit?"

"No." Niemann shook his head. "Kristian was the best."

"In what way?" Pendreigh pursued. "Was he also passionately dedicated to the cause?"

"Yes!"

"But doctors are healers, essentially peaceful," Pendreigh persisted. "We have heard much evidence of his caring for the injured and the sick, tirelessly, to the exclusion of his own profit or well-being, never of him as a man of action, or any kind of warfare."

Mills stirred in his seat.

"If we are to believe you, Mr. Niemann," Pendreigh went on more urgently, "then we have to understand. Describe Kristian Beck for us, as he was then."

Niemann drew in a deep breath. Hester saw his shoulders square. "He was brave, decisive, unsentimental," Niemann answered. "He had an extraordinarily clear vision of what was necessary, and he had the intelligence and the will, and the moral and physical courage, to carry it out. He had no personal vanity."

"You make him sound very fair," Pendreigh observed.

Hester thought Niemann made Kristian sound cold, even if it was not what he intended. Or perhaps it was? If he wished to exact a revenge on Kristian for his winning of Elissa, this was his perfect opportunity. Had Monk brought him here for that, unintentionally sealing Kristian's fate?

Or was it possible, even probable, that Niemann believed Kristian guilty?

"He was fair," Niemann said. He hesitated, as if to add something more, then changed his mind and remained silent.

"Did he fall in love with Elissa von Leibnitz?" Pendreigh asked. His voice was thick with his own emotion.

"Yes," Niemann replied. "Very much."

"And she with him?"

"Yes." This time the word was simple, painful.

"And they married?"

"After the uprising, yes."

"Did you ever doubt his love for her?"

"No. No, I didn't."

"And you all three remained friends?" Pendreigh asked.

Neimann's hesitation was palpable.

"You didn't?" Pendreigh asked.

"We lost touch for some time," Niemann answered. "One of our number was killed, very violently. It distressed us all profoundly. Kristian seemed to feel it most."

"Was he at fault?"

"No. It was just the fortune of war."

"I see. But he was the leader. Did he feel perhaps he should somehow have prevented it?"

Mills half rose to his feet, then changed his mind. Niemann was painting a darker picture of Kristian than the dedicated doctor that had been shown so far. It was hardly in his interest to stop Niemann, or to question his veracity.

"I don't know," Niemann answered. It was probably the truth, but it sounded evasive.

Pendreigh retracted. "Thank you. Now may we come to the present, and your recent visit to London? Did you see Mrs. Beck?"

"Yes."

"Several times?"

"Yes."

"At her home, or elsewhere?"

"At the studio of Argo Allardyce, where she was having a portrait painted." Niemann looked uncomfortable.

"I see. And were you in that vicinity on the night of her death?"

"Yes, I was."

"Where, precisely?"

"I was walking along Swinton Street."

"At what time?"

"Shortly after nine o'clock."

"Did you see anyone you knew?"

"Yes. I saw the artist, Argo Allardyce." Niemann drew in a deep breath. "I also saw a woman who has since conceded that she was there, but unfortunately she does not remember seeing me."

"Argo Allardyce?" Pendreigh affected surprise. "What was he doing?"

"Striding along the pavement with an artist's case under his arm. He looked very angry. The woman was following him and spoke to him while I was there."

"Thank you. Your witness, Mr. Mills."

Mills bowed and rose. He did not ask more, but with a few skillful questions he drew from Niemann a picture of Kristian as a leader in the uprising which was even more self-controlled than before, a man who never lost sight of the goal, who could make sacrifices of all kinds, even of people, in the good of the greater cause.

Hester sat cringing with every new addition, and felt Callandra stiffen beside her. She could only imagine what she must be feeling.

"And you were in London and saw Elissa Beck several times, is that correct?" Mills enquired.

"Yes." Was it defiance or embarrassment in Niemann's face?

Mills smiled. "Indeed," he observed. "Always at some place other than her home? Was Dr. Beck ever present, Mr. Niemann?"

The implication was obvious. Niemann blushed. "I came because Elissa was in some financial trouble," he answered, his voice thick with emotion. "I was in a position to help her. Kristian was not. In deference to his feelings, I did not wish him to know what I had done."

Mills smiled. "I see," he said with only a whisper of disbelief in his voice. "I commend your loyalty to an old ally, and a woman with whom you were in love. I am afraid there is nothing you can do now to help either of them." Mills thanked Niemann, and withdrew. He had caused the damage, and he needed do no more.

The luncheon adjournment was brief. Hester saw Charles and Imogen only as they disappeared through the farther doorway. She, Monk and Callandra ate in a noisy public house, where they took refuge in the difficulty of hearing amid the clamor to avoid speaking of the trial.

It was on the way back, on the steps going up to the court, that Runcorn caught up with them, his coat flying, his hair damp from the clinging fog.

"What is it?" Monk demanded, turning to him.

Runcorn looked at him, then at Hester. Callandra had gone ahead and he did not recognize her at this distance. "I'm sorry," he said, and the weight of it was heavy in his voice. "We found the cabbie who picked up Allardyce outside the gambling house. He remembers it pretty clearly. There was a nasty scene. A woman snatched some drawings from Allardyce and tore them up there on the side of the footpath. He says Allardyce seemed glad to get away from her before she drew everyone's attention to the fact that he had been drawing people without them knowing. He was into the cab like a fugitive, he said, and he took him all the way to Canning Town." He sucked in a deep breath and let it out in a sigh. "There's no possibility he went 'round to his studio and killed those women. I'm sorry." It was an apology, as if he felt somehow at fault that he could not have given the answer they all wanted.

Monk put his hand on Runcorn's shoulder. "Thank you," he said thickly. "Better to know that now than later." Too wretched to find any more words, he put his arm around Hester and went on up the steps and inside.

Pendreigh did not call Monk to the stand. He realized that there was nothing he could usefully ask him, but to his amazement Mills called him in order to confirm or rebuff Niemann's evidence. The request seemed reasonable, even helpful to the defense. Pendreigh had no cause to object, and no grounds. If he had tried to prevent it, it would have served against him. Why would he wish to? Monk was in his employ. Pendreigh had no possible choice but to concede. He did so graciously and seemingly at ease. After all, Monk would confirm what Niemann had said.

Monk climbed up the tight, curling steps of the witness box and stood facing Mills, a neat, diminutive, unthreatening figure. Monk swore to his name, residence, occupation, and why he had gone to Vienna at Pendreigh's request. He did not correct Mills that it had actually been Callandra's and that Pendreigh had concurred. It was close enough.

"Presumably, you made all the enquiries you could regarding both Mr. and Mrs. Beck during their time in that city?" Mills said politely. "I say that because you have the reputation of a man who seeks not only the truth that serves his interests, but all of it that he can find."

It was a compliment. It was also a reminder, like the twist of a knife, of exactly what Runcorn had said.

"Time was short, but I learned all I was able to," Monk agreed.

"Short?" Mills raised his eyebrows. "I estimate you were gone seventeen days. Am I incorrect?"

Monk was startled that Mills should have cared to be so exact. "No. I think that's about right."

"I imagine that what you learned is broadly the same as what Mr. Niemann has told us," Mills continued. "Nevertheless, it would help us to hear it directly from you, and know the sources from whom you obtained it. Where did you begin, Mr. Monk?"

"With listening to stories of the uprising from those who fought in it," Monk answered. "And you are quite correct, they confirm what Mr. Niemann told you. Kristian Beck fought with courage, intelligence and dedication to the cause of greater freedom for his people." He chose his words carefully. "He cared deeply for those he led, but he was not sentimental, nor did he favor those who were his friends above those who were less close to him."

"He was impartial?" Mills asked.

Monk would not be moved. "I meant what I said, sir. He did not favor one above another because of his own feelings."

Mills smiled. "Of course. I apologize. No doubt you heard many tales of great courage and self-sacrifice, of heroism and tragedy?"

"Yes." Why did he ask that? What had he heard? What did he suspect?

"And did you follow them up, pursue them to be certain what degrees of truth they held?" Mills shrugged very slightly. "We all know that terrible conflicts where there are profound losses can give rise to legends that we . . . embellish . . . afterwards."

"Of course I followed them up!" Monk said tartly. "One-sided, they are of little use."

"Naturally." Mills nodded. "I would not have expected less of you. With whom did you follow them, specifically?" The question was gently put, almost casually, and yet the silence in the room invested it with unavoidable importance.

"With Dr. Beck's family still living in Vienna, and with a priest who had helped the fighters with comfort and the offices of the church," Monk replied.

"Offices of the church? Perhaps you would explain?"

"The sacraments: confession, absolution."

"A Roman Catholic priest?"

"Yes."

"A number of the revolutionaries were Roman Catholic?"

"Yes."

"All of them?"

Monk suddenly felt guarded, uncomfortable. "No."

"The others were Protestant?"

"I didn't ask." That was an evasion of the truth. Would Mills see it in his face?

"And yet you know they were not Catholic?" Mills persisted.

Pendreigh rose to his feet, frowning. "My lord, can this possibly be relevant? My learned friend seems to be fishing without knowing what it is he seeks to catch!" He spread his hands wide. "What has the religion of the revolutionaries to do with anything? They fight side by side, loyal to each other, united by a common cause. We have already heard that Kristian Beck played no favorites!"

The judge looked at Mills. "Since you did not apparently know of this priest before Mr. Monk spoke of him, Mr. Mills, what are you seeking to show?"

"Merely confirmation, my lord." Mills bowed and turned, raising his face to Monk, in the stand. "Is that also what you learned, Mr. Monk, that all were treated alike, Catholic, Protestant, atheist and Jew? Kristian Beck treated all with exact equality?"

Could Mills possibly know about Hanna Jakob? Or was he so sensitive to nuance, skilled to judge, that he had perceived something, even though he could not know what it was? What had he learned from Max Niemann in that short conversation before court this morning? Runcorn's face kept coming back to Monk, his quiet, almost accusatory insistence on the truth.

Dare he lie? Did he want to? If he looked at Hester now, or Callandra, Mills would see it. The jury would see it.

"You hesitate, Mr. Monk," Mills observed. "Are you uncertain?"

"Of course I'm uncertain. I wasn't there. I'm only working on what others tell me."

"Exactly. And what did this priest tell you? Has he a name one may call him by?"

"Father Geissner."

"What did Father Geissner tell you, Mr. Monk? It cannot be se-cret under the bonds of the confessional, or he would not have re-peated it to you. I assume you were honest with him as to who you were and what your purpose was in enquiring?"

"Yes, I was."

"Then tell the court what he told you, if you please."

Pendreigh rose to protest, and sat down again without having said anything. The fact that he was unhappy, but had no legal cause to object, did more harm than good. Monk saw it in the jurors' faces.

"Mr. Monk, you must answer the question," the judge ordered, although there was courtesy in his voice, even some sympathy.

Monk was the last witness. There was no one else to call, no other suspect to suggest. They were all but beaten. And yet he still could not bring himself to believe that Kristian would have killed Sarah Mackeson, even to save himself. It was the act of a coward, an innately selfish man, and every evidence there was, whether from friend or stranger, said Kristian had never been that.

"Mr. Monk!" the judge prompted again. "I do not wish to place you in contempt of the court, nor to allow the jury to assume that whatever it is you learned is to the discredit of the accused, so much so that you, his friend, and employed by his defense, would rather suffer the penalties of defying the court than to tell us."

Monk made the decision with the same wild sense of despair that he might have felt while overbalancing off the ledge of a cliff.

It was almost a physical dizziness, a knowledge of disaster rushing up towards him. And yet they had nothing to lose—except loyalties, dreams, illusions of what had been good.

The judge was about to speak again.

Monk dared not look at Kristian, or at Pendreigh. He would face Hester later.

The court was in stiff, scarcely breathing silence, every face staring up at him.

"He told me about Hanna Jakob, who was a member of Dr. Beck's group in the uprising." Monk's voice fell into the waiting room like a stone into dead water. It was as if no one understood the meaning of his words. Even Pendreigh's pale face was completely blank.

Mills frowned. "And what meaning has that for us, Mr. Monk? What caused you to hesitate so long before committing yourself to an answer?"

"It is a tragedy I would rather not have disclosed," Monk replied, staring straight ahead of him at the carving on the wall below the dock.

The waiting prickled in the air like tiny needles in the mind.

It was too late to turn back. Maybe it was reasonable doubt. It was all there was left, no matter how many dreams it shattered. "She was in love with Kristian Beck," Monk said softly. "As was Elissa von Leibnitz. They were both brave, generous and young. Elissa was English, and one of the most beautiful of women. Hanna was Austrian . . . and Jewish."

No one moved. There was no sound, and yet the emotion in the room seemed almost to burst at the walls.

"They were both fighters for the revolution," Monk went on. "Because of her Jewish background, Hanna knew that many families, before the emancipation of the Jews, when they were still forbidden many occupations, excluded from society, denied opportunities and living in constant fear, had changed their Jewish names to German ones. They had taken the Catholic faith, not from conviction but in order to give their children a better life. The Baruch family was one such." He breathed in deeply. "They changed their name to Beck. Three generations later, the great-grandchildren had no idea they had ever been anything but good Austrian Catholics."

At last he looked up at Kristian, and saw him start forward, disbelief blank in his face, his eyes wide, aghast, as if the world he knew was disintegrating in his grasp.

"No one knows the conversation between the two women," Monk went on. "But Elissa was made aware that the man she loved, and had presumed to be of her own people, was actually of her rival's, although he himself did not know it." He was aware of faces in the room below him craning around and upward, staring.

"It was necessary to carry dangerous messages to warn other groups of revolutionaries," Monk said, continuing the story, "in different parts of the city. Hanna was chosen to do it, for her knowledge of the streets of the Jewish quarter and her courage, and perhaps because she was not so closely one of the group, being a Jew. Father Geissner told me that Dr. Beck afterwards felt guilty, even that the ease with which they chose her for the task troubled him. Apparently, he spoke of it outside the confessional as well as within it."

Mills's eyes were fixed on him. Not once did he glance away at Pendreigh, or at the judge. "Continue," he prompted. "What happened to Hanna Jakob?"

"The other group was warned by someone else," Monk said quietly, aware of how strained his voice was. "And Hanna was betrayed to the authorities. They caught her and tortured her to death. She died alone in an alley, without giving away her compatriots. . . ."

There were gasps in the room. The upturned face of one woman was wet with tears. A voice muttered a prayer.

"By whom was she betrayed?" Mills asked hoarsely.

"Elissa von Leibnitz," Monk answered. At last he looked at Kristian and saw nightmare in his face. He had not known. No one could look at him and believe that he had.

"No!" Max Niemann struggled to his feet. "No! Not Elissa!" he cried. "It's not possible!"

Two ushers of the court moved towards him, but he sank back down again before they reached the row of seats where he was. He, too, looked like a man who has seen an abyss open before his feet.

Pendreigh stood with difficulty; only the table in front of him supported his weight. He looked like a pale taper of light with his bloodless face and white wig with thick, golden hair beneath it. His voice came between his teeth hoarsely.

"You lie, sir. I, too, would like to believe that Dr. Beck is innocent, and have done so to this moment. But I will not have you blaspheme the memory of my daughter in order to save him. What you suggest is monstrous, and cannot be true."

"It is true." Monk answered him without anger. He could understand the rage, the denial, the unbelievable pain too immense to grasp. "No one thought she meant Hanna to die," he said softly. "She was certain she would yield up the names long before that point, and would be released, humiliated but uninjured." He found it difficult to breathe, and to keep control of his face. When he resumed, his voice was harsh with pain. "Perhaps that was the greatest injury of all, the insult. She was betrayed, and yet she died without giving her torturers the names of any of them."

There was silence, as if every man and woman in the huge room were absorbing the agony into themselves. Even Mills did not move or speak.

Finally, the judge leaned forward. "Are you suggesting, Mr. Monk, that this is relevant to Mrs. Beck's death?"

Monk turned to him. "Yes, my lord. It is obvious to us here that Dr. Beck is as shattered by this terrible story as Herr Niemann, or indeed Mr. Pendreigh, but there are those in Vienna who were aware of it and could piece together the tragedy, as I did. Surely their existence raises more than reasonable doubt that one such person, rather than Dr. Beck, may have been guilty of a fearful revenge?" He found his hands shaking as he held on to the railing of the box, palms wet. "If you convict Dr. Beck you will never lie easily in your beds that you have hanged a man innocent of his wife's death, and that of poor Sarah Mackeson."

"Mr. Monk," the judge said firmly, "you are here to give evidence as to what you have seen and heard, not to make defense counsel's summation speech, however well you are able to do that." He turned to the prosecution. "Mr. Mills, if you have no more questions for your witness, you might offer him now to Mr. Pendreigh. . . ." He looked at Pendreigh. "If you are well enough to continue? In view of the extraordinary nature of Mr. Monk's testimony, and the way it cannot help but affect you personally, the court will be happy to grant you until tomorrow to compose yourself, if you wish?"

Pendreigh looked bewildered, as if he hardly knew where he was. "I . . . I will question Mr. Monk!" he said abruptly, swinging around to stare up at the witness box. His face had no vestige of color, and his eyes were bloodshot.

"What you have said of my daughter is a damnable lie, but I give you the credit that you may have been led to believe it. Therefore I must suppose that those who told it to you may also imagine it to be true. I concede that in their sickness someone might have felt it motive for revenge, and made this parody of justice a last, dreadful act. If so, as you say, this court cannot, in any semblance of honor, convict Dr. Beck. The defense rests, my lord."

He made his way back to his seat like a man walking in the dark, almost feeling his way. His junior stood as if to guide him, but did not indulge in the familiarity of actually reaching out his hand.

Mills had little more to say. He pointed out that such an avenger of Hanna Jakob was entirely imaginary. No one had named such a person nor was there any proof that he or she existed. Dr. Beck, on the other hand, was very much there. He summed up all the evidence, but briefly, knowing that in the emotion-charged room he could lose their sympathy if he appeared too tied to reason.

The judge instructed the jury and they retired.

Kristian was taken down to the cells, and the rest of the court was left to wait in an exquisite suspense. No one knew whether it would be minutes, hours, or even days.

CHAPTER
FOURTEEN

Callandra left the courtroom without any clear idea of where she was going, except to where she could be alone without the pretense of courtesy or that she was more or less all right. She had been as shattered by Monk's testimony as had the rest of the court. She had seen Pendreigh stagger as if seized by a physical pain, but it was Kristian she had turned to. She had wanted to find Elissa human, not a heroine she could never equal, but she would never have wished this searing tragedy, this desolation which left only a broken and terrible grief for what had once been so beautiful.

She could understand being so in love it robbed you of your balance, your judgment of good and evil, but she could not make the leap to acting out the passion or the violence as Elissa had. There was nothing worth winning at the cost of your own being, the soul, the integrity that was the core of who you were. The act of doing such a thing made it impossible for you to hold the good, even if you could grasp it for an instant.

She pushed through the crowd, oblivious of individuals, wanting only to escape for a while.

Had Elissa submitted to a moment's insanity when she was exhausted, frightened, pressed in by danger and threat on all sides, then spent the rest of her life regretting it, and unable to redeem any part of herself because she had kept the prize?

Callandra had expected to feel loathing, and yet, walking slowly out of the courtroom entrance and down the steps with the rain in her face, she was amazed that it was pity that stirred inside her for all that had been thrown away.

She stood on the pavement alone as people brushed past her. When would they bring in the verdict? Monk had taken a terrible chance. He had been brilliant. She knew why he had done it. It was like him, a desperate throw when all else was lost. He would have known how it would lacerate to the core and create scars for which there was no healing.

She did not know whether she would be allowed to see Kristian. The verdict was not in yet, so he was technically still an innocent man. She could lay no claim to be family, but she was a representative from the hospital; Thorpe had never taken that from her. Surely if they would permit him to see anyone at all, other than his lawyer, since he had no relative, it would be a colleague from his place of work.

She should hurry. They could bring in the verdict at any time, and then it might be too late. She turned and began to climb back up the steps.

She did not know if he would even wish to see her, but she must try. Whatever happened, and she refused to think it through to the end, he must know now, before the verdict, that she believed in his innocence.

She had feared he could have killed Elissa. The provocation was so great it was too easy to understand a moment of fear overcoming a lifetime's morality and restraint. The act could be over and irretrievable in moments, before the brain had caught up with the action of the hands.

But she did not believe he could then have gone on and deliberately killed Sarah Mackeson. No fear whatever would have driven the man she knew to do that. She must look him in the face and he must see in her eyes that it was so.

"Can't give you long, ma'am," the guard said reluctantly, his voice tense, his eyes glancing back to be sure he was not observed by any higher authority. He was doing this as an act of compassion, and it made him nervous.

"Thank you," she accepted sincerely.

"I can give you ten minutes, that's all," he warned.

"Thank you," she said again. Ten minutes seemed desperately short, but then ten hours would have been, too. Whatever the time, there was always an end to it, a parting which might be the last. If that was what she had, then she must make every second of value.

He unlocked the door and pulled it open with a scrape of iron on stone. "Visitor for yer!" he said, and allowed her to go in.

Kristian was standing, staring up towards the high window where a square of gray daylight was visible. He turned in surprise, but when he saw Callandra his expression was closed, unreadable. He had no idea what to expect from her, and he was exhausted in mind and spirit. He had no reserves with which to face her needs or doubts. Every certainty had been torn from him, even his own identity was no longer what he had believed. His heritage had been an illusion, and the reality was alien, worse than alien, because it was known and faintly, subconsciously, held to be inferior. He was no longer one of "us." Without his having changed or done anything, he was inexplicably one of "them."

The wife he had admired for her courage and honor had committed a fearful act of betrayal, and kept it secret from everyone, seeing him, talking to him every day, and hiding it.

Callandra knew he was not able to discuss any of it. As happens to someone who is desperately ill, everything in the world had changed and he was no longer supple or strong enough to react to it.

She smiled at him, as if it were a normal day. Should she say anything that mattered, say that she believed in him? That it made no difference whatever to her whether he was a Jew or a Christian? That she was not outraged by Elissa's acts, nor did she hold him accountable for how he reacted now?

He met her eyes, his own hollow, skin blue around the sockets as if he were physically ill. He was searching her, and not able to find the words to ask, perhaps not knowing whether it was unfair, expecting of her something she could not give. Perhaps he was even afraid of the answer. Was she here from pity, loyalty, anything that was half a lie, and entirely a hurt?

She made herself smile at him fully, without reservation, and felt the tears brim her eyes. "I cannot imagine what you must be suffering," she heard herself say without thinking first. "Or how you can absorb what you have heard. But families are not who you are, good or bad. You cannot judge why they did what they did. We were not there to see the passions or know for whom the sacrifice was made. What you believe, how you behave towards others, and within your own truth, is who you are. No one can alter that except you. And you should not try, because who you are is good."

He bent his head to hide the well of emotion in his eyes.

"Is it?" he said, his voice choked.

"Yes," she answered with certainty. "Maybe you were not always wise with Elissa, or even fair to her boredom or lack of purpose. But you cannot have known the guilt within her, because it sprang from an act beyond your imagination."

He looked up suddenly. "I did not kill her!"

"I know," she answered, and he saw in her face that she did know. She smiled very slightly. "I never imagined that you could have killed the artists' model, no matter what provocation there was to hurt Elissa, or to stop her destruction of both of you."

"Thank you," he whispered.

She leaned forward and kissed his cheek. His skin was only just warm. She ached to do something more, to reach him in an infinitely comforting way and take some of his pain and tiredness to herself, and bear it for him, but she could already hear the guard's footsteps and she knew time was up.

She stepped back so their intimacy should not be intruded upon. She would not say good-bye; she would not use those words.

She just looked at Kristian for a moment, then as the door opened, she faced the guard and thanked him for his courtesy. She left without looking back or speaking again. Her throat was aching too much and she was blind with tears anyway.

Hester and Monk also left the courtroom and went outside into the hallway.

"Where is Callandra?" Monk asked, looking around and failing to see her. He took a step forward as if to search, and Hester put her hand on his arm to stop him.

"No," she said quietly. "She'll find us if she needs us. I think she may prefer to be alone."

He stopped, turning to meet her eyes. For a moment he seemed about to question her, then he saw her certainty and changed his mind.

People were milling all around them, trying to decide whether to leave and find supper, or even to go home. Would the jury return tonight? Surely not. It was too late, after six already.

Hester looked at Monk. "Could they still come in tonight?" she asked, not knowing if she wanted the verdict sooner or if it would be even worse to wait all night. "Is it better if . . ."

"I don't know," he answered gently. "Nobody does."

She closed her eyes. "No, of course not. I'm sorry." She started to push her way towards a clearer space a few yards from the door and was just short of the entrance when Charles came striding towards her. His hair was falling forward and his cheeks were flushed.

"Have you seen Imogen?" he demanded, urgency making his voice rough-edged. "Is she with you?"

"No," she answered, trying to ignore the fear she felt in him. "Did she say she was looking for me?"

"No . . . I thought . . ." Charles stared around, searching for sight of Imogen.

"Perhaps she has gone to the cloakroom," Hester suggested. "Is she all right? Was she a little faint, or distressed? It was very close in there. Shall I go and look?"

"Please!" Charles accepted instantly. "She was . . ." He swore under his breath, his jaw clenched.

"What?" Monk demanded. "What is it? Charles?"

Hester saw in her mind's eye Imogen's white face and staring eyes. "Why did you come?" She caught Charles's sleeve. "Not for me!"

"No." Charles looked wretched. "I thought if she heard what had happened to Elissa Beck, the tragedy and the waste of it, the terrible way she died, she might be shocked enough never to gamble again. I thought if I brought her today . . . just at the end . . . the summing up . . ."

"It was a good idea," Monk agreed vehemently.

"Was it?" Charles seemed almost to be pleading for assurance. "I'm afraid I might have frightened her too much. She excused herself when the judge adjourned, and I thought she had just gone to . . . but that was fifteen minutes ago, and I haven't seen her since." Again, as if he could not help himself, he craned around to search for her.

"I'll go," Hester said quickly. "Stay here, so that if I find her we don't lose each other again." And without waiting she moved away to find the cloakroom and the convenience. Perhaps Imogen just needed a little time to be alone and compose herself after the distress of what she had heard. In her place, Hester felt she would have herself. If the trial had had the effect on her that Charles had desired, it would produce a change which could hardly be accommodated in a few moments.

She pushed her way against the crowd, who were now leaving for the night, and ended up in the cloakroom, but Imogen was not there. There was a woman in charge. Hester described Imogen as well as she could, her clothes, particularly her hat, and asked if the woman had seen her.

"Sorry, ma'am, no idea." The woman shook her head. "All I can tell yer is there's no one 'ere now, 'ceptin' us. But nob'dy 'ere bin wot yer'd call poorly."

"Thank you." Hester gave her a halfpenny and left as quickly as she could. Where on earth could Imogen be? And why would she go off alone, now of all times? Suddenly fury boiled up inside her for the sheer thoughtlessness of causing more grief and anxiety at a moment when they had almost more burden than they could bear.

She marched to the clerk she saw standing at the top of the stairs to the nearest entrance.

"Excuse me," she said peremptorily. "My sister-in-law appears to have gone looking for her carriage without us." It was the first lie which sprang to her mind. "She is about two inches less than I in height, she has dark hair and eyes and is wearing a green coat and hat with black feathers. Have you seen her?"

"Yes, ma'am," he said immediately. "Carrying a green umbrella. At least it sounds like the lady you describe. She left several minutes ago, with Mr. Pendreigh."

"What?" Hester was stunned. "No, that can't—"

"Sounded like the young lady you described, ma'am. Sorry if I made a mistake." He inclined his head towards the open doors. "They went that way. Almost ten minutes ago, walking quite quickly. I think he was helping her. She seemed a bit upset. I daresay one of the trials had affected someone she knew. He might only have been taking her as far as her carriage, just making sure she was all right."

"Thank you!" she said abruptly, and swinging around, she ran back to where Monk and Charles were still waiting. They saw her and started towards her.

"What is it?" Monk said breathlessly. "Where is she?"

Hester looked beyond him at Charles. "Did she have an umbrella, a green one?"

Charles was ashen. "Yes! Why? What's happened?"

"I think she left with Pendreigh. A clerk at the door over there says someone exactly like her went out with him about ten minutes ago."

Charles lunged forward and ran across the now almost empty hallway and down the steps, Monk and Hester racing after him, feet flying, clutching the rails to keep from tripping. Outside was that unique darkness of very late autumn and fog. It was almost like disappearing into a muffling layer of cloths, ice-cold and gripping as if a solid touch, except that it parted in front of you and closed behind, leaving you without sense of direction. Even sound seemed swallowed by the wall of vapor.

"Why would she go with Pendreigh?" Charles said from a few feet away in the gloom. "What could he do for her? How could he help? With what he's just heard about his daughter, how could he even think of anyone else's grief?" He spun around, almost colliding with them in the thick darkness. "Do you think he's trying to save her, because he lost Elissa?" His voice was wild with hope, soaring up out of control.

"I don't know," Monk said roughly. He swore as he stumbled on the edge of the curb. "But why in God's name did they leave the courthouse? She must have known you'd be frantic with worry for her."

"Perhaps she's still angry with me for bringing her to see just how gambling can destroy everything she loves," Charles said, trying to choke back his emotions and hold on to some kind of control.

Hester was beginning to shiver, as much from fear as cold. There was something profoundly wrong. Imogen did not know Fuller Pendreigh. Why on earth would she go out into the fog alone with him? No matter how distressed she was over Elissa, or gambling, or anything else, no matter how much she might grieve for Pendreigh because they had both known Elissa at wildly different times of her life, she would not have left Charles and walked off into the fog.

Then a terrible thought assailed her. Could Pendreigh in some insane way blame Imogen for Elissa's gambling, just as she had once feared Charles might blame Elissa for Imogen's? She swung around and gripped Monk's arm so hard he winced. "What if he thinks it is her fault that Elissa gambled?" she said urgently. "What if he means her harm?"

Monk started to protest her foolishness, but Charles broke away and, churning his arms, trying to feel his way through the shifting patterns of the mist as it thinned and then rolled together again, he lurched towards Ludgate Hill.

With awful certainty Hester knew where he was going ... Blackfriars' Bridge, and the river.

Monk must have known it, too. He clasped her hand and pulled her along, forcing her to run blindly through the white wall around them, along to New Bridge Street, then left with muffled hoofbeats of cab horses behind them and the dismal sound of foghorns from the water ahead. The mist smelled of salt, and it was moving in patches now on the wind off the water.

It cleared, and they saw Charles ahead of them, still trying to run, swiveling from right to left as he searched desperately for a sign of someone, anyone he could ask. The gas lamps were barely visible, just one before and one behind, giving the illusion of a pathway.

They overtook a hansom, which was almost soundless in the gloom, just a faint creak of leather and wood and the hiss of the wheels on the wet road. It was invisible until they were almost on top of it, and then only a darkness in the paler mist.

"Imogen!" Charles shouted, and the night swallowed his voice like a wet sheet. "Imogen!" he called, louder and more desperately.

There was a faint murmur and a slurp of water ahead, and then suddenly the boom of a foghorn almost on top of them. The road was rising. The bridge!

It was stupid, pointless, but Hester found herself calling out as well.

There was a gust of wind; the fog cleared a few yards. Half a dozen lamps were visible. They were on the bridge, the water below a black, glistening surface, looking as solid as glass, and then gone again, rolled over and vanished in the choking vapor.

Another hansom passed them, moving more certainly. A moment later the driver called out, a thick, sharp cry of alarm.

Monk sprinted in the brief patch of light from the lamps.

Hester picked up her skirts and ran after him, Charles catching up and passing her. Even so she saw the dark heap on the curbside between the lamps, almost as soon as they did, and only the volume of fabric around her ankles prevented her from reaching it at the same time.

Monk fell on his knees beside the body, but in the fitful light through the vapor he could see little, except the ashen pallor of her face.

"Imogen!" Charles cried, all but collapsing on his knees and reaching out for her. "Oh, God!" He snatched his hands back, covered with dark, sticky liquid. He tried to speak again, but he could scarcely breathe.

Hester felt her heart choking in her throat, but it was too dark to see anything to help. She swiveled towards the roadway and scrambled to her feet. "Cabbie!" she shouted, her voice high and thin like a scream, except she had not drawn in enough breath. "Bring the carriage lamp! Hurry!"

It seemed like an eternity in the mist and darkness before she saw it wavering towards them, but actually it was only a moment in time. He made his way at a run, carrying the lamp high, and held it over the body on the ground.

Charles gasped and let out a sob of horror. Even Monk gave a low moan. Imogen was gray-faced, and the whole top of her body from the waist up was scarlet with blood.

The cabbie drew in his breath with a hiss between his teeth, and the light in his hand swayed.

Hester steeled herself to touch Imogen, to search for the wound and see if there was anything she could do. There was no blood pumping, no movement at all.

Blinded by her own tears, she felt for Imogen's neck and pulled away her collar. Her fingers touched warm skin, and a definite beat of pulse. "She's alive!" she said. "She's alive!" Then immediately she realized how stupid that was. There was blood everywhere, scarlet arterial blood. The whole of Imogen's jacket front was soaked in it. But where was the wound? Was there even any point in trying to find it when so much blood had been lost?

With fumbling fingers in the juddering light from the carriage lamp, she half pulled, half tore at the fastenings until Monk reached over and took them from her, ripping the jacket open. Underneath on Imogen's white blouse there was only a single bright stain.

Hester heard Charles sobbing.

Less blood . . . not more. The blood was from outside. It was not Imogen's! Just for a last assurance she pulled the blouse out of its anchorage in the skirt waist and pushed her hand underneath. There was no blood at all, no wound to the smooth skin.

So why was Imogen unconscious? Quickly she replaced the clothes, wrapping them around her. "Coats!" she ordered. "Give me your coats to put around her!" And instantly Monk and Charles threw their coats off and handed them to her. The moment after, the cabbie offered his, struggling to keep the light high at the same time.

Hester felt very gently under Imogen's head, exploring, terrified to find broken bone, more blood, a soft indentation of the skull, but there was only a swelling. Her heart beating faster and faster, her mouth dry, she covered the last few inches. Still no splintered bone.

"She's struck her head," she said hoarsely. "But her skull seems whole." She looked up at the cabbie. "You'll take her home, won't you? Now . . ."

"Yeah! Yeah, o' course!" he said quickly. "But wot abaht all that blood, Miss? If she ain't stabbed . . . 'oo is?"

Charles let out a long, shuddering sigh.

Monk stepped forward and took the lamp from the cabbie and held it high. It was Hester who saw the green umbrella lying on the pavement beside the bridge rails. It was still rolled up, and the long, sharp spike of it was thick with blood, and more had fallen in spots along the path.

"Oh, God!" Charles burst out in horror.

"Pendreigh . . ." Monk gasped. "Why?"

"He must be very badly hurt." Hester tried to gather her wits. Whatever had happened, someone was severely injured.

"I can't do anything more for Imogen," she said, climbing to her feet. She turned to Charles. "Take her home, keep her as warm as you can, and when she comes to, try to get her to take a little beef tea. Call the doctor, of course. Don't put her into sheets, put her straight into blankets, and sit with her." She watched to make sure he had understood, then she faced Monk. "We must find Pendreigh, if he is still alive. I may be able to help."

"We've no idea where he is!"

"We'll begin at his home. That's where most people go when they're badly hurt." She started towards the roadway again.

"No!" Monk said instinctively.

She ignored him. "And we must take a constable or someone with us! Apart from anything else, you haven't any authority. And . . ." She gulped, the ice-cold vapor hurting her chest. "We have to know what happened, for Imogen's sake. We have to protect her!" It was hideous, and still totally inexplicable. Why had she attacked Pendreigh? There had to be a reason, something that would excuse her in law.

"I'll get Runcorn," he answered. "But you're going home."

"No, I'm not! It's my duty to help the injured, just as it's yours to answer the law. Don't stand here wasting time. We need a cab, and we need Runcorn!"

Charles had already bent and picked up Imogen very carefully. Now he straightened his back and his legs to carry her across to the waiting cab. The cabbie suddenly galvanized into life and scrambled after them, waving the light, leaving Hester and Monk alone in the darkness.

"Don't argue!" Hester said.

Monk swore, then bit it back and started to run towards the near end of the bridge, where he could see a cab looming up from New Bridge Street. He shouted at the driver, and saw the man turn in surprise and disapproval, silhouetted in his high-collared coat and stovepipe hat.

"It's an emergency!" Monk said breathlessly as he reached the cab, half lifted Hester in, then scrambled in behind her. "Take me to Superintendent Runcorn's house in Lamb's Conduit Street, and go as quickly as you can."

After only the slightest indecision the driver obeyed, and Monk sat beside Hester shivering, praying that Runcorn was at home. If he had to direct the cab to go looking for him, he had no idea where else to search but the police station, and even that was time wasted. Pendreigh must be badly wounded—from the amount of blood on Imogen, perhaps even fatally.

"What on earth had they been doing on the bridge? Why did she go with him?" Monk said in the darkness as they sat together and the cab moved forward.

Hester did not bother to answer. Nothing made sense, except that they had fought, wildly, desperately, leaving Imogen senseless on the footpath and Pendreigh bleeding so terribly he surely could not get far.

The fog was thinning away from the river, and the cab picked up speed.

"He must have attacked her," Monk said in the fitful light as they moved from lamp to lamp. "But why? In what way could she possibly have threatened him? And don't say to blame him for Elissa. He's not that big a fool. Elissa was gambling from her own need. It had nothing to do with anyone else at all!"

"Imogen was in Swinton Street on the night of the murders," Hester replied. "We know she saw Allardyce. . . ."

"Pendreigh?" he said in astonishment. "Why?"

"I don't know."

The cab pulled up abruptly, and after telling Hester to wait, Monk leaped out and ran across the rapidly icing pavement and pushed open the outer door. He went up the stairs two at a time to reach Runcorn's apartments. He lifted his fist and banged so hard the door itself rattled against the frame.

"Runcorn!" he shouted. "Runcorn!"

The door opened and Runcorn stared at him. "What is it?" he said almost calmly.

Monk swallowed. "Pendreigh took Imogen Latterly out of the courthouse and through the fog to Blackfriars' Bridge. They quarreled about something." He all but pushed Runcorn inside, looking around for his coat to hand it to him. "We found her senseless and covered with blood, but no injury on her. Her umbrella point was used to stab someone, and Pendreigh's nowhere to be seen. We've got to find him. Come on!"

Runcorn opened a cupboard and took his hat and coat out, then made for the door still carrying them in his hand.

Monk ran down the stairs again on Runcorn's heels, and across the pavement into the hansom, calling out Pendreigh's address in Ebury Street as he went. Runcorn showed a moment's amazement that Hester was in the cab, but there was no point in arguing about it now.

Once again the cab started forward and picked up speed. The fog was drifting in patches and the hiss of tires on the wet roads was muffled as they swung through the alternating light of each lamp and into the spaces between.

It was several moments before Runcorn spoke, and when he did it was with intense feeling.

"What are you not telling me, Monk? Why was she there? What did she know about Fuller Pendreigh and his daughter that we don't? Or at any rate, that I don't?"

"I'm working it out!" Monk said tartly, looking sideways at Runcorn's face in the glare of lamplight. He saw no hostility, only puzzlement. "She was the woman in Swinton Street that night," he began his reply. "At the gambling house." He heard Runcorn's quick intake of breath. "She must have seen Pendreigh there, too. That's about the only thing that would make him take her down to the river and, we presume, attack her. She must have been at least half prepared for it, and she went for him with the spike of her umbrella. In spite of his clothes, she must have given him a fearful blow, from the blood all over her. Don't know how she managed it."

Runcorn muttered a blasphemy under his breath, or perhaps it was not. He might even have been praying.

The hansom careered its way through the streamers of fog and sudden glittering lights. The wind was rising.

"Will she be all right?" Runcorn said at last.

"I don't know," Monk admitted.

Runcorn drew in his breath to say something, then could not make up his mind.

Monk could feel the warmth of his body beside him. In the intermittent light he could see Runcorn's indecision, his waiting to offer some kind of pity, and all the memories flooding back of envy and distrust, all the petty unkindnesses of the past.

The cab stopped at Ebury Street and they both got out, Monk turning to help Hester. Runcorn paid the cabbie and then went up the front steps. He pulled the doorbell hard, and then again. They stood impatiently for what seemed an age until the butler came.

"Yes sir, madam?" he enquired with just a hint of disapproval for the lateness of the hour.

"Superintendent Runcorn, of the police," Runcorn said icily. "And Mr. William Monk, and Mrs. Monk."

"I'm afraid Mr. Pendreigh is not receiving at this hour, sir. If you come to—"

"I'm not asking, I'm telling you," Runcorn snapped. "Now be so good as to step aside, rather than oblige me to arrest you for obstructing the police in their duty. Do I make myself plain?"

The butler quailed. "Yes sir, if . . ." But he was elbowed aside as Runcorn walked in with Monk on his heels.

"Where is Mr. Pendreigh?" Runcorn asked. "Upstairs?"

"Mr. Pendreigh is not well, sir. He was attacked by robbers in the street. If you—"

"Yes or no?" Runcorn snapped.

"Yes sir, but . . . Mr. Pendreigh is ill, sir . . . I beg you . . ."

"Come on!" Runcorn ordered, ignoring the butler and gesturing to Monk as he began to climb the stairs, again two at a time. They met a startled maid at the head of the flight, carrying a pile of towels. "Mr. Pendreigh's room?" Runcorn asked. "Is he in there? Answer me, girl, or I'll arrest you."

She yelped and dropped the towels. "Yes . . . sir!"

"Well, where is it?"

"There, sir. Second door . . . sir!" She put her hands up to her face as if to stop herself from screaming.

Runcorn strode to the door indicated and banged on it once then threw it open. Monk was at his shoulder.

The room was very masculine, all paneled wood and deep colors, but it was extraordinarily beautiful. They barely had time for more than an impression. Fuller Pendreigh was lying on the bed, his face gray and his eyes already sunken. He clutched a folded towel around his throat and neck, but the scarlet blood was seeping through it and the stain was spreading.

Hester moved forward to him and then stopped. She had seen too much death to mistake it easily. He had more stamina than most men to have made it this far. There was nothing she could do for him, even were it in mercy rather than a prolonging of pain.

"She saw you in Swinton Street the night of Elissa's death, didn't she?" Monk asked softly. "She didn't know who you were then, but she recognized you in court, and when you saw her looking at you, you knew it. It was there in her face, and it was only moments before she would tell someone. What were you hoping to do? Make her look like a suicide? Another gambler driven beyond sanity? But she's not dead. We got to her in time."

"Why did you kill Elissa, sir?" Runcorn asked in the silence. "She was your own daughter."

Very slowly, as if he barely had strength to lift it, Pendreigh let go of the towel and put one hand up to his face, trying to waken himself from a nightmare. "For God's sake, man, I didn't mean to kill her!" he said in a whisper. "She flew at me, lashing out with her fists, clawing at my face and screaming. I only wanted to fend her off, but she wouldn't stop." He struggled for breath. "I didn't want to strike her. I put my hands on her shoulders and pushed her away, but she kept on. She wouldn't listen." He stopped, his face filled with horror as if a hell of reliving it over and over again had opened up in front of him, always with the same, terrible inescapable end, worse now because he knew it was coming.

"I stepped back and she lunged forward and slipped. I tried to catch her as her feet went from under her. She turned, and I caught her face in my hands. I couldn't hold her. I meant to take her weight . . . I . . . she broke her neck as she went sideways. . . ."

Hester wet a corner of the sheet in the pitcher on the table beside the bed and touched Pendreigh's lips with it.

"Why did she attack you?" Monk asked.

"What?" Pendreigh stared at him.

"Why did she attack you?" Monk repeated. "Why were you there anyway?"

Runcorn looked at Hester, his eyes wide with question.

"Why were you there?" Monk said again.

"I had an appointment to see Allardyce," Pendreigh said hoarsely. "I was going to give him an interim payment for the picture. I know he needed it. But I was delayed. I was late." He gasped and was silent for a moment.

Hester bent forward, then looked at Monk, shaking her head minutely.

Seconds ticked by. Pendreigh opened his eyes again. "He'd grown tired of waiting for me, and angry, and he'd gone out. But I wasn't going to pay him without seeing the picture first." His voice faded to a whisper. The scarlet stain was soaking through the towels. His face was gray. "It was beautiful!"

Runcorn drew his brows together. "So why was Mrs. Beck lashing out at you?"

Pendreigh's face was a mask of horror. "When I got there his model answered the door to me. She was alone, half dressed, and staggering around with drink. She fell over and her robe slid off, leaving her half naked. I tried to help her up. I . . . I was sorry for the woman."

He stopped while Hester wet his lips again.

"She was heavy and kept sliding away," he went on, determined now to talk. "I had her in my arms when Elissa came in. She misunderstood and assumed she had interrupted some sexual assignation. She worshiped me . . . as I did her! She couldn't bear it . . ."

Monk could picture it easily. Elissa's own shame of her appetite beyond control, suddenly finding her adored father, who she believed had so perfectly mastered his own life and virtue, in the arms of a drunken, half-naked woman. "She flew at you in rage for shattering her ideal of you, for betraying her dreams. The idol was clay all the way up to the waist!"

Pendreigh's voice was no more than a sigh. "Yes."

"And you killed her accidentally?"

"Yes!"

"But you killed Sarah Mackeson on purpose!" Runcorn burst out, his face ravaged by fury and an anguish he did not know how to express. "You killed that woman only because she'd seen you! You took hold of her and you twisted her neck until you broke it!"

Pendreigh stared at him. "I had to. She would have told Allardyce, and it would have ruined me. She would have prevented all the good I could have done."

Runcorn shook his head. "No she wouldn't. Any real friends would have stood by you. . . ."

Pendreigh seemed to find a last strength. "Friends. You imbecile. I would have made Parliament! I would have changed the laws. Do you know how easy it is for a greedy man to take everything and leave a woman destitute? Do you?"

Runcorn blinked at him. "That's got nothing to do with it."

"It's got everything . . ." Pendreigh sighed, and his breathing grew more labored, his chest rattling. The shadow of death was on his face. "One woman sacrificed . . . I wouldn't have chosen it, but it was unavoidable . . . to get justice for millions."

"And Kristian?" Monk asked. "Is it worth it for him to hang for murders he did not commit? What about all the sick he could have cured? What about the discoveries he might make that could heal millions? What about the fact that he is innocent? What about truth?"

"I could have . . ." Pendreigh began. He did not finish. He let out his breath in a long sigh and his eyes ceased to focus.

Absolute silence filled the room, and Hester leaned over and passed her hand over his face, closing the lids gently.

"God help us," Runcorn said in a whisper. He swallowed hard and turned to Monk. "I'll go and tell them . . . and . . . and get a constable."

"Thank you," Monk said. He reached across and touched Hester's arm. He felt an ease inside that resolution always brought, but no victory yet. Kristian would be freed, of course, but he still had shattering truths to accept. He himself was not who he had believed he was. His heritage, his very blood, was different. He was one of the people he had been brought up to think of as outsiders, somehow inferior, and yet a people who had given the Western world the core of its soul, and so of its culture also. The thought was almost too big to grasp, but he would have to.

As he turned it over in his mind, Monk became aware of an intense need within himself to know his own roots, the meaning of his identity that hung only in shadows and pieces in his own mind. Who were his people? Where did they fit in the history of his land? What had they believed, lived for or died for? What had they given anyone?

It was not enough to ask; he must begin to look for the answers. The truth about everyone else was important. It was his job. What of the truth about himself? Who were the people he should have felt the bond with that Hester felt for Charles? Where was his blood tie to the past?

Runcorn came back, closing the door behind him. He looked first at Hester, then at Monk.

"You all right?" he asked.

"Yes, of course," Monk replied, tightening his grip on Hester's arm.

"Good," Runcorn replied. "I've got a constable with me, and another coming." He glanced at the silent figure on the bed. "What a terrible waste," he said, shaking his head a little. "He could have done so much." He turned back to Monk. "Cook's got up and made us a pot of tea," he added. "Look like you could take a cup."

Monk saw kindness in his face, even a flash of the old friendship.

"Thank you," he said, smiling, although he had not meant to. "That's a very good idea. Let's do that." And guiding Hester in front of him, he went out of the room and along the passage side by side with Runcorn.

ANNE PERRY is the bestselling author of two acclaimed series set in Victorian England: the William Monk novels, including *Dark Assassin* and *Execution Dock*, and the Charlotte and Thomas Pitt novels, including *Buckingham Palace Gardens* and *Long Spoon Lane*. She is also the author of the World War I novels *No Graves As Yet, Shoulder the Sky, Angels in the Gloom, At Some Disputed Barricade,* and *We Shall Not Sleep,* as well as eight holiday novels, most recently *A Christmas Odyssey.* Her stand-alone novel *The Sheen on the Silk,* set in the Byzantine Empire, was a *New York Times* bestseller. Anne Perry lives in Scotland.

www.anneperry.net